ALL THEIR ASTRAL LIGHT

Tome One of the Starbrary Archives

QUINN CASLAN

For those who are insane enough to remember who they are.

And for my three-year-old self; we did it, little one.

CONTENT WARNINGS

Content Warnings, from the author

This is an adult epic fantasy novel, and it addresses some very sensitive and serious issues, including explicit scenes involving graphic violence, sexual acts, suicidal thoughts, and harm towards children. (Full list of content warnings is on the Amazon and Goodreads pages.) Please read with caution and awareness for your own triggers and sensitivities.

A NOTE ON SELF-PUBLISHING

All Their Astral Light is a self-published novel. Self publishing is a labor of love in every sense of the word, and is an all-consuming process, in terms of the author's heart, time, and finances. Due to many resourcing roadblocks that indie/self-published authors face, our books may be more likely to have minute errors or hiccups. However, your love and support, both emotional, and financial, through the purchase of this book, give us the chance to access more resources for future books, and print cleaner second editions of earlier ones. Thank you for supporting a self-published author!

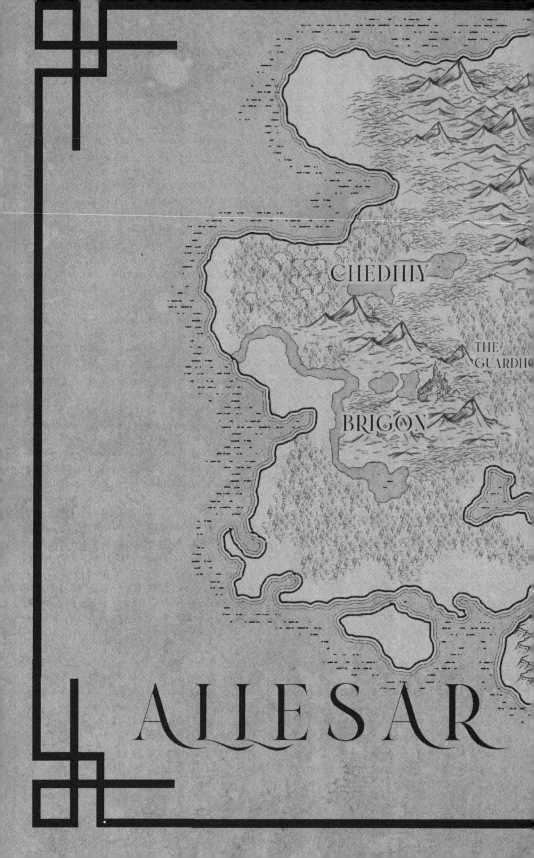

CHEDHIY

THE
GUARDHO

BRIGON

ALLESAR

CONTENTS

THE LANGUAGE
AND
PROVINCES OF ALLESAR

PROVINCES & PREMIERS

~~Strike through~~ - deceased

Canestry
Premier: Canryn
Wife: ~~Lorrel~~
Children: Indra

Meirydh
Premier: ~~Jofsa~~
Wife: ~~Marrylett~~
Children: Jauyne, ~~Astra~~

Nareilë
Premier: ~~Hadadh~~
Husband: ~~Jashar~~
Children: (none)

Pallydh
Premier: ~~Nalaliy~~
Husband: ~~Agret~~
Children: Alis, Quinn, Barlow *-missing, assumed deceased-*

Jopaar
High Priestess: Reinah
Partner: (none)
Children: Adras, Lumen [*adopted*]

Chedhiy
Premier: Mara
Wife: Shettel
Children: (none)

Brigon
Premier: Herran
Partner: (none)
Children: (none)

PRONUNCIATION GUIDE

FOR NON-NATIVE ALLESARI SPEAKERS

dh~ pronounced "th" as in "there", not as in "thunder"

ch~ pronounced with a "k" sound as in "loch", not as in "church"

iy~ pronounced "ee-ah"; Chedhiy is pronounced "Keh-thee-ah"

au~ makes an "ow" sound as in "wow", not as in "row"

ei~ pronounced "ay" as in "day"

J~ pronounced like an h; Jopaar is pronounced "HO-par"

Y~ pronounced like "uh" unless paired with an "a".

E~ always pronounced soft, as in "left", never as in "keep", unless followed by an "i"

I~ usually pronounced soft, as in "lift", not as in "ice", when on its own, but pronounced "ee" when ending a word

MAIN CAST
OF
CHARACTERS

Jauyne
Pronounced: HOW-*un-eh*
Age: 25
Home Province: Meirydh

Zechariyh
Pronounced: ZECK-*ar-ee-uh*
Age: 23
Home Province: Chedhiy

Osiys
Pronounced: OH-*sigh-us*
Age: 30
Home Province: Brigon

Indra
Pronounced: IN-*drah*
Age: 17
Home Province: Canestry

Lumen
Pronounced: LOO-*men*
Age: 21
Home Province: Nareilë (but grew up in Jopaar)

Adras
Pronounced: AH-*dras*
Age: 27
Home Province: Brigon (but grew up in Jopaar)

THE FIRST CRYSTALLINE SACRAMENT

Nothing is the same as it once was, and nothing is the same as it will future be. We remember.

77TH & CRYPTCALL

YOUR HAIR IS GREEN. You do not dye it; it grows this way, out of your head in kinky curls that zig-zag the peripheral of your vision.

There is a gaping, aching pain in your gut. It has always been there, since the day you opened your eyes and you were five and Kip was four and Eoin found you on the street, covered in mud.

You know that aching pain is hunger, and that you have never once been satisfied.

You know that satisfaction is coming.

Kip shakes your elbow and grins, all teeth, inches from your face. Waves a hand. "You're always going places, Quell. Come back."

You are back. You are never back. You palm him directly in the face, wrinkle your nose, and he flails away, overdramatic as usual.

The coffee shop blooms back to your senses, all warm polished wood and gleaming windows. Brilliant blue light shines, tossed at length through the panes of glass by the dipping sun. A patron in the left leg of the horseshoe-shaped seating area flicks a fifteen-cent coin into the air, and it glints blue where it catches the sunlight.

He is reading a newspaper printed in Vaughnketi, and his boots drip melting snow. He has slung his warm wool coat and scarf across the chair opposite him, drying. The woman two tables down from him chats in Karresk with her friend, both in short outfits made from a single length of linen that is belted at the waist. They drink their coffee iced, in tall, faceted glasses and chitter like birds. The teenagers at the large center table meet here once every month to excitedly share news from all their corners of the world. They are dressed in short linen and heavy wool and billowing high-waisted pants, and they speak in at least six different languages.

You understand all of them. Everyone does, here.

Because this is Cryptcall Coffee.

A belching hiss erupts from the huge, domed espresso maker. Its reflective copper surface takes the yellow lamplight and throws brownish-gold beams into the wild contest of light.

Fiadh is pulling a shot of espresso into a white ceramic cup, little to no attention paid to the way the espresso is dripping onto the rim and streaking the outside; she's too deep in ecstatic conversation with a patron who grips a newspaper with headlines from Silghkë. A gentle but stern scold comes from Roan— something about how Fiadh ought to tie back her wild ginger curls. Snorting laughter pops and dies like the bacon crackling in the pan being tended to by Ailbhe, and Callum's brows knit in oblivious concentration as he gently swirls foamed cream across the top of a mug.

This is your family. This is your home. What would life even be, without the soft grey and white stripes of the aprons, without the earthy-sweet aroma of coffee beans being roasted and the grand world map pinched between plaster and pins from your patrons?

You look down at your fingers, warm brown against the off white of the typewriter keys, and at what you have typed. You wrote the menu in multiple languages again; even with the magic of Cryptcall Coffee, it is disconcerting. It will need to be retyped. A larger, darker, rougher hand than your own squeezes gently around your wrist. When you look up, Eoin winks at you from behind wiry grey brows and smiles wide in the kindest way you think a human might be capable of.

This man is as good as your father. This is your family. This is your home. You are hungry all the time.

In the box beneath Eoin's desk is a black crystal with rainbows in it, which he does not know you have seen.

You want to eat it.

You smile back.

I

1

THEY'RE GETTING CLOSER

OSIYS, CANESTRYN HIGH HOUSE
4 days until the sack of Meirydh

The Starlight trapped in the walls had stopped screaming for help years ago. Or maybe the high shriek had only ever been the guilty, terrified part of him. He kept it locked somewhere deep and horrible inside himself. It was somewhere so deep and so horrible that not even the vile tyrants who frequented Osiys' waking moments could stumble upon it.

Screams or no screams, the chamber hall bore countless gashes and scars down its ancient, rock-hewn length. Great gashes sliced through the sacred stone. No one here spoke of that oddity. The old tapestries, crawling and garbling with distorted Starlight sewn into them from the days of the Old Order, embarrassingly attempted to hide the crude markings left by instruments of forged and beaten metal.

The Starlight here was wrong. It was a constant, creeping feeling, a near-silent stretching contortion. A decade later, it still had Osiys looking over his shoulder when he passed through the places where Premier Canryn had woven it through the veins of his High House and city.

Still, Osiys walked these dim halls with numb confidence. It had been so long... Were there still truly High Houses that celebrated sacred Starlight? He knew it was a foolish question, but still he asked it. He had to ask it. He would go mad if he didn't ask it.

Nine... no, ten; it had been ten years since the beginning of the division, when he had chosen to leave Brigon and come to Canestry. Osiys could scarcely remember the sunlight sighing softly through the great peaks of Onar's Spine, the sky-scraping mountain range his own people called home. Why had he chosen Canestry?

He reached out a leather-gloved finger to trace a particularly deep gash in the wall. There were slightly blackened streaks in it, too. Burn marks. From harnessed, possessed, enslaved Starlight. The Canestryns had not called upon it to heal or to grow crops or to light their way. No, they'd stolen it, poisoned it— wrestled it into cleaving, clawing, wrenching things which tore limb from limb those of the Old Order who populated the Provinces. Canestry was desperate to be rid of them. To purge the earth, all of Allesar. Swords had done this. Axes of wood and steel had set their wishes in motion.

He didn't flinch at the sacrilege of it anymore. He couldn't afford to if he wished to live to see his own province again. Osiys rested a hand on the hilt of his sword; the other tugged a dangling strand of copper hair, the same strand that always loosed itself from the black hood all Night Walkers of Canestry wore.

He had done his time. He had worked his way through the layers of trust and secrecy to the esteemed, elite crew of Night Walkers. They were perhaps the fourteen men most whispered about and feared in Canestry— stealthy shadows who crept, unseen and clad all in black, among the cities of their Province and beyond. The rumors of the Night Walkers were nothing short of godlike, stories of invisibility and invincibility that turned up the corners of Osiys' usually-concerned mouth into a humored smirk. Soon, though, it would all be behind him. Two short weeks and he'd be home to his mountains, his forests, his family, his friends, his Elessid.

When the northernmost star of the Chedhiy starscape reached the Canestry skyline, he would march out with the Canestryn army. They said they were representing the rise of a new order, and that for new life to happen, there first must be death.

He would be nothing but a faceless corpse as far as Premier Canryn and his bloodthirsty army were concerned.

"Osiys!"

He turned, a grin splitting his face when he saw Indra.

She had only been seven when he had arrived in Canestry, barely a man of twenty and already doubting his pained choice to be in a hostile foreign land. She had offered him a flower from her garden. He had snuck her chocolate oranges from the kitchen. Soon enough, she was a little golden shadow, smelling of oranges and shimmering in his footsteps whenever his commitment to the Premier allowed him to remain in the High City.

Still a little thing at 17, she sprinted towards him, shining silver eyes glancing about to be sure no one was around to see her hurrying with gauzy skirt in hand. The curious glow in those silver irises was the betrayal that her father, Premier Canryn, sought to hide by keeping her entrapped in the grounds of the High House. They were a shining signal of the Old Order, the Starlight of her ancestors gleaming stronger than it had been seen in generations.

Of all the backwards and hostile people in this damned Province, Indra was good-natured and quick-witted, and, as Osiys well knew, wiser than she let on. Women had to be resourceful here in the three easternmost Provinces, where the guidance of the Stars had been abandoned, and Osiys had the strong feeling that Indra was very resourceful indeed.

"Indra," he grinned at the way her boundless gold curls flung themselves across her face. "What are you doing in this hall?"

"I knew you'd be here!" She was breathless, pushing ringlets out of her solemn, glowing eyes. "I have news."

"Oh?"

She nodded fiercely and twisted a heavy rolled scroll of paper in her little hands. Her eyes took full inventory of their surroundings before grabbing Osiys' hand and tugging him towards a little door in the wall, nudging him through and into the closet. Osiys floundered in panic and tried to tug his hand out of her surprisingly strong grip, frantically looking around them, lest his hand be removed from his body for touching the princess.

"What are you—"

"Hush!" Indra clicked the door latch closed behind them and began to speak in a hoarse whisper. "I learned a while ago that our Astronomers have not been entirely honest with our people." Her Starlight hummed fiercely; he could see it working silver through the tiny veins around her eyes. "At the start of the division the Stars began behaving strangely, but their charts, open to the public, did not show this deviation from the predicted, and published, routes. So, for the past three years, I've been making my own star charts."

"Your own star charts!" Another wave of panic — he'd lost count of how many had crashed into him today — and he gaped in the dark at the little creature before him. "Indra, that's..."

"Illegal, yes I know. Ever since the New Order was established." She said it like she might have stated an item on a very boring list, only the smallest quiver to the tone of her words. Osiys wanted to shake her.

They stood in the dark room, shocked silence and patient pause soaking up the air, and would have been nose to nose in the smallness of it if Indra had stood taller than his chest. Indra smiled — not as reassuring as she seemed to think — and closed her eyes, tilting her head upwards and pulling down dangling strands of light into existence to illuminate the cramped space.

This was Starlight in its pure, unadulterated form. This was the sacred stuff he so easily forgot when the befouled, cloying tendrils reached for him in the halls. This was what her father was so desperate to extinguish, and, looking at Indra's shining face, he would never understand it.

Osiys was going to be distraught to leave her when the time came for him to go. He helplessly wished he could tell her about Brigon, about the place he came from, where she might have been loved and taught and honored for the Starlight she'd been born with. Instead, he shook himself and reoriented to this strangeness that was them, huddled in a closet with illegal Star charts.

Indra turned and began to unroll the chart, fumbling with the length of it in her small arms. Osiys took the other end and stretched it as wide as the space would allow.

"So," he surrendered to her entrapment, keeping a hand fixed on the doorknob and his voice hushed, "what are the Stars doing?"

Her eyes gleamed silver in the cool light that hung like tangled threads above them. "I already knew that Nareilë, Jopaar, Chedhiy, and Pallydh had begun to orbit us more quickly. That much was clear when Nareilë first appeared in the summer, far before harvest time, seven years ago. But there's something else, Osiys... something very strange."

That Starlight in her eyes dug into his own something fierce as she paused, fumbling for the right words.

"The Stars... they're getting closer."

"Closer?" Osiys whispered it almost unintelligibly. It wasn't possible was it? The ancient texts, which Canestry and her neighboring Provinces had banished as the Old Order, spoke of no such thing as far as he knew. More than that, she was still a curious child, brutally bored, terrifically lonely, and endlessly imaginative. "It isn't possible, Indra... Is it? Neither the Old Order nor the New ever speaks about it."

"I swear to you, Osiys, it's the truth!" Her whisper was strained with desperation. "I've measured the sky countless times. I didn't sleep at all last night, and barely at all the whole past month. I know it's unbelievable, but there's no way around it. The stars are coming closer. They have been for years. And it's been hidden from us all."

He trusted her despite himself, and that trust gouged caves of misery into his heart. Indra was one of the few whose eyes still gleamed with Starlight. She had an uncanny connection to the celestial, and it was a connection that a lesser creature like himself was drawn to— a pitiful moth to brilliant flame.

"Why would they hide this? What would that reasoning possibly be?"

"I don't know." She sighed, and it was a sound that belonged to someone far older than she. "I know it makes no sense for the upcoming attack. I know it spells disaster for any Meirydhi honoring the Alignment on that day. I suspect... I suspect it's why I feel them more clearly all the time, why my father's fear is getting stronger every day." There was a watery pause, one that tasted like withheld tears, and it drowned Osiys in rage. "But I can't take this to the Canestryn Ring, Osiys. You were right; Star charting is illegal for anyone not an Astronomer. Not even my own father could protect me from these laws. They will kill me."

His body fought the urge to crumple. Indra was right. She would die if she was found out; this was the carelessly pained act of a caged child. Her Starlight felt like the sprinkling of cool water, and he clamped down on the way his blood curdled at the thought of her father watching sternly as she poured blood onto the polished stone floor, the Starlight in her eyes fading out.

Meirydh would be just fine. His spies, already on their way across the Tanaraq plains to deliver the date of the planned Canestryn attack, would make sure of it.

"We will not put you in danger." His voice was more gritty than he'd expected when the words came out. "Now you take these charts, and you throw them in your fireplace, and you ensure that they burn to nothing. You ensure that no one ever finds these."

Her face fell and she swallowed back her evident disappointment.

Osiys' time in Canestry had made him tender to Indra. He tried not to think about the day he'd come back to invade her Province and end the war, when he'd have to lay out the slain and bleeding bodies and find hers in line with the rest. How many other innocents were there? How many would he slaughter unknowingly? His stomach surged in protest as the guilt and anxiety rose in his throat. He said a brief prayer to the

Seven Stars and massaged the bridge of his nose between forefinger and thumb, the frustration building like a furious darkness inside his mind, as it always did.

Indra's soft hand lighted on his shoulder.

"Osiys?" Her voice was stern and concerned. "It's going to be alright."

"Yes. I'm sure you're right," he lied, and she smoothed her hand over the arm of his robe in what seemed to be reassurance.

He almost flinched away from her touch. He didn't deserve a friend, or even a kind word... certainly not a touch of any kind from the caged Princess of Canestry.

He knew what he really was—a boy playing hero, the lives of a hundred cities dangling from his shaking hands. How bitterly he regretted his own courage, the enthusiasm with which he'd leapt at the chance to do something of consequence all those years ago. It was certainly of consequence, but perhaps in a much more grave and terrifying way than he had realized. He could scarcely look at himself. No matter what he did, his actions ended in both death and life for masses.

Indra chided him as she peeked out of the door into the great hall, ensuring their safe departure. "It will be alright." She looked back at him with ancient, childish eyes. "Don't you dare doubt me, Osiys."

He waited several moments in the darkness of the closet, willing his breathing to slow, swearing softly at himself as the image of her mangled body came unbidden to the inside of his eyelids. Ribs locked the softness of his heart away, pinned down the horrible feeling of failed responsibility, and refused to let it escape his chest.

It's not you I doubt, he thought.

DON'T

2
A TERRIBLY STUPID THING TO DO

Long iron chandeliers dripped down from where the vaulted ceiling came to a point, their light cool and shimmering. The fourteen men, all draped in their black hoods and wearing their black leather trousers, stood stoic in two parallel lines of seven, but the heavy circles under their eyes were evidence of their exhaustion. It was unusual for a Gathering to be called so late, long after moonrise.

Osiys tugged his hood further down and bent his head to disguise a long yawn. He was concerned, if he was honest. He could feel it in his bones; something was not quite right about the whole thing. They'd been given only ten minutes warning prior to the Gathering which explained why some of the men had arrived disheveled, their hoods wrinkled and shirts half-tucked.

The Premier was off to the side of his High Seat, in deep discussion with a huddle of those in his Circle. They were each dressed in battle wear—long leather trousers, arm bands dotted with obsidian and agate, hair pulled tightly back into knotted buns at the base of their necks, heavy vests of interwoven metal. None of this was according to the usual proceedings.

Osiys turned his eyes away from the Premier's High Seat. The dais which it sat on, as well as the seat itself, was made of some strange metal, arranged in a sleek, geometric pattern that made his skin crawl. It felt like nails being dragged slowly along his spine, begging him to turn around.

A sudden nauseating image flashed before his eyes as he blinked, and it was as though the High Seat disintegrated into ash, forcing its floating fragments into sticky smoke that wrapped around his wrists and clogged his throat. His hands were shaking; he jammed them together in the sleeves of his robe, focusing on the crawling metal of the dais which was, at least, a whole thing and not actively attacking him.

It was the stress. All of this was stress.

The Premier walked with purpose to the High Seat and stood in front of it, his broad shoulders and upturned chin commanding attention. He raised a hand, though all fourteen pairs of eyes were already locked, dutiful and obedient, onto him. "Men of Canestry, the time has come."

He outstretched a second hand, both reaching outward, palms facing the sky as though he were lifting up a great and sacred thing.

"It is time to rise and give the gift of our enlightenment to the rest of Allesar. The Province of Meirydh is still in the dark, hopelessly following a Fractured Order. We can lead them in the way of honor. We hold their liberation in our hands!"

Osiys' heart pounded. The Premier was readying them for battle, but they were not to ride out for another nine days. Sick was rising in his throat, and his breath shuddered. They were leaving early. The Premier may have fooled the rest of his Province about the movement of the stars, but he was no fool.

He knew the truth: he knew not only that tonight the sky would be an impenetrable dark, but also that it was the night of Black Moon Rites for those of the Old Order. He would exploit it in order to massacre an entire city. Osiys clenched his fists, nails digging into the soft flesh of his palm as the horror of this reality sunk into his gut.

The messengers won't arrive in time... They are all going to die.

"This is your birthright." The Premier's voice rang out against the chamber's stone walls, echoing around the hooded men. "You are the chosen men of Canestry. It is your duty and your joy to fight and die for the flourishing of the New Order. And you will fight today. Even Provinces must die. Even the Stars must fall."

Osiys pounded his feet on the glossy stone floor in solemn celebration with the rest of the hooded Night Walkers, but beneath the folds of deep black fabric, his chest heaved, and his mind spun with horrified panic.

Premier Canryn sat and gave an abrupt pound against the arm of his throne, at which signal the Night Walkers filed out of the hulking entry doors, down the corridor with the walls of convoluted Starlight and battle scarred stone. He stepped out into brittle-cold night air, depthless in its moonlessness. The Night Walkers filed around him, swift and silent feet carrying them out the gate and towards the southwestern military halls.

The Stars gleamed, Meirydh climbing the starscape to its eventual alignment with the rest of her sisters. Their light bored holes into him as he arced his head back to take them in, to remember what they looked like on the night he failed. He would never be forgiven. He would never be welcomed into the Eternal House of Brigon's light.

But if he was to be unforgivable, he would drag as many of these Canestryn bastards with him into the void as he could.

It was my responsibility. I failed. I failed. I failed... He wanted to weep but dared not. Couldn't. Not now. Not yet.

Osiys steeled his face and forced himself onward to his personal ready room. Each of the Night Walkers had their own, as they were individually preparing and commanding a group of 50 men in their division. His nail had dug into his palm as he clenched his fist tightly, and it dripped beads of blood when he opened his fingers to clasp the door handle.

Inside, he walked to his table, which sat sturdy before a small fireplace, and sorted through the neatly organized containers for a small bandage, quickly wrapping it around his hand to keep the blood from dripping on the polished wood.

The grey-painted wooden wardrobe, the blank walls, the stone floor and metal table—it was all so cold, harsh, impersonal. The coals in the fireplace were still golden and ruby and gave off the mere suggestion of heat. He snorted— those coals were the warmest thing in this whole fucking place. He wouldn't be coming back here again, thank the Stars. His eyes rested again on his table and grazed a small strand of burgundy ribbon protruding slightly from its drawer.

That's odd...

He glanced out of the small window in his door into the hall; men half-dressed in battlegear anxiously jostled one another in their haste to rush this way and that. The sounds of scrambling and scuffling mingled with the occasional clipped voice of irritation.There wasn't much time...

Hurriedly, he stepped forward and opened the drawer. The ribbon was tied around a folded paper, crumpled up as though it had been stuffed inside of someone's pocket. He tugged on the ribbon and roughly unfolded it, spreading it flat in order to read the flourished scribbles that made up the strange little note:

Osiys, you are in danger, and I am the only one who can help you. Look for the stars on the hide of my stallion. Stay close to his flank.

Osiys glanced again at the door with an involuntary shiver, folding the note and jamming it between his teeth while he slipped his arms out of their sleeves. As he stripped off his wrinkled ensemble, his mind ran stumbling through the details of the letter. The flourished scratches, the stallion he'd never seen in their army, the lack of revelation of the writer.

He pulled on a clean pair of black leather trousers fresh from the storage wardrobe and pulled the laces tight at the waist before strapping on his leather waist-hilt and thigh knife sheath. Over his shirt sleeves he buckled the long leather half-gloves that hooked between his thumb and forefinger. Each glove had a secured pocket and was littered with various tiny, stitched-in crystals which he'd charged the night previous, using the scarce remainder of the small bottle of sacred spring water he'd brought with him those ten years ago.

He snatched the note from between his teeth and tucked it into the pocket on his left glove before pulling on his black hood, buttoning it to the leather strip across the shoulders of his shirt. His sword, knife, and darts slipped snugly into their sheaths.

He could see the words of the letter even though they were tucked safely in the pocket of his glove: *I am the only one who can help you.*

Stars and voids... I hope this fucker's confidence pays off, or we're both dead men.

Snatching a key from a small, concealed pocket in his hood, he reached beneath the table and fumbled about until the key found its lock. He turned his wrist and a wooden door no more than six inches wide opened; a silk drawstring bag and a thin copper chain threaded through the drawstring loops tumbled out into his ready hand. Swiftly clicking the door closed and relocking it, he slipped the chain around his neck and tucked the silk bag inside his shirt over his heart.

Osiys tossed the key into the embers of the fireplace and walked out the door, not looking back as the handle ticked shut behind him.

Making his way to the stables through the clamor of men clad in leather and grey cloth, he felt the silk pouch cool against his warm chest. He'd kept it carefully treasured, hidden away in this strange Canestryn High City for all ten years. Now, saddling his warhorse, the feather-light pouch felt like a boulder around his neck, so heavy he could scarcely breathe.

Osiys tucked a foot into the stirrup and swung his leg over the huge creature. The horse was as black as the inky metal which fashioned their weapons, just as each of the other Night Walkers' horses were. The

Premier claimed they were symbols of the night sky, the true sacred space, unlike the sacred Stars of the Old Order.

Only children's tales lived in the spaces between the Stars— creatures of terrible myth and obscene legend. It seemed a fitting place for the despicable myth and legend that was his history. Osiys frequently spent his nights urging himself to put out of his mind the atrocities he had committed as a Night Walker.

He nudged the horse's flank and trotted out to the training field that bordered the stables, eyes straining in the inky absence of moonlight for the horse with the starry hide. Nothing...

He'd have to move soon, get his division in formation and ready to ride out towards Meirydh. He didn't have time to be searching for some lone rider. The horse snorted and he patted its head in agreement.

"It's a damn joke, isn't it?" he commiserated to the creature, who tossed its mane with indifference. The rider was probably just luring him to a trap, ready to slice him neck to gut for being a traitor. But considering his life was no longer terribly valuable, he let curiosity edge him onward, let it sharpen his eyes.

Pulling the reins to the left, he took them to the crest of a gentle slope where he could look out over the amassing army. His head pounded with guilt, the growling darkness ramming into his skull. Patience was leeching from him. The star-flanked horse and its unaccountable rider were stubbornly missing from the seven-hundred men on horses.

From the corner of his eye he saw the Premier and his High Circle riding out from the stables on their horses clad in silver and crystal-studded harnesses and knew the rider's time to reveal himself was over.

Osiys' division was nearly in formation, their horses an unforgivingly straight line. He trotted down to join them, circling in front of them briefly to confirm their presence and readiness. Their faces were uncompromising and lashed with hatred and terror. His stomach turned.

The Premier raised his beam, a long steel rod, at the end of which was a large piece of raw crystal encircled by a leather cord. It emanated a sickly energy, the screeching squirm of violated Starlight. It warbled Osiys' vision, ripples running out from it in a near-invisible dark glimmer.

He had heard Canryn punishing and praising his various mages over the past several months. Something looming and terrible would be unleashed, he knew, but it wasn't until he overheard one of the mages swearing tearfully to himself that he realized what the Premier was attempting. He believed there was untapped potential in Starlight, if only it could be controlled, and he had been experimenting with the Stars' power over time itself.

A brief, bright flash shot out into the sky from the crystal and the long, low drone of something yet unknown set the air abuzz.

The wide expanse of plains in front of them shivered... shuddered as though it had been subjected to something which intimately disgusted it.

And then it began to fold. The sky heaved forward and down on itself, the plains lifted into a wall of green and dusty brown. The air was thick with the squirm of something tangibly execrable. Such heaviness leaned and groaned in on itself until Osiys was sure they would be crushed under this impossible earth-sky.

Sepulchral darkness bloomed into being as the earth and sky contracted. His chest constricting with numb dread, Osiys watched with unbelieving eyes as Canryn sent his horse into a gallop, driving them both into the cancerous black that had consumed the world.

Nothing prepared a man to watch his world be snuffed out by a mere tilt of crystal and metal. No seasoned warrior could bear the extent of this loss. But Osiys had already committed to changing the plan. He was going to die honorably, pay for the mortal mistake he had made, the doomed lives for which he was responsible. Perhaps this void would take him, or perhaps it would spit him back out. That was no longer his concern.

There were no Stars in this void as he led his division for it, so he filled it with the memory of the ones he had stopped to gaze at just an hour before. He filled it with the distant memory of stars caught in the mountain trees, of Elessid's hand pointing out the Brigon Star, of his first funerary trip to the Spire of the Dead— the place his ashes would now never travel.

As the void loomed closer, its blackness flickering with hunger, Osiys felt a hot, steaming breath against his left thigh. He jerked his head towards the offending soldier.

A rider clothed in the midnight purple hood and the deep brown leather boots and gloves of a page was gaining ground at his side. The rider sat atop a polished saddle, blood-red crystals embedded into the trim, and a large chunk of obsidian on the pommel. The dark purple cape that flowed from the hood covered all but a glimpse of the horse's grey and white speckled hide. Osiys raised an eyebrow.

Stars...

The rider's face was fully concealed in the depths of the large hood, and Osiys hadn't spent time among the Canestryn pages. But there was no doubt in his mind, cleared of distraction by the nearness of death: this was the writer of the note. The wind tugged at his ill-fitting clothes, ripping the cape this way and that.

As Osiys heaved his dread-weary gaze to the blackness ahead, the rider inched closer, drawing his horse nose to nose with Osiys'.

Together, they leapt into the void.

Osiys gagged on the ear-crushing silence that hit them like a hostile pressure.

Then...

Their presence seemed to elicit a heinous screaming from the dark. Worse than an injured animal. More unearthly. More lost. More vengeful. More despondent.

Flashes of light. Silver. Flickering out.

A wailing reach— the darkness thrust itself down his throat. Aimless panic. Utter surrender? What else was there, but this clawing, shriveling cold?

Razing silver light. Again. Once.

Gagging. Retching.

A sudden presence of being. The sound of sound. No crushing silent pressure. No horrid screaming dark. No crawling blackness in his throat.

They were at the Meirydhi border—he could see the first outpost jutting from the white grass of the plains now— and the barely visible moon was fully raised in the sky, a slivered whisper amongst a field of tiny, pinpricked stars. It was truly, dreadfully dark.

But the Meirydhi border was more than a week— nearly two!— from Canestry on horseback.

The Premier had violated the sacred Stars to repudiate the boundaries of time. Osiys puked all over the grass. It hit his boot with a distasteful splatter, and black smears dragged through the vomit.

In front of him, the three outermost divisions on each side of the army broke to the side and separated, soldiers lagging and trailing as they, too, emptied their stomachs. None dared stop; none dared question their all-powerful Premier.

Osiys looked behind him to where his division had just made it through the darkness. He recalled the plan as he motioned for them to follow him, shifting to cover the outer left edge of the cavalry.

These separated divisions were to neutralize each of the outposts surrounding Meirydh, keeping the guards from running for help to neighboring Provinces or coming to the aid of their High City. Effective. So inhumanly effective.

A hand brushed his arm. The gloved hand of the cloaked rider handed him a small stone.

FOLLOW was painted on the grey of the stone. A nod.

Ten of his men whipped their horses into a bolting gallop, riding up against the watchtower to their left. Four of the riders notched their arrows, sent them flying towards the now-scrambling lookout men. Two fell from the small tower with cries that cut through the dull thudding of hooves against dirt. The riders dismounted and began storming the small tower. Even as Osiys passed, the Meirydhi flag atop the outpost was stripped down and replaced with a Canestryn one.

Moments later they surged past the second outpost to the right, a rolling sea of manes and glinting metal, watching the Meirydhi soldiers emptying of blood on their own soil. It wasn't long before the outpost was disappearing behind them and their sight was fixed on the High City, with its reflective white marble walls that spiraled high into the sooty atmosphere and gates framed with geometric curls.

The page was riding hard, close to his side. They would arrive at any moment. There were three divisions ahead of Osiys', and he knew the plan. The three initial divisions would circle back to the northern side of the city, dismount and enter a series of tunnels, the locations of which had been obtained through the long-term project of a spy. The strategy had been flawlessly dreamt.

When they were merely a few hundred yards from the city, a loud bell rang out, and the great gates began to creak open, pouring out a swell of riders and foot soldiers from Meirydh's High City. Energy cracked in the air above them, sending out unforeseeable bouts of blue sparks and violent flashes of white light. He heard a horse somewhere in front of him scream. The clash between them was coming... it was so close it was as though he could hear their breathing.

Ten years... And it ends in failure and death.

They collided.

Instantly, he was reacquainted with the sound of metal sinking into human flesh. To his right, a Meirydhi foot soldier was dragged under the waves of horse hooves, his skull crushed until his screaming ceased.

They soared ever closer to the gates, now billowing with desperate citizens fleeing the harbingers of death that had crept into their city. The Canestryns cut them down as they ran, a soldier beside Osiys severed the head of a man in fine robes leading a young woman by the hand. In the trailing upswing, her face was bisected in a river of blood.

Osiys' chest heaved, grief and rage boiling up in undeniable lurches. He rasped his sword free of its scabbard and buried it in the soldier's chest. As he turned for the other Canestryn within reach, his horse bolted.

It refused to be redirected and continued charging for the westward side of the city away from the thick of the battle. Clinging to its back with his legs and irritably trying to soothe its terror over the cacophony of war that now rose behind them, Osiys faced no choice but to go where the enraged creature took him.

The page raced beside him.

The horse began to calm and, despite Osiys' death oath, the traitorous part of him that still wished to live raced the steed onward beside the page, the battle roar dimming in their wake.

Osiys chanced a glance back towards the massacre. A fire had already started in the High City and armor glinted in it like jewels; Meirydh had been sacked. He squinted into the night. A lone rider had broken from the battle, riding out for them. He returned his gaze to the page beside him.

"There's a rider. We will have to face him."

The page briefly bristled before giving a silent nod.

They rode hard, yet the lone rider was gaining ground behind them. Osiys was not afraid: just today he had faced the butchery of a people and gagged on a void created by man. It was the prospect of some possible hidden pursuit which made his stomach turn. He cradled the hilt of his sword.

"I will deal with this." He glanced back again to see the rider nearly closing in on his flank. It was time. He brought his steed to a halt, turning the two of them round to face the soldier riding towards him, the great bloodbath like a macabre curtain behind it all. Osiys drew his sword.

The rider was one of the drafted: a simple peasant with a bit of armor and a sorry excuse for a sword. Vomit streaked his chest and his pants were stained where he had urinated out of fear, likely during his trip through the void. This man had received little formal training in the art of war. He was probably looking for the reward that came with slaying deserters, and he certainly didn't deserve to die. He would die anyway, though, because nobody ever got what they deserved.

At least I can make it quick.

Osiys gritted his teeth. The man's eyes swam with emptiness and terror as Osiys easily disarmed him with a single swift blow. With a second swing, fast and deadly as Meirydhi lightning, he removed the man's head from his shoulders, the remainder of his neck spouting blood that stained the tawny mane as his body slumped against the horse.

His head fell at the feet of Osiys' horse, eyes still open and glazed with misery. The horse bolted, and the peasant's body fell from the saddle, dragging beside the galloping horse by a reign-entangled hand.

"Let's move." Osiys quickly turned to face the page, and once again they kicked their horses into a brisk gallop.

They rode hard for nearly an hour, until the High City of Meirydh was only a faded shape, slowly engulfing in fire on the horizon. They slowed their horses to a brisk walk. Morning light grew like a flame behind them, illuminating the smoking city and casting long shadows on their path.

A fresh burst of wind rushed at them, stopping the shuddering horses in their tracks. Osiys looked over to the page, who remained silent, and squinted against the plains dust being blown towards them.

His throat was raked sore and his tongue dry and parched. He didn't want to think about the last thing that had passed between his lips.

"I think the horses need a rest," he rasped.

The page tilted his head towards Osiys when a wild gust blew back the deep purple hood and a mess of blonde curls spilled out over the cape.

Osiys visibly jolted and tumbled out of his saddle.

"You precious little brat!" he laughed, rushing to grab her hands and dragging her from her horse to press her against his chest in relieved shock. She wrapped her arms around him briefly before tugging herself away.

"You didn't know it was me? A dreadful spy, you are." Indra smirked, taming her bouncing hair by wrapping it behind her head with a length of fabric.

Osiys watched her, his temple throbbing, her lighthearted voice not masking the reality of her words to him. He shuddered, but not from the wind that whipped his hood flat against the side of his face.

She could have died. Why would she do this? His mind flooded with her Star Charts, with her father's summoned void, with the way she shadowed him, smelling of oranges. Of course she would do this. Death is better than that.

"Indra..." his gravelly voice faltered. "That was a terribly stupid thing to do."

She smiled softly and pulled the oversized gloves from her little hands. "It was less stupid of me to leave that place than it was for you to come to it in the first place. But, selfishly, I'm glad you did."

He looked at her hard, but found no insincerity in her eyes. There never was any.

Osiys glanced behind them. What was once the High City of Meirydh was now a smoldering ruin, belching black clouds of smoke into the air and casting a foreboding shroud over the enchanting blue of the Tanaraq plains. Sweat dripped down into his eye, salty and pinching, as he squinted towards the smoking expanse. Nothing— at least not yet. There was no sign of further pursuit, but he couldn't be sure. Now that he knew Indra was with him too... He watched her tend to her horse, nuzzling its velvety nose before pulling herself up into the saddle. Osiys followed suit, clicking his steed forward encouragingly.

"We've got to move, Indra. We've got to move quickly."

KNOW

3
THREAD BY BLOODSTAINED THREAD

JAUYNE, HIGH CITY OF MEIRYDH
3 days since the sack of Meirydh.

Smoke.

She remembered smelling smoke.

And burning.

Even beneath closed eyes she knew: the High Circle of Meirydh was burned. Her home was ashes. Everything was gone.

And the pain—slicing, torturous pain—it cut across her face from temple to lip.

A hoarse cry escaped from her mouth. Her sorrow boiled over and slid from squinted-closed eyelids as her hands dug into the blackened ground beneath her body. The dry, moaning cries skidded over the fallen stones and scattered bodies until her parched throat could no longer vocalize her grief.

Seconds, minutes, eons later, Jauyne opened her eyes to a hazy sun. She saw the smoke rising like a morbid offering to the heavens from the Tanaraq Plains all around her, the grey haze softening the distant mountain range into smudges of charcoal and ash.

In stunned anguish, she gasped for breath. The silence was harrowing. Forcibly, she blinked. Hard, and with physical ache. With great effort, she rose to sit, where she promptly wretched at the sight and stench of the dead strewn all about her in numbers vast and sickening. Belryn, her father's closest friend and High Priest of Meirydh, lay beside her, his head a separate entity that haunted the bloody ground at her feet.

Beautiful Meirydh, home to the wildest of all the Startouched. Meirydh—where they danced in the flashes of lightning storms and meteor showers, and the children ran strong and unafraid with feral creatures

creatures. With its soaring circular rings of white marble and finely detailed stairs and gates; it was gone, and her own sorry ass was all that was left.

Her home had been flayed and burned, and its blood turned the bluish-white plains red. The ache was too great. The taste of bile was still on her lips.

Jauyne wiped her mouth on the back of her shaking hand. Recoiling in pain, she saw on it a stripe of blood—too bright. Turning slowly, the reflection which met her eyes from a splattered shield was devastating. Her face was gashed deeply from her right temple down to the left side of her trembling lip. Her nose was broken. For a moment, she could feel the earth whirling. She was losing blood too quickly. She was going to die—die with all of her fallen people. Die an ugly, pointless, stupid death. Although, in her dwindling and feeble state, at least it would not be slow.

Resolve and hatred rose up in the form of vomit, and again she wretched on the charred grass. The strength that anger brought pulled her to her feet where she stumbled headlong through the ruin, forcing herself onward through the cadaverous tangle, eventually collapsing in the doorway of a crumbling apothecary which stood just inside the broken city gates.

Her mind reached stark-wild through the hum of hazy clouds, her energetic senses dulled by weakness and pain; yet still she strained, reaching into the heavens for the Starlight which her mind could feel as the dangling threads of the light of a thousand stars. They called to her, a memory, a familial burst of want. She pulled the threads toward her, her mind flaring with a surge of strength as her senses soared, flooded with Starlight. Cool and bracing the Meirydh Star felt as she reached for it. Silver light laced with the promise of a storm. A friend to her since childhood, her very first memory, its radiance had always filled her mind.

Her shaky hands rummaged through the stones and torn-down shelves, coming to buried bits of gauzy cloth and an assortment of chipped bottles. Blotting the cloth with the contents of a small jar, she placed it on her battered and broken face. Only the dead heard her scream with agony.

After binding her face and sipping some chloronynë for the pain, she slept in an anguished heap on the apothecary floor, the stones still warm from the fire that had ravaged its southern wall.

Jauyne woke again as the sun was slipping down with fiery protest between blood-red clouds. Her face fucking ached, but her mind's clarity was growing. She steeled herself and perched on the apothecary stoop, taking in the depravity of the genocide. She swallowed hard as the rays of angry sunlight glinted off the crystals inlaid on the fallen stones and metal work of the countless buildings, and rested her head softly against the broken doorway.

She was starting to remember...

She'd been with her father in his study, the smoke from his Pallydhan cigar curling around them and making her nostrils burn delightedly before winding upward towards the high ceiling. She was often here in this lavishly snug room that brought her joy until it didn't. It was where her daily lessons took place, where she learned to hone her Star-given gifts into sharp edges and clear words. It was where she was taught the role of leadership, taught her place in her world, her Province, her family— never a daughter, always a student. She loved it, and she loathed it. Tonight, though, she'd been pulled from her bed and brought to her father in a scattered rush.

Her papa's eyes glinted in the lamplight with the hint of remnant Starlight like they always did, but they were red around the edges, concerned. She'd felt a dull roar in the city, felt it so deep it was as though her bones were grinding against one another. Their midnight lesson had felt jagged and strained— awkward reminders of things she'd known since she was small.

"The Stars give us their light to carry it into the world. They stretch out to us, Jauyne, but to you most of all. You are a rare jewel in Allesar. You must always think of your duty. You must always reach for the Stars. You must be ready in the least seemingly of times to do what must be done, regardless of your own feelings or wants. Do you hear me? Your desires have no place in the life of one so Star-blessed, or one of a Premier. Get rid of them. And do what must be done."

She had known this her whole life. She had spent her twenty-two years in service to it. She needed no reminder. So she said, "As I always do, papa."

He had finally clasped her face in his hands and whispered, "There are those who were born to speak the language of the Stars, and you, Jauyne, are among them. It is the language that birthed the world. It is written on your mind. The whole fabric of Allesar is written in it. The Stars are part of your blood and their light flows through your veins, even now." He kissed her on each eyelid, a blessing— or a claiming, she could never be sure— on the part of her that was evidence of her gift. "I love you so very dearly."

Belryn had taken her hand then, as the dull roar grew, surging through the nearby hallway, accentuated by screams that turned her blood to curdling. He'd pulled her along as she realized what was happening, dragged her away from her father and into a tunnel behind one of the sacred tapestries. As they huddled on the other side of the concealed door, Jauyne heard the unmistakable thud of metal meeting flesh, and knew her papa was dead.

Jauyne covered her mouth with her hand, her stomach lurching at the memory. A silent cry parted her lips as salty tears soaked through her bandage and stung the wound. She hunched against the doorway, convulsing with the untamable sobs of an agonized girl who had never had anyone to comfort her. Not really.

She must have drifted off again.

She needed a new head bandage.

The sun was so bright...

Again she cleaned the ugly wound on her face, crying out as the cold and stinging ointment soaked into the cleaved skin, and again she bound it with fresh cloth. It was irritating, painful, and awkward work. Exhaling sharply, she knew it was time to salvage what she could of her home. Jauyne collected the bottle of chloronynë ointment and folded up some strips of gauze, tucking them into the small pouch secured around her waist.

Climbing the debris-littered steps towards the central ring of the city, she stopped to take a large leather pack from the back of a young man's corpse. His hair was long and blond, except for the ends which were dyed a verdant green and pulled into a rumpled knot at the base of his neck. On his face was a full beard, partially scorched from the flames of the burning city. Crushed against the city wall, there were arrows embedded in his side, and—could it be?—tear stains in the bloody muck and grime on his dirty, grief-stricken face. He was certainly not Meirydhi. He looked as though perhaps he hailed from the Chedhiy Province, what with all his smattering of freckles and the green and white and brown he wore. She prodded the body with her foot until it turned over. The embroidery on his shirt was sure enough an arrow-strung bow—the mark of the forested Province of Chedhiy. Their people were strong and gentle, hunters deeply in tune with the earth and its creatures. Why would a Chedhiyn man have been in Meirydh instead of capturing game during the season of hunting?

It was no business of hers, and he was dead anyway, so she sat on a large granite stair covered in an unfathomable amount of dried blood and rummaged through his pack. It seemed to buzz and hum when she had hauled it from his body, and now the hum was a soft tingle spreading through her fingers.

Dried venison and a large chunk of famed Jopaar Province bread wrapped in brown paper were the first items she found. She'd at least have some decent food to last her a while. She continued to dig into his pack: three leather bound books, Pallydhan coffee, a glass jar of something that smelled like chloronynë, carved bone pan pipes... It was a strange assortment of items, she thought. She reached in for the last thing in this Chedhiyn man's pack. Her fingers curled around a large, soft leather pouch, and something in her sternum murmured a wordless, sibilated greeting. The pouch was pulled closed with a braided cord. She tugged it and tilted the contents of the bag into her hand.

Her body was met with a feeling like wielding lightning, like the fiercest storm raging in her ribs, like every star in the sky was pouring into her their glittering, endless light.

Her mind was assaulted with a vibrancy that hurt, with a curiosity so strong it made her livid, with a familiarity that made her want, made her yearn.

Her un-bandaged eye was met with a sight she did not understand.

A large, sky-blue crystal point rested in her palm, set into a hunk of melted foreign metal from which burst several skinny, multicolored protrusions. On the back, several thin strands of wrapped metal stuck out in all directions, as though it had been ripped from something larger and then discarded. She turned it over and over in her hands, attempting to make sense of it.

Its hum was steady and forceful, a deep vibration. It emanated from the crystal as though it pulsed along with the rhythm of her blood, as though it was listening for her blood. Jauyne clutched it, deeply inhaling, making a very failed attempt to steel herself and collect her scattered mind, before sliding it back into its pouch.

Shaking her head, Jauyne piled the items back into the leather pack and slung it over her shoulder. The crystal hummed still even through the carrier on her back, and she felt it in her bones, and in the very beat of her heart. Making her way further up the corpse-littered steps, she stepped over Meirydhi citizens with gaping, shiny rifts in their throats or wetly punctured chests or gashes blooming into repulsive flowers of blood on their clothing. A limbless, unrecognizably mangled man bridged the gaping gateway of her home. The meat of his severed torso shone foul and sticky in the harsh sun. Flies congregated on the wounds.

This is a slaughterhouse...

There were still places that smoldered, embers and little flickering flames that had yet to die out in the parts of the city that were built from wood and from the pile of bodies which had been incapacitated and burned alive. She knew this because she had heard the horrors of what had happened to Nareilë seven years prior. It had been taught to her, sparing no detail, just after it had happened. She had been fifteen. She had swallowed her puke and then emptied her stomach when lessons were over and she was out of her papa's sight. This would never happen to Meirydh, she was told. They were prepared. They were in contact with spies within the Canestryn Province.

Well, fuck those spies, and fuck Canestry. They hadn't been good enough, and now she was the last living Meirydhi.

The last living Meirydhi.

With tears boiling in her eyes, Jauyne entered the courtyard of her home, waving at the smoky air. She forced herself forward, planted one foot in front of the other, took another step and then another. The strange crystal hummed at her back as the Stars hummed invisible in the daylight sky, and it was just sustenance enough.

The doorway. The hall. The kitchen. The bodies of her mother and little sister were slumped against the wall of a torn-open pantry where they'd been hiding. Her mother's arms were still clutching Astra to her, her glazed eyes open and gazing with terror upon a long-gone Canestryn soldier. Covering the floor, poured out from their navels and throats like a bastardized wine, was their blood, dark and thick. A despairing urge welled up in her to pour the blood back in, to scoop up the organs gushing from her mother's belly and press them back into place, to just fucking undo this. Instead, her feet pounded on, silent on the decorated carpet running the length of the hall, further into the desecration.

She could remember how the air smelled sweet of her mother's perfume; how the birds would fly in and out of the west-facing windows in the long hall; how little Astra would prance in and out of the opposite kitchen and study doors, batting her lashes for sweet things from the cook and clinging to their papa as he studied or instructed Jauyne or met with people from other Provinces. She could almost see her mother, arms filled with fresh cut flowers, stepping in her flighty way, almost dancing down the hall, humming an old ballad and calling for Jauyne to come fix her untidy bedroom.

She closed her eyes and ran her palm along the great, smooth marble wall of the house, seeing warm golden light in her mind's eye and hearing her father calling them to dinner as the smoke from his Pallydhan cigar swirled after him down the hall.

But again she opened her eyes and saw cold and crumbling stone and smelled the fetid death all around. She nearly vomited on the rug under her feet at the thought of her sweet sister never again clinging to her papa or her mother never again humming gentle songs under the clamorous city sounds.

Was this what it meant to survive? She slapped at the tears on her face and gritted her teeth. Sorrow was a knife in the belly.

Crossing into her war-rummaged room, she stripped it of the clean and comfortable clothing and peeled off her blood-caked wrap shirt and pants. They clung to her skin, sloughing off with shucking noises. Tugging on her heavy leather riding boots, she crammed a warm sweater and cap made of firecat fur into her pack. It was the beginning of autumn, and winter would be well on its way soon.

Venturing to her parents' quarters, she paused. She had no love for these people, who had only ever instructed and refined her, reserving their tenderness for her sister. Still, this was her legacy. She was what was left. So she took a gold bangle of her father's, marked with the simple and comforting sign of her people—a jagged bolt of lightning—and slid it up her arm underneath her shirt before fixing an ear cuff of her mother's to the wide outer curve of her left ear.

After filling her sack with the remaining food from the large pantries, she turned to survey the sight one last time. With tears swimming in her vision, she blew a swift kiss goodbye, and with hard resolve turned her back on her home.

She briefly stopped at the stables to gather a metal water canteen and her uniquely crafted Meirydhi dagger, carefully concealed in a special plank of wood at the side of the horse stall. She ran her hand along the naturally smooth-ridged flat of the obsidian dagger, avoiding the craggy edges. It was comforting, the way it mimicked what thrashed inside her, and she tucked it into the scabbard at her thigh before making her way back to the outskirts of the city.

Jauyne faced the cool tones of the Tanaraq Plains with a shaky gaze—it stretched wider than she remembered before her sorrowed eyes—and her heart faltered. Not just the city, but all of the grassy tufts in the desert were smoked out, reduced to ashes and bitter sorrow. She could still see the small, distant lights of little fires dwindling on in the teasing breezes that kissed the grass, and, on happier days, had made it sway and dance.

Where is there to go?

She brushed her father's bangle on her arm with her fingertips. She had her answer: To anyone. She would go to anyone who would listen, to anyone who would join her. She would speak the truth. Men in black clothing had attacked, and she knew their faces. She knew the whispers of corruption that had swept through the people, years before their annihilation. She would go to whoever would listen, and she would face the corruption, look it in the eyes with the deadness of her own, and sever it limb from body, unravel it thread by bloodstained thread. She would hold tight to her rage and with it, build her Province—tall, proud, beautiful Meirydh—back from the ashes.

One step. Another. The crystal at her back. The Stars in her blood. She was the Premier of devastation and death. She was the last Meirydhi. She trained her eyes on the massive forest that sprawled far northwest across the plains. Chedhiy was as good a start as any.

IF

4
A TRILLION STARS EVERYWHERE SCREAMING

Once, when she was feeling infinitely alone and profoundly sad and terribly brave, she had seen them do it to other children born with eyes far less shining than her own.

She had tugged on a worn, discarded page's cloak that she had stolen from the laundry several months before, and crept down the smooth-finished stairs to the entry that led to her garden. Ducking behind the ornamental shrubbery that grew out of the ground where gate and wall intersected, she slid through the space she had carefully cut away at the only remaining section of wooden gate.

The guards should have been more attentive, yes, but who was going to break into the highest-guarded layer of the Premier's city? And who would want to break out... It hadn't happened yet, and so Indra had, rather a bit too easily, been able to creep up the stairs to the top of the wall surrounding her father's tented meeting chamber.

A real Star Chart report: this was what she had been hoping for, considering this was where Canryn's upper circles came to give their announcements and hold ceremonies. Instead, she saw children.

There were nine of them. Their eyes shimmered faintly, some flaring between bright silver and ash grey. Indra felt their pull. She felt the way the Stars reached for them, reached back with a vengeance. She felt their little bodies, felt them as an extension of her own.

Never before had Indra seen another person with eyes like hers. Never before had she felt Starlight curling and flowing in veins that were not her own. Her whole self lurched with familiarity, with some deep, overwhelming emotion that clawed its way up her throat and pin-pricked her

She felt the children, and she felt the Stars, and she wanted to echo them. Wanted to reach back. Wanted to be reached for. Instead, below her, something in the bold curlicues of stone groaned and flinched away from her with a loathsome murmur.

Surrounding the children were her father's High Circle and several guards. So many guards. They circled them in revolving ripples, hemming them in. The smallest child began to weep; the others began to back towards one another in terrified, twitching movements. White stone streaked through where their bare feet shuffled on the dirty floor.

Her father stood on the open-air dais, blond hair cut close but curling around his ears. A ring-clad hand raised, and Indra felt a glaring brightness scream within her from the Stars. Her fingers gripped the stone so hard they ached, keeping her body pressed to the spot, forcing her to stay, in opposition to the panic lurching in her lungs.

Soldiers dragged the crying child forward, his little knees scraping against the pebbled ground. His Starlight was thrashing; Indra could see the silvered strands on which he pulled and lurched, arcing out into the night sky, unmoored.

Beckoning with his extended hand, Canryn reached for the boy. He grabbed the front of his skull, thumb and smallest finger grossly bridging his temples. The boy went limp. There was a flash of silver— not Starlight; no, not Starlight— and that little silver thing was nestled into the child's neck.

Canryn dropped him, and the boy crumpled.

He was so small.

The Premier— her father— descended on the small body, prying open his eyes and barbarously peering at them. "Let's take the eyes on this one. He's too small to channel much, anyhow."

The other children flailed in a useless swell of panic. There was nothing they could do. There was nothing... Indra's chest was surely splitting open; her heart wailed.

A nod to the soldiers. The small body was moved to the side. Someone crassly pulled open the boy's eyelids and reached between them, clawing out the eyeball and stringy optic nerve.

"Put him down with the others while we take care of the rest. Separate the blinded ones and the eyeless ones from the rest. They're much stronger than the last crop." Canryn reached for the next child.

Her lungs were failing. She was being pulled apart. Everything went nova. Starlight everywhere in her vision. Sparking behind her eyes till it burned down into her throat. A trillion stars everywhere screaming out to her. Six marvelous orbs of shrieking light, hopelessly disconnected. A baring anger that stripped her whole. Nausea burning a forceful blare from navel to throat.

A hand curled around the back of her neck.

A voice.

"Wake up."

A scream was strangling her tongue, gluing it to the roof of her mouth as she blinked up at a sparse canopy of green splattered over a sunrise-mauve sky. She sobbed a gasp.

Osiys tucked a cloth-wrapped copper mug into her hands. He awkwardly petted a soft circle into her upper back. No words. They watched the sun rise over the puckering stacks of smoke.

What was real? Which reality was this? Was she really here, or would she wake up again, trapped in a house without hope or escape, save that of watching other Starlit children being rounded up and routinely tortured?

At last, "What do you dream about?"

Swallowing the tea made her body real. Made her hands real. Made the pinking sky and the tree branches and the dew-damp ground and Osiys real. She met his eyes.

"The day I decided to leave." A pause, a fluttering of something sick with hope in her chest. "It's a strange dream to have when I've left."

"You've done it. You left."

"I know. Now I only need to figure out how to get back."

There was a beat of time that felt closer to a hiccup. She could feel his eyes boring into the side of her head.

"What?"

A deep breath drenched her lungs in dew drops and smoky humidity. "I have to go back for them."

"You can't— for who?" Panic clung to his voice.

She met his eyes. "For the children. It's my responsibility. He is my father. I am his blood. And wrongs written in blood must be rewritten."

"Listen to me, Indra." Osiys leaned forward, his hands gripping one another in his lap. "Nothing that your father has done— nothing— is your responsibility. When I say that your father will pay for his crimes, when I say that my soul will not be at peace until I am confident he cannot hurt another living person, I am telling you the truth. We will end this. But you, you will not make another stupid move and try to run yourself back to Canestry. All that's going to do is get you tortured and killed. It's not going to solve a thing. It is certainly not going to rewrite any of his wrongs."

She stared him down, ever-aware of her smallness, of her youth. "When we end this, I want to be there."

"Indra..."

"I want to be there!" She knew she'd spilt her tea, knew her eyes were lit unbearably bright, knew he could see the Starlight creeping along her veins.

He swallowed. "Okay. Alright. I just... You don't deserve to ever have to set foot within those walls again."

"No one in that Province deserved anything they have had to endure."

"You were always too big for that place. There's too much in you for that oppression."

She felt hot all over. "There is too much in everyone for that oppression. There's nothing special about me."

He sighed. "Well, you're right on the first account— I suppose being surrounded by cruelty for long enough made me a bit cruel as well— but you're wrong on the second, and you know it."

A feeling twitched in her chest. The only thing being special had managed to do for her was keep her locked behind walls and separated from anyone who might have had a fighting chance at teaching her about who she was and what the Starlight that ran through her veins was capable of.

And yet... she had seen the eyes of the children her father tortured. She had seen them flare and swell with the same thing in her own... but it was less. It was so much less. None of their eyes glowed silver before it surged up in them. Some of them did no more than ever so slightly shimmer, even as they pulled on their Starlight. No one else she had ever seen had shimmered from the inside out the way she did. She knew she hadn't seen many people, and no one outside of her own Province save Osiys, but still... Still...

Yes. She was special. She hated it. She changed the subject.

"Tell me about the Stars, Osiys. And Brigon. And all the Provinces. Tell me the things I would know if I hadn't been his child."

The grass tickled the back of her neck as she lay back in it like a nest. They would get up in a few minutes. They would pack up their camp, and they would mount the horses, and they would ride towards the mountains, turning their back on the blackened sky behind them. But for now, she was Indra, the child who had been trapped behind walls, and he was Osiys, the Night Walker who had tossed her chocolate-covered oranges.

She didn't want to tell him how she'd gotten them out. She didn't want to tell him what had happened in the darkness of her father's power. She didn't want him to ask. She wanted to hear forbidden stories.

Pointedly ignoring the question his face was asking, with a skyward expression of her own that she hoped looked like innocence instead of heartache, she watched the place where black smoke merged with white clouds. She watched the Seven Stars, nearly aligned, wink brightly against daytime blue. She clawed her fingers into the dirt, anchoring herself to Meirydhi soil, to anything sturdy that wasn't stone walls and half lit, mutilated children. To anything that wasn't her bloody city.

The Stars mesmerized her. They didn't buzz with fury. Instead they sang out here in a way she hadn't been able to hear in Canestry, a lilting astral ballad that kept time to Osiys' words about myths of astral dragons she might have been told as a toddler, and the history of how Allesar had come to be— children of the Stars called up from dust and soil. He pointed to the mountains, looming and shrouded in forest to the west, showed her the peak that held the High House and the town in which he was raised. He told her about how the houses and shops clung to the mountainside, about the thin trails they'd climb on horses, about the guard houses they'd pass and the native plants she'd be able to find— how there wasn't a garden as she was used to, but he'd teach her to forage instead.

She rubbed her eyes. Even though the sun was creeping higher in the sky, the world was growing dimmer, the light diffused by the smoke and ash. It was time to go.

Osiys continued without pause as they tucked away their things into packs and saddled the horses. Indra cradled the velvety muzzle of her steed, murmuring encouragement into the horse's mane before awkwardly pulling herself up into the saddle. She had never had cause to learn more than the barest hint of riding, as she'd never been allowed more than a turn or two around the High House on her horse.

Riding the day before had left her stiff and sore, her muscles squealing for relief as she hauled herself up. She grimaced at the thought of at least four more days of the trek. Surely she'd be nothing but a pained board by the time they reached Brigon. They'd have to tilt her into a bath, for Stars' sake. She groaned.

"And then there are the myths of Starchildren, or Starseeds as some like to call them." Osiys was still rambling on. She would certainly forget half of this later on, but she was glad for it, anyhow. "They're considered to be those who, for some reason or another, possess more Starlight than others. Their blood is truer to those first Starchildren that the Stars raised at the beginning of Allesar— their eyes shimmer, their veins are bright, they are so much more powerful than the average channeler. The last ones died years before either you or I were born."

Starchildren... Something light and tingly started at the base of her skull. Something familiar and foreign, all at once.

YOU'RE

5

IF YOU RUN,
I WILL GUT YOU

JAUYNE, HIGH CITY OF MEIRYDH
9 days since the sack of Meirydh

Golden sun beat down on pale skin. Jauyne pressed the back of her hand to her forehead, then traced a finger down the mangled bridge of her slowly healing nose, wincing. She had just replaced the bandage to her facial wound, which was soon to mend into an ugly scab if she was lucky and woundrot didn't set in. Jauyne scarcely recognized herself in the small mirror she had taken from her mother's armoire. She hated it.

The cool grey dust which the breeze continuously kicked up from the road and swirled with the lingering traces of smoke made her cough. The coughing stung her injured face. But the further from Meirydh she trudged, the less dry and smoke-polluted the cold, bluish plains became, and the sweeter the smell of the occasional lone, curled sytril tree.

She was six days out from Meirydh, and she hadn't met a single human being on the long road to Chedhiy, which was often scattered with conversational travelers. For a day and a half, she had veered away from the stamping footprints of the dark army where they had left evidence of pursuit, and of cutting down the families who lived in the outskirts of the Province.

Eventually, she reached the marker where the road swerved with intention in the direction of the Chedhiy Province. The marker was engraved with the sigil of Chedhiy—an upturned bow strung with an arrow, encircled by a crown of leaves. She was growing steadily closer to the great mountains which separated Chedhiy from Brigon like a great arched spine, and the mists that rolled down from them smelled green and alive. It was as though she could breathe again, and how sweet air not tinged with fire and melancholy was!

Jauyne stopped for a moment to rest under the scant shade of a twisted, swirling sytril tree, her pack nestled up against the grey-barked trunk. These trees, like everything else in Meirydh, responded to the intensity of the land's magic in strange and wonderful ways. they warped and curved in spherical dances of bark and leaves. With fingers salty from sweat, Jauyne unlatched her water bag and took a deep drink of the sweet Meirydh spring water.

Home... it tastes like home.

And reality tasted bitter, almost in actuality, on her tongue. She broke off a chunk of the bread with unnecessary aggression and chewed a bit of the gamey strip of dried venison. It was an odd and slightly disappointing experience for her Meirydhi tongue so used to spice, and she worked the unnervingly chewy meat around her mouth before taking a second swig of water.

She stretched her feet out in front of her towards the looming grey and green palette of the mountains and let her head lull back lazily against the trunk of the tree. Gazing up at the branches, she saw birds and realized she had somehow missed their singing. Her ears drank it in. Returning the bread and venison to her pack, her hand brushed the pouch containing the foreign crystal device, and a tingle of warmth sang up her arm with a fiery urgency.

Jauyne paused, her hand still on the pouch, her arm still buzzing. There was kinship there, and fear, too. Her pride rested on remaining unaffected by things meant to rattle her, and this crystal— this thing— was plucking at parts of her she allowed no one and nothing access to. No one and nothing but the Stars.

Pressing her lips together and casting a brief glance around the empty plains, she tugged the pouch from the pack. She felt the strange thing leaping with light under her fingertips before she even pulled the drawstring open. There was Starlight in it; she could feel it seeping into her bloodstream, in a way stronger than any training, exercise, or conductor had ever brought to the surface. She gently slid the crystal from its pouch, the weight of it resting in her palm.

Pin pricks. A heady emanation of myth itself. The Stars. An effulgent swirl of silver, bleeding upward through her hands, sliding beneath the pale skin of her arms. A tangle of Starlight along the ribbons of her insides. A brilliantly cosmic, terribly human venation of all Their astral light.

A shiver ran the length of her spine. She knew enough to know she was in the presence of something sacred.

She remembered her father's lessons, turning the crystal over and over in her hands. They spoke of celestial guidance and communication, a network of their spiritual past, present, and future. Jauyne, like all believers in the Old Order, believed that the Stars guided and cared for all their creation. All of Allesar was born from them, and all of the inhabitants of the world were their children; she knew her slaughtered people were now living in the Garden of Stars, the home of the star Meirydh, who mothered her Province.

"The ways of the Stars may be enigmatic, but their communication is always simple: if Starlight is calling you, you must always listen." Jauyne whispered her father's words to herself as she gazed at the crystal, stroking its tiny horizontal lines and strange, triangular etchings with a fingertip.

She closed her eyes, and she could still see the Starlight branching through her. She could still see the shape of the crystal, the little markings and patterns in an intricate spatter across its surface. Lungs filling with prickling warmth, she brought the crystal, this piece of the Stars, to her chest, and a radiant shock slammed into her as though she'd been struck by lightning.

Vision stuttered in blaring silver and stunting darkness. She heard her own voice, so young: *Papa?*

His brusque reply: "It isn't time for your lessons."

"Can't I just sit with you? I'll be very quiet."

"Jauyne, you know the rules. You are not to speak to me outside of lessons."

"But you let Astra sit with you!"

"Astra doesn't have to be Premier someday." He shook his head at her, gaze brimming with an unsolvable disgust where his eyes met hers above the spine of his book. "You need to learn how to react appropriately when someone gives you an answer you don't like."

The rage, the one feeling that had always been coiled up inside of her, leapt up her throat with hot tears. "I SAID I just want to SIT! I just want to SIT with you!"

He slammed his book on the desk, and her little nerves flinched. "You will not raise your—"

"My VOICE?" The crackle of light and heat was flickering in her chest, the study illuminated in hues of starry silver. "I WANT to raise my voice! I WANT to sit with you!"

She flung her little finger towards him, and Starlight streaked over the distance between them. She saw fear in his eyes— real, genuine fear— and at least it wasn't disgust. At least it wasn't grating displeasure. At least it wasn't apathy.

He dropped to the ground.

The raw abrasiveness of a whip slapped against her neck, lashing her throat to the tree behind her and bringing her back to the present.

Jauyne's eyes snapped open. She stayed motionless, heart clattering against her ribs and silent, stunned tears sprouting in the corners of her eyes. Her vision scrambled to rearrange, but her rage had come back with her, clear and hot as ever.

"I am Jauyne Everforth." Her voice did not betray her. "Premier of the Province of Meirydh. Remove your whip, or Stars alive I swear I will string you up by your balls with it."

"Liar!" the disembodied voice scoffed, and the whip tightened with a rough jerk that made Jauyne gag. "Meirydh was burned. Premier Jofsa died with it, as did his daughter, Jauyne. Now you will tell me: where is Aeron, messenger from the High Circle of Chedhiy?"

Jauyne's eyes flitted to her pack. Her dagger was beside it, inches from her fingertips. She wriggled her fingers towards it as she choked out a reply. "Aeron? Blond and bearded? He burned with Meirydh, you fucker."

She could reach it... She could... The crystal tumbled from her other hand.

"You still lie!" The raspy voice was close to howling, and the whip yanked tighter. "You have his pack! What did you do to him, Meirydhi bitch?"

Her fingers found the leather handle of the dagger. In a single, fluid motion, she slashed the whip restraining her neck and whirled to her feet around the tree, yanking it out of her attacker's hands and tossing him to the ground from the force of it. The man hurriedly picked himself off the ground and, eyes boiling into her, drew a small knife of his own from a sheath on the outside of his thigh. Jauyne rushed at him, his shaky stance telling her all she needed to know.

She silently called to the sky— reaching for the endless strands of light that hung there for her and her alone. The crystal sang out, too, and she called back to it in her mind's eye, letting it pour Starlight like hot pricks of energy into her veins. She pressed it into her fingertips; her eyes lit up like shining silver.

Something in the man called out to her, too, an incandescence that recognized, just a moment too late, what exactly she was. Her fingers kinked in a beckoning to the Stars, then struck in the man's direction, flicking Starlight towards his body, a perverse and unheard-of action fueled by fury hunting for release.

He didn't go down like he should have— there was Starlight in this little shithead— and she lunged forward, knocking his knife away with her dagger and facing him. They were nearly the same height, and, fuck, she devoured her own satisfaction at the surprise that lit up his face when he was close enough to see hers.

She grinned, a vicious snarl clutched between her teeth. A hand splayed intimately on his chest, she let the Light in her palm release with a solitary pulse, and he dropped hard to the ground. The breath rushed from his lungs, and his mouth gaped up at her.

She straddled his chest, her knees holding his arms at his side. Pressing the obsidian blade to his throat, she leaned down till they were nearly nose to nose; her eyes drilling into the misty shimmer of his grey and green ones. They were like mirrors to the mountains behind them. He coughed and heaved a breath under her gaze, equally as cutting as her knife.

"Who are you?" Her voice was flat. Cold.

"I'm Zech— from Chedhiy." His eyes were shocked saucers, but she saw grief somewhere in them as well.

"Understand me well, Zech of Chedhiy. Your friend, Aeron, is as dead as my Province. My High City is ashes. My people are murdered. Now, I swear to you—I am Jauyne, daughter of Meirydh's fallen Premier Jofsa, sole survivor of the violence against us, and therefore the rightful rebuilder and ruler of the fifth Province." A pause. Her father would have chosen his words precisely. But she never was one to intimate her father. She chose hers wrathfully. "If you are here to fuck with me, I have an abundance of vengeance which I would find highly satisfying to exact upon you."

She smirked.

Zech met her eyes with a sincerity and boldness she was unused to. "Forgive me, Premier Jauyne. I didn't recognize you. It's been so long since I've seen you... It was my assumption that you would have been among the first to die in the attack. I have nothing against you, I swear." His eyes flicked to the red stripe rising on her throat. They flinched. Back to her face. "I'm so sorry I hurt you. I can help, if you—"

Jauyne's eyes narrowed, a burning surge of confusion in her gut which she refused to give voice to. "Turn over." Keeping her knife at his throat, she rose slightly from his chest. "You strike me, you die."

Compliantly, he rolled onto his stomach and she placed her boot on his head, not gently, as she snatched the rope from across her shoulder. Dagger between her teeth, she straddled his back to bind him. She bound his hands, then stretched the length of the rope down to his feet and bound them individually so that he could still walk while keeping his hands and feet connected by the stretch of rope between them. Rising from her crouch, she retrieved his knife and stored both weapons on her.

"Get up."

Fumbling awkwardly through his restraints, Zech righted himself and shrugged, brows raised, "Now what?"

"Now," Jauyne gestured for him to follow her to the other side of the old, gnarled tree, "I ask the questions, and you answer them."

She glanced at him sideways as she began to return the various array of goods to her pack. "Why were you coming to Meirydh?"

"I came searching for Aeron. Once I heard about the attack, I..." His voice fumbled, and he bit his lip, looking like he might cry. There was a pause before he took a deep breath and continued with resolve. "I cannot imagine the losses you have endured. I came searching for Aeron because I feared the worst... or maybe I refused to believe it. He was sent to deliver precious items of huge significance to your father—for you."

"For me? I—"

"Please allow me to explain." His voice was low and husky, and now she thought it might be with exhaustion or grief. He squatted down on the ground, hands still bound behind him. "Your father, as well as others of the final five Provinces, suspected for some time that there was corruption in the High Cities of the first three. They knew they needed to act, but there was no way to do that without risking war. It was coming, though. Everybody could feel it, so spies were sent to the three fringe

Provinces to gain information on why the Old Order was being deserted and what could be done to restore it.

"Then, two unmistakably miraculous signs happened. Firstly, the Oracle of the frozen Province to the north uncovered a book unlike any they have ever come across in their libraries. It spoke of two sacred relics called The Deathless and The Reaper which can be found in Meirydh. When these relics are brought together, they will be like a force of nature and will form a weapon unlike anything seen before, which can bring to their knees anything that comes against the Stars. And then, almost immediately after the book was discovered, those started falling from the sky." He pointed to the thing she had just plucked from the ground, the thing that buzzed, almost painfully and certainly addictively, in her hands.

Jauyne blinked down at the crystalline device as Zech continued, "The Premiers believe they're connected. The Stars have never sent us anything like this before."

Incredulous, Jauyne shoved it back into its pouch, before tucking the pouch into her pack, frustration seething inside her. She glared at him from around her bandage. It would be easier to do away with him now. She didn't have time for this. "What the fuck are you talking about?"

"I know it's strange," Zech adjusted in his uncomfortable position, "This isn't how you were supposed to find out. I'm definitely not who you are supposed to find out from. I know that. I'm just a Starsdamned border watchman! I'm not even supposed to be here!" Bitterness raked through his laugh and he glanced around, pained. "But it's the truth. The Stars are speaking to you, Jauyne. You've been given a task, and it's up to you to—"

Jauyne yanked the pack's clasp tightly, "Oh, fuck off. I am not going to save you or anyone else. I'm going to build my damn Province back. That is what I am meant for. That's what a Premier does. And that is why I am traveling to Chedhiy."

"You're wrong."

Jauyne leaned forward again, her body quivering with scarcely-contained anger. She shouldn't bait him, shouldn't push the boundaries of whatever she possessed that masqueraded as patience. "Is that so?"

"Yes." The intensity of his gaze, though veiled in softness, matched her own.

"Why should I trust a fucking stranger who tried to bind the Premier of a High City to a tree?"

"Stranger? Jauyne do you not—" He interrupted himself with a harsh noise of frustration. "It doesn't matter. You should trust me because the closer this army presses in, the more Provinces that burn, the more heightened your clarity of the truth becomes, the reality of this void we're in will sink in, and you'll understand that you don't have a choice. Yeah, it's fucked. You won't see me pretending it isn't. But you will have to trust me if you want to survive this, Jauyne. You'll have to trust me if you ever want to see a single stone of Meirydh rebuilt."

Jauyne's stomach lurched, sick creeping up her throat at his exasperation and apparent familiarity, but she shrugged, feigning indifference. "We should get going. I planned to be at the edge of the plains in four days, and you've held me back."

She heaved the pack over her shoulders as she strode back onto the path and snapped her fingers at Zech like her pet. She didn't let him see her wince at the pain her face was in.

"We can't go back to Chedhiy," Zech stumbled to his feet near the tree.

Jauyne spun on her heel, the last thread of her patience fraying. "Stars be damned, Zech! Either come with me now or wander about on your own, bound hand and foot, and wait for a firecat to grow hungry."

"At least I won't be waiting for woundrot to take me," his lips curled upward with a satisfied smirk as he awkwardly made his way in the opposite direction.

"You don't know what you're talking about!" Jauyne's voice was little more than a growl, "My wound has been treated, and I am more than capable of caring for myself."

Zech sighed. "Jauyne, I'm a healer by trade, and I can tell from here that your face is in trouble. Anyway, you'll have to trust someone sometime. Yes, I'm the asshole who thought you killed my best friend, but I'm also the asshole trying to help you."

A single, furious tear slipped out from behind her black lashes, despite her willing against it. He was right in one regard; the pain that striped diagonal across her face was vile, and she had very little chloronynë left. Woundrot wasn't an unthinkable possibility. "Why go back to that wreckage? I've been there... I've just come from there; I can tell you. It's all blood and ashes."

His voice was dripping in sorrow when he spoke. "I know how this sounds. I know what I'm asking. I just...If you could keep anyone else from feeling the way you feel right this moment... wouldn't you?"

"I don't want to go there." Jauyne swallowed back her shame for the cowardice she could feel her father scrutinizing in those words, even as her chin jutted out with pride, but Zech shuffled over to her with something that resembled compassion in his eyes.

"Neither do I."

His honesty made her want to stab him.

He turned with difficulty in his bonds and began to shuffle down the road. Jauyne chewed her lower lip. Her heart pounded with indecision behind the linen shirt she wore. For all she knew, this impulsive fool could have a trap waiting for her, or could be waiting to murder her in her sleep the moment she took rest. Her grey eyes, sharp and flashing as flint, narrowed towards his shuffling figure.

He grated on her like metal on slate. Then again, if she let him go, who knew what stories he'd tell of her, how he'd disgrace her and her Province. Worse yet, what would he do; what was his true reason for this inconvenient trek back to a sacked High City?

Jauyne turned her face to the mountains, rising like huge, glorious gems of green and silvery grey from the rolling mist. She could almost taste the hope and clarity the High City of Chedhiy, its giant white-barked trees only partially concealed among the mist, would bring her. Pressing her thin lips together and steeling her slender shoulders square, she turned her back on the mountains and faced the dwindling smoke of what had been her home.

She easily overtook Zech with her unbound stride, and he smirked at her with that quirking mouth, her loathing of which was steadily growing.

"Ah, so you've decided not to leave me for the firecats?"

"I've only decided it might be more satisfying to see your demise myself." She spoke flatly, but still he laughed. "Stop walking."

He stopped, and she pulled his knife from her belt, cutting the lower rope and loosing his feet. Zech grinned, and shook his legs a bit, stretching them in a lunging sway. Jauyne stepped in his way, her knife in front of her; the point of the blade almost nicked his chin, and he stilled abruptly.

"If you run," she whispered against his cheek, her voice as simmering as the molten lava of the Meirydhi volcanic springs, "I will gut you."

She turned on her heel and marched in the direction of the rising smoke, her steps sure and heavy with intention. She'd thought she was a different woman the day she'd hauled her weary body away from this wreckage, but she hadn't the slightest clue then. She knew now exactly what she was willing to do for her Province, and herself, the last blood of the Meirydh High Circle. She knew now what she was capable of: it wasn't just that she could walk away from a stinking, bleeding void and heave herself back to life through force of will.

She could also carry herself back into the cavernous mouth of death.

GETTING

6

HE HAD STOOD IN THE WAY OF HER VENGEANCE

ZECH & JAUYNE, A SHACK IN THE MEIRYDHI PLAINS
2 weeks since the sack of Meirydh

The red sun dwindled lazily just above the dry grasses, seemingly lighting them on fire, from where Jauyne rested in the doorway of an abandoned shack near the outskirts of Meirydh's High City.

She sat on a patch of yellow moss which had overtaken the doorstep, the heavy cloak she'd taken from her old quarters wrapped around her.

Zech sat inside against the left wall of the small hut, his head hanging back and jaw slack in sleep. His hands, still bound, were bunched awkwardly at the small of his back, and his knees were tucked, as he had attempted to get into a more comfortable resting position. A small creature, which had been hiding in the rafters until now, scampered daringly down the wall and across Jauyne's feet, out of the shack.

Jauyne ran a hand through her hair, massaging her fingers over her scalp. She had relented, after two days of his insistence, and allowed Zech to properly heal the wound that slashed across her face.

She'd felt the Starlight running through his body during their violent introduction, but had apparently underestimated how skilled he was. She had learned, as she frantically searched for conversation to steer her mind from the discomfort of his hands and eyes paying her face so much attention, that he had once studied under some of the most prominent healers in Allesar before being unceremoniously relegated to border watchman. When she had asked why, he'd simply winked one of his green-grey eyes at her and said, "I can't believe the rumors haven't reached Meirydh yet. Everyone knows I'm crazy."

It had certainly been worthwhile, despite all the face-touching and eye-winking. She trailed a finger along the length of the scab. She could still feel the cold tip of the sword clip her temple. It was a mercy, probably, that her wound had appeared fatal; a dead woman need not be killed. The near-fatal wound had, in truth, saved her life.

She'd bear the mark forever; there wasn't a way to disguise a scar that ran the length of her face. It was ugly, she knew, but she wasn't particularly pretty to begin with. She knew she was a jagged bundle of angles and hollows. She knew her hair was always frazzled, and her hands were always cold, and her eyes were always haggard. She knew the names she was called behind her back— skeleton girl, wraithling, and the occasional frigid bitch. It would have bothered her if she weren't already used to verbal abuse.

It often begged the question: did she suffer their bladed tongues because she was made of sharp edges, or did she grow herself sharp to ward off their blades? Her mind never stuck around for the answer.

She stared into the lively night; the darkness was hovering, illuminating the orange glow of the lava springs to the south. She remembered her father taking her there as a small child, back before Astra had been born, excitedly telling her the lava was the liquid stars of the earth. She had walked between the springs, holding her father's hand, listening to the wisdom he taught her of the Celestial. The other Provinces feared the unpredictable spouts of fire, but the Meirydhi danced beside them. Jauyne had liquid fire in her blood, and it burned all the brighter now.

Zech's breath was growing quicker and heavier, and his eyes, though still shut in sleep, winced, and darted back and forth beneath their lids. Jauyne watched him suspiciously out of the corner of her eye as he flinched. He shook visibly, a terrible chill roving over his whole body, and began to mumble incomprehensibly. Jauyne swallowed back the fear which threatened to creep into her mind and instinctively found the hilt of her dagger, which lay beside her on the weathered wooden floor of the shack. A silver glow appeared beneath his eyelids, riotously surging and stalling.

Jauyne leapt to her feet, moving to wake him from his strange and disturbed slumber, when he started violently, his upper body lurching forward and glowing eyes blinking open with a hollowed-out scream that rattled Jauyne's bones.

She froze. Her body absolutely froze.

Bent over his knees, Zech vomited and then continued to dry heave; panting like a wild animal, his still-glowing eyes eerily wide and unblinking as he stared forward. His breath rasped between heaving and frantic, unintelligible muttering. The length of his torso still twitched and curled. Jauyne was still frozen in aghast confusion, poised in the doorway, her hand clutching the dagger and her mind scrambling to make sense of the disturbing scene.

"Zech!" Her commanding voice refused to betray her fear.

The muttering went instantly silent. There was a pause banked in tension.

Then his head twitched in her direction, those unblinking, glowing eyes boring into her with an otherworldliness that made her bones cold.

"You," he said, and his voice was an echoing whisper that shook the rafters as he snapped the bonds from his hands with ease. "Why are you back here? I told you to leave me alone."

Jauyne slowly raised her dagger higher and pulled Zech's knife from her belt, brandishing a weapon in each hand. "Zech... If you attack me, I will not hesitate to kill you where you stand."

"It wasn't enough to die, was it? Now you have to haunt me, too?"

Zech's face was covered in streaming tears, though there was no distortion of sobs in his voice. Jauyne watched the tears as they dripped, trembling, from his nose and chin.

It's Starlight... His eyes are flooded with Starlight.

Jauyne had no time to think; her actions were primal.

Tossing the knife and dagger to the ground at once, she outstretched both her hand and the shimmering strands that connected her to the Stars. She sent the glowing threads of her Starlight through her fingertips flying forward towards Zech, calculating the pockets of Starlight in his body that were sourcing this absurd surge. The strands found their mark.

Connecting her Starlight to his, every hint of rage, confusion, and grief that she saw on his face ran unleashed through her own body. Tears budded in the corners of her eyes. Her breath was dragged shallow. It was as though she herself was Zech. His sorrow was her sorrow; his remorse was her remorse; his fury was her fury.

Slowly, Zech stood, his eyes beaming points of light in the night-dark room, fully fixed on her. He crossed the room, halting here and there, to stand mere inches away from her outstretched hand. Their breath was synced, a mirrored companionship in the rise and fall of their heaving lungs.

Jauyne was thrust headlong through his mind.

She saw a woman with eyes like orbs of ice, framed with luxurious black lashes; her hair, curly and black as a starless night, swirled around her warm brown face "Darling..." She pulled Zech close to her where she stood on a rocky outcropping, and Zech was just a child, just a little curly-haired thing. The woman's finger tugged lightly on one of his curls.

Jauyne blinked, and the woman was an arm's length away, just out of reach. There were giddy tears in her crazed eyes, and her fingers were still outstretched where they'd slipped from his grasp. The woman blinked the tears away, and a scream tore from Zech's throat, high and childish and full of pain.

The woman ran.

They were high on a wall, a lookout post situated on the rocky crag of the great mountains. Mist hovered along the mountainside, obscuring the ground, thousands of feet below.

"I love you, Zechariyh." Her voice was calm, but shrill as she turned, so close to the edge, her back to nothingness.

Zech screamed again, his feet pummeling the rock below him as he ran. Jauyne felt the burn in her own legs, the tears on her own face.

"Don't forget me." It was a whisper, but still it made it to his ears. "Don't forget me." The woman tilted backwards, even as he flung out his little hand to snatch hers. The mist swallowed her up. She didn't make a sound. Jauyne felt a cry rising up in her throat, and it exclaimed in Zech's voice. "Mama!"

Jauyne was surrounded by heavy space, an overwhelming inky blackness.

A single voice penetrated the void. "You didn't think I'd ever leave you, did you, darling? I can't have you forgetting me."

There was a rush to her head, and Jauyne saw clearly— a message written in blood, echoing spectral voices, those eyes over and over and over...

Those crystalline eyes jolted clarity into Jauyne, and she clamped down on the connection between herself and Zech, closing her fist in tandem with her extended Starlight. Zech winced and fell to the floor, weeping; Jauyne could hear his mother scream.

The Starlight in her hand vibrated and glowed silver, and it was as though a weight in her palm sought to pry open her clenched hand. Screaming with effort and pain, Jauyne slammed her fist into the doorframe of the shack, splintering the wood and extinguishing the concentration of Starlight with a massive crack.

The whole structure collapsed around them.

Zech stepped out of the shelter he'd fashioned from the splintered wood of the shack into the downpour. Quickly fetching the tin pail he'd left out to gather water, he ducked back under the haphazard collection of boards, leaves, and a large cut of waxed fabric. He'd woken up with Jauyne in a heap on top of him, one hand fisted in his shirt and the other a swollen mass of bruising and broken bones. The ruins of the shed had collapsed on and around both of them. Fixing a shelter from the oncoming storm clouds in the dark of night had been damn near impossible, as weak as he was.

His visions had never manifested before. They had always stayed firmly inside of his mind, silently torturing him, a constant companion to his grief.

His mother was his most frequent ghost. When she was alive, she had been his best friend, living in a pretty little treehome on the outskirts of Chedhiy, far from their High City. She'd never been the same after the rockslide that had killed his papa and sister. Less corporeal, more fitful. He'd find her weeping and howling about going home, and she would brush him off. She told him all sorts of fantastical stories; she'd been such a dreamy and quixotic woman, always telling him to keep believing in the fantastical.

And then she had killed herself.

Leapt from the heights of the mountain that served as the Chedhiyn/Brigonan border during the Festival of the Sacred Grove, ten years ago.

And no one remembered her name. No one even remembered that she had existed. And, despite the chaos that had ensued when the crowd watched her jump, no one even seemed to remember her death. They never looked for her body. They listened to Zech's story a dozen times, and each time the expressions they shot his way were more piteous and more condescending than the last.

So he stopped talking about her. And he began to see her. Hear her. Everywhere.

Jauyne had shattered her constant, hovering voice, splintered it like the hut that sat in wreckage around them now. His mother's voice no longer throbbed inside his skull like a headache. He didn't let himself really believe it. She'd come back. There was no way this was permanent.

But in this moment, here and now, he felt more at peace than he had been in years. He looked down at Jauyne. Both of them still held the faintest glow in their veins; hers were so fine and tangled at her wrists, an aftermath of their celestial encounter.

She hadn't awakened yet. If he was honest with himself, he was terrified. What the fuck was he going to tell her?

Uh, sorry my dead mother tried to make me attack you! Thanks for getting her out of my head for a few minutes!

Stars-be-damned. Surely she'd kill him; she had made it evident where her priorities fell, and they were definitely not with him. He had stood in the way of her vengeance. More than that, he had put her in danger. He should never have put her in a position to bear his gruesome burdens, but he had, because he was an asshole.

They just needed to return to the High City of Meirydh. Aeron had been shrouded in mystery, preferring to keep his own secrets, but there was one thing he had assured Zech of before his departure for Meirydh: There was a war in the cosmos, he'd said. The Stars were battling for their world, and They were looking for the weapon that the two ancient relics would produce.

These two relics sat in Meirydh, Aeron was convinced, and had gone to find them himself. He was planning to discuss the fallen crystals with Premier Jofsa, and had brought the Chedhiyn device with him. All he'd wanted was to prevent war, to make it all okay.

Zech's chest tightened at the thought of Aeron being so brutally slaughtered in the streets— no second thought, as though he were nothing, no one. Aeron had been the only true friend in his life, and now he was gone.

He would probably be gone soon enough at the hand of Jauyne. He knew it would be smart to run, to try to gain a few hours of distance between them before she woke and inevitably slit his throat to let his blood pool with the rain out here on soil that was no home to him.

But where would he go? And to whom? No, running was not an option.

Zech jumped as she stirred beside him, and the fear pricked at his skin. Starlight power like hers had not been witnessed in a thousand alignments of the stars, and how was he supposed to fight something that wasn't supposed to exist?

He also hadn't stripped her of her weapons. That would have been the act of a coward and, for all his insanity, Zech was no coward. If she wanted to gut him she would have an easy time of it. Whatever was coming to him, he most likely deserved, anyhow.

Jauyne's face contorted in a grimace, and, not quite awake, she moved with a groan to cradle her left hand, which had been the one to wield her Starlight and splinter the doorframe of the shack. It was puffy and bruised, already a painful mosaic of blues and purples, and from the odd-angled shape of it, a few bones were certainly broken.

Her eyes fluttered open, instantly took in the sight of the makeshift shelter and observed Zech's exhausted form and shaking hands. Hugging the injured hand to her stomach, she shuffled herself upright and pushed her tangled and muddy hair out of her face. Finally, her still-glowing eyes met his with a weight of steel.

"What did you do?" she asked, hoarsely.

His voice cracked from exhaustion when he spoke, and he loathed how small and childish it made him feel. "I'm not sure."

Jauyne snorted, "You're not sure?" A laugh boiled up from her belly and rang out in the darkness, mingling with the shushing sound of the downpour. It startled Zech, bones nearly leaping out of his skin. Her laughter died with an amused sigh, and she looked at him again.

"That was the strangest thing I have ever seen." Her voice was flat, and, terrifyingly, tinged with humor. "I have never seen or heard of anything like it, Zech, and I have spent my entire life studying Starlight."

Zech shook his head, his fear shifting to discomforted suspicion. "Are you going to kill me?"

She raised an eyebrow. "No. No, I am not going to kill you. I don't know why. I feel like I should. You're definitely not making my trek easier. You almost killed me."

He grimaced, "I'm sorry."

He was always making things worse. The ghosts were always making things worse.

"You said you could fend off woundrot." Jauyne abruptly changed the subject, examining her swollen and broken hand with a wince. "You said you're trained as a healer. You fixed my face."

What did she want him to say? "Uh, yeah."

"Will you help with my hand? I suppose..." she looked around them at the broken pieces of the shack once again, "I did this."

Zech nodded and reached for her hand, taking it in his own. He was surprised at the smallness of it, at the muscles that knotted and corded around the little bones. Calling the Starlight was still instinctual, but it was tiring. His exhaustion was a force of nature. Though he tried to hide it, his hands shook as he extended his mind to the Stars. Jauyne raised an eyebrow at the grimace he hadn't felt creeping across his own face, but said nothing, watching him work.

_____

She told herself she loathed the soft lines which bookended his lips and those dusky grey-green Chedhiyn eyes, when the truth was that his face was the warmest distraction from the jagged pain of her hand. He felt like a cool summer night spent round the roaring lightning pit fires of her High City. His eyes were deeply focused on her fist, which was growing considerably less swollen in the ever-increasing Starlight surrounding it.

She trained her gaze on his eyes, on the way she could feel him measuring out Starlight like a rule of deprivation. She could see the budding power that slept behind his skull, and she was ashamed at the guttural need to grab and pull that rose at the base of her throat.

"You're holding back," she found herself saying. The beads of sweat forming on his temple were not a sign of difficulty summoning Starlight; they were a sign of difficulty containing it.

Zech released a fractured exhale. "Holding back?"

"That's why this is difficult."

His face twisted, released her wrist, whole and well. "You just saw the result of not holding back. I don't think there is much of a choice."

She wanted to fight, but she wanted to sleep more.

She hadn't felt exhaustion like this in all her life. She needed rest. They both needed rest. The deep thrum of the rain was dulling, and the sky would soon be empty. Her first plan, a long night march along the chilly plains road, was forfeit, and her mind was too foggy with the incontestable siren of sleep to remake their plans at the moment.

"Does it feel alright?" Zech's voice was close to her ear where he had laid down, heavy with weariness.

"Yes. Thank you," she whispered. She could feel her words beginning to spill out, uninhibited by the mental faculties of clarity and energy. "Aeron... He seemed like someone worth grieving."

"Everyone is worth grieving. But I'll grieve him most."

"Everyone, Zech? Really? I can promise you, I won't grieve Canryn when I crack him open with lightning fire."

Zech chuckled. "What, will you also bring a cup with you, to drink his blood from right out of his veins? Monstrous creature."

She tried, and failed, to ignore the way she tensed low in her belly at the slight coo to his voice when he said *monstrous*. "My whole life was designed so that I would be monstrous. My father knew the thing he was creating."

There was no response, but Zech brushed her arm as he shifted beside her.

It was eerily silent now; the rain had pattered out to nothing, the clouds thinning and parting. The faintest Starlight filtered in between the boards of their makeshift roof. A chill was spreading through the plains, and Jauyne watched their misty breath rise, mingling, to the Starlight in the cracks above them.

She was actively aware of Zech's closeness to her side, and his half-closed eyes which darted over her face. It was that realization of closeness, and not the cold, which made her shiver. Scooping her cloak around her, Jauyne rolled away from him, her breath separating from his and finding its lonely way up into the night.

Anger and grief boiled up like a bubbling pot in her gut, fury all ablaze over her own neediness. Fuck this damned Chedhiyn boy, showing up at the least opportune moment, only to derail her journey and drag her into his nightmares and blast her hut to splintered bits. And for him to then have the gall to heal her hand and breathe gently beside her... It was too much!

She roughly tugged her cloak over her eyes, hand against her thigh, resting on the grip of her knife. Exhaustion demanded an end to her consternation and she helplessly relented, falling into a dark and troubled sleep.

THESE

7
ALL MUST BE MARKED FOR A COMMISSIONING

JADRAS, HIGH CITY OF JOPAAR
2 weeks since the sack of Meirydh

Who can breathe the icy flakes?
One with Jopaar's blood in his veins!

It wasn't snowing, but Adras still remembered the tune. The other schoolchildren used to chant that solitary line from the ancient ballad in crude, sing-song mockery. The next line was one which those small, unkind humans had devised out of their own ignorance:

Who shall be buried beneath their weight?
Only the halfsie he-she fake!

A smirk crept up into their cheek, and the frozen metal rail only excited the warm veins in their black-painted fingertips. What was winter to one raised in a land of crystal and ice, and what were cold words to one adopted by the frozen Evernorth Province? Adras didn't need Jopaari blood; they had learned to breathe the snow all on their own, though it had at first felt akin to breathing underwater.

They took a drag from the rolled blunt of herbs pinched between their fingers. Felt the smoke singe its way down their lungs. Exhaled it into the wintry air.

Some had despised them for their inability to conform, while others worshiped their transcendence. The High Priestess honored them as the next evolution of the Revealed Stars, though inevitably, worshiping an oracle who bound themselves to no single gender had proved impossible for some. As many as adored them, also expressed their disgust with vigor.

Only Lumen could come close to understanding the strange, twisted way in which Adras had learned to exist in their world. He stood beside them on the balcony. His solidly black eyes and glassy white hair were a close to perfect counterpart for the chips of ice Adras wore as eyes, and the deep brown hair they kept cropped close to their skull.

Lumen's icy hair and black eyes, deep and unflinching as a moonless winter sky, were the accidental gifts of the lifesaving Starlight that he had been doused in as a toddler. He didn't talk about it much, didn't speak to what it had felt like to have been abandoned by confounded parents when their son was returned to their arms a different creature. How he had extended his arms to them, wailing, while they recoiled. Adras shot him a sidelong look as he frowned down at the city beneath them, his hand absentmindedly brushing the pommel of the dagger strapped to his thigh.

Adras was accustomed to the whispers, the taunts, even the death threats which had for years been found slipped under the door of the High House. Lumen was less accustomed to them, scowling and thin-lipped for the remainder of the day after the mornings they'd discover a new one. This had been one such morning. He looked as though he might brave the multilevel drop to the city below if he could see the culprit from his perch.

Seven years younger than Adras, Lumen had come to the High Priestess' palace when he was just three. It was where Adras had spent their days while their father worked as notetaker for the highly secretive audiences the High Priestess held with her Circle. Wandering the halls, they used to bring Lumen treats from the kitchen and show him the massive murals lining the palace walls. He'd followed Adras like a wounded fox pup, and their lonely soul devoured the love and silently adopted him as a brother.

Adras was an unafraid, otherworldly creature, raised solely by a grieving father in a cold and untamed world, far from their Brigonan home. There was no set path for children who killed their mothers by entering into the world, no instructions on how to hold the weight of it, all the while surviving the absence and vacant eyes of a mourning parent. It had been nearly twenty-seven years since the day their father had first set foot on Jopaari soil with that small bundled toddler clinging to his legs, and three months since nearly three decades of grief and toil had finally broken and withered his body into the grave.

Their grip on the rail grew tighter, ice-blue eyes squinting out over the shades of white and grey that stretched endlessly out to the north and east. Another drag of herbs, tapping off the cinders. Frost gathered where their breath misted over a heavy knitted grey cowl, wrapped hastily round their neck and tucked into the buckled breast of a leather jacket.

The sleeve's buttons had been left undone in their rush, and swirling tattooed scenes of stars and astral dragons were half-bared on their arms. A small arrangement of simple dots—the home constellation of their sacred Jopaar— surrounding an inked dragon with outstretched wings, revealed itself under their chin when Adras tilted their face skyward to take in the grey of the atmosphere.

They'd felt the pulse, a surge of energy taking place throughout the holy Starlight that flowed in their veins. It had happened once before, not even three dark moons ago, shaking them from a deep sleep. Adras still remembered that day well. The High Priestess had come to find them, and hurriedly they had cloaked themselves in their warmest furs and gone out into the deep Winterlands, where the strange crystal device had fallen from the sky.

The Winterlands were a wild place, the northernmost point of all Allesar. Creatures of ice and snow lurked there between curtains of ever-falling snowflakes. It was a fearsome place that any sane person feared, and no one had any cause to traverse it. But Adras had indeed traveled it, alone and with quiet confidence, as they always had. They had brought back the odd prize to the High City, this mass of crystals and metal veins. And a book, a terribly strange book that made their skin crawl and head ache. Even now, in another corner of Jopaar's High House, they could feel a connection to it, an ever-humming strand of energy that thrummed beneath their skin.

Lumen had quite nearly had a fit when the High Priestess had forbidden him from assisting Adras in their trek. Adras fought the twisting of their lips a bit; he was the only one who could growl and stomp at the wise woman without consequence. But Adras had returned, and he'd scooped them up into a crushing hug while scanning them for injury or pain.

Five more pulses had been felt since the first— spread out around the Provinces. It was causing a bit of a stir in the Circle of the High Priestess. A pervading sense of unease and wariness had sunk into all its members, and questions were sifting through the High House.

Soon, the High Priestess would arrive in the sacred hall once again and Adras and Lumen would leave the expansive balcony and go in to meet with her. There were disturbing messages from the south, rumors and whispers of a great violence, licking like hungry fire through Provinces and destroying High Cities.

Adras shivered, though not from the cold. They even preferred the biting cold of the outdoors; at least it was free and unpredictable, as they were. Within the sacred halls and huddled groups of diplomats, there was an expectation of propriety, a demand to conform in order to make a difference. The wild outdoors held no such pretense or expectation, and Adras dreaded having to leave it.

A young man, outfitted in leather and heavy white furs cinched together by a reflective blue stone at the left shoulder, stepped onto the balcony and into the yellow light being thrown from the open doorway.

"The High Priestess has arrived." White puffs of warm breath gushed from his lips as he spoke. "She is waiting in the Hall of Ice."

Adras pressed the end of the burning herbs to the icy railing and watched as the little puff of smoke mingled with their breath and dissipated into the grey sky.

Lumen dragged his eyes from the city below and huffed a sigh, taking long strides toward the doorway. He tugged back the white hair that hung around his shoulders— a silvery-slick gleam on it as though he were a pythfox slinking from the water— in a band of black leather. Adras turned their back to the cold and made their way across the wide slate balcony to the door, still held open for them by the page. The warmth hung heavy in the air, and Adras tugged the knit cowl off over their head as they made their way across the room to another set of doors.

These were great, hulking, wooden things, carved with images of falling snow, great mages from the old stories, sacred symbols, and the sigil of their Province: the pythfox. These creatures were silver-furred, black-eyed foxes which stood at least to the height of a grown man. Depictions of great northern beasts lurked on the lower borders. They had been painted white long ago, and the paint was wearing around the edges and in the grooves of the carvings. Adras ran a finger gently along the indentation of a pythfox before grasping the curled, old iron handle and pulling the heavy door open with a soft heave.

The room into which they stepped was an oval space, the walls built in white marble, with a tall spiked seat at the end of it. The throne was three times as tall as Adras and made of a jet black stone with an enormous polished opal set into the back rest. Small yellow lights dripped from the domed onyx ceiling like the summer fireflies in the southern Provinces, of which Adras had heard from the few travelers who made their way this far north. Luminescent paint had transcribed every star and planet in the night sky across the length of the ceiling. Tall banners, a deep purple with the pythfox sigil stitched in silver, hung along the curved walls of the room. The Jopaar motto "We are the frost" read above each pythfox in that same silver stitching.

Adras' boots clapped against the white marble floor as they walked towards the end of the room and towards the woman who sat upon that great throne.

She was a relatively small woman in stature, perhaps appearing even fragile, but her presence soaked into every inch of the cavernous room. At fifty-nine years old, she still looked scarcely older than Adras, despite the thirty years that separated the two. An ancient sort of wisdom blossomed behind her unblinking amethyst eyes, an expression that was as gentle as it was regal. Decades of peace and pain looked out from behind her long lashes, which were a frothy blonde, unlike the short-cropped curls dyed a light, silvery lilac color. The neck of her deep purple dress was stitched with silver constellations and collared, except at the front where it plunged to reveal a section of nearly translucent white skin down to her waist. Fine silver chains connected the neckline to the sleeves, which began just above her elbows and hung, long and flowing, down to the silk of her skirt, gathered round her legs in swaths. The High Priestess stood, a small smile on her lavender painted lips, and reached out tattooed and ring-laden hands to Adras as they closed the distance between the two of them.

Adras grasped her hands, "Reinah! It's good to see you."

"And you, my friend. Trouble has kept me from you for too long. All those messy southerners wear on me. You are refreshing."

Adras smirked before growing serious. "And what did these southerners have to say about the Starstone? Did they try to deny it?"

"No," the High Priestess, Reinah Il Firloch, shook her head solemnly, gesturing for Adras to rest on the throne's adjacent seat. "They did not. Southerners may be tiresome, but we do have friends among them. However, Adras, what we may be facing is far worse than denial."

Adras' stomach churned, though they steeled themself. "What is it, Priestess?"

"Not long ago, the Province of Chedhiy was given a Starstone like our own," Reinah began. "It fell into the mountains of Onar's Spine and was taken to their Premier. Their High Circle determined that it should be taken to Meirydh based on an old prophecy which spoke of the united destiny of their two Provinces, as well as what was written in the book you recovered with our own Starstone. However, just a week after their ambassador, Aeron, left for Meirydh, a massacre ravaged the High City. Canestry's alliance with Pallydh and Nereilë has finally bred war, as we always knew was inevitable. As soon as word reached them that this had happened, one of their outlying border guards, and a friend of Aeron, disappeared. The Chedhiyn Premier assured me that this man, Zechariyh, is trustworthy, and will return the Starstone if he finds it. But we must prepare for the worst: it is likely that this sacred gift has fallen into the hands of those who decimated an entire High City without conscience."

The last of her words hung trembling in the air, reverberating through Adras' bones. They could scarcely make sense of the vastness of the horror. The south seemed so far away, so unreal, like an occasional distraction to the grand beauty of their northern home. Jopaari people kept to themselves, and Adras was no different; they loathed the thought of leaving their dear friend and mentor and venturing deep into the sweltering land of tamed custom and judgmental Province dwellers to fight a war that did not concern them. Yet their heart ached at the thought of this sacred gift from the Stars being claimed as a spoil of some petty tyrant's war.

"There is something else."

Adras' brow arced in devastated surprise. "Something else?"

"The seers of Brigon have claimed that Jauyne, heir to the Seat of Meirydh, was not among the fallen. She is thought to be the crucial component in the prophecy surrounding her Province. And the Province of Canestry has sent out a demand for the return of their Premier's daughter, Indra, who has disappeared, though to the surprise of both Chedhiy and Brigon. He wishes to make an example of her to his Province, to show them what happens to those who desert their Premier." Reinah shook her head. "Chaos is seeping into the earth, over all of Allesar."

"Allesar cannot stand against an army who massacres entire High Cities as though it simply breathes," Adras murmured.

"Stars forbid it," Reinah muttered instinctively, shaking her head, "It cannot, not without divine intervention."

"What do you want me to do?" Adras searched their mentor's face earnestly. Their voice was barely above a whisper, the solemnity and horror of the moment demanding a hush.

Reinah met their eyes levelly, cold steel in her own. "I want you to find Zechariyh and, together, retrieve the gift of the Stars," she said. "I want you to locate Jauyne so she can fulfill her part of the prophecy and call upon the Stars on behalf of her Province. I want you to keep Indra from the clutches of Canestry and bring her here to be safely cared for by a people who will champion her."

Adras swallowed hard, then bowed their head. "As you say, High Priestess, so I manifest."

———

The seven priests and priestesses of Jopaar were gathered in the Hall of Ice, their seats lining either side of the opal throne where Reinah sat. Each of them, in their flowing purple robes and their jet black hair, held a whitewood staff with a large chunk of raw, flashing labradorite at the end. The blues and greens and purples glinting from the stones cast small fractures of colored light around the long hall. The priests' arms were bare and heavily tattooed with scenes of myths and stories in the sacred texts of the stars painted in black across their skin.

As Adras walked towards these wise men and women with sure steps, the gravity of their journey began to sink into the pit of their stomach. This was no small task which had been asked of them. It would require all the fortitude and bravery they had acquired in their many years of surviving in a land not their own. But now that Adras was returning to their native home, it felt much more like entering an alien planet, and leaving the place where they'd once been a stranger now felt like a piece of their soul being torn from their body.

They didn't know much of the south, only of the visitors who rarely strayed miserably into their borders. Those visitors were generally the kind who looked down their noses at the northerner's unrefined and untamed tendencies, raising an eyebrow and keeping their distance. Adras felt no excitement at entering a land full of these nose-wrinkling people, nor at the heat they were likely to encounter there. They'd only ever known the cold and ice.

Their black leather pants were laced tightly up the sides and tucked into thick grey socks and then into sturdy black boots. A belt crisscrossed over their waist, and the axe which hung from it clinked against the knife in their leg holster. They wore several layers of cotton and wool under the thick cowl and a buttoned leather vest, which hung open in the warmth of the indoors. The heavy pack they would soon carry out into the frozen lands on their journey southward had been deposited temporarily at the entryway.

The seven holy men and women, along with High Priestess Reinah, stood as Adras approached the steps leading up to the throne and additional seven seats. They raised their staffs high, and Adras could now see the small, shining needle each of them held in their opposite hands.

"Adras, child of the north," the High Priestess began, "the second commissioning of the Seven Stars is here upon you. We send you out into all of Allesar. You are the cold hand of Jopaar. You are all wisdom and mystery. You are the protector of the edge of the world. You are the light in the dark. You are the frost."

"You are the frost!" The priests and priestesses shouted.

"Jopaar has called you, and Jopaar shall guide you on your journey southward."

"Jopaar has called! Jopaar shall guide!"

"You are to find Zech, the seeker of Chedhiy. You are to retrieve the gift of the Stars. You are to call the heiress of Meirydh to her prophetic destiny. You are to bring the daughter of Canestry home."

"This is your commission!"

Adras knelt to their knees. They knew the ritual. It was not so long ago that they had been commissioned to find another Star-gift. They closed their hands into fists, crossing their arms so their fists rested across the front of their shoulders.

The High Priestess and her priests slowly descended the cold marble steps, their bare feet noiseless. They circled around Adras, their staffs tapping against the white and grey swirled floor. Their tattooed hands, which held the silver needles, outstretched towards Adras.

"Adras of the frost, the Stars command that all must be marked for a Commissioning." Reinah's rich voice rang out to the ends of the room and came back towards them again in a ringing echo.

The first priestess stepped forward, coming to face Adras. She held her needle outstretched, and slowly pin-pricked Adras' right cheek, striping a short straight line of black ink vertically under their eye. Adras did not flinch, or even blink, as the needle weaved its way in and out of their skin. Beads of blood swelled out of the tiny punctures and joined to trickle down their jaw. The priestess pulled the needle out of the final pin prick and slowly knelt before Adras. Reaching out her hands to hold Adras' face, she brought their foreheads together, repeating the Jopaari blessing given during Commissioning rituals.

"My blood goes with your blood, and my spirit with your spirit."

The priestess released Adras' face and stood once again, taking her place back in the circle of holy women and men.

One after another, the priests came forward to mark Adras as one of the commissioned and to bless them. The thin black stripes, dripping blood, grew on their right cheek— five, six, seven of them, a matching set to the ones on their right— and soon they felt the slow trickle of the red drops splashing from their chin to the white marble floor. The red spatters looked as though they were seeping into freshly fallen Jopaari snow.

At last the High Priestess presented herself from out of the circle. Kneeling quietly with an air of gentle dignity, she held out her own needle between her left forefinger and thumb. She raised her right hand, covered in dozens of identical, small semi-circle tattoos, and began to stain yet another tiny crescent among the others with the needle. When she was done, and dark blood dripped from the knuckle on her thumb where the freshly tattooed crescent was, she leaned forward.

Adras' breath caught in their lungs. This ritual may be familiar, but the journey it heralded was not. This was not another venture into the familiar climate of cold and snow, or a trek in uncharted frozen wasteland. Despite the danger and the unknown, it had still felt like home. It had still been Jopaar. This new commission would take them only Stars knew where, into some mysterious southern weather and confusing foreign tenor. A ball of molten heat felt stuck in their throat.

There were seven new stripes on Adras' left cheek and beneath them, like a little bowl, Reinah meticulously carved out a slender semilunar curve, akin to the one she'd just made on her own hand. Her soft brow ever so slightly furrowed in concentration. Then, as blood leaked once again down Adras' cheek, Reinah lifted her freshly tattooed hand and pressed their twin wounds together in solemn feeling.

Adras' icy blue eyes met Reinah's lavender ones as she parted violet lips in a benediction.

"My blood goes with your blood, and my spirit with your spirit."

MESSAGES

8

A DISTANT SENSE OF SAFETY

Indra had never before left Canestry, and certainly had never traveled to a Province which observed the Old Order. Born at the high tide of Canestry's conversion to the New Order, only the tales from her childhood caretaker had forged in her a connection to the ancient wisdom of the Stars and those who worshiped them.

Her mother had been a follower of the Old Order. Vile tales and gossip about the gentle woman who had birthed her often reached her ears in her home Province, as her father conveniently turned his ear away. Indra was just seventeen years old, and raised in a bizarre corner of the world where women were softened and pressed into whatever shame the demands of men called for. But Indra was as wise as she was innocent, and as strong as she was soft.

Brigon was a strange place to her young eyes, accustomed to the gardens and shining silver and clean white stone of the High House in Canestry. Here she was surrounded by near-vertical dirt roads which wound up steep mountainsides, lush green trees and rich brown soil, and old stone-block buildings which seemed to defy time itself. There were no sweeping gardens or grassy knolls with ponds tucked into their cambers.

And yet, Indra found her traitorous heart missing the familiarities of home. Perhaps it was the finality of it all, the continued realization that she could never return to her homeland, unless it was with her father's head removed from his shoulders. There was a certain pang of sorrow to it.

Her body and mind recoiled in fear and disgust from both the High House where she'd been trapped for so long, as well as the man she'd called father, yet some small, childish part of her missed both. Even now, as she soaked in the bath, suds nearly up to her nose, she wondered what would have come of things, had she not ridden out to Osiys on the field of battle. It wasn't that she regretted it, but that she had come to a distinct crossing in the road and had made a firm choice, one that carried with it the weight of action and responsibility and the taking of her destiny into her own hands

One's own fate was not a thing one had control of in Canestry. The New Order was clear about what each person had to offer their world. It was set in stone, predictable, disempowering. Leaving wasn't what she had thought it would be, though she hadn't really had any idea of what to think at all these last few years as she dreamed and charted and waited and planned.

I suppose empowerment is something you have to forge yourself...

She did not understand the horrific void her father had summoned. She did not understand how they had been on the outskirts of Canestry one moment, and the next at Meirydh's gates. She did not understand the way she had protected Osiys, the way the Stars had filled every pore of her skin with light and given her strength so much greater than what she had thought she possessed.

Indra lifted a hand from her bathwater, little bubbles cloaking it like an odd mitten. They caught the dawning shafts of sunlight which shone from the window, glinting curved rainbows up at her. A pointed exhale, and they drifted off into the air, bursting as they touched walls and soap dishes and folded towels.

At least bubbles popped the same in Brigon as they did in Canestry. Nearly everything else seemed different... The food was heartier, favoring root vegetables and thick stews and game meats with earthy herbs and seasonings. There was no trace here of the light seafood and citrus fruits and bright spices of her native cuisine. Even the walls surrounding the bath were built from archaic stone, rough and hewn from the cliffs and mountain escarpments. Huge, thirteen-pointed stag antlers were mounted above the hammered metal wash basin and its corresponding mirror.

The only thing which felt remotely familiar was the bath itself, a massive, oblong basin of carved and polished rose quartz, with more than enough room to stretch her slender legs to their full length. That was where the similarities ended, however, as this bath was built directly into the stone wall, which hung from the face of the mountain. A small metal plug could be pulled from the end of the bath when she was done, and the bath water would spill out over thousands of feet of rock and empty air. Despite the warmth of the water, Indra shivered to think about plummeting to her death in the bath. Evidently, none of her Brigonan hosts ever feared the same.

She stood, water dripping from her eyelashes and elbows, and reached for the tin bucket full of clean water with which to rinse. The warm water swept away the last of the soapsuds from her skin, whisking them into the smooth, pink basin. Stepping out of the shin-deep soapy water onto the plush rug, she wrapped her hair in a towel and patted her body dry with another. She was surprised at the softness of the fabric. It was easy to forget how sensual the Brigonans were– true creatures of comfort, despite how coarse their western sort of comfort felt to Indra's eastern sensibilities.

Squinting her silvery eyes closed and fumbling with her fingers in the sudsy, lukewarm water, her hand closed around the stopper's chain and she pulled it free, wincing at the sound of water freefalling down the sheer rock face. Turning her back on her fear with a shudder, she took a small tin tube from the vanity and gently applied the pink color to her lips, before brushing a bit of color on her cheeks .

There was a set of clothes hung in the open arch which led to her bedroom, a deep green and gold and cream ensemble with a long sleeved, fitted brocade shirt, which bared three solid inches of skin before the hem of the pants began. The pants were a deep green with large, thin outlines of blooming flowers and were so loose and wide they could have been mistaken for a skirt, a necessity for the equestrian ladies of Brigon who wished to remain in the latest fashions while still hunting on the steep mountain ledges with ease. Indra resisted the urge to dig around in the drawers for a sash to cover the stripe of skin left under the delicate gold-stitched hem of the cream shirt, but instead fastened the highest hidden closure on the green collar and straightened her shoulders.

Breakfast would be ready shortly, a meal that Indra had been forgoing over the past week and a half in favor of the tray that was brought to her room a few hours later. Yesterday, however, the Premier had returned from his hurried visit to Chedhiy where he had met with both the Chedhiyn and Jopaari Premiers in an audience shrouded with strict confidentiality. He had sent word to both Indra and Osiys yesterday evening as they sat by the common room's massive fireplace, requesting that they break their fast with him the following morning.

Skin still soft and smelling like pine and berries from the bath, Indra slipped her feet into the gold brocade slippers waiting for her by the heavy wood plank door. Pulling the enormous iron handle, she heaved the door open and stepped out into the wide hallway, lushly carpeted with ornate rugs and thick furs. At least a dozen more mounted antlers, some with skulls attached, lined the length of it from end to end.

She padded down the hall towards the great twin doors at the south end. They looked older than the rest of the Brigonan Premier's home, primeval and mysterious, etched with countless carvings of creatures and sacred symbols, things she did not understand. The closer she came, the more she was reminded again that she was just a foolish child in a foreign land, at the mercy of her father's most bitter enemies. To them, she was probably little more than a bargaining chip to be preserved so that she could be utilized in case of emergency. Osiys she trusted; the other members of the Brigon High Circle, she was more than a little wary of.

The attendant at the large doors, a tall, thin young man with mussed fiery hair, stepped forward as Indra approached, turning towards the door to push it inward with his entire bodyweight. As he did, Indra's eyes took in the large dining quarters where the Premier entertained guests and met with visitors of honor.

At the end of a long carved wooden table there was a fireplace, taller than her, with a golden fire crackling and hissing in its hearth. In front of the fire, at the head of the table, sat the Premier. His hulking shoulders were haloed in amber and ruby by the glowing flames behind him. Osiys had talked about him as though he was a legend; the man was over seven feet tall, and even while sitting was at least a head taller than anyone else at the table. A warm laugh bellowed out from behind his thick copper beard, a riotous sound that was accompanied by the pounding of his fist against the table at some joke it appeared Osiys had been telling.

Three others sat at the table with them, opposite of Osiys. A lanky, pale woman with small, dark eyes and hair the color of coiled autumn leaves, which was pulled back into a bun at the nape of her neck, patted a napkin over her quiet smirk. The man beside her, a stunted fellow with muscles rippling in the patch of bare chest his loose shirt revealed, snorted laughter as he nearly spit out the drink he had just swilled. He wagged a stubby finger of fake irritation at Osiys that was smacked away with a laugh by the nearly identical man to his left. Their similarities were striking, though the second man was of a more average height. They both had the same warm brown hair and eyes, like they had sprung from the mountain soil itself. Osiys noticed her then, where she had paused just inside the door, and lifted a hand to her.

"Come on in, Indra! Don't you want any breakfast?" He still grinned, and his words were colored with the remnants of laughter.

Indra felt she had never shook more than this moment, with all those eyes boring into her, not least of all, those of the Premier.

How is it that riding into battle is less frightening than meeting an enemy at his own dining table?

She swiftly winced to herself, chiding her thoughts as she realized she still felt like this man's adversary. She felt very small indeed in this great cave of a room, walking quietly towards this great mountain of a man, resisting the urge to pick at the strange clothes that seemed to sit the wrong way on her body. Meeting the Premier's eyes was an impossibility, so she fixed her gaze on Osiys and his smiling face instead, which steadied her a bit. It seemed to take her a year to cross the room, step by agonizing step, and come to the seat next to Osiys' at the long table.

She took the seat, which Osiys had risen to ready for her, and flicked her eyes nervously around the table before staring down at her empty plate. Osiys returned to his seat next to her. The Premier looked down at her with what could only be read as gentleness, and passed her a cloth-lined basket of brown bread rolls, still steaming from the ovens.

"Hello, little daughter." His voice was as warm as the bread she broke in her trembling hands. "I am Herran, the Premier of our great Province of Brigon. I trust you have been well cared for here? I must apologize; there were matters of grave importance which kept me away. But now that I have returned, I look forward to hearing the strange story of this unlikely escape you made with my old friend."

He glanced sidelong at Osiys with a thin smile.

Indra bravely met his eyes, feeling the tremor in her voice as she responded. "I have been exceptionally well attended to, Your Grace, and I thank you for your hospitality."

The short man sputtered into his coffee, while the woman raised an eyebrow. Indra swallowed hard, embarrassment and confusion coloring her neck as Osiys patted her hand.

"Oh dear," the woman smiled kindly at her through thin pink lips, "don't mind this little fool beside me. You're new to the place, is all."

Indra's face nearly stung with heat as she felt the flush creep up from her neck, feeling stupid and still confused. "I'm so sorry..."

"Don't be!" Osiys interjected. "The New Order is all you have ever known. I'm sure there are a thousand little things that will take a bit of getting used to."

She managed a weak smile.

"Well, that isn't at all comforting, is it?" The woman laughed. "Though it's most likely true. But you mustn't worry about all of that with us, despite this one's sorry sense of humor."

"Dammit, Elryh!" The small man yelped as her elbow jabbed him in the ribs and some of his coffee splashed against his shirt. He rubbed the sore spot woefully, before shrugging. "Eh, I probably deserved it— if not for this, than something else."

Elryh sipped her tea as she replied. "If it was what you deserved, Berg, my elbow would have found your balls instead of your ribs."

Berg spun to her with a feigned expression of shock and offense. "You wound me, my dear!"

"Mm, I just might," she pursed her lips.

Osiys snorted, and Premier Herran chuckled at the crude gesture Berg made in response to Elryh before turning his attention back to the blushing Indra.

"There is no need for formalities or titles such as 'your grace' here. In Brigon, we are all equal. I, as the Premier, am only here to serve and guide our people when they need my guidance... as I am now here to serve and guide you."

"We all are," the taller man sitting beside the Premier said, his eyes smiling. "I'm Baird. This sarcastic little twat is my twin brother, Berg." He flicked Berg in the back of the head with a laugh. "He's the best human I know, better than you for sure, Osiys."

He winked at Indra's copper-haired friend, who smirked at Baird. Indra was thankful for Baird's presence, which hung, kind and humorous, in the air around her. Even as these people were warming her to the Brigonan comforts and way of life, she still felt safest near Osiys.

Elryh piped up cheerily, peering over her cup of tea, "I am Elryh. It is certainly a great pleasure to meet the marvelous Indra who brought home our Osiys in one piece."

"Oh," Indra gave a small, awkward laugh. "I don't know about all of that. I think we were... there for one another. When he gave up faith, I helped him restore it. And when I was weary, he was strong for the both of us."

"You seem like a very humble person." Baird noted sincerely, then nodded to Osiys. "This one has always had a bit of a self-destructive streak. Don't downplay your part in his story, my dear."

Osiys shrugged. "It's true, on all accounts— my faults and her strengths. I'd most certainly be a corpse rotting in the mud if it weren't for her intervention."

Herran nodded, "It was not your time."

Indra let the smooth coffee roll over her tongue, warming her from the inside. It was mixed with cream and a dash of honey, and there were hints of Pallydhan cinnamon and nutmeg in the dark, frothy drink. Cradling the earthenware mug in her hands, she watched the interactions of these five Brigonans with growing warmth and curiosity. The cold-as-steel feeling of animosity, which she had assumed would be present, was slowly dissipating from her nerves, as quickly as the coffee was draining from her mug and filling her belly. There was a kindness, a familial quality to these people, and their love for Osiys was evident, despite his long absence from his homeland. Whatever kinship had been forged between these companions a decade ago was alive and well still today.

"We still haven't heard the story of this blossoming unexpected friendship and daring escape," Berg said with a sarcastic flourish, reaching awkwardly with his short arm to take another ladle of oatmeal from the little cauldron of it in the middle of the table. Slapping it into his bowl and tossing the ladle back into the huge cast iron pot, he looked up eagerly at her and Osiys. "Well? Do we have to strangle it out of you two?"

Indra exchanged a glance with Osiys, a small smile on her face.

"Where to begin?" she laughed.

Osiys grinned at her. "Where, indeed?"

Berg rolled his eyes at their waffling exchange. "How about you both stop silently reminiscing and start moving your mouths, eh?" He shoveled the oatmeal into his mouth as he gestured impatiently towards them with his free hand.

"I think we may need another carafe of coffee," Herran nodded to the round-faced girl standing in the corner of the room, a soiled apron tied round her wide waist.

The girl skipped away through the small wooden door beside her, and returned momentarily with two large carafes of the frothed coffee in hand. Setting them on the table, she scuttled back to her corner to await any further requests from those seated. Baird took a carafe and poured himself a mugful of the coffee before looking up towards Osiys and Indra once again.

"Go on, kids." He waved his hand at them as he took a sip of the mug, its billowing steam rippling over his face. "We've two carafes of coffee and a table full of food to keep us satiated through your inevitably long winded tale."

Osiys nodded to Indra. "You first."

Indra bit her lip. "Me? I don't quite know where to start."

"We want to know everything," Elryh squeaked excitedly. "How you two met, for starters. And how you knew."

"How I knew?"

"How you knew he was a spy, of course! And how you succeeded in that wild escape, too."

"Oh, well, alright." Indra twisted her hands in her lap as the five pairs of eyes affixed inquisitively to her. "Osiys came to Canestry ten years ago, when I was only seven."

"Goodness, child, you're a little thing, aren't you!"

"Stars, Elryh, she's barely a sentence into the story. Let the girl speak!" Berg glowered exaggeratedly at the woman, who promptly hid her face behind her mug of tea.

"Sorry!"

Indra let out a little laugh before continuing. "I think I suspected, even as a child, that there was something different about him. He used to bring me chocolate oranges from the candy shops when he came to meet with the guard, before he was a Night Walker. It wasn't in a malicious way, though, as some of the other men would do the same."

Her eyes flickered down to her hands, which twisted her cloth napkin nervously in her lap. She abruptly straightened herself, lifting her eyes once again. "He was kind. Before long, he was in the High House always, having been raised to Night Walker. I was rarely allowed to leave the High House grounds, and I was often bored there, with nothing much other than my tutoring or gardening to pass the time, so I'd go find Osiys. He talked to me, treated me like a whole person, told me stories about far-off Provinces. I always had those childish hopes where I would escape my father's house and run off and visit the places he told me about. Before long, we would meet in the long hall and eat those chocolate oranges and whisper about the Old Order, almost daily."

"You're leaving something out," Osiys remarked.

"Am I?"

"You were so damn curious and wouldn't let me alone about the Provinces and the Old Order... and the chocolates, you greedy creature."

Indra huffed good-naturedly . "I think you're simply too proud to admit that your loneliness got the best of you, and the only person you were able to confide in was a small child."

Berg laughed. "Ha! There she is! Now I see the fierce woman who rescued a grown-ass man from the most secretive Province in all of Allesar."

"She's a much better storyteller than you, pal," Baird grinned at Osiys as he nursed his coffee.

"You all really know how to charm a fellow, don't you?" Osiys raised an eyebrow and surveyed the group, who now grinned at Indra, excitedly.

She gulped in their curiosity, confidence waxing as she readjusted herself in her chair and splayed her fingers, gesturing intently as she continued the story. "Soon enough, I suspected secrecy—more than usual, mind you—from my father's Priests of the New Order. They had always been rather unforthcoming, but I caught them once, desperately snatching back a Star chart they had shared with a lower-ranking official, and switching it with another they had in their collection. I had studied minimal astronomy with my tutor, and decided to chart the Stars myself."

"Illegally chart the Stars," Osiys interjected.

Herran raised a bushy eyebrow, his eyes widening. "Illegally?"

"Yet," Indra confirmed. "In Canestry, the charting of Stars is designated solely to the Priests of the New Order. To chart them as one outside of the Discretion is illegal. Now we understand why."

Osiys nodded. "About a month ago, Indra showed me what she had charted. What we shockingly discovered was not only that the Discretion was concealing the truth of the Stars. It was also the truth itself."

"What do you mean?" Herran pressed.

"It sounds very strange," Indra paused, looking to Osiys as she forced out the impossible words. "The Stars are moving more quickly than the Canestryn Star charts would have their people believe, it's true. But there's more than that. They're also... moving closer."

Elryh choked on her tea.

"Closer? I doubt that very much," Harren shook his head. "Did you not say you studied minimal astronomy? Isn't it possible that your measurements were wrong?"

"No." Indra lifted her chin, squaring her slim shoulders as she stood from her chair, trying to hide the shakiness she felt and the skittering of her nervous heartbeat.

"No?" Harren's eyes widened, and he leaned back in his chair, as if he were backing away in stunned silence from her audacity.

"No," Indra repeated, with an equal amount of mettle in her voice.

"Indra...How can you be sure?" Berg's hands gripped the edge of the table as he leaned forward with skeptical curiosity.

"Because I stole a copy of the Canestryn official Star Charts. And their records confirm my work."

She walked around the back of Osiys' chair, catching a glimpse of his dumbfounded expression, jaw agape and unblinking stare. Reaching into the back of her short shirt, Indra pulled out a folded section of thin, ivory leather.

She had agonized over whether or not she ought to tell Osiys about her recent thievery when they had first made camp after escaping the Canestryn army, but still her anxiety had simmered, despite their growing proximity to the safety of the Brigonan High City. If they had been captured, her plan was a simple one: hide the Star Charts in the Brigonan forest and barter for their own release. She planned to take full responsibility for the charts' disappearance, having no desire to implicate Osiys in any further treason against her murderous Province. *When we arrive,* she had assured herself, *then I will tell him.* Still, when they finally did arrive in Brigon, her fear had taken hold in the pit of her stomach. A Canestryn girl in an enemy Province had no guarantee of safety, regardless of who her friends may be. These inexplicable Star Charts were her only hope for ransom if they had chosen to turn on her. It felt foolish and infantile now, all her restless fear, as she looked into the astonished eyes of the people around her and walked, posture tall and graceful, to stand beside Premier Herran.

Herran and Baird hurriedly pushed the dishes away from the end of the table, sending them clattering and ringing against one another. Spreading out the sheet of soft leather onto the cleared space, the three others clamored around her to get a better view of the chart. Berg climbed onto the table and squatted at the top of it, facing them.

"Indra, can you, ah, translate for us?" Osiys pressed against her left shoulder, brow wrinkled with fervent interest.

"Yes, please!" Elryh insisted, barely above a whisper, somehow still clutching her tea, which was assuredly cold by now.

"Certainly." Indra gestured to the large wheel, delineated in the center of the chart. "This is the sky as we know it. These various rings in the wheel indicate months, days, and finally the seasons on this outermost ring, as they correspond to the horizon ascension of each sacred Star. These staggered curves stipulate the movement of each star in relation to Allesar."

"I'm afraid you have already left me in the dust in terms of your astronomical knowledge," Berg winced from his perch on the table.

"Perhaps if you weren't looking at it upside down, my little twin...?" Baird smirked at his brother.

Berg cocked an eyebrow. "Don't tell me you understand astronomy now?"

Rolling his eyes, Baird tapped the chart. "Continue, would you, Indra? Help us understand what this bit means."

"The curves are aligned around the wheel in correlation to the months the Stars appear and disappear on the horizon. See here: the outer curve simulating the Star of Brigon begins just outside of the wheel segment representing the month of Brigon. But the beginning of the curve is further from the wheel than the end of the curve, as is the case for each of the other surrounding curves. The measurement between the curve and the wheel represents the distance between the Stars and Allesar, so, as you can see, their measurements show the Stars moving closer."

Indra felt the silence like a weight upon her back, pressing her forward towards this evidential truth. She had kept the chart hidden and secret since the moments she'd taken it, and looking at it now felt real in an eerie, unsettling way.

Her pleading words cracked the empty air. "It takes skill and practice to read Star Charts. I am sure if you take it to your priests, they will be able to compare it to their own, therefore verifying my translation."

Herran rested a hand on her shoulder, his broad fingers looking mammoth on the narrowness of her bones. "Our priests do not measure distance. It has never been a thought in their minds. Rest assured, Indra, that we trust your honesty and your mastery."

Somehow, the weight of his hand, and his trust, relieved, somewhat, the weight of her solemn realizations. For the first time in her recent memory, she felt a distant sense of safety rising in the horizon of her soul. She was no enemy here.

"Well," Herran sighed, leaning back into his chair and dragging a hand across his face, "I suppose it is time for some news of my own."

Wordlessly, the group filed back into their seats, an air of urgency and importance in their blood.

"I have just returned from an assembly with the Premiers of Chedhiy and Jopaar. It would seem that the Stars are not only moving more quickly and drawing nearer to us. They are also sending down to us their shattering astral home."

An intense terror seeped into Indra's fragile hope of momentary safety, drowning it in a slow, agonizing death. Her father's words warbled in her ears as she felt the world around her growing dim and hazy:

"Even Provinces must die. Even the Stars must fall."

OR

9
BOLSTERING ALL HER FRAGILE COSMOS

JAUYNE & ZECH, EDGE OF MEIRYDH'S HIGH CITY
3 weeks since the sack of Meirydh

It had been a full week since the Starlit explosion had leveled that small hut, and Jauyne was still exhausted. She refused to let on, though she knew Zech had noticed. The sooty black soil had stained two of her three changes of clothes by now, and she was desperate for a bath.

If they had continued to Chedhiy like she had originally planned, she would surely have arrived at the watchtower by now, where they'd have received horses to make their way to the High City, arriving in less than a day.

Instead, she was on her way back the very same way she'd come, nearly having reached the heaps of wreckage and death, and certainly no hot bath to soothe away the grime of grief and days on the road. She glowered at Zech ahead of her, his gate somehow still bright and steady.

Bastard watchman... At least he fended off the woundrot. Jauyne absentmindedly raised a hand to her face where she traced the nasty scar which remained. She had to pause to regain her breath for a moment, her heart attempting to lunge out of her chest as she felt all over again the sword which had cut down her father's right hand man, before slicing her face.

"We can slow down for a bit."

Shit. He'd taken note of her halting steps.

"I'm fine," she quipped, quickening her pace to match his gate defiantly.

"Well, that's definitely a lie." His left eyebrow was raised at her.

"Maybe you should stop assessing my motives and begin deciding how you plan to pull apart the already ransacked remains of my home to search for these two sacred, ancient relics or whatever nonsense Aeron begged you to look for." She tossed him an exaggerated flourish with a roll of her eyes.

Jauyne knew she was being unkind and felt a hint of guilt, but she was miserable, angry, and Stars, she just wanted a hot bath.

She wished he would be unkind. It would be easier to snap at him that way, but he'd been so gentle— if not mouthy— since discovering she was not, in fact, the enemy. She rolled her eyes again, seemingly incapable of halting the motion, kicking a small stone down the road ahead of her as she brushed past him, her shoulder roughly jostling his arm.

Should have let him think I was a fucking Canestryn.

"It isn't nonsense," he insisted, long strides bringing him quickly back to her side. "It's the truth. I believe it."

"Believing in something doesn't make it true. Or do you still believe the tales your parents told you about the dragons made of Starlight who live in the swirls of dust out there between the Stars?" She widened her eyes and waved her hands with some melodrama, emphasizing his insanity in a way that made the guilt inch back into her gut.

"I have seen a lot of things in the past few years. Who's to say there isn't a dragon Province in the Stars?"

She snorted, and Zech grinned, an inkling of self-consciousness pricking at the edges of his mouth.

"I tease, Jauyne." He continued in a tone which made her feel as though he hadn't been teasing at all, when she responded with only silence. "I suppose it doesn't help, though, when I'm trying to convince you of things that aren't children's tales."

Jauyne stopped still in her tracks. "If you enjoy teasing so much, humor me. What do these two relics look like? Where will we find them? And what are we to do with them once we do?"

Zech looked down at the settling dust that his feet had kicked up. "I don't know."

Jauyne shook her head. "You're right. You are hilarious." She briskly turned on her heel and began walking even more swiftly than before, "This was a mistake. We should have continued on to Chedhiy. I could be rallying support, summoning men with strength to rebuild my home.

Instead I'm letting you drag me back into the ashes of it. Some leader I must be, if I can't even command a single man."

"Jauyne—"

"Stop. Speaking." Her teeth ground together painfully under the force of her rage.

He nodded quietly. Silence had never been his strongest suit. Looking up at the sky, he couldn't help but remember all the wild stories he'd heard as a child, myths of astral dragons and ancient wars between Stars in the great beyond, eons before the Provinces of man had been born. Oh, how he'd been fixated on those stories– obsessed, really. What child didn't want to believe in mystical creatures and adventurous realms outside their own?

What grown man doesn't want to believe in them? It's damn well better than reality.

Zech stole a glance at the woman walking beside him. Despite her light, little frame, he could feel the heaviness of her energy as it emanated from her in a dark, rippling wave. The look of her stoic sort of grief sent a chill of awe down his spine, and he wanted to reach out, take her hand, though he wasn't stupid enough to try a stunt such as that. He was funny, but he wasn't a fool.

He was also intelligent enough to know that people like Jauyne Elenfor, if there were any other people like her, were incapable of being forced into anything they didn't wish to do. Perhaps she was fooling herself into believing that his claims were nonsense, but somewhere in her, she knew the truth. Zech was convinced of that. He would let her voice her doubts and mock him, but she would let herself believe in it all, sooner or later. And when that happened, he had no doubt in his mind that she would be an indomitable, stunning sort of power.

They walked away from his beloved mountains, the sun sinking towards those great stone summits, as they went on their solemn way. It had been a long while now. Perhaps his skill in keeping his mouth shut was growing, after all. He grinned to himself. If only Aeron was there—he'd be impressed with this new-found talent. He would also do anything to push the limits of it.

The shadows were stretching long in front of them. Jauyne took in their surroundings in the dwindling daylight, the heap of her High City growing ever-closer on the horizon. They'd need to make shelter soon, and possibly hunt; the little food they'd had with them had been quickly depleted, and there was still close to a day's journey before reaching Meirydh's High City.

Her feet were growing tired of the trek, and they ached in tandem with her head. Journeying by foot was hard enough, but holding onto her anger for Zech was somehow equally exhausting. Even more infuriating was the nagging suggestion that he was right, that this was a good choice, that these two ancient, mysterious pieces of their history were, indeed, a necessary detour.

A small clump of trees grew out of the invisible distance, a hundred yards off to the east. She pointed to it. "There. Let's set up shelter and find a meal. We're close enough to the city to take the rest of the journey in a day, if we begin early."

He nodded. "I expect it's not the sort of scene you want to arrive at after nightfall, anyhow."

"Wow, you really do put belief in those children's tales."

He smiled. "In Chedhiy, we have a tradition we practice when death comes for our loved ones. After they die, we burn the bodies. Once the embers have died, we collect the ashes and bottle them. We make the journey to the sacred clearing, and we climb the tree of their clan. Then we take the bottle, and we hang it from the branches, so that even their bodies from this life will be bathed in the light of the Stars..." He took a shaky breath, broad smile fading. "I hate that Aeron died so far from his tree. There's no way to honor him, now."

Jauyne was silent for a few moments. This was not what she had been expecting; it tweaked at a place in her spine, a place that held her legacy and her grief. When she spoke, it was with the only voice she trusted not to break, scarcely above a whisper.

"In Meirydh, our mages preserve the bodies until the next storm. It's never long, a couple of weeks or so at most. We carry them out to the molten springs in a coffin made of metal. The lightning always strikes true, catching their bodies on fire. We offer them back to the place where the fire of the heavens kisses the fire of Allesar, into the sacred lava pools."

She trailed off as they reached the little grove of trees.

"I'm sorry. It's hard. I know."

That stupid, infuriating kindness...

"I only wish I didn't need to see them again... their decaying faces, buzzing with flies, stinking. It isn't the thing I want to see when I close my eyes to remember them." Jauyne roughly wiped her nose on the sleeve of her shirt and set her pack on the ground, nestled in the gnarled roots of what appeared to be an ancient tree.

Zech nodded softly as he knelt at the edge of the path to begin collecting firewood. "I've never had to look into the dead eyes of someone I love. It isn't something I ever wanted to experience."

"Didn't you see your mother, after her..." She wasn't sure how to end her question, and realized she was being horrible and insensitive. She stood under the branches, digging her nails into her palms with a new feeling of embarrassment.

"No," Zech paused, looking back towards the hulking black outline of the mountains. "No, they never found her body."

"Stars... I'm sorry."

He nodded his thanks. "I've come to peace with it. Mostly. I've lost family. I've lost my friend. I know what this is like."

He reached for her hand; without a thought, she let him.

Fuck, she missed Lissa and Merech and Hana. For the briefest minute, he wasn't Zech. He was each of her friends, in one body, in one hand. It was only after she met his eyes that she realized what he'd done. She held his earnest gaze steady. A thin sheen of milky Starlight swam over his eyes; he was looking at her with wonder. It was silent between them before she withdrew her hand and massaged it with her other.

Her cheeks filled with color, and she was thankful that he had abruptly turned round to collect more firewood, sparing her flushed cheeks the embarrassment of being noticed. She pressed her cool hands to the side of her face, trying to banish the mysteriously appearing pink color from them.

Why in Allesar had he done that? And where had her courage gone—she'd warned him that if he touched her again she'd put him in the ground, so why is he still standing, Starsdamnit? Why wouldn't her fists comply at the command to place one of them between his eyes? *And for Stars' sake, why am I nauseous?*

There was a throbbing of energy around and inside of her, a heightening of everything that set her on edge and soothed her simultaneously. She remembered the Starstone in her pack and the glimmery light in his eyes, and she felt a yearning start in her nerves.

Inhaling deeply and blinking hard, she forcibly pressed Zech and the Starstone out of her mind and set out to search the dry grasses for birds' nests to strip of eggs for their dinner, ignoring his existence behind her under the trees.

Jauyne followed Zech into the rubble of what was once her home, cursing under her breath. She had never meant to come back here, not like this, not without a mass of people to rebuild while she rode further east to gut that murderer, Premier Canryn, in his own great halls. Her hand instinctively wrapped itself round the hilt of her mostly concealed dagger as she pictured what Canryn's guts might look like, spilling out of his belly all wet and steaming.

She watched this man in front of her move between the masses of fly-covered bodies that led the way to the broken front gates. The whole area still reeked; they had smelled it soon after beginning that morning's final stretch of road. It was all part of the humiliation, proof that Meirydh had been taken purely for punishment and not out of need. Canestry had not taken the city or removed the corpses strewn about. It was an altar to death itself.

Zech seemed to itch with purpose the closer they came to the gates. He hopped about, nearly vibrating with an intense nervous energy. She cursed him silently even as her gaze paused on his strong hands studying something he'd found in the dirt, on the cords of muscle lashing through his arms, on the sweaty curls of auburn hair that brushed the top curve of his ears.

She dragged her own hand across her forehead, where her hair stuck to her skin with sweat. It was by no means warm in Meirydh, but the punishing pace of the day's trek prevailed over the cool air.

Zech continued towards the gates. They weren't far off now, a hundred yards or so maybe, and the sinking sun glinted off the polished metal like diamonds. The gold and amber light danced in his auburn curls and set them on fire. Jauyne followed it like a beacon, keeping her eyes on his back to avoid the sight of the putrefying bodies piled around them.

She came to a patch of grass soaked brown with dark blood, and noted with disgust the sick on the ground beside it. Her bones screeched in distant recognition, and she crouched there, taking in the sight of death and fire from this new vantage point. Her breath shuddered in her lungs. The realization hit her with a crumpling nausea that squirmed and raked its way through her belly.

Scenes of horror battled for attention in her vision, and only half of them made sense. The rest were filled with flashing silver doorways, crisp lines of Starlight lighting the blood-streaked floor beneath her, some inhuman scream blaring consistently overhead. People were crying out for her, and the Starlight webbing through the veins of her hands felt close... so close, so strong. There was a hand on her back, and that hand bridged every memory, every moment. She had the feeling of an infinitely important and precious thing being torn from her by her own will. The sword that had cut her down, cut her again and again and again...

Zech glanced over his shoulder mid-sentence, expecting her to be directly behind him, and instead found her several yards back, kneeling in the dirt.

"Jauyne, what is it?"

Her eyes were far-off and pearlescent with light, lips trembling so hard that her voice was a thin and jittered vibrato. "This is where they tried to kill me."

The pit of Zech's stomach went cold and hollow; he watched her hand distractedly trace the still-healing scar along the length of her face.

"It is where I fell, where I bled, where I woke up." Her voice seemed devoid of herself, distant and detached from her quivering body.

He could see her chest heaving and hear her ragged breathing as he moved towards where she sat in the dampness of her own blood, mixed with soil and rainwater. Her hands shook violently in her lap, eyes glued to the faded splatters of vomit.

Is she in shock?

"Jauyne," he knelt beside her, taking one of her hands. It, like her face, was pale and cold. Her pulse thrummed fast beneath his fingers on her wrist. He repeated her name. "Jauyne, look at me."

Could he anger her out of it? He prodded. "Come on, little *firestarter.*"

Her eyes remained locked on the ground, her breathing growing more shallow and rapid. "They are taking something from me. It is going to kill me. I don't know where I am."

She swallowed and gagged, nearly vomiting on top of the old splatter of bile. Zech grabbed her chin and pivoted her face to look into his own, but her pupils were dilated and confused.

"I was... I'm... I died... I think..." she muttered nonsensically.

Zech swallowed back the swell of fear that crashed towards him, at her blank face, her disjointed thoughts.

She needs to lie down, to breathe. He looked all around them at the ocean of war-bloodied bodies and winced. *Not here. She needs to go home.*

Placing one arm around her shoulders and swooping the other behind her thighs, he raised her from the ground. He began the stumbling journey towards the center of the city, following ring after inner ring of the streets toward the High House, as her head curled unconsciously towards him. She muttered incoherently.

It took years, or so it felt.

By the time he laid her on silken purple bed coverings and dragged the heavy pack from her shaking shoulders, the sun was nothing but a streak of melted orange behind the distant mountain peaks through her window. The muscles in his arms were a searing burn, and his legs twitched when he collapsed next to her, his breaths coming hard.

She blinked, slowly and repeatedly, at the high domed ceiling decorated in large flowers and stars done in gold work. Air began to flow more steadily through her lungs, and he watched the soft, reassuring rise and fall of her chest. Her fingers absentmindedly stroked the silk beneath them, until they found Zech's hand, and she abruptly started.

It was as though she'd forgotten where she was in time, as though she'd forgotten he was there, or that he existed at all. But now she remembered. His presence was a catalyst for reality, for the grief that barreled in with it, and her eyes silently brimmed over in the dusky amber light.

"I'd forgotten," she whispered. "I didn't know you could forget pain like that so quickly. It was just... there. Waiting for me."

Zech wasn't sure what to do, so he entwined his fingers with hers. His whisper was cracked through with labored breathing. "Heartache is nasty in that way."

Jauyne nodded as she pressed her eyelids shut sharply, silently squeezing out tears in a tidal outpouring of sorrow. He felt her hand grip his till their bones ground together at the knuckles, like she was motionlessly floundering for something to hold onto. Daringly, he turned on his side to face her; he rested a hand on her opposite arm to tug her towards him. She rolled into him with a rattling sob.

Zech couldn't believe how small her bones felt clattering against him like this as she cried. Her spirit was so huge, so all-encompassing wherever she was, he had never considered the possibility that she might be thin enough to snap like a twig in a summer storm. The scent of her sweat from their long tramp through the plains still lingered in her hair, and it twined with the salty smell of her tears.

He found himself in an odd suspension between wanting to rock her like a devastated child, and wanting to worship her like the wild goddess of grief and rage that she was. He decided on clutching his hands in her hair and bolstering her fragile cosmos in his arms.

Long after her eyes dried, they stayed curled on the purple silk in the darkened room. Zech wasn't sure when she fell asleep, or if she ever did. But they stayed there, quiet and still through the night, desperately exchanging the comfort of breath and warmth in the center of a city inhabited only by the cold dead.

NOT

10
AN OLD WOMAN.
ALSO THE GROUND.

The little silken bag still hung around his neck. It still felt as though it weighed a thousand pounds, as though it would drag him like an anchor over the edge of the flimsy wooden railing. That was the only barrier between him and hurtling down the mountainside.

He absentmindedly stroked the bag with a rough finger. There were perhaps more important things for him to worry about than this errand, though none were more important to him.

Osiys could still see that little home in his mind's eye long before he reached it, carved out of the stone, with yellow curtains fluttering in the windows. Even as he plodded woodenly down the steep stairway that curled against the rock face, he dreaded the direction it took him. It was a strange mixture of misery and stomach-fluttering elation.

Turn around. Oh for Stars' sake, turn around, you fucking idiot.

His feet refused to obey.

It was getting closer now, and he could see the curtains waving. Ten years. They were still bright yellow. Surely she wouldn't still be there, in her parents' home. She'd be on her own by now, but he hadn't had the courage to ask anyone in the High House. So onward his feet dragged, and closer the yellow curtains waved.

The wooden door was more weathered than it had been the last time he'd seen it. More gashes in it from the branches and small stones that the storms kicked up, this high on the mountain. He was coming home with a few more gashes, too, and a weathered spirit.

He reached out, knuckles forward to knock, when the door was preemptively pulled open from the inside. He blinked.

A girl, probably taller than her age warranted, grinned back at him, teeth bright white on her smudged, round face. She was probably nine or ten, and her kinky copper hair was all a mess, coming loose from the sloppy way she'd pulled it onto the top of her head.

"Woah!" she gaped, awestruck. "Who the hell are you?"

"Language, Verve!" A scratchy, female voice hollered from somewhere further inside the little house.

She rolled her amber eyes dramatically and huffed a little. "Yes, Gamma!"

Osiys wasn't quite sure what to do, or who this fierce little person was. "Uh," he trailed off before he could even begin.

"Well, then, go on!" Her eyes widened eagerly and she gestured him to continue, even as she kept babbling on. "I know everybody— and I mean everybody— in Brigon, and I don't know you, so who *are* you?"

"Oh, ah, I am Osiys, from the High Circle of the Premier. I'm here looking for... for someone. But, um, I must have the wrong place. Verna and Grend—they used to live here."

He shook his head, full of foolishness, as he turned away.

"What do you mean, you got the wrong place?" She laughed, as though it were the funniest thing she'd ever heard, which only served to turn Osiys's mood even sourer than it already was.

"They're just inside there. I'll get 'em for you!" she continued, turning her head back to bellow out a call. "Gamma! There's some fancy High Circle man here at the door looking for you!"

The air in Osiys's lungs went stale.

Gamma... *They have a grandchild... So she has moved on, after all. As she should, you selfish ass. As you should.*

He had never felt more stupid or more exposed, shaking there on the edge of a mountain as a child called for her grandparents. And yet, as the graying woman appeared at the door, and her face drained of all color, he felt smaller still.

Starsdamnit, she's going to die right here.

Verna clutched her hands together, gritting her teeth as tears budded in her eyes and streamed down her face. She shook her head rhythmically and muttered a trail of anguished words from behind the tears.

"No... Oh, Osiys... I knew you'd come. I knew. But... Stars, I can't bear it. I can't bear it!"

"Gamma?" The girl glanced worriedly back and forth between her grandmother and Osiys, obviously trying to sort out what could possibly elicit such a reaction.

Osiys stumbled backwards and gripped the weather—smoothed wooden railing behind him for support, his heart throbbing up into his ears. His memory abruptly assaulted him: visions of deep brunette curls pooling on his chest as she rested her head on his shoulder with a soft sigh, laughter like music, a screaming argument followed by a night of furious fucking when he told her he was leaving...

He wanted to feel badly for the child, for the position Verna was now in, to tell her granddaughter that the man at the door was her mother's lover, all those years ago. Yet the only feeling he could muster was depthless self-loathing and a gripping nausea.

Verna pulled the girl close to her, softly running a hand over her tangle of hair and attempting to cradle her with work-roughened, maternal hands, though Verve stood a few inches taller than she. With a nervous, sidelong glance back to Osiys, she spoke to Verve in a trembling voice, which somehow still held a heavy hand of strength.

"Verve, darling... Do you remember when I told you about the man who your mother loved so very much? The one who... who left?"

Verve held Osiys's gaze as she answered gingerly. "Yes, Gamma..."

"Osiys is that man."

The girl blinked slowly. Paused for a moment. Then her breath seemed to stop, and she stammered, looking rapidly between her grandmother and Osiys.

"But, Gamma... That means. *That means*..."

Verna tore her gaze away from her granddaughter to look back at Osiys, her eyes rimming over once again with glossy tears. "Yes, love. Osiys is your father."

It was as though something had deafened him. Choked out his air. Dizzied his mind. There was no frame of reference for him to categorize this scrawny, wide-eyed, wild-haired girl who stood in front of him, hysterical with shock.

"Osiys."

He could see Verna's lips mouthing his name, but he still struggled to hear her. Even through the madness of Verve's shocked wailing, he could feel tendrils of hope weaving their way into his heart.

Maybe she's still waiting for me... with her— our —child. Our child...

"Osiys!"

He blinked. Verna was stepping towards him as Verve fled into the house. Her hands were outstretched towards him, calloused and chapped from mountain air and hard work, like any Brigonan woman's. They grabbed him with a harshness he'd forgotten, hauled him down into an embrace that felt anything but tender.

"Verna, where is she? I've got to see her. Apologize for everything. Hear her tell me about our—our! —daughter. I have to—"

She whispered suddenly from where she had crushed herself against his ear, cutting off his excitement mid-sentence. "Shut up, you wicked boy, and listen to me."

Osiys froze in the vice grip. "Verna, what's the matter?"

Verna pulled away from him and dug her fingers into his shoulders with a surprisingly painful grip. She looked him square in the eyes, resentment glittering there. "Elessid died. Six years ago."

The ringing wave of grief and overwhelm took hold of his mind once again, dragging him through its murky undercurrent. She was talking, but it wasn't important. What could be important now? What could be important ever again?

Elessid... Darling...

Nausea and blind vertigo crumbled him, slamming his knees to the stone. The pain was nonexistent, though he watched the blood squirm out in swirling lines from under them. His own wrenching breath and the angry groan of his heart were all he could hear in his silent universe of sorrow. His knees were wet. The grey stone was growing black, but there was no rain.

It was then that he felt the hot tears on his face and his hearing returned in a jolt as he heard his own howling sob echoing off the mountain. Fury drove his fist into the wooden post beside him, splintering the wood and bloodying his knuckles. It felt good though, to watch the grief escape like this. It felt good to hurt in a way that could only tear his skin. It felt good to see the despair mark his body. There was so much relief in it, that he pummeled the post a few more times, his own blood spattering his face.

"Osiys!"

A sharp smack landed on the back of his head, sufficiently reviving him. He flinched up towards where Verna stood. She glared down at him, sternly.

"Stars–be–damned, Osiys, *get your fucking shit together.*"

"What?" he hissed, seething.

How dare she?

"I said, get your *fucking* shit together. You have a daughter in there who has suffered all of this pain once already. If you are here to subject her to it a second time, then it is time for you to leave."

Osiys could scarcely force it to compute. When he did, the shame made him gag. He was out of control, and he had no ability to reign in this kind of quantity of misery.

"Where is she?"

"Verve is in the house, but you—"

"Elessid." He interrupted her. He didn't deserve to hear another word about Verve. He'd leave her alone. She'd be better off if he joined her mother in death. "Where is Elessid?"

Verna blinked, livid. "In the spire."

He nodded repetitively, unable to stop the movement. His knuckles were beginning to sting, and the blood was running down his arm in long, vibrant stripes.

"I'll leave her alone. I won't come back."

"It should have been you instead," the greying woman spat. "With the pain you put my girl through. After you abandoned her, I prayed every day to the Stars that you would never leave that fucking Province alive."

Verna stalked away, her receding gaze a viscous poison, leaving Osiys in his own blood by the wooden railing at the edge of the mountain face. The reverberation of the slamming door rattled his bones.

He stood, slowly, shaking.

You vile, ignorant little fucker. Lover-killer. Selfish Starsdamned asshole. She wouldn't have died if you hadn't abandoned her. Given up on her. Like you give up on everything, like you gave up on Canestry. Like you gave up on yourself.

Blood dripped from his knuckles as he gripped the rail, the perfect beads of red endlessly suspended in cold mountain air as they fell thousands of feet to the ground below. He stood, leaned precariously over the side, the dizzying height beckoning. He swayed. A ball of heat swelled in his stomach. Even his body wanted to be rid of his soul.

The lurching vomit surprised him. He wretched over empty air and then staggered away, wiping his mouth and then wincing in pain when he realized he'd used his battered hand. Blood mixed with bile in his mouth, and he stumbled onto his ass to sit on the hard ground.

He curled his knees to his chin and buried his face in his hands, sobbing into them with practiced silence. Salty tears stung his knuckles and knees as he wept there, no care paid to how much time passed.

Eventually, with a deep sigh, he leaned back his head against the stone and lifted his eyes to the darkening sky. It was growing pink and orange in the dusk, and clouds passed around and below them here, high on the mountain spires. The blood on his hands and knees was drying dark and caked on his skin, and was probably streaked across his face from the crying. His tongue still tasted like puke.

Eyes still lost in the sky, he slowly reached to the little pouch around his neck. He traced the cord which kept it around his neck, then ducked, pulling it over his head. The little thing was so small in the palm of his hands. He stared at it for a moment, before tugging at the drawstring and loosening the neck of it.

A small silver ring tumbled out into his hand. The stone was a brilliant emerald, cut in a teardrop shape and set into the silver band with delicate prongs. She'd never worn it. Hadn't even known it existed... though she had known of his feelings and intentions. It was his promise to himself, even more than it was to her. A vow to come back and do right by her.

He hadn't wanted to spy for Brigon, not really. Never been able to convince Elessid of that, though. He should have listened to her. He knew that the minute he'd stepped foot outside of their home province and began walking east for Canestry. He'd never stopped feeling like a fool for the woman he'd left behind and the stupid headstrongness with which he'd thrown himself into his mission.

He was in the wrong. He knew that.

He'd never not known that.

And a daughter?

Shit. How did I never question? After that night? The poor child... My poor child.

Elessid had near plastered herself to him the week of his deployment to Canestry. He'd only left her bed to eat and piss, and she'd drag him right back in and under the covers again. How had he never even considered the possibility that they'd made a child together in all that time?

He leaned his head back again, and the cold mountain breeze swept over his face, soft... like her skin had been. He could still feel her, still hear her chiding, high voice and rapturous giggle. Oh, he missed her. It was all so Starsdamn final now. His body felt heavy and limp with the kind of damp exhaustion that comes with excessive crying.

Dropping the ring back in its pouch, he strung it around his neck and pushed himself upright. He didn't know what kept him from leaping over the wooden barrier, but whatever it was, it kept him alive the entire long climb back up to the Premier's home, where he stumbled into his bedroom and instantly collapsed on the downy mattress.

A sharp rapping on the wooden doors of Osiys's room shook him awake. The grogginess of agonized sleep clouded his eyes and left a dull throb in his temples. He dragged a hand over his face, but the movement reopened the scabs on his knuckles and sent fresh blood rolling down his hand.

He sucked on it to keep it from dripping onto the sheets as he rolled to standing. Stars, he looked a mess.

"Yeah?" His voice was so raspy.

The door creaked open just a little, and Indra stepped into the small opening. Her eyes went wide at the sight of him, but she quickly hid her worry. Stepping forward into the room, she pulled the door shut behind her and walked to the adjoined bath. She reappeared a moment later with a bowl of water and a wet rag.

"We should fix all this up." She nodded to his bloody knees and streaked face. "There are some important developments that the Premier wants to meet with you about."

Osiys looked at his feet, the deep shame suddenly returning.

"You don't have to—"

"No. I don't." Her voice was soft, but firm. "But you look like shit, and I'm willing to bet you feel even worse."

He smirked. "Since when do you curse?"

"Since I became a turncoat runaway and realized it doesn't actually matter," she shrugged.

He sat on the edge of the bed. Tugged on a spiraled strand of auburn hair. Sighed a sigh that emptied his lungs. Indra produced an extra wet rag from the bowl and wrung it out, then handed it to him to use on his face and hand.

How did all this grief become our normal?

She was looking at him now. Shit. He'd been staring right through her. Quickly, he patted his red knuckles with the cloth she'd given him.

"Who was the unfortunate soul that bloodied you up?" Indra broke the silence. "From the looks of those knuckles, you must've at least got a few swings in."

Should I tell her it was an old woman, or the ground? Even his thoughts dripped with sarcasm towards his piteous situation. He was too tired to lie. He had been lying for ten years.

"An old woman. Also the ground."

Indra snorted a laugh, before looking at the misery on his face and coming to the realization that he was speaking seriously. "Stars, Osiys! What happened to you?"

She dropped the wet rag back into the bowl with a resounding splat and dried her hands on the flowing pants of her burgundy ensemble. Easing down on the bed beside him, she looked at him with an unflinching gaze that demanded he speak.

This child... She's not even a child anymore, not after what she's seen. Has she ever been a child, really?

"There was a woman, before I left for Canestry." The words started spilling out before he could stop them. "A lover. Her name is— *was* —Elessid. She told me not to go."

He almost choked on the ball of tears that occluded his throat. *I am so fucking done with this. Don't bawl. Do not bawl.*

"I kept this ring," He pulled the chain over his head and handed the silk pouch to Indra. "to give to her when I returned. I went to find her today. She's... gone. But not before she had our child."

Indra pinched the ring between her forefinger and thumb, lost in the sadness of his story and the glittering jewel of the ring. Tears filmed over her eyes as she looked up at him.

"I... I'm afraid I don't know what to say. 'I'm sorry' doesn't feel adequate." A tear splashed off the point of her chin as she nodded towards his bloodied knees, which he now busied himself with washing off, in order to avoid her teary display of empathy. "How did you manage that?"

He shrugged, trying to banish grief with nonchalance. Numbness took over as he recounted the events like they had happened to a different burdened soul. "Bawling like a child. Elessid's mother smacked me pretty good on the back of the head to get me to shut the fuck up. She seemed to think Elessid and I should swap places. I punched the guard rails a few times."

What he wouldn't tell her was the fact that he'd agreed with Verna. Or how good it had felt to bleed. Or the moment he'd almost tilted himself forward into the empty air. She pitied him enough.

Indra gaped a bit, then clapped her mouth shut properly and stood. "I think you should get into clean clothing and then come have a drink. I also heard rumor of Berg making popped corn."

"Indra, I don't really want—"

She raised her chin with an air of authority and snapped at him. "Change, and get your ass to the dining hall."

There was no time to protest before she'd flitted out of the room and closed shut the huge door behind her. Osiys watched her go, loneliness eating at his bones. He put his face into his palms, etched reddish in the lines with blood that still hadn't come out from the rag washing. Fingers massaged his temples and forehead, where a thumping ache was beginning to form.

Fuck.

The loneliness was the worst bit.

With some mental effort, he tugged his shirt over his head and kicked his pants to the corner of the room. He finished scrubbing the blood from his raw knees and plunged his hands into the bowl of water, vigorously going at the dried bits under his nails and in the worn lines. A splash to the face shook him awake a bit. He didn't bother to pat dry, and the water streamed down his neck and over his chest, trickling down his stomach into his navel.

There was a large chest of drawers along the far wall, and he dug out a fresh shirt and pants, which he pulled on, slowly. His body felt stiff and achy as he stretched to dress. Slicking back his hair with a bit of the hair paste in the bath, he gave himself a brief once-over in the mirror and stepped out into the hall.

He didn't know how to hold his self-hatred or his shame or his sorrow. He didn't know how long it would be before his body and mind won over whatever scrap of self still clung ravenously to life. He just knew that in the dining hall there was a drink and popped corn and a circle of friends who hadn't bothered to tell him his lover was long-dead.

BUT

11
SHE'D FREEZE, BODY AND SOUL

JAUYNE, HIGH HOUSE OF MEIRYDH
23 days since the sack of Meirydh

They had searched everywhere.

For four days, they had sought out these two halves which were stated to be here, somewhere, in the High City of Meirydh. Jauyne could not think of a single other place to look, and the smells and sights of this sunbaked massacre had long been filling her with an inescapable dread.

It hadn't been discussed, what had happened that first night in the High City, though she couldn't shake the gnawing emptiness of the places in her that childishly demanded to be cradled again. Zech had wordlessly taken his sleep on the floor beside her own bed on each of the last three nights, and her pride hadn't been able to bring herself to ask otherwise of him, though she'd wanted to. She didn't want him, not really; she just wanted to not be alone, to have the comfort of another warm and living heart beating near to her own. It was deafening, the silence of the dead. What she wanted, needed, was the pounding sound of life.

She slumped against the door frame and pressed a hand to her throbbing temple.

They were down in the lower ring of the High House for the third time, and Zech ran a grimy hand through his mess of waves. He was warm, even his coloring. That honeyed, ruddy skin and hair like magma tempered with brown earth; it was too much.

For some unbearable and irritating reason, in the jolting wretchedness of the place surrounding them, just looking at him soothed her in all the places she felt isolated. She felt the contrast between his warmth and her own frigidity like a solid thing. She could attempt to blame it on the recent horrors her eyes had seen, but the truth was, she'd always been too serious, frighteningly angular, strangely wrapped in the dark distractions of her own mind. This man introduced an openness to her intensity that both comforted and frightened her when she thought about him for too long... as she was doing now.

It made her want to hiss and snarl and sarcasm her way out of his presence. But she was really fucking tired.

He dragged a hand across his face and looked at her with green-grey eyes underlined in rings of exhaustion. "Should we check your home one last time? They did say it was something to do with you directly."

There was no mention of what might happen, should they not find what they were looking for, but Jauyne shrugged tiredly from where she stood in the doorway, unsure if it was anger or hunger or just the sheer eeriness of the place that made her want to crawl out of her own skin.

Zech made his way over the decapitated body of a man who had once been one of the most deeply revered mages in all of Allesar. Cringing wasn't even a reaction any longer. There were too many to grieve for. He had found Aeron on the second day they'd been there, and had dragged his body away from the main stair so he wouldn't have to pass it again. Jauyne had covered the corpse with a blanket and set fire to it, a gesture that still surprised her, in a makeshift tradition of her people. He met her eyes with mutual weariness, and as he passed her in the doorway, he wordlessly took her by the hand.

Jauyne wanted to recoil, but it was warm and firm and didn't grip her like a belonging, so she begrudgingly allowed herself to accept it. It steadied her, grounded her somehow, as they wound their way up two broad flights of carved stone steps to the highest and most secluded place in the city. She wasn't sure how many times she had walked the bloodstained halls of her home since the slaughter had taken place, though this time it was with a hand gripping her own.

The closer they got to the broken front doors of what had once been her home, the colder and emptier the rage in that familiar pit of her stomach grew, seeping into her heart, her shoulders, her knees. Her eyes avoided the splattered blood that painted the threshold of the house, but squinting them closed just swathed it across the inside of her eyelids. The empty cold poured into her cratered palms.

He buzzed beside her like the Starstone buzzed in her pack, and it made her dizzy and overwhelmed. She yanked her hand from Zech's and rubbed it roughly with the other. He could pretend all he liked that he was a friend, that he had her best interests at heart, but it was he who had dragged her back here, who had put some stupid prophecy on a higher pedestal than the vengeance and justice of her city. Higher than the breaking of her heart. How could he expect forgiveness for that? Perhaps he didn't; perhaps his tenderness was a scheme. It would seem fitting.

He walked slower after she removed her hand from his, and it flexed and relaxed a bit at his side, as though it missed hers. She could have spit. A sigh loosed from his lips. Exasperation built in her chest. Everything about this was stupid.

Pausing in the grand marble foyer, Zech gave her a sidelong look. Jauyne kept walking.

"Where should we look next?" His voice sounded tired— but rimmed with that warm buzz she hated so much— and the rasp of it grating on Jauyne's irritation was the last straw. She whirled.

"I don't know!" She splayed her hands wide, not bothering to keep the exasperation from her face. "You wanted us to come here. You are chasing this apparent prophecy that I've never heard of, despite years— *a lifetime, even!*— of studying. You figure it out."

He was still humming like a magnet in front of her, still buzzing with the kind of energy that she knew would ignite, explode, incinerate, if she were to touch him again. No shit. Jauyne was the Premier of Meirydh, Premier of the chaotic and wild and feral. It was her birthright, and she knew she wore it in her eyes, crackling like silver lightning. But Zech was chaotically genuine, wildly honest, a feral sort of vulnerable, and it was so damn dangerous. It enraged her, that she was capable of feeling any glimpse of magnetism at all, when she was wading through corpses, let alone for a grinning Chedhiyn watchman with kindness in his heart.

She turned on her heel, not entirely sure where she was headed, but knowing, wherever it was, that it wasn't here, wasn't next to him, wasn't where she could feel her already frayed heart coming undone.

"Where are you going?" He snapped behind her, exhaustion the edge to his irritation.

"I'm going where I damn well please." She stalked down the hall, trying not to look at the little corpse girl by the pantry, the little girl with the flies lighting on her, the little girl with the still-open, dead eyes.

A catch on her hand. So warm. That igniting hum. She nearly snapped. Spun. Nearly slammed her whole body into Zech's. "What are you doing?" He asked, his head quirked to the side, a smile tugging on one corner of his lips. His voice was so quiet.

"I told you already." She met his eyes with vicious frustration. "I'm going where I damn well please."

"Oh, come on... That's not even a real answer."

Glaring at him, she tore her hand free from his and flung herself away from him, further up the hall. She hugged her arms to herself, furious and heartbroken and— Why was she even still here? Why had she followed him back to this place? She couldn't remember what he'd said that could have swayed her, couldn't believe how stupid she'd been to follow. She cursed her failure as a Premier, less than a week into her premature reign, and forced a tear away with the heel of her hand. She was twenty-five years old, and she still felt like a child.

The stairs she'd taken in her haphazard fury wound round to a balcony overlooking the city. She hadn't meant to come here. It felt like a cruel joke played by her subconscious, to lead her to the place where she used to enjoy tea and fire cakes with Lissa, looking out over the carved stone and guessing what each person bustling below them was doing, saying, where they might be going.

Jauyne missed how they'd shared everything in hushed whispers, despite how this balcony was deep in her array of personal rooms and they were never disturbed. She missed the kisses, Lissa's wandering hands that drew feather-light trails across her body. She missed the times when Hadlen would join them, how he'd cover her mouth so the people below wouldn't hear her and how Lissa would watch with lust in her eyes.

Most of all she missed how they'd both hold her, how she could let her softness free with them; how Lissa's hair slid silky between her fingers while she braided it, or how Hadlen made empty threats of violence against her father after particularly trying lessons. She knew it was why some part of her leaned gravitationally towards Zech— he tugged at the remaining flecks of softness locked so deep inside herself. Fuck. *Fuck.* Stars, she missed them so badly, her heart was a gaping wound. She was going to fall apart.

She gripped the stone rail— once polished white marble, but now coated with soot— with white knuckles, gasping for air between sobs and the wind. The freezing wind stung her eyes, but she refused to close them to the carnage below her. She needed to remember this. She needed to remember what she was made of— what she was made for. This was her job, to rebuild this city, and this Chedhiyn boy was tearing the heartbreak of her reality to giddy shreds with his fairytales.

She'd half expected him to be running after her, all worried and sarcastic. He didn't. So she sat on the cold stone, let it run shivers up her spine and numb her ass as the sun sagged in the cold blue sky. She splayed her hands on the marble where she'd once sat with her dearest friends, soaking it up.

Who cared if she was cold as the stone? Who cared if she was unmoving and hard as granite? If it got her Province back, so be it: she'd freeze, body and soul. The words felt hollow in her mind, but she clung to it— the lingering shreds of self.

At last, she picked herself up, stiff and sore and pale as ice from the cold, and turned her back on the wreckage below her as she wiped the remaining tears from her cheeks. She dusted her hands off on the riding pants and her shirt, leaving ash-black streaks. Then, she ran a hand through her hair, brushed the last of the dampness from her eyes, and wound back through her sitting area and bath and personal study to her room. Her feet fell flatly on the rich teal and silver carpet.

The door to her room was still open from where she'd barreled through, and she walked in. Zech stood beside her bed, the contents of both of their packs spread across the purple silk. He was smoothing one of her shirts as he tucked it back into the leather bag.

"What are you doing?" Her voice sounded more tired than she'd expected, scratchy from crying.

He started, as though he'd been deep in his own thoughts until that moment. She watched him take in the streaks on her pants, the strained pink of her fingers and nose and eyes, her mussed hair. There was a pause. "I thought I would pack up, since you seemed to be intent on leaving." Another pause. "Are you alright?"

Jauyne swore internally. "I'm fine."

A long look at her face. "You're a mess."

"Excuse you?" The nerve of him!

"You've got dirt all over your face... Were you crying?"

She scowled, strode over to the bed and began jamming the rest of her items inside the pack. "Don't touch my things." Her hands grabbed a small bag, the mouth of it drawn closed with a cord. Energy hummed through her bones. She leveled a glare at him. "Especially not this."

A hard, warm hand intercepted hers as she went to place the Starstone in the pack. The presence of a second person on the Starstone heightened the hum to a buzz that made her feel as though her bones would vibrate out of her body. She gritted her teeth. Zech's expression was a challenge, eyes pointed and lips pressed stubbornly together.

"This was Aeron's. I have as much of a right to it as you. We may not have found anything here, but that doesn't mean there's no explanation, no clue, somewhere in what he carried. That doesn't mean there's not still a chance for me to finish what he came here to do and find the two ancient—"

"As Emissary, like he was?" Jauyne snorted, interrupting him. "Fine job you're doing at that." She didn't let go of the pouch. The buzz was under her skin, rolling like a second pulse over her muscles and behind her eyes. She'd never touched it for this long, never with the intensity of a second person's magic flowing with it. It made her dizzy with... with strength, light-headedness, power, rage, need, sorrow... warmth...

Zech gritted his jaw at her, fury growing in the pupils of his eyes. "I'm sorry I mistook you for a deserter, alright? I'm sorry you decided to shackle me, and I'm sorry you're back here." There was a sarcastic edge to his voice that sent a heated crackle of anger to Jauyne's chest. "I'm doing the best I know how. I have his legacy to think of. I have the whole Starsdamned world to think of, considering you can only see as far in front of you as your own Province. Don't stand here and feign honor, playing at being so high above me, when you're running away to some freezing balcony to cry because you cannot imagine that I would have enough *humanity* in me to understand your grief!"

He was inches from her face, breath heavy and hand still gripping the Starstone. The fury in his eyes wavered, and she realized she was gaping at him. There was a vibrancy clinging to his skin, his eyes, that hadn't been there a moment ago, an almost glowing quality that made his face flushed and eyes bright. It was Starlight, she knew, but so much of it...

Heat radiated from his body towards her, and she remembered how cold she was, how much her hand ached from the chill, but also from the buzzing Starstone it was clenching. It more than ached... it *hurt*. And despite her pride, she released the pouch, wincing.

His eyes followed her trembling hand as she pulled it to her chest, cradling it with the other. A silent swear shot into her mind, and she looked away with what she hoped was one last scathing expression, turning to sit on the edge of the bed. Fuck him for being right— he was an insufferable prick about it. She tried to massage the hand that had held the Starstone and then thought better of it when the action only seemed to inflame the vicious, tingling pain.

The soft creak of leather folding against itself preceded Zech's feet coming into her line of vision, facing her own dusty shoes. He slowly knelt, gently resting his palms on her knees. He was so warm. He bit the inside of his lip, looking at her.

"I'm an ass."

"Yes," she agreed, coolly. It was so unexpected that she almost wanted to laugh, but swallowed it down. "You are. I am, too, though, a little."

The edges of his mouth tweaked slightly. "A little," he echoed, with a hint of a question.

Jauyne pressed her lips together to keep from smiling. He was melting her, and she was letting him, and she was trying not to smile. She tried to rekindle the anger he'd sent crackling through her chest, tried to remember how inadequate his honesty made her feel, tried to summon the blind rage that had caused her to wrestle him to the ground and hold a knife to his throat just a few weeks prior. But now the thought of staring down at him from atop his chest just sent a shiver of enticement through her.

Starsdamnit, don't be perverse.

Honestly, she'd hadn't gone this long without a decent fucking in years. No wonder she was such a disaster. She wasn't about to be above hate sex, either, when she was this desperate, for Stars' sake. She was, however, above giving away another measure of her power to this human inconvenience.

"Jauyne, you've— You've seen the sort of memories I have. You saw what I've seen. Just because I am not driving Starlight into your mind, doesn't mean I can't see what you've seen. It doesn't mean I can't see *you*." She was keenly aware of how his thumb stroked the inside of her knee as he continued. "You are freezing cold. You've been crying. Let me help."

He was being daring. She knew he knew it, but she frostily held his gaze for a moment to be sure. At last, she gave him a curt nod. He gave her a small smile, a sense of victory shooting through his eyes that made her want to rescind that nod and smack him instead. "Wait here." He stood, absentmindedly skimming the top of her thigh with the tips of his fingers, the feeling of which seemed to her to mimic the hum of the

Starstone. She made a rude gesture at his turned back with her unhurt hand— the foul part of her mind was unlocked, though, and she knew *exactly* where else she wanted his fingers, *Starsdamnit*— and scooted herself backwards, further onto the satin-clothed bed.

A moment later, he sauntered back through the door to the bath, a small wet towel in his hand. He gave it to her. It was warm. She raised an eyebrow at him. "What's this for?"

"Wash your face." His eyes dragged along her body from her face to the streaks of ash on her chest and stomach and thighs. "You're filthy." Something in the humored curl of his lip, and the way he lashed that last word towards her, dragged the heat of the cloth into the pit of her stomach. She glared witheringly as she put it to her face.

"And you're a bastard." She muttered it into the warm damp of the cloth.

The warmth felt reviving, seeping into her cheeks and eyelids and tingling pleasantly. She took her time, inhaling deeply behind the towel until the burn of the cold in her lungs subsided. Zech was rummaging for something on the bed beside her. With a final pass with the cloth over her face, she looked down at it and saw the dirt and dust it had washed her face free of. Embarrassment flushed her cheeks at the realization he hadn't been simply teasing her. A clean pair of riding pants and a velvety top with tight sleeves and a loose tie-front was set in her lap, and he extended his hand to take the cooling cloth. She handed it to him, still with her good hand. He frowned.

"Is that from the Starstone?" He nodded at the hand still curled to her chest.

"I was fine until you grabbed it," she quipped.

He shot her a look, but held out a hand to her. "Let me see." At her pause, he gave an exaggerated roll of his honey eyes. "Whether you give in now, or tomorrow when it's really hurting, you know you'll let me heal it. Save us both the time."

"It's just tingly," she protested. Then: "Did you really not feel that?"

Zech dropped the cloth and snatched her hand from her chest, hooking her forearm between his arm and body so she couldn't pull it away. She hissed.

"Zech! Let me be—" she sucked in air as she felt the heat from his body, and he painfully splayed her fingers with his own, ignoring her in favor of focusing on his craft. Silver light flooded the veins of his hand and he held it above hers, hovering back and forth, seeking out the source of the injury. Indra ran the other hand through her hair, helpless to do anything and feeling stupider by the moment.

"I felt you," he said finally, so quiet she almost didn't hear him.

She blinked. "What?"

His eyes were shimmering silver with Starlight as he worked. "In the Starstone. When I touched it, when you decided to order me to drop it—" a sideways glance "—it felt like you. All sharp and blazing and silver and zapping."

Jauyne tried to search his face for hints of a joke, but found none. She recalled the feeling of the stone as his anger had built... the rage and sorrow and warmth rippling from the strange object and under her skin like a heartbeat. She recalled the soft hum rising to unbearable heat. The need that had swam in her gut. "I felt you, too," she murmured.

The Starlight faded as he looked down at her, held her hand in his. Some unknown question rippled in his eyes, stray remnants of Starlight shivering there. "I can't fix your hand this way. But I have an idea."

Jauyne crooked her brow at him.

"I'm sorry I hurt you." He looked down. "I keep doing that."

She wasn't sure what to feel at that, much less say, so she didn't say anything.

More of that unsettling vulnerability...

But he didn't dwell there, instead pushing the clothes and packs aside to sit on the bed. He crossed his legs, and pulled the Starstone out of the pack. "I think we need to use this."

A hoarse little laugh barked out from her lips. "I'm not touching it if you are."

He shot her an irritated glance. "Just listen. I think— I think it hurt you because I was hurting you. When I felt you through this, It was so raw. I could feel what you felt, as though it was some sort of... channel, or..." He gestured vaguely. "Or link or bridge. I think I can use it to let you feel my Starlight. If my Starlight can get right to you in such a direct way, I think it might work." He rubbed the back of his neck.

She wanted to say no, even opened her mouth to form the word, but the tingling pain seared sharp and hot, and Jauyne sighed heavily. "Alright." The light that filled his face caused her to shrink back. This territory was pure jeopardy. "But for Stars' sakes be *careful*. If you ruin my hand, I'll—"

Auburn brows raised mischievously, dancing above a grin. "You'll what?"

A smirk got the better of her. *Fuck.* "I'll gut you."

Zech shrugged, "The threat sounds familiar, and yet, here I am, guts fully intact."

Shaking her head, Jauyne swiveled to face him on the bed, mirroring his crossed legs, close enough their knees almost touched. She watched with a twinge of nerves in her stomach as he lifted the small pouch out of the bag and held it in his hands.

He met her eyes.

"Ready?"

Her silent response was the extension of her hand, shaking a bit, to rest above his on the pouch. The reaction of her body was sudden and intense, and she bit her lip to avoid gasping, internally cursing the outward reaction that had revealed her anxiety. Zech leveled his eyes with hers.

"Take a deep breath," he said softly. "Close your eyes and find me."

As if to demonstrate the safety of it, his eyes closed, his face stilled. She sat watching him for a moment, warily, then closed her own.

Her hand was still on fire, and her body was still crawling with inconvenient lust, but she breathed.

PLEASE

12

I'VE ALWAYS BEEN COLD

JIAUYNE & ZECH, HIGH HOUSE OF MEIRYDH
23 days since the sack of Meirydh

Close your eyes and find me...

She exhaled. A release. A cautious invitation. And there he was.

The space behind her eyelids bloomed with green and gold— swirling, windswept patterns of it that carried the scent of mountain breezes and earthy forest floors. And in the bursting and flowing colors, his eyes. Green-grey irises flecked and suspended in silvery-gold Starlight. Like light dappling through a canopy of trees, like the feeling of brown earth between her fingers, like a playful breeze tugging at the loose laces of her riding pants.

She saw their hands over the Starstone, and his was a kaleidoscope of green and silver swirls. Warmth beamed from his colors as though they were the sun, and some primal, innocent part of her that had not thought existed in a very long time wished she could curl up in the beams of it, like a cat. It nearly took her breath away.

"There you are." His voice murmured beneath her skin, as though it came not from his mouth, but from those shining, warm eyes.

"Hello," she said, because she didn't know what else to say. His soft laugh curled through the color around her. Humor gleamed in his eyes. "What is this place?"

"I don't know." The lightness in his voice didn't seem to mind the mystery. "You have enchanting eyes."

"What do they look like?" The question tumbled through the space before she could stop it, her curiosity entirely provoked.

"They look like... lightning striking the ground. And sheets of ice over swiftly moving water. And flickering candles."

Jauyne bit her lip as a warm hum spread through her body, so different from the jolting buzz of last time. She hadn't thought through what the answer to her question might be, hadn't considered that it might stir up that agitating need in her gut.

She never had that problem. She *knew* better. *Fuck.*

Swallowing thickly, she trained her thoughts back to what was familiar: pain. "What about my hand?"

A pause. A wincing voice. "This is complex. You'll need to have some patience. Relax. Are you ready?"

She nodded.

His thumb shifted, brushing beneath hers, and it was as though her every nerve lived there, in that stupid curve below her stupid knuckle; the sensation echoed into the rest of her body. She let it ripple her open wide, let it expand her until she was alive and churning with feeling.

This was familiar, a sense of looking through eyes that were not her own. This was *Zech's* feeling. She felt his hesitancy at pressing towards her, eagerness to feel into her, shame at the way he'd accidentally harmed her, a gnawing fear that she might pull away, the rippling glow of his healing Starlight, the writhing of unhinged chaos, the spiking of her own pain in his hand, and then... something deeper... warmer... She could feel him reaching for her here in this space, the familiar soothe of the way his Starlight worked, but beyond that there was desirous, hungry, helpless heat.

Images— memories?— dashed across her vision. It felt like what had happened in that shack in the Meirydhan plains, when she'd found her way inside his mind and seen his mother. But this was... *her.* She— he— was barreled over, and Jauyne saw herself perched atop his chest, felt the chill of her knife on his neck as shock and realization barreled into his mind. She saw herself in the shack, starlight sprinkling her tired face, watched through his eyes as they darted over her lashes, the part of her lips, the mess of her hair, and a strange mixture of awe and apprehension and desire brewed between his hips. She saw herself scowl, and felt affection rise in his chest. She saw herself half-conscious in his arms, his feet stumbling over bodies and rubble, felt panic swirl in his gut. She saw the pitiful streaks through the dirt on her face, her red eyes and frigid-pale skin, and a surge of protective concern lodged itself in his throat.

She couldn't breathe, the shock was so unthinkable. A hot tingling rolled down her spine, melting her bones into reverberating, aching desire.

Tenderness and surprise and laughter brushed over her senses, and she could *feel him in her head*, could feel him feeling the comfort and exasperation and lust and repulsion and that humiliating feeling of being exposed that had been surging through her the past few weeks... that was surging through her now. She could feel him feeling her, her memories of him. She gulped in air as though she were drowning.

"I can't—" her voice strangled the rest of her words, and she grasped empty air, losing her grasp on his hand below hers. She felt trapped in her own inability to catch her breath. There were no swirls of green and gold, no green-grey eyes; it was all just turbulence and drowning.

"Jauyne. Jauyne! Open your eyes."

She peeled her eyelids open, gasping. Zech was leaned forward, his face close to hers, brow crinkled. She felt steadiness bracing her and realized his hands were on either side of her face, cradling her jaw, thumbs skimming her cheekbones. One of her hands was hooked into the neckline of his shirt, knuckles white and fabric taut, as though she'd grasped onto him to break a fall. Abruptly, she released him, mortified. Her mind was reeling... the things he'd seen. She tried to look anywhere, fucking voids *anywhere*, except for into his eyes.

"I'm sorry, I— I don't know what to—" Her emotions flailed, helplessly.

"Jauyne, look at me." His voice was a gentle command. She avoided his eyes. "Look at me, right now."

She knew what she'd find when she met his eyes face— unbearable compassion. She wanted to hit him, just to escape it, but her hands were shaking. This was *not* what she had asked for; she wanted him in her cunt, not in her head. Dreading the shame and fear which was inevitably swimming in them, she dragged her eyes to his... and found she'd been wrong.

There was compassion there, in his eyes, certainly, but it sat thinly over the hurt and guilt and hunger that broiled in the grey and green. A stunned mirror erected in her own mind.

"You're alright. You're safe. Stop looking away from me. *Stop* that. How does your hand feel? Think about your hand."

She flexed it, keeping her gaze steady. "It's better," she said huskily. "You saw—."

He interrupted. "So did you."

The memories of his affection and arousal bled through her body, pulsing. She chewed her lip. Nodded. He released her face from his hands, sighed, his hurt poorly hidden now that she was no longer in such a panic. It bit, unexpectedly, at her heart, to see it. But she was shit at comfort.

"Zech," she began. "Are you alright?"

He said nothing for a moment, massaging his jaw. At last, he sighed, and looked at her as though for once, vulnerability cost him something, the way it had always cost her. "I knew who you were the minute you pounced on me beside that tree. I knew you hated me. I never expected anything from you. I didn't— I didn't expect you to feel anything other than that. And to know you do," Jauyne felt a flush fill her cheeks. "but that your loathing is enough to shutter it..." He laughed rather bitterly, and shook his head, ruffling his hair with a hand.

A sick sadness settled in her. Zech dropped her gaze, but she hadn't yet grasped what he was saying. She was rigid as he picked up the Starstone and placed it carefully in the pack. He shrugged, shifted.

Jauyne had had so few choices that were actually hers to make, and the ones she'd had, she'd fucked up so spectacularly that she would never forgive herself. Stumbling across Zechariyh hadn't been her choice, but *seeing* him could be. *Touching* him could be. *Trusting* him could be. As he leaned towards the edge of the bed to leave, she grasped his arm.

He looked sideways at her, wearily, questioning. She took him in for just a moment— The broadness of his shoulders, the auburn hair curling on his forehead, the scent of his sweat and the soft curve of his mouth.

Her blood quickened, marginally less from lust than from fear.

"It wasn't you." Her voice was barely higher than a squeak. She swallowed, tried again. "The problem— it wasn't you. I am... intense. Unpredictable. Cold..." A gulp. The baring quality of her words clogged her throat. "I like those things about myself. I'll never apologize for them, but... You are— Zech, you are none of those things. Light. Grounded. Fucking *insane*. Warm..." That last word... She couldn't keep the want out of her voice as his heat-filled memories rolled over her. She watched Zech's eyes deepen with a shadow of that same hunger, as if he heard himself echo from her.

But she was floundering now, not sure what else to say, uncharacteristic embarrassment creeping up into her cheeks, heat melting into her hips, somehow incapable of looking away from this damn Chedhiyn border watchman, so far from his home. He shifted his hand so hers slid into it, turned to face her.

"What did you say?" he whispered, leaning in front of her.

She shivered, murmured. "You're so warm." Starsdamn. His hands were on her knees again. "I've always been cold." She leaned toward him as though he was a center of gravity equal to her own.

"I love when the frigid bitch comes out." His laugh was barely a huff of air. "But Jauyne... You don't need to be cold all of the time." His voice was nearly guttural, and it grazed against the last shreds of her speculative stubbornness. She knew what he'd seen in her, knew he was speaking to both her scarred face and her scarred soul. He lifted his left hand from her knee, brushed his thumb over her chin. Heat spiraled down the front of her throat. "Are you cold now?"

She nodded silently, terror and something giddy thrilling through her at the sly sordidness of his words.

Sweeping away a strand of her tangled black hair, Zech leaned yet closer to her, bringing his lips to her ear, just close enough for her to feel his breath. "Where are you cold?"

Goosebumps raised across her skin. She knew what she was doing. What was she doing? She hated him. Had she ever hated him? Stars above, she wanted him to tear her to pieces until she came.

"Here." She pointed to her forehead, and he placed a slow kiss there, his hand on her knee beginning to sweep softly across her riding pants. "Here," she breathed, running a finger over her cheek, and his lips followed. "Here... here... here..." her nose, her other cheek, her chin.

"Here."

He watched her finger dance across her lips, and looked straight into her eyes— waiting, searching, for what she wasn't sure. He hesitated, and Jauyne closed the space between her mouth and his. His lips responded immediately, a rough press on hers that felt like kindling.

The fingers on her leg dug in, sending sparks skittering up her thigh, and her breath hiccuped. She nudged her knees wider. Zech hummed into her mouth when he felt it, taking his other hand to run up the side of her arm, over her shoulder, until it slid behind her neck with a claiming grip.

Ravenousness rocketed down her spine.

"Where are you cold," he repeated, whispering against her mouth.

Jauyne felt a groan roll up from her chest. "Everywhere."

He shuddered against her.

Violent, heavy kisses swam behind her ear, at the sharp point of her jaw, at the hinge of her neck. Then, a soft bite on her clavicle. She shouldn't be doing this, shouldn't be sidetracked by a haunted Chedhiyn boy with a penchant for believing in fairytales, shouldn't be— His hand slid over her gaping ribs, under her shirt, his mouth buried in the soft hollow of her collarbones.

"Getting warmer?" It was a rumble against her sternum, and she knew she could end this now.

I could walk away, and he'd pull me to my feet. Instead she tugged on a fistful of auburn hair, gleaming gold and flame-red in the sunset beams that striated the room.

"Don't stop." Her startled mind wanted to rail against it, ignore how this was something more nuanced than the hot sear of lust, pack her bags... He pressed into her, scooping his arms around her lower back to tug her forwards into his lap. She straddled him, knees tucked, his mouth inching lower towards the swell of her breast. She arched towards him, her criticism powerless against instinct, drowning in heat as his body tingled against hers like the brilliant buzz of Starlight.

A final attempt to grasp her practicality surfaced, and she flattened her hand on his chest, lifting her chin. "This changes nothing." She meant for it to sound menacing, commanding, like the Premier she was; but as his thumb grazed the skin beneath her breast, it came out like a gasp. And she hated, hated, *hated* it.

His laugh rumbled soft against her neck, where his mouth had since angled. "Don't worry. I haven't forgotten your warning— if I run, you'll gut me." He pulled back abruptly, leaving cold air to prickle the skin where his lips had been. Eyes glittering with stubbornness or lust or challenge or some combination of all three, he leveled his face to hers, so close his breath heated her lips. "I have no intention of running from your bed, *Premier.*"

She couldn't stop the visible shiver that ran the length of her body, vibrating under his hands, but she only said, "See that you don't."

He fisted her hair, knots tangling in his fingers, and yanked her mouth to his. The breath was driven from her lungs, and he bit her lower lip, dragging it away from her teeth.

Not to be outdone, she rolled her hips against his lap, pressed herself close against his body before pulling away, forcing space. Her shirt was ripped over her head, and she tossed it aside, reveling in the heated surprise on his face and the twitch of him under her.

The way his eyes devoured the small peaks of her breasts made liquid pool between her legs. He twitched again and slid his eyes to hers, not breaking their gaze as he braced her ribs with his hands and, with excruciating slowness, brushed the calloused pads of his thumbs over her nipples.

She refused to be the one to look away first, and it was positively *stupid* how this made her whimper. He was *barely fucking touching her*. Worse, he splayed a hand across her upper back, the other behind her neck, and tilted her back to devour her. When he experimentally pulled with his teeth, she cried out.

She closed her eyes and gave herself over to it, then— the primal need surging under the surface of her skin. She could see it, feel it. It glittered under her pores, escaping in tiny cracks of light, like Starlight static, everywhere he touched. Green and gold swam in her vision. He kissed every inch of her bare skin, pleadingly, worshipfully.

Lunging for his mouth again, she fumbled with the edge of his sweater and yanked it up, running her hands over the dips and bulges of the muscles that ran taut under his skin. His hair was wild and messy when the sweater tugged over his head, and she filled her hands with those auburn curls as he pressed his skin to hers. He was stiff under her, and she moved her hips with an expert tilt as his hands slid into the back of her trousers, gripping her ass for rougher traction.

Their bodies echoed one another. She bit at the meat of his neck. He slid his hand around the front of hers. A brusque stroke over the confined length of him. A harsh tweak to her breast. His skin was crackling with silver, and she bowled him over backwards, baring her teeth in a sinful grin when his eyes went wide.

She was alive in a far-off, brilliant way, and she was on the prowl. Hands planted on his chest, she dragged herself across his cock. The tease of their closeness was agony. Firm hands encircled her wrists; she realized she was shaking.

"Jauyne." His grip was merciless and reverential. His eyes were wicked and tender. She was taken aback.

"Yes?" Her breath heaved in time with his chest.

A tug on her wrists had her flattened to his body.

"Take off your fucking pants."

She obeyed without question, which caused her to briefly wonder if she had gone utterly, bat-shit mad.

He watched her strip them off, propped on his elbows, restraining the constant groan of need that kept gnawing at the back of his throat. That dark patch of hair between her legs was so fucking distracting. He wanted his face buried in it. Instead, she splayed a hand on his stomach to still him, and with exaggerated slowness untied his trousers. He bit his lip and watched her work.

When he stretched free of the fabric, she did a little appreciative hum. A quick glance at him, and she bent her head forward, licked him from base to tip.

"Oh, *fuck.*"

She laughed, pumped him once with her hand, took him in her warm, wet mouth. Molten rapture flooded his body. He'd never been touched like this, not like *this.*

Back in Chedhiy, one of the supply delivery women had got him off outside the guardhouse one night, saliva coating her hand and her movements an excited, scandaled rush. She'd wanted to say she hand-fucked the crazy boy who saw ghosts. Every once in a while the boy who made the rounds to check in on the state of the border would get on his knees in front of Zech's bunk and do outrageous things with his tongue and fingers until Zech was biting down on his own fist to keep quiet.

But none of them wanted to be close like this. None of them *wanted* him. None of them wanted him to *want them*. Not like this. Not like her.

He grabbed her wrist. "Keep that up, and this is gonna be over real quick."

They were both breathless. He drew her up against him. Up close, her eyelashes were dotted with sweat. There was so *much hunger* in him.

"Let me touch you."

Her hands hooked around the back of his neck. She nodded. He slid a hand down, slow, between them— over the silky damp of her skin, into the curled, dark hair. Her slit was dripping; he stroked a finger the length of it. He watched her draw her lip between her teeth. Catching her earlobe in his lips, he sucked softly as his finger found her cunt and eased inside. She moaned, loud and animalistic. Her wetness dripped into his palm, and he pressed it against the base of that mound of hair. He fucked her with his fingers, adding another, grinding the heel of his hand against the most sensitive part of her.

This was new to him, and he ate up every sound she made— these little whimpers and cries and groans that he was drawing out from her with three fingers and his palm.

She was getting louder, and she propped herself up on his chest, riding his fingers, her soft little tits bouncing hard with every thrust.

"*Fuck, Zech!*"

His name in her mouth. He was undone. She could slit his throat; he'd still worship her. Her breath ran ragged; she twisted her nipple. With a wail, the walls of her tightened, and her body seized and shook.

Closer, I want you closer...

Yearning pulled at him, sat him up, pressed her against him. Without a thought, he pulled his fingers from inside her and put them in his mouth. She watched him, mouth slightly agape, waiting for him to react. The taste of her was tangy and warm and sweet. Pulling his fingers free, he kissed her, let her taste herself.

"*Delicious.*" He said it into her mouth, her tongue on his. Had he always been so starved? She tasted so damn good, he wasn't sure he could ever stop tasting her, wasn't sure if he could ever get enough of her against him.

"Fuck me," she whispered back.

He tipped her backwards, took in the sight of her, as she gazed at him with a smirk, naked, except for the golden lightning bangle around her upper right arm and the short leather boots she'd stripped her trousers over. She lay breathless and pale-skinned there under him on the silken purple blankets, the white fur beneath her scarcely lighter than her skin. She was sharp and concave, all of her: her long nose, her jutting hip bones, her skinny little fingers and pointed pink nipples. Sharp and cold, breathing heavily, with skin as white as ice and hair black as the volcanic soil upon which her city was built.

There was something electric about the way their skin met. Bits of golden static, like the wild lightning of Meirydh, cracked and sparked between them. Everywhere he touched came alive with it, this energy all their own. It was as though he was creating Starlight out of every pore in her skin, out of every raised, fine hair and every trembling muscle; they all hummed with the thrill of it.

He wanted to live in every detail of this moment—the gape of her lips, her fingers electric on the small of his back, her little leather boots whispering against his shins as they moved.He returned slowly from traversing her body to nuzzle her jawline with his nose, to feel her shallow breathing on his cheek, to hear her heartbeat thundering in his ears.

JAUYNE LEANED INTO HIS gentle nudges. The bright sparks of energy snapped under the light touch of her fingers as she trailed them down the length of his bare spine, and she watched her caress raise bumps on his skin in contented pleasure.

His eyes were full of Starlight when Jauyne looked into them, and for a moment, it stole her breath away.

"I mean it," he breathed. "I'm not going to run."

His words rippled with Starlight, a heavy, truthful weight that forced her to recognize the honesty of them. Goosebumps raised over her whole body.

"I know," she said. A smile danced on her lips. And then, "I'm probably not going to gut you."

She felt him stiffen against her hip, even as he laughed into her neck, his lashes brushing her cheek as his eyes crinkled closed. Lifting his head, he met her gaze and trailed a hand through the midnight of her hair. The tiny sparks of energy twinkled across the strands as his fingers ran through them.

Mere weeks ago, she'd sat atop his chest with a dagger at his trembling throat, fully prepared to kill this threat to her cause— this dirty Chedhiyn border watchman who had wandered far past Province borders— with no hint of contrition. Now he hovered over her, his skin making hers come alive, his hands and his mouth doing Stars knew what to every inch of her shivering body as she laid in the wreckage of her home.

Life was strange.

His eyes watched the way the golden static shimmered through her hair, the way it leapt from his skin as she took a slender finger and traced a faded scar down his bicep. The look across his face was wonder and bewilderment.

"What is this?" She whispered.

"I think... it's the Starstone. The artifacts—"

Realization sprinted through Jauyne's body, dragging behind it a surge of fractious craving that had her catching his open mouth with hers before he could finish, stealing his words with deep, heavy kisses. She was frantic with desire now, and overcome by his profoundly tender attentiveness.

Closer, closer, closer... Stars, if she could have crawled inside his very skin, she would have. She could tell it drove him mad, the way she clung to him, responding to every sensation, her noises panting in his ear.

She gasped as he shifted over her, and her arms curled around him, shooting off golden fireworks where their skin met. There was a heat in her stomach that was blossoming to fill her entire body, and the memories that had threatened to so irreversibly stitch shame and anger into her mind just minutes ago were suddenly scorched into beauty and delight by this Starsdamned heat that was swallowing, *just swallowing-*, her whole.

"Zech, I swear..."

He smirked roguishly as he slid into her. She'd never known sex like this. This was raw passion, and exquisite worship, and all his mischief and curiosity dancing over and inside her. He thrust into her again, and her body responded in shiver up her spine, arching her body towards him. Her eyes rolled back as he took a nipple in his mouth, and golden electricity sparked from where his mouth touched her.

His body moved in rhythm with hers, one hand curled in her hair and the other stroking between her legs. The electricity on their skin was like a lightning storm, pricking the hair on the back of her neck and filling her lungs with hot, tingling air.

The room felt like sweltering summer, the swirling magic beamed through with the magenta and gold of the setting sun. She could smell the sweat on his skin, taste it when she kissed his shoulder. His skin rippled with a glimmering molten gold, and where their bodies met, the crackling sparks became a river of gold and silver, a shimmering film of magic.

The energy crackled in between and around them, more vibrant and brighter with each of her husky, belabored breaths. It shone in the room around them, in the dwindling light of dusk coming in slanted orange rays through the window. She groaned, and his thumb responded, stroking slow circles around the bundle of nerves between her thighs.

His other hand held her face, and his kisses found her mouth— deep and savoring— as the heat exploded in her and she came. He swallowed all her moans as though he was starving and they could fill him, his fingers stroking her through the height of it, her hands tangled in fistfuls of his hair.

He kissed her roughly as all the Starlight in him surged, and she felt him, rigid and gasping, in her arms. Jauyne felt it, too; a thousand threads of light to a thousand stars in the universe, all shooting out from her body. It was sheer pleasure, a rolling wave of blinding fever, crashing over her again and again, and she wished it would never end.

RETHINK

13
ENOCH DERNACH OF THE PALLYDH PROVINCE

INDRA, HIGH HOUSE OF BRIGON
24 days since the sack of Meirydh

She was waiting for Osiys when he arrived in the dining hall. Berg and Baird were seated next to her on soft furs, with the massive fireplace to their backs, engaged in an playful argument.

Baird's elbow kept jabbing her as he gestured wildly, and Elryh, who sat across from them in a chair, inconspicuously rolled her eyes behind her third mug of tea. Indra scooted a few more inches away from the wildly gesturing twins, and patted the fur beside her, beckoning Osiys to sit.

He padded over the wide-planked wooden floorboards in just his stocking feet, which felt strangely intimate, and sat beside her.

Indra could feel him emanating a stiffness and discomfort she hadn't seen before in his home Province. The presence of his childhood friends always seemed to have a near immediate soothing effect on him, but today he just stared downward, twisting and tugging at the fur that fluffed up between his folded legs.

He must have loved her so deeply...

Indra wanted to reach out, to put a hand on his shoulder or wrap him up in an embrace, but she refrained. People had already begun to make suggestive comments on the nature of their relationship, despite the difference in their age.

Teeth gritting, she recalled one elderly woman in particular who had pulled her aside in town to warn her about being so intimately involved with a man who had held a secret identity for so long. "You'll never know who's really in your bed, child," she'd said, and Indra had just blinked and gaped before sputtering out "Oh Stars, he's never in my bed at all." The woman had just giggled as Indra's face turned a dark shade of pink.

It was all such nonsense. Osiys had just... been there. For her. For such a long time. He was foundational in so many of her childhood memories. She had grown up with him there, his shadow protecting her as she quietly metamorphosed into her power. He was a solid thing, a constant presence in the process of her personal evolution, and she couldn't imagine her life without him in it.

And yet... thinking of him as a lover... it made her blush, certainly, but only out of sheer mortification. Others would never understand the depth of the love and joy she felt when she looked at Osiys, or her complete lack of desire for that love to manifest as anything other than what it was—an unspeakable bond between two intertwined survivors that had nothing to do with carnal attraction.

Overcoming the fear of how others might gossip, she reached out and rested her hand on his scabbed one. "You are not alone," she whispered as he jumped from her sudden touch, and his eyes met hers. He nodded. Shrugged.

Baird finally gave up his argument and turned his attention instead to Osiys, taking in the sight of the bruises and scabs that littered his skin. "Oh Stars, what happened to you?"

The others briskly turned their heads to see what Baird was talking about. Elryh raised her eyebrows, cupping her steaming mug in both hands. "Indeed, Osiys. Look at yourself—you're all scraped up! Who have you been tousling with?"

Indra could see the muscles working in his jaw and feel his hand tense under hers as Berg joined the curiosity, sarcastically querying if he could get a few punches in.

Osiys slowly raised his head to face them, brushing Indra's hand away. Tension ripped through the jovial mood of the room, rage rippling from Osiys in ways that Indra could almost physically feel. There was a score to be settled here, somehow, and she hadn't realized it until the room was full of this simmering rift.

He spoke, finally, after meeting each set of curious eyes. "I have a question for you, before you get any answer... Why didn't you tell me about Ellessid?"

Baird's eyes went wide, and he pressed his hands to the top of his head. "Oh shit, Osiys."

The horror in Baird's voice hit Indra like a cold, sick feeling in her stomach. *Stars... They knew?* She shuddered, suddenly wishing to be anywhere but in that room. Inching towards the fire behind her, she tried to remove herself from between Osiys and the friends he was questioning.

"Why didn't you tell me?" It was a hiss behind gritted teeth, and Indra could see the tears pricking in the corner of his eyes. His hands were bawled into fists, tucked against his stomach as he leaned forward.

"I..." Baird swallowed hard, his eyes, too, filling with tears. "I was hoping you wouldn't go looking so soon. I was going to tell you...But fuck, Osiys, when is the right time to tell a friend their lover is long dead?"

His voice was cracking now, as he stood and then came to kneel in front of Osiys. Tears were splashing down onto his hands. There was a loving sort of desperation in his mannerisms, a need to have Osiys understand that he hadn't been betrayed. It was so gentle and so markedly different from his usual sarcasm and wittiness, and Indra's heart ached to witness it.

Indra felt distinctly out of place in this emotional display of their personal history, yet deeply connected to Osiys. They knew the headstrong boy who had left out of duty when his passion told him to stay; she knew the man who had endured for years and remained kind and gentle. It was so odd, each of them understanding and appealing to these different facets of who he was, and Indra felt it keenly. She also felt the intensity of the tension in Osiys— the rage and the grief and the blame that rose up as a low growl in his throat.

"You could've..." His attempt at a steady voice was failing him, and he shook his head, shoving the heels of his hands into the tears that had budded in his eyes. His breath was heavy, and Indra could see how hard he was working to maintain control of himself, how he was trying to slow his breathing despite the anguish.

"Osiys, I am so sorry." Baird nearly lunged at him, wrapping his arms around his friend, letting him fight against the stubborn sobs while tucked away in an embrace.

Indra hugged herself a bit, the comfort they wrapped Osiys in seeming to find its way to her, too. She nearly jumped when a hand rested on her own. It was Elryh, who had come to sit on the furs alongside her, silently wiping tears from her own eyes with the edge of her sleeve. Indra clasped her hand, and they silently squeezed together with this solidarity of grief in which they found themselves. Indra was glad for it. Loneliness could be crushing sometimes, especially when she felt selfish for acknowledging it. Having a hand to hold was wildly comforting.

Osiys lifted his head, softly croaking out "I have a daughter."

His three friends nodded silently.

"We know," whispered Elryh. "She's just... She's both of you. So beautifully."

Berg nodded. "That hair... just like Ellessid's."

The great doors at the end of the room creaked open, and Herran entered through them, his hulking figure an instant point of focus in the room. Osiys pulled back from Baird's embrace with a start, straightening his shoulders and squaring his jaw. His eyes were still puffy and glassy from tears. Baird dusted off the front of his shirt and stood so he could sit at the table instead of on the furs.

None of that really mattered... they couldn't have fooled a puppy with that mad scramble anyhow. The Premier instantly raised his brows. "What's happened here?"

Elryh looked him straight in the eyes and spoke softly, but also with directness: "Ellessid."

The sigh that Herran released could have rattled foundations. It was full of heaviness and sorrow. "Oh, my young friend..."

He clapped a hand over Osiys's shoulder, patting him heavily before crossing his arms. Osiys kept his face forward, but Herran moved to look him directly in the eye. "You must grieve her, Osiys. That is only right. Tonight you will go to the Spire of the Dead and give offerings and honor her memory. But here, right now, you must be strong, focused, present. We need your expertise. We need you."

Osiys nodded. "I am here."

"Good." Herran's brow creased. "Because unexpected guests have arrived, and I believe that the information they bring is crucial to the survival of the Old Order, and the people within it."

Indra cautiously straightened her back with interest, still half-absorbed in giving attention to Osiys's pain. Part of her pricked with fear at the panicked thought that perhaps someone was coming in disguise to capture her for her father. But mostly, she felt curiosity and excitement at the prospect of new information that could further their cause. Her mind reeled at who these strangers might be. It was a limited existence that she'd had in Canestry. Sheltered beyond belief, with the exception of the nighttime escapades she'd rather forget, her knowledge of the other Provinces was imaginary at best, and the idea of meeting these people in the flesh felt more like fiction than fact.

Would it be a forest-dwelling Chedhiyn messenger? She'd always wanted to meet them. She couldn't imagine living in houses perched in trees and being comfortable in the constant damp of the forest. And she thought Jopaar was most likely too far away to send more than a letter, but how she wished she could see one of their mystical and mysterious priestesses. Her heart thudded faster.

At the same time, she held Osiys' squirming grief in her chest, and the two feelings together in her body were a confusing mix. She grasped at the juggling of it as they all moved to sit around the table, and the kitchen workers brought out hot drinks and freshly baked brown rolls with butter and a variety of jams.

The twins were asking questions of Herran, and Elryh was asking one of the kitchen workers if they perhaps had any Pallydhan spiced tea in their pantries. Indra watched Osiys beside her, as he made a conscious effort to center himself. She spread a roll with butter and berry jam. Placing it on one of the small plates, she slid it slowly to him and tapped his arm gently to let him know it was there. He met her eyes for the first time since he'd walked in the room, and there was ashamed thankfulness there.

"Indra?"

"Yes?"

"Would you come with me tonight?"

She blinked. "With you? Where?"

"I'm going to the Spire of the Dead, like Herran told me."

Fortunately, he read her blank expression and expanded: "It's where we go to honor our dead. There's a tall spire carved out of the crown of the mountain, and we light incense and carve our tributes and scatter ashes. Well... I don't have any ashes to scatter. But I'll still honor her with the rest."

Indra knew he was genuine, but still felt the pang that told her perhaps she didn't belong in this delicate conversation, in this part of his life that was all foreign ritual and agonizing familiarity.

"Osiys, I didn't know her like they did. It wouldn't be right..."

"No, you didn't know her. But you know me just as well as any of them. And you know things they don't. The person I was in Canestry. I'm not," he fumbled for words. "I'm not the same man who loved Ellessid. I mean, I still love her of *course*, but Stars I'm such a different man than I was."

Indra watched the way the pain crinkled in the soft lines at the corners of his eyes. She smiled softly. "Alright. If you want me there, I'll go."

He nodded his thanks to her and tucked into the roll she'd spread for him. Buttering another for herself, Indra watched as Herran took his place at the head of the table and one of the doormen skittered over to speak to him. Herran nodded to the boy, who looked younger than Indra herself, sending him back across the room.

"It appears our first guest is ready to speak with us, friends." The Premier's low voice hushed the remainder of conversation, and all their heads turned as one to the great carved wooden doors at the end of the room.

The doorman stepped forward and called out loudly, "High Circle, I introduce Enoch Dernach of the Pallydh Province."

She heard Osiys nearly choke on his food beside her, and her own breath caught in her lungs as she waited. Heavily, slowly, the huge doors creaked open, and in the long shaft of light that stretched into the room, stood a man both Indra and Osiys had seen many dozen times before.

He wasn't a tall man—Osyis stood head and shoulders over him—but he had always carried himself with the confidence of an entire army. Thick black curls hung round his face to graze the top of his shoulders, and his mustache and closely trimmed beard were that same jetty hue on his brown face. His dark eyes, usually dancing and proud, were cast down to his leather moccasin-clad feet. Indra had never seen him in clothing from his native Province. That was not allowed in Canestryn-ruled territories, so the soft creases of his cropped white linen pants, and the shirt embroidered in Pallydhan style with oranges and reds, knocked her off guard.

Her mind felt thick and heavy and buzzing.

Stars, I was right... They've come for me. Indra gripped the edge of the table till her knuckles turned white and she couldn't feel her fingers any longer. She felt Osiys place his hand lightly at her back, heard his breath quicken as he looked around the room for something with which to defend them.

Enoch was moving towards them slowly, almost nervously. And when his eyes lighted on Indra, astonishment and wariness jolted through them, bringing a pause to his step and causing the thick gold bangles on his left arm to jangle harshly. Their gazes locked, both Indra and Enoch frozen tense with fear, though she didn't wish to admit that was what she saw in his face. Osiys, too, seemed to have frozen behind her, as the three of them were caught together in shared alarm.

"No need for nerves," Herran belted out behind her, "You are among friends here, dear guest."

Enoch's eyes finally tore themselves from Indra's gaze to face the Premier. He bowed briefly in a squatting genuflection with the fingers of his right hand brushing the space between his brows. "My apologies, Premier Herran. But I..." he glanced back to Indra and Osiys. "I do not understand the presence of these two."

Herran raised an eyebrow.

"Us?" Indra's disbelief found her voice. "Our presence?"

The buzzing in her head was growing into a headache that made the inside of her eye sockets hurt and her vision strangely layered and lagging. Her skin felt thin and tight-stretched. Was she going to be sick?

"What is the meaning of this?" Herran turned to Osiys, who didn't take his eyes off Enoch as he answered.

"We are all rather familiar with one another, Herran. This fellow made dozens of journeys between Pallydh and Canestry to meet with their Premier, during my time there."

Herran dragged a hand over his face and tiredly gestured for Enoch to take a seat. "Ah, yes. I ought to have predicted this. Enoch, please share what you have to say with my High Circle."

Shakily, Enoch took his seat, nodding. "Of course, Premier." He clasped his hands together in front of him, squeezing till the fingertips went white. "All those years ago, when Pallydh was taken... I volunteered to do the unthinkable. I committed to make everyone—Canestryn and Pallydhan—believe I had turned on my own people. I was joined and supported by a very small circle, including my brother in nearby Nareilë. Our hope was that we would be able to gain intelligence that could turn the tide of the war, and also that we might warn our own people of potential new dangers before they arose. In the attack on Nareilë, my brother was murdered, and his wife and young children went missing. My circle felt…" He shrugged away tears, "that I had been compromised by my grief. They felt I was putting too much effort into finding his family; they were worried I would be discovered. I had one man, Finnan, who was as concerned about them as I, and he is currently risking his life to bring them to safety… All except my brother's wife. She was killed. But her children are still alive. My circle was correct, however. A letter we sent was intercepted, and Canestryn forces now know that my brother's wife is being brought by escort to my home in the High City at Pallydh. My plan was to escape from there with the fallen Starstone, taking my brother's family with me, but when my Circle discovered that I was going to be assassinated by Canestryn NightWalkers—" He shot a look of dread at Osiys. "I had to leave immediately. I had no choice. Finnan has not been made aware of this danger, and he will lead my family into the teeth of it, unawares, unless he can be intercepted on the road. I have come for help… And I have brought the Starstone."

A bright burn of pain lanced through Indra's spine, but her wince was overshadowed by Elryh coughing on her tea.

"You have it! Here!" She sputtered.

Indra could not make sense of the scene around her. Attempting to categorize this man as anything other than the enemy was proving more than difficult, although the familiar wash of empathy was rising in her, despite herself and the gritty pain that had taken up residence in her head.

She inhaled deeply, relinquished her grip on the edge of the old table, and closed her eyes for a moment. She needed strength. Reaching out to the Stars with the tendrils of light in her mind, she exhaled the deep breath she'd been holding. The energy flooded her, and she allowed it in, directing it at the gaping ache in her head, at the space in her stomach that felt as though it might collapse in on itself. It only took her a single breath, and yet she reopened her eyes to see Enoch looking directly at her with calculating curiosity.

Elryh was still sputtering in shock about the Starstone, and Baird was massaging his temple in an attempt to process it all, when Enoch spoke to Indra.

"How did you come to find yourself here?" His voice was quiet.

Osiys shrugged beside her. "As it turns out, you were not the only one pretending to be someone you weren't."

Enoch tilted his head at Osiys. "I know," he said. "I could feel in you what I could not bear to feel in myself. I was glad for it, all those times I came to the Canestryn High City."

"You knew?"

Berg laughed a little "Guess you weren't as good of a pretender as you thought, pal!"

Osiys shot Berg an annoyed look and a jutting middle finger, which only caused Baird to snort some of his coffee and elicit a smirk from Berg. Herran just rolled his eyes.

Enoch looked at Indra once again. "Believe me, while I am curious and delighted that Osiys fellow is with us here, I am even more interested in how you found yourself in Brigon, Princess Indra."

As all eyes found themselves on her, Indra bit her lip. It was a strange thing, to hear herself referred to so genuinely as 'princess' after all that had happened over the past few weeks. It was evident that her new companions also had surprising feelings about it. There was an air of awe in the room that hadn't been present just a moment before. She had nearly forgotten what it was like to feel oneself separated by class and relegated to role, at just a word. A shaky breath sucked in more Starlight as she replied.

"I was born in Canestry, but it was never my home." The image of children thrashing under her father's torture came unbidden to her mind. "That place is no one's home anymore.

A solemn, lopsided smile stretched the left side of Enoch's face as he nodded. "You are as much a refugee as I."

Indra looked around the table at the five pairs of kind Brigonan eyes that met hers without irony or condescension. "I was. But I think I have a home now."

Elryh beamed at her with tear-rimmed eyes, and Osiys squeezed her hand.

"Enoch," Herran once again drew their attention. "Thank you for coming to us. We will certainly discuss how we may help you retrieve your family and Finnan. But for now, where is the Starstone?"

Herran's final word echoed, muddy and underwater, as Enoch bent to the side of his chair where he had set a leather pouch. He grasped it in both hands and lifted to the table. He looked to Herran, and after a nod from him, pulled open the mouth of the sack.

A wave of intensely cold air slammed into Indra, and she gasped softly, panting a bit as all the pain surged back into her head and chest. It felt like her lungs were vibrating, and it stole her breath. There was a ringing in her ears.

He pulled out a large, awkward thing from the sack, wrapped further in some soft cloth and red cord. Untying the cord, the cloth fell away to reveal an odd contraption—a twisted mass of metal, protruding from a vibrant golden-orange crystal.

The ringing in Indra's ears became a scream so loud that she cried out, scrambling to cover her head. Her vision blurred and brightened. She watched Elryh's mouth move, her face warped with worry, but no words reached her ears. She couldn't even hear her own voice, though she was desperately trying to cry for help.

There were voices now, in the high pitched scream, voices yelling and commanding and barking orders; her father's voice was there, curdled with rancor, and it spoke to her. As long as you live, may your footsteps leave death in their wake; may your tongue be saturated with blood as your birthright.

Indra found herself amongst two great commotions as pins and needles began to shoot through her limbs, and she felt tears leaking from her eyes. Osiys reached out to her arm, but his touch was like fire and she recoiled, flailing.

Stars, what's happening? What is that thing?

Desperate to put as much distance as she could between herself and this Starstone, she pushed the table away from her and clamored out of her seat. However, the shooting pains that ripped through her limbs had taken her ability to walk, and she collapsed onto the floor, convulsions shuddering through her. She bit her tongue, and blood filled her mouth, running out from between her lips. May your tongue be saturated with blood as your birthright.

As she stared up at the high stone ceiling, and the faces that soon crowded over her, it all began to blur to white, and Indra lost her vision.

The voices dulled into a single chant that erased the pain. She had no feeling anywhere. She was no body.

The chant was so foreign, and so familiar, and she leaned into it. Starlight became her limbs, became her body, and she was a being of nothing and everything. She could feel herself pulsing with the light and the chant, with the rawness of this universal force that she had always found comfort and kinship in.

She did not so much hear the words as she felt them, the way she'd felt her skin and muscle and bone mere moments, mere eternities, ago. *Fear and trembling, Galaxy-maker, fear and trembling, home at last...*

Indra reached out to the chanting voice with determination.

You have answers. It wasn't quite a question, but a need for validation.

Yes. I do have answers. The chanting halted when the reply came, and Indra felt the shock ripple through her. *You are not the Stars... Who are you?*

Indra hadn't fully expected the voice to reply, and she paused there, blind and nonexistent and shaking on the floor, unsure of what to say.

I am the Canestryn princess.

More silence.

You found a Star gift... The voice sounded breathy with surprise and awe, and perhaps wariness.

The Starstone? When it was unveiled I fell to the ground. It's hurt me. I've lost my eyesight. And— and I heard you chanting.

Chanting? Indra, I will come find you. We will unravel this. I am coming to you, do you hear me? I'm on my way, as we speak.

How do you know my name?

The high pitched ringing cut into to Indra's ears after a sharp clap as the voice dissolved. It was so strong and painful, that for a moment she forgot her confusion as she struggled just to breathe; and even as she finally sucked in a breath, she felt her consciousness be torn from her.

THIS

14
IT COULD HAVE BEEN PLANTED

Rain and snow together slanted down from the grey sky. The slim and barren tree, against which's trunk Adras leaned, dangled a wild tangle of ice—slicked branches above them.

Already, the frozen tundra of their homeland was giving way to southern climates, and they hadn't yet crossed the border into Meirydh. Adras narrowed their eyes at the cutting drops of rain diving between the snowflakes.

One week; that was how long it had been since they had exited the doors of the High City and begun their journey southward. Adras loathed the fact that they were reluctant. This commission was a deep honor, one which they had earned with dedication and accepted with pride. In two days they would reach the border between the Provinces of Jopaar and Meirydh. From there, it was another three days' worth of travel to the High City, where Adras would begin their search for the disappeared Zech and Jauyne.

Perhaps it was foolish, to go looking for an unseated heir in the ruins of the city she had been born to govern, but the Meirydhi were an unpredictable people. The very words of their banners read "Untamed and Unburnt", the declaration of a people nearly as wild as the Jopaari themselves.

Hunger stabbed at the inside of their belly, and a knowing exhaustion forced them to admit that it was time to stop pressing their body for the day. They had hoped to continue after a short rest, but knew it was better to conserve their strength for the long days ahead.

They rested their head back against the wet bark of the tree, blinking their eyes closed against the snowflakes that caught on their lashes.

But how long...?

This was no short trip, and there was no defined end to it; that truth gnawed at Adras more intensely than their hunger.

As the remainder of the falling snow melted into a cold drizzle, they knew how difficult, even impossible, this task would be. Usually, it would be lonely, to be gone this long in foreign territories where they would be relegated to an elevated, if misunderstood, guest. But this time, due to the length of the journey and the new threats of insidious violence, the High Priestess had sent Lumen with them.

He'd fallen asleep— how he could fall asleep anywhere, Adras was sure they didn't know— with his back to the trunk of the tree, and his head lolling onto theirs. They could just hear the sound of his slumber-heavy breaths rising and falling in the pattering raindrops. Adras was unused to traveling with anyone else, but they'd found it was comforting; he knew them well enough to keep his nuisances to a level that still left them considering him somewhat endearing.

They tugged their cavernous hood further over their face to close out the rain and reached a slender hand inside the heavy coat. It was waxed cloth on the outside, with fur sewn within for warmth. A large inner-breast pocket held some strips of dried game meat and dried winter fruits, and Adras took a bit of each, quietly tucking into the small meal while Lumen slept.

At the steady increase in the icy rain, they at last prodded Lumen with an elbow.

"Wake up, we are both getting soaked."

He groaned and wriggled closer. "Five minutes."

"Absolutely not." They stabbed him with their elbow again. "How are you comfortable?"

"You," he yawned, and rain poured from his hood. "are very rude."

Adras snorted.

The two of them lashed together some long branches with a length of rope from the leather pack they carried, using well-practiced knots to create a flat surface from them. They then tied a large waxed cloth to the underside, effectively waterproofing the half-finished shelter. Rain dripped down the bridge of Adras' nose as they took the flat surface and wedged it between two of the lowest branches on the skinny little tree. Unfastening a heavy, woven square of fabric, which had been rolled and attached to the top of the leather pack, they spread it out under the newly erected makeshift shelter. It covered very little ground, only about half of the now-drying area, but Adras didn't mind.

They wedged themself onto it, next to Lumen. The few extra branches, which had been too small to use in the covering, they scrapped together in a tiny pile in the other half of the shelter. Lumen dug around in his pack, looking for the flint.

There was small *clink* noise before he said, "Huh," and pulled out the flint, as well as something else.

He frowned down at it in his hand, and it was cold and shiny-looking. Adras peered at it, an ugly squirm in their gut, before he handed it to them.

"I didn't pack that. Did you go rearranging my pack? Because you *would*." He struck a flame.

Adras turned it over in their hands. "I would *not*."

It was a pouch, but instead of being sewn from fabric, it was made from the tiniest intertwined metal links that Adras had ever seen. The metal was dark but shiny, almost blindingly so where it caught the orange firelight, which seemed to grow increasingly brighter as the hazy grey around them dimmed towards nightfall. The pouch seemed to respond to the energy in their hands, curling against each finger and warming to their touch. It felt surprisingly heavy for how small it was, as though whatever was inside was nearly bursting out. There was a little metal closure at the top—a sleek, hinged little door of sorts which, Adras realized upon trying to pry it open, had been sealed with Starlight.

They paused. It was all a bit too mysterious.

"It could have been planted." It was a bad thought to allow into their head, but it was not impossible.

They met Lumen's inky gaze, huddled close behind the catching kindling. His eyes reflected eerie flames, glinting gold on midnight black.

The countless letters of protest and death threats which repeatedly, anonymously found their way into Adras's possession flitted through their mind, their heartbeat rising with the realization of just how on their own the two of them were out here, in the middle of the Jopaar wilderness. Adras was a powerful wielder of Starlight, it was true, and Lumen's skill with his swords was unrivaled, but against weapons of stealth, or coordinated group attacks from the hateful anti-alloy gangs... well, there were limits to their power, after all.

Their breathing quickened. Lumen's hand tightened around the hilt of one death-sharp blade. Reaching out into the mist with their tendrils of Starlight, Adras felt for the presence of others who might be gathering their own Starlight to use against them. It would be blasphemy, but that had never stopped their kind before.

"I don't sense anything."

Lumen expelled a breath. It took a moment for their heartbeat to slow. Any hint of hatred always left a stale sourness in their lungs. Many times, they'd encountered the Anti-Alloys, but always within the safety of Jopaar's High City, where there were as many who supported Adras as there were who opposed them. The Anti-Alloys' message was one which protested the very existence of Adras and those like them, an outraged dissent against the veneration of those who walked with feet in a world transcending gender.

Hatred always escalates into violence, and violence into oppression. This was what Reinah had told them, after a High Council meeting in which the priests had expressed their displeasure at the great lengths she was willing to go to, in order to put an end to the Anti-Alloy factions. Adras had felt so safe and proud when they heard those words, felt a hope for those like them who lived in fear of those who would spit on their dignity.

Out here... there is no one to stop the violence. There is only us.

A few side-blown raindrops hissed into the fire, causing Adras to start. The chill of the ground beneath them and the sudden gust of wind which bit at their nose, brought a grounding sort of weight to their mind.

"Hey." Lumen nudged them

Adras peered a bit closer at the metal link pouch, examining it for evidence of whom it might belong to. Holding it just out of reach of the flames, where the orange and gold flickered close to their fingers, a small, thin etching above the hinges of the closure became visible.

The pythfox of Jopaar... with a crystal crown.

The fine lines etched in the silver were clear as the glassy ice fields of Jopaar's western wastes. Adras brushed the tiny sigil with their thumb, a stiff lump of emotion balling in their throat. It was from Reinah, they were sure. This hidden, altered version of the Jopaaran sigil was one she'd used in the past, snuck into places where it had no business being. It was always a sign for Adras, a reminder or a confirmation or a comfort. And now, it was an assurance. This was no Anti-Alloy plot; it was a gift.

Carefully, Adras placed a finger on the lock, focusing the Starlight they'd gathered, holding it in their veins like a winding network of gleaming power. Pressing the Starlight against the warm metal, through their finger, Adras felt the firm pressure of the opposing Starlight, which had been used to seal the lock. Probing their own a bit further into the shield of energy, they felt a sudden release, the opposing Starlight voluntarily melting away from their own.

A giddiness shuddered through them.

"Damn," Lumen whispered.

With a flick of their finger, Adras clicked open the little latch, which had now been unlocked. As soon as the latch lifted, a sudden surge of familiar Starlight jolted them so hard that they tumbled backwards, juggling the metal pouch. Lumen gave a little jump. Righting themself, Adras blinked at it.

"The fuck is in there?" Lumen peered over their shoulder.

With a determined exhale, they roughly opened the pouch, only to start as they peered inside.

The Stargift...

There it sat, cradled in fine mesh metal in their hands, its twisting form of metal veins and faintly glowing crystal looking like the innards of some nonorganic beast. Adras could feel in their very bones the fine vibrations that the Stargift sent into the air around it. Tiny bumps rose on their skin at the feeling of this holy object in their hands, and at the humming vibrations that seemed to residually ripple through their blood.

They weren't sure how much time went by before they snapped the lock shut and returned the pouch to the bottom of the pack. They hugged their knees, gazing into the gold and orange flames in front of them. Even Lumen had grown quiet as soon as he'd seen what was inside the little mesh pouch. There was so much to think about, now. The entire tone of this expedition had shifted, and Adras felt a bit overcome by the gravity and sacredness of it. Why Reinah had smuggled it into their pack was a mystery.

Adras absentmindedly traced the tattooed semicircle on their cheek, the scarring line raised and bumpy against their soft finger. Perhaps they were needed to be together—the two Stargifts. Adras was on their way to find the bearer of the second known Stargift, and it would make sense that the two ought to be in proximity to one another. They closed their eyes, calling to mind the description of the three people they had been sent to find.

Zechariyh: Chedhiyn, dark auburn hair, medium build, travelling on foot, unpredictable Starlight, most likely gone in search of missing friend Aeron. Jauyne: Premier Heiress of the fallen Meirydh, tall, thin, black hair, very powerful Starlight wielder, widely presumed dead but wondered alive by many Premiers. Reinah had also high suspected that Jauyne may have in her possession the Chedhiyn Stargift, as Aeron had been sent to deliver it. Indra: slight, curly blonde hair, missing only child of Premier Canryn, most likely either in disguise or dead.

Adras tried to picture them in her mind, though having never seen the three missing persons, it was a stream of endless variations on the few descriptors they had been given. They rolled onto their side and stared into the flames. Keeping their eyes open was becoming a struggle. Lumen rested his hand on their shoulder. Silently, Adras closed their eyes and sent their Starlight into a swirling band around the haphazard shelter. As the comforting band of their own connection with the Stars turned endlessly around them, Adras's eyes closed slowly into a tumbling, dreamful sleep.

The smallest hint of dawn was creeping over the edge of the horizon, but already the sogginess of the ground had lessened immensely from the past week and a half, which had been filled with nonstop downpours. The still-glowing coals at Adras's side gave off more heat in their dying moments than they'd expected, but they welcomed it, cozy against the chill of the clear dawn air. Adras gave them a bit of a poke with a nearby stick, nudging them back to life as they added a bit of grass and twigs that they had reserved under the shelter for just this purpose.

Lumen was curled around the opposite side of the fire, his face childish in the slack of sleep, one arm hooked around the strap of his pack.

The few fingerling potatoes which were still left in their food supply, were tucked into the outside section of the pack, and Adras patted them down into the edge of the coals before retrieving the tin cup they'd set out to collect rainwater, and hanging that above the little flame to heat.

As they waited for their breakfast to cook, they squatted down just outside the edge of the waxed fabric cover, surveying the landscape as they drew their Starlight back from its circular path round the shelter. It felt good to have a semblance of a routine out on the road.

The panorama wasn't quite as bleak and ugly as it had appeared in the several days prior, now that the rain had stopped and things weren't so waterlogged. A thick fog was rolling down over a far-off hill, and it looked lovely, in the melancholy sort of lovely way in which Adras appreciated things.

Adras kneaded the palm of their hand with the opposite thumb. Soon, they'd reach Meirydh's High City. They hoped their hunch wasn't wrong. It had been a big risk—heading straight for the one place everyone else was certain the missing people surely wouldn't be. But Adras couldn't help but follow their intuition. It hadn't been wrong yet.

The gurgle and hiss of boiling water splashing onto open flame, accompanied by a yelp from Lumen, tugged them away from surveying the rest of the local scenery.

"Are you trying to boil me alive?" He was wiping at the side of his face, where a single drop of the spitting water had landed. He was still sleep-groggy and rubbing his eyes between the attention he gave his cheek.

Adras tried not to laugh. "Breakfast's almost ready." They plucked the little mug from its dangling perch over the fire. The water still bubbled as they dropped in a tiny pouch of strong tea leaves.

It was the same ritual tea they sipped before sacred ceremonies and Commissionings. Hundreds of generations of Oracles, Priestesses, and Wise Ones had brewed this tea before them. Now, Adras brewed it in preparation for the most important thing they'd ever done—a mission utterly strange and surreal.

Adras scooped out the little pouch of tea leaves with a couple of sticks. They held it to their nose, letting the steam bathe their face and fill their nostrils, fighting a sneeze.

This tea was pungent and spicy, and certainly not one which was drunk for its taste. The herbs and spices which made up this tea were ones which altered the mind, prepared the drinker for sacred work. Foxear was a focuser, which helped narrow the drinker's attention. Lavender was simply for taste. Moon dust was a stiller, which helped to rid the body and mind of anxiety. And Priestess' flower lifted the mood and heightened the senses. For this final reason, it wasn't uncommon for boys in Jopaar's high city to attempt to steal the higher quality Priestess' Flower plant from within the high gates of the Priestess's own garden.

Adras took a long slurp from the still-steaming liquid, feeling it sear its way down their trachea. Their lips pursed to keep from being ill, but already they felt the effects of the tea, washing over them in a familiar sort of way, with a comforting sort of burn, like fine whiskey. Hurriedly, Adras gulped down the rest of the small cup and placed it back into their pack.

Lumen was fishing the potatoes out of the embers with a little pair of metal tongs from his pack and placing them onto the tin plates they had both brought. They steamed, and the steam swirled upwards, entrancing Adras.

Their head was beginning to feel light and airy, their hyper-focused mind ready to find itself in a self-induced hypnotic meditation. Adras was keenly aware of the way the grass tickled as they rested their hands on it, and of the heaviness in their jacket's inner pockets as the contents of them pressed against their chest. Breathing came easy and steady now, amidst the spiraling purple light they saw behind their eyelids, and a pinpoint of heat pulsed between their eyes.

Just as they had done before leaving Jopaar, Adras sat with closed eyes and reached out with the tendrils of energy that connected them to the Stars. But Adras did not reach for the Stars. They reached for Jauyne. And for Zechariyh. And for Indra. Focusing, effortlessly due to the tea, on what little they knew of the three missing persons, Adras began to feel a Starlight signature grow in their mind's eye. They let the signatures grow stronger, feeding them with their own power until the Starlight from each was distinct and intense.

Jauyne felt like snapping lightning—all white and silver and full of sparks and unpredictability. Hues of jetty black and crimson glowed as they crackled and spat like fire.

Zechariyh felt soft at first- deep greens and browns swathed his energy, cut with unexpected gashes of silver. There was an unsteadiness to him that unnerved Adras. He was steady and strong on the surface, but the inner turbulence often broke all of that up into choppy, careless slabs.

A wave of silver crashed, so intense and drowning that it caused Adras to flinch, panting lightly. They could see a pair of eyes. Grey. Silver. Shining. Adras stared into them, unafraid and curious. The Starlight that accompanied them was like a river— swirling cool hues of blue, flowing through Adras's mind, and glinting with silver and gold.

You have answers, the eyes said.

PLEASE

15
A PANG OF JEALOUS WONDER

She had woken up before him. He hadn't seen her for hours.

When she came back, nose and cheeks red and wind-whipped with cold, and pressed herself against him in a hug, she was far away— unreachable and frigid. Zech rubbed long strokes into the roped muscles of her back where she sat near him in her father's study, her body rigid and eyes shadowed.

While she'd been out, doing Stars-knew-the-fuck-what, he'd dragged out the bloated bodies, their joints loose and sludgy when he tugged at their arms and legs. He had rolled up the rug, richly patterned with thread and blood, and mopped up the long-dried gore from the stone floor beneath. Supposing Jauyne wouldn't appreciate a heap of dead father in the hall, he shoved the dead bodies and blood-stiffened rug into the tunnel hidden behind the tapestry on the far wall.

Now she was poised and unyielding beneath his hand as she inspected the room from her vantage point on the floor.

"Can you stop that?" She bristled, chewing her scarred lip.

Zech flinched, despite himself, and withdrew his hand. "Of course."

She fastened her gaze to him a moment too long, dragged it away almost angrily, and ran a hand through her hair, the tangles ripping away as her fingers snagged in them.

A rattling sigh heaved from her throat. "Well, let's get to work looking for these mythical objects, I suppose."

Zech opened his mouth, closed it again. Something like hurt or indignation flared in his chest. She really was not going to give a fuck about him cleaning this entire room. He wanted to grab her hand, yank her back, ask her if last night's fucking had just been a crazed illusion of his obviously untrustworthy mind. Instead, he pushed himself to his feet after her.

"Yeah."

Had Aeron been wrong? It nagged at the back of Zech's mind as he picked at a callous on his thumb. The worse thought: Had Jauyne been right? Was he really just the foolish, stupid boy who believed in myths and legends and was willing to risk everything for a make-believe foretelling that didn't seem to exist anywhere outside of a small circle of believers?

She evidently was back to reminding him of the absurdity of this fact, although she had not, as of midday, threatened his life, which seemed like some sort of progress.

There was still half the day to go.

For him, their night had felt touched by something cosmic. For her, evidently, this was not the case. At the time, she'd been unclouded and open— or at least he'd thought so. Unless she was toying with him, which he was stupid and desperate enough to fall for.

Maybe he just wanted to be wanted, to be seen as something worth wanting. What was so wrong about that, anyway? Why wasn't he supposed to want that? Because he was crazy? Untrustworthy? He felt that even fucked up people must deserve a little love.

She ripped open the drawers of her father's desk, tearing them from their casters and letting them knock woodenly against the stone floor. There was something violent bristling under her skin, and he didn't know what he'd done— or hadn't done?— to bring it about. She sunk to the floor, a pile of angles and scars, clawing through the spilled-out drawers of documents and trinkets. Hands stilling on a small metal figurine, she stroked it with a thumb, then gripped it in a furious fist and flung it across the room, where it crashed through a window.

Frozen to the stone beneath his feet, Zech watched as she pressed her fists to her eyes and screamed out a frustrated sob. Something in his chest squeezed with familiarity. If she wasn't such a self-protective little bitch, he'd have rushed to hold her.

"Jauyne...?"

"What?" It was bitter and muffled.

"I..." What was he going to say, exactly? Huh? Could he maybe think for a second and not get himself stabbed? "It's okay. We'll figure it out. We don't have to—"

"It isn't you, watchman."

Now it was his turn to ask it. "What?"

A frustrated little grunt left her mouth as she scrubbed her beautiful, ruined face with pale hands. She straightened and looked him in the eyes so directly he nearly started. "I don't like it here. Not just because it fucking reeks and it's where I nearly died. I've never liked it here. I'm not a moron, Zech. I know I'm a bitch, and I know people don't like me."

At the way his mouth opened, she glared silence into him.

"My own parents hated me. I was a necessary irritation, a firstborn child, existing only to be taught to rule. Stop that. Don't get all soft about it. It's reality, Zech. I spent more than twenty-four years knowing that the only reason I was tolerated was because I was a quick learner and enough of a cunt that people would do what I told them to. They knew I'd do the job well, so they let me exist. My sister was perfect and pretty and kind and good, and they loved her. And now she is dead, and I am alive, and I have one fucking job." Her slim chest was heaving, eyes crazed, hands shaking with what he could see clearly as adrenaline.

He opened his mouth, which was probably stupid, and then he said something, which was probably stupider. "I don't hate you."

"I know." Teeth gnashed. "But you don't even know me! You're just like she was, except..."

A step closer seemed stupid, too, but he was already well beyond smart. "Except what?"

The raspy snap of her voice made him jump. "Except you're more fucked up."

Charged air connected his gaze to hers. There were only feral creatures in this room. Dark clouds outside painted the shadows in purple.

Without warning, she laughed.

She was fucking *laughing*. Stars and voids, she was almost as crazy as he was. He chanced an unsteady smile. Evidently, his insanity was the most hilarious thing she'd ever seen, as her laughter howled out of her, high and wolfish.

He was used to being the punch line. Used to his mental instability being the theme of the joke. Didn't mean he liked it. He turned on his heel, some fine crack inside him growing wider. The laughter stopped abruptly.

"What's wrong?"

"Nothing." His teeth grit together, and he bent to pick up a stray piece of paper.

"Stop that." Bony fingers encircled his wrist. When he turned, he was eye-to eye with her. "Tell me what's wrong. You don't hide."

Anger warmed his chest. "I don't hide? That's rich, coming from you! You can't mock how fucked up I am and then ask what the fuck's wrong. Don't be stupid; that's my job."

Slate-grey eyes blinked. "I wasn't mocking you."

"No?" Anger was still heating him up, and the slime of it crept into his voice. Starsdamn her.

"No." Her grip on his wrist tightened. There was a cautious firmness to the soft rasp of her voice. "Everybody's fucked up, watchman. Anyone who says otherwise is a liar and a kiss-ass who wants something."

A tremor ran through his heart. Her veins hummed where their skin touched.

"And just because I fucked you and it felt... important..." Her eyes flicked away, a momentary surrender. "It doesn't mean I want to bare my soul. Let me be the kind of fucked up I am, and I'll let you be the kind of fucked up you are. Deal?"

He slid her hand from his wrist to his fingers. "Deal, firestarter."

A repulsed wrinkle of her nose at the nickname bent the pinkish scar that bisected her face. "No."

New, softer warmth made him reckless, and he shot her a shit-eating grin. "You'll get used to it."

She opened her mouth, but the crackle of thunder lanced through the shattered window. A deep breath filled her chest. The fight in her was replaced with something like anticipation. Her veins flickered with Starlight as lightning screamed from cloud to cloud before lashing out at the far-off ground.

A curiosity wormed its way into him.

"What does it feel like?"

Her glance was sideways and skeptical. "The storm?"

"Yeah." Her body was illuminated with Meirydhi magic, a cosmic quality to the light that always bloomed around her, something only his healer's eyes could see. His mouth felt dry.

"Come here." It was a command, and he obeyed.

They stood almost level; some part of him loved the way he squirmed when she looked him easily in the eye.

"Be still." Her voice was a near-whisper, and her eyes were shimmering and conspiratorial. Taking hold of his hand with hers, she raised it to the plane of her sternum.

His fingers splayed, spreading across her clavicle. Beneath his palm, her heart beat in an erratic thrum. She was watching him, holding an invitation at bay.

"Feel," she whispered, and thunder rumbled under his hand, an echo to the groaning crackle that burst outside.

Despite himself, his breath caught. Silver light spread through the spiderwebbed veins in her chest, through the ones in his hand. She dipped her head closer to his, and static built in the room until his ears popped.

"I feel it," he felt himself whisper, awe bleeding through him.

She grinned in a way that felt terribly unlike her, in a way that said just wait without any violence.

Lightning struck.

It burned through her, a buzzing so brutal and a rush so wild, and it slammed into him with a giddy unleashing. Her eyes flared, Starlight surging in pure delight, and his whole body tingled. A laugh cracked out of him. A second bolt of lightning branched out, and he felt this in his blood where his skin was pressed to hers.

But her eyes turned blood-hungry. In a buzzing motion, fueled by the wild thrash of lightning, she swept her arm across his, and pushed him behind her, body whipping towards the door of her father's study.

She was terrifying. Raw power unfurled and lashing.

In the doorway stood two hooded figures.

"Who are you, and why are you here?" It was less a question, more a demand, scraped from the hollow of her throat.

The shorter of the two figures reached up with hands bound halfway in leather gloves, fingers half peeking out and pinching a smoking blunt. The hood fell back. The person who stood there, face bared, was tattooed and sturdy, feet planted firmly despite the smallness of their stature. To their credit, they looked only slightly frightened, instead of shit-their-pants-terrified, and that alone was cause for concern over just how powerful, or how stupid, they might be.

"My name is Adras," said the not-as-scared-as-they-probably-should-be person. "I am Jopaar's Oracle. This is my brother Lumen. We've been sent by the High Priestess of Jopaar to find you and ensure your safety."

The other figure pulled back his hood, and Zech felt his inhale flip his stomach. The man's eyes were solid black, no distinguishable iris or sclera. His skin was the toasty warm color of brown sugar, and his tangled hair, dripping rain against his shoulders, was brilliantly white. The hilts of crossed swords peeked out above his shoulders. Grinning, he looked from Zech to Jauyne.

"Did we interrupt something? We can always come back later."

Zech felt Jauyne flinch, then stiffen. Panic moved his body, jolting in front of hers.

"No, no, everything is fine." He fumbled for her hand behind him. "But I don't understand. Why would you be interested in us?"

The tall one with creepy-ass eyes (Lumen?) gave a shrug and elbowed his companion— sibling? "I mostly follow this one around. Can we start a fire in here or something? I'm Starsdamned freezing."

He pushed his way into the room, making for the neglected fireplace. Zech gripped Jauyne's hand harder behind him. Adras' gaze bored into them, inquisitive, before they stepped across the threshold of the doorway and looked around the room.

"Well? You've found us!" Jauyne's voice was a grating shrill. "You can leave now. We are safe. I think it is evident I can keep it that way."

"Ah, yes." Lumen opened his mouth before Adras could. He was poking at the old, dead logs, rearranging them in the stone fireplace. "That magnificent, permanent decoration across your face tells me your self-protection skills are impeccable."

Oh no... Stars, no.

Jauyne tore her hand from Zech's, and he floundered for her.

"Shut your mouth when you don't know a damn thing about me or what I have survived. I have survived more than you can *imagine*, Jopaari foxshit."

Fuck fuck fuck. Zech flinched at the slur.

Lumen turned away from the fireplace, his humored features flattening into fury for the sharpest, shortest moment. "Don't think you're the only one who's seen death, little Meirydhi, just because you are the only one who still clings to it."

"*Fuck* you." It was spat.

"Perhaps instead of insulting one another, we could instead create a plan together." Adras' voice lilted from behind them all.

They folded their cloak over one arm, patting down a thick, knit cowl that tucked into a well-worn leather vest. The sweater beneath the vest was rucked up to their mid-forearms, and visible on their skin were swirling tattoos—astral dragons and Star patterns and pythfoxes. Setting their cloak on the floor, they sat on top of it, tucking their knees in a fold in front of them.

A practiced calm radiated from them, and Zech felt weirdly *observed* when their icy blue eyes met his. He licked dry lips roughly, glancing toward Jauyne and Lumen, who gave a huff and something that might have been an eye roll, if he could've seen his fucking eyeballs.

Tentatively, he pressed a hand, gentle but firm, to the middle of Jauyne's back. "Let's sit," he found himself saying. "Figure out what the fuck is happening before you spill anybody's guts."

Her face was rigid, skeletal anger stretched against muscle and bone, but, stiffly, she sat. Zech crouched beside her, and moved his hand, not wishing to press his luck.

Adras looked at each of them, tired but with intent. "We know you have the Chedhiyn Starstone."

Jauyne bristled.

"We have the Jopaari stone. We have reason to believe there is one fallen in each Province. We know that Aeron brought the Chedhiyn one here, and that is why you are here, Zechariyh. You, Jauyne, are a surprise. I did not hold out much hope that you survived. It's good to see you did."

"Alright, Oracle," Jauyne interjected, tone acidic. "If you know so much about us, tell me this: how do I build back my Province? How do I kill the Canestryn Premier?"

COME

16

THE SPIRE OF THE DEAD

INDRA, BRIGONAN SOUTHWEST MOUNTAIN SPIRE
1 month since the sack of Meirydh

One foot in front of the other, Indra climbed the roughhewn stone steps. There were no railings here, on the oldest buildings of the Brigonan city, so she hugged the side of the rocky mountain face and desperately avoided peering down over the thousands of feet of empty air to her right.

She'd never understand how the Brigonans were so comfortable with dancing on the edge of nothingness. Osiys looked back at her, sheepishly.

"I'd forgotten how steep this was..."

Everyone had been especially concerned for her since she'd gone unconscious and been injured by the Starstone. Her hearing still had not fully returned in her right ear, although the bandages were off and everything else seemed normal as could be. The healing mages gently told her she must not have too high of expectations for a full recovery.

She was still a bit weak, it was true, but she knew she was capable, and there wasn't the heaviness settling over everything, as she had feared there would be.

"I'm alright." She waved him off. "I just need a moment to breathe."

He backtracked a few steps to be closer to her. Squinting out across the sparse mountainous forest beneath them, he pointed out little landmarks to her as she slid down to sit, with her knees at her chest and her back to the mountain rock. She watched him gesture wildly to all the various points far out beyond her and smiled to think that perhaps if she'd ever had a brother, this is what he might have been like. Eventually, Osiys extended a hand down to her.

"Come along. We'd better get moving if we don't want to be up here all night."

Indra nodded, a shiver wriggling down her spine at the thought of being stuck in the dark, at the top of this Spire that seemed to brush the clouds. A new energy pounded through the trembling muscles of her legs, and she climbed with fresh strength, keeping her eyes focused on Osiys's leather-clad feet, padding up the stairs in front of her. The two continued climbing for some time, as the sun eased down into the crook of the two largest peaks of the mountain range, casting shimmering orange flares across Indra's vision.

"Look." Osiys' words nudged Indra out of her focused trance, and she nearly bumped into him.

His rough hands grazed the mountain wall beside them as carved words began to appear, the solid grey rock slowly giving way to an ancient, hand-hewn tower, which was decorated and inscribed. The tower was simply the pinnacle of the lower peak itself, hollowed out and then engraved with beautifully detailed inscriptions. She looked to Osiys.

"What do they mean?" She breathed, running a finger along one of the engravings, a swirling text that rippled into the image of a flower. Her finger looked small and pale, even to her, against the darkness of the stone.

"They are finalities." Osiys's face seemed oddly serene in the warm light, as he climbed the culminating stair and rounded the corner into the hollowed tower.

There was a sudden awareness of her heart thudding in her chest as she followed him.

"This place is so full of love and grief..."

"Yes," he murmured softly, coming to stand in the center of the circular room, "It truly is. It is etched with a thousand, thousand words of memory. There is more love here, than anywhere else in the world."

He began to move round the room, circling her as she came to stand in the center, tracing words and images in the stone. There were low stone benches protruding from the curved walls, lining the base of tall windows which came to a gentle point at the top. Mountain views sprawled majestically outside of them, purples and greens of the earth tangled with the golden light of the setting sun streaming through their foothills. The ceiling was arched, a hollowed-out sphere ten feet above her head, and it radiated a cool, earthy air that felt all at once calming and chilling against her skin, damp from sweat. Her feet scuffed against the floor, and she looked down, noticing the engravings of the sun, the stars, the mountains, circling the floor in rings.

Osiys continued in his orbit around the circumference of the room, until he came to the bench alongside the doorway through which they'd entered. Placed on the bench was a small mallet and chisel, and he picked them up, thumbing the worn, leather-wrapped handles of the tools.

"In Brigon, we burn the bodies."

His voice was rougher, raspier than before, and she turned to see his brows creased together. Her heart ached with a helpless wanting to soothe the pain so evident in his words, but this was a man she didn't know—not really. This was a grief from a life he had lived so far outside the scope of their friendship, that she didn't know how to reach out to him, didn't know how to respond. So she just stood, nodding, existing, there.

"We burn the bodies," he repeated," and we come here—whole families—to throw the ashes from these windows." His hand skimmed the opening of the window beside him. "Their bodies can join their souls, singing over the mountains, over their home. In the sky, you know, with the Stars." He shrugged.

"That's beautiful." Indra's voice was scarcely more than a hoarse sigh, but it seemed to grate off the stone. She winced.

"I remember coming here as a child," he continued, as though he hadn't heard her. "It was winter, steps were all slick with snow and ice and all that. I slipped on the stairs."

A lump formed in Indra's throat, half with the emotion she could sense emanating from him, half from the terror that surged in her with the thought of slipping on stairs of that height. She remained silent, however, as Osiys gestured wordlessly out the window. Sunshine flared around his shoulder, and she refused to blink, making her eyes water.

"I'm not quite sure why I'm saying all that." He turned from the window back to her, and his eyes were red.

She shook her head. "That's alright. I don't think we always need to know why grief remembers the things it does."

The mallet and chisel were visibly shaking in his hands, but he smiled haltingly. "Would you like to help me?"

"Help you?"

Osiys's eyes scanned the room till they returned to the window he had been gazing out of previously. His hand smoothed the stone of the sill and beckoned Indra over with a soft curling of his hand. She padded hesitantly over to his side,

"She loved the sun... This window is perfect for her."

"Will you engrave memories for her?"

He nodded. "They say the souls of our dead visit this Spire one night each year. I want her to know... I want her to know I've met our daughter. That she's perfect."

"She will be so pleased." Indra smiled, and she felt it all the way into her blood. Perhaps she did not know what was true about death, whether the dead of Brigon truly visited this Spire or not. But she knew the surge of emotion in her heart. There was no beauty after death in Canestry—more honor and glory, surely—but no beauty, no love. It struck some deep well in her which she had no words for, something which rimmed her eyes in tears.

She watched as Osiys closed his eyes for a moment, lips muttering silent rites, before he placed the chisel to the stone, and the clear, sharp clink of metal on stone rung out over the mountains. It was quite some time before the final high-pitched clink echoed back to them and then drifted into silence. The words weren't recognizable to her, but she smiled softly at Osiys nonetheless as his eyes lifted from the windowsill to meet hers. There was an exhaustion in them that had never made so much sense to Indra as he wiped sweat from his brow with the hem of his dark blue sleeve.

"Well," he sniffed, a bead of sweat dropping from the tip of his nose, "It is done."

"You ought to have a drink of water," she observed, nodding to the light pack slung across his back, which he'd never taken off.

He blinked with a flinch, like he'd been elsewhere—Indra suspected he had. "You ought to have some water. I hadn't even thought about it. You're still recovering!" He untangled himself from his pack, wriggling pitifully like a toddler till it was off, before rummaging through it to find the water.

He handed the skein to her, even as she shot him a cross look, and watched her carefully as she took a small drink before shoving it back in his hands. When he looked as though he were about to refuse, she shook her head. "Grief is exhausting," she said softly, pressing the skein completely into his hands.

Lips pressing together in a surrender of his stubborn protest, he lifted the skein to his mouth and drank deeply. A single droplet splashed from his lip to the stone floor as he sighed, ran his hand through sweat-plastered strands. A ragged sigh scratched its way out of his throat.

"Thank you."

Indra shook her head. "Nonsense—you were thirsty."

"No." He smiled humorously. "Thank you for coming with me."

She reached for his hand and squeezed hard. They were familiar with loss, with death, the two of them. He was her brother in grief and darkness, her friend in death and horror. There was no need for thanks, she thought, when her heart acknowledged this truth so fervently. But instead she simply said, "Always."

BACK

17

STARCHILD

He'd been glad that Indra had accompanied him up the Spire of the Dead. He'd needed her there, even if his proposal of it had been presented more as a gesture.

His grief had abated from a stabbing, open wound to a dull ache that followed him wherever he went, and he knew that this was in great part to Indra, and her gentle, reassuring presence. He felt guilt, too, for depending on a child of seventeen for the emotional stability he, for some infuriating reason, felt incapable of. She both was and was not a child, though- she'd seen more than any child should see, and it had at once scarred her and caused her to bloom into adulthood with an unnerving tenderness.

Tugging a crimson shirt over his head and jamming the hem into his trousers, Osiys ran a scarred hand through reddish amber hair and opened the great wooden door of his chamber. Padding softly over the thick rug which ran the length of the long hall, he at last reached the massive, carved doors of the council hall where they met daily for meals, as well as to plot their next moves against the army of Canestry. He stepped through them with an anxious heaviness though, for today was different. The plan was different. The future would change after what was decided here.

Indra was already waiting for him here, along with Elryh, Baird, Berg, Herran, as well as Enoch. Indra sat tentatively across from the Pallydhan messenger, holding a mug of steaming tea in front of her as though it were a shield against every traumatic memory of the man.
Enoch looked deeply uncomfortable in the presence of these old friends and a Princess who was no longer a Princess. Osiys sunk into the high-backed wooden chair beside Indra as Berg nearly spit out his drink at some wry comment from Elryh. Indra looked sideways at him, her concealed anxiety at the situation reading as irritation.

"Ah, finally the wanderer joins us!" Herran spread his hands wide from the head of the table, and the fire in the hearth behind him the shape of him all aglow with golden warmth.

Osiys smirked at the familiarity. "Well, I suppose I had to crawl from beneath the bedcovers sometime today."

Baird chortled. "A rare occurrence indeed, eh Berg?"

The man's twin replied only with a laugh which snorted out of his nose without care for dignity.

Elryh rolled her eyes, disguising her smile behind the brim of a mug full of tea.

"Well, if we are all present and accounted for, we must begin." The seriousness washed out from Herran like the tides bathing the white Canestryn beaches, and Osiys felt it settle in him as a collective nod responed to the Premier's words. "Enoch, please relay your account of the situation in Pallydh and the location of their Starstone."

Enoch cleared his throat uncomfortably, glancing around the room. He nodded curtly, hands twisting together on the table top as he began. "Pallydh has been taken for many moons now. It was... the kind of horror I didn't know was real. Men and women who resisted the New Order— as they call it— beheaded in the streets in front of their families... Women taken as slaves for the High Court of the Premier..." He was trembling now, though a raw numbness glazed his eyes.

Osiys' stomach wrenched at the gross recognition he felt. The kind of horror I didn't know was real... Yes. Yes, he knew it well, emblazoned onto the synapses of his brain like the tattoos he'd seen on some High Priestesses and Oracles of the Jopaar Province. Impossible to remove, or scrub off, or claw out. Just seared into him like they had always been there.

"Many fled the Province and tried to take up residence in some old hunting lodges outside the city in the marshlands," Enoch was continuing, his voice high and strained. "They were burned to death inside the lodges or forced to buy the silence of the Patrolmen through illegal rape deals. I know..." he trailed off, attempting to compose himself before beginning again. "I know people who have died- so many. My own brother murdered in the street. His wife and children somewhere in hiding, maybe dead by now as well. This is about more than some strange mystery from the skies." He sounded spiteful there. "This is about a whole people being exterminated like insects. This is about dignity and survival for me and my people. Do you know what that is like? Do you?"

Indra trembled beside Osiys, tears rolling silently down her pale cheeks. "I am so sorry." Her voice was so small, Osiys could scarcely hear her. "I am so sorry for the wickedness of my family. For my father's cruelty. I feel like it must be my job to end this."

Osiys shook his head, rage echoing back from the horrors in his memory. It was her job to do nothing. None of this was her fault. How dare she think she had some sort of debt to be repaid? She was among the first to deserve repayment!

Her tears splashed into her coffee as Enoch struggled to meet her eyes. "It is good to see that his lineage has not continued in violence. This is why I'm here- why you are here. We must end this, and now."

"You," Indra finally looked directly at Enoch without fear in her eyes, and a chill ran the length of Osiys' spine. How he ever forgot she was no longer a little seven year old looking for oranges, he'd never know. "You have given me something to fight for. And I want to thank you for that. I am going to do all that I can to end the violence and unravel the mystery. I'm... I'm just one girl. And I know I'm young and naïve and don't know the first thing about anything. But I will do what I can."

A smile so small it was barely noticeable turned the corners of Enoch's lips. A little secret thing that seemed to ask itself a question. "I am thankful," he nodded, licked dry lips. "I would guess there is more to you than even you yourself are aware of."

Her smile was equally small. "Perhaps."

Herran missed not a single moment. Hesitation clung to the corners of his eyes. "Are you prepared for this, young one? You still are not fully healed from the incident with the Starstone."

She took a breath so deep it was as though she were inhaling all the air in the room. "Yes. Yes, I'm ready."

Herran nodded, matter-of-factly. "Tell us, Enoch, where is the location of the Pallydhan Starstone, and how are we to retrieve it?"

Enoch brushed tears from his cheeks as he answered. "It is being kept by the secret members of the original High Circle. A new member of the High Circle is entrusted with its safety each day, so that its exact location is never clear. There are seven members of the High Circle-

Locke, the Treasurer of Pallydh; Charys, the High Mage; Allych, the Master of Agriculture and Distribution of Sustaining Goods; Lydhea, the High Court Preservationist of Lore; Cheadh, the Captain of the Guard; Dallan, the Headmaster of the School of Pallydh; and Pyrfan, the High Circle Strategist.

"They are each highly skilled and trained masters of their crafts, and are deeply wary. They have managed to maintain communication between one another despite being in hiding due to having the city taken by the Canestryn forces. The High Circle was once a location as well as the people within it, but the buildings and gardens are now being used to house the Captain of Canestry's guard. The High Circle will be unwilling to hand over the Starstone- all except perhaps Dallan and Lydhea. These are the two who I hope to retrieve alongside the Starstone, and bring back here to work with you on unraveling their mysteries." He gestured to Indra here, and Osiys watched her bristle.

Concern spiked in his gut. Indra? Study those strange things? Images flooded his mind of her writhing and screaming on the floor of this very room. "That can't be safe!" He couldn't help but interject. "We have seen what happens when a Starstone is brought near her. It would be cruel to ask her to bear that again!"

Enoch shook his head. "She does not need to be near them in order to study their mysteries. Don't you all see? Look in her eyes. All that silver gleam, shining even in the dark, needing no light but their own... She is a Starchild."

Osiys blinked hard. Starchild... He'd heard the word before. Retold it in stories he'd recounted to Indra to distract her from the nightmares. *Children's* stories. *Folklore.* Not reality. Baird had beat him to the snide comment, querying Enoch on whether or not he believed in those wild tales.

"I suppose you believe in the Silver Starbirds, too? And great worlds such as our own, battling above the sky? And astral dragons? And Merydhians who can shoot true lightning from their palms?" Berg was nearly howling with laughter, but Enoch remained still and unruffled.

Herran hushed the twins and nodded to Enoch. "What is all this talk of Starchildren?"

"My own great-grandmother was alive to see the birth of a Starchild long ago. A powerful woman who could shatter creatures with a flick of her wrist or make the sky dance with colors. No one knows what happened to her or to where she disappeared. But she lived, and so does Indra.

Perhaps the Stars have seen fit to tip the scales against Canestry. Either way, Indra holds a sacred gift- an ability far surpassing any of us, with which she can communicate with the Stars. She has the very best chance of understanding their gifts."

The room was silent. Worry still nagged Osiys' stomach in a way that nothing else did. War, he could understand, despite all its horrors. Tactic, extraction, the safety of home, sitting here in sturdy chairs with mugs of coffee... they all made sense to him. But this strange, unearthly suggestion left him utterly unmoored in a strange feeling of unknown and helplessness, as if she was about to go to a place where he could not follow. It frightened him in a way he hadn't been prepared for- losing this creature of light and softness threatened to smother the last pieces of light and softness in him. He peered at Indra, trying to read her expressions, her silence.

Slowly, her glowing silver eyes raised from her mug to Enoch, wide and innocent, wise and ancient. "I am a Starchild." Her voice was a husky whisper. "Aren't I?"

And despite the terror raging in his belly, an inescapable knowledge settled gently in Osiys' mind. Yes. Yes, she was a Starchild. The ancient innocence. The wide-eyed wisdom. The gentle rage. How had he avoided that truth until this moment? The way she'd looked up at him oh so solemnly at just seven years old, told him he looked like a nice man when he stalked past in his flowing Night Walker robes. She had been like a magnet, like her own force of gravity. The thing that had always felt so untouchably confusing about her, the thing he'd constantly questioned and wondered about... it had been right there this whole time.

Starchild. Yes, yes she is.

Perhaps this had always been his mission after all, to find the Starchild, protect her, and extract her from a land of monsters and petty god-men. If he believed in fate it would be so easy to accept, but here he was, wrestling his mind to make sense of it all.

Enoch nodded at her, a true smile tugging at his mouth. He ran a hand over his dark face, the stubble make a rough scratching sound as he itched his chin with his thumb. "Yes, you are."

There was a strange quietness, then. A hush down in the bones of all who were in the room. Osiys knew it was some sort of sacredness they were witnessing, and it made his heart ache for reasons he couldn't quite put his finger on. He looked at the girl sitting beside him; she had never been a child, but now, in this moment, she looked more gentle and more invulnerable than ever. Her eyes were shining brightly with Starlight, and her skin was so pale and soft it appeared nearly translucent in the firelight, where the echoes of flame played on her skin. Her somber face had a new sheen of purpose to it that danced behind her eyes and toyed with the corners of her lips.

It was a good look for her, he thought, his heart softening even as it ached. She was always meant for something far more grand than the confining evils of her home Province. But then again, she'd reminded him only days ago that everyone was meant for more than that. Perhaps that was true, but she was meant for more than most. He was convinced of it. It was a relief, really that there were others who saw her greatness, saw her wisdom, saw her deep love for humanity and chose to honor that instead of squandering it.

He knew then what the grief was all about- she would no longer be accompanying him to Pallydh. He'd known this anyway- it was no place for someone as good as she was, to be on the front lines of a war her own father was waging, but this felt more permanent, more final, and it hurt his soul to bid farewell to the child that had been his companion for a full ten years— a decade. He didn't quite know how to get on without her, and it pained him to know he would need to figure that out for himself. He took a deep breath, sucking the warm, tense air in the room deep into his lungs. It was less soothing than he'd hoped.

Herran was gesturing to Osiys now, suggesting they needed a secure plan in order to breach the defenses they'd surely find. He was questioning Enoch on how they might go about finding the High Circle, putting things together, and moving small pieces of metal and clay about on a large map which had been unfurled over the tabletop. Elryh was waving over one of the young boys to get her some fresh hot tea. They'd all moved right through this news that had pummeled him over.

He looked back at Indra, and this time she turned to look back at him. He knew she could feel his inner conflict; she'd always had a knack for that. Guess he knew why, now. She rested a little hand on his knee and scooted a bit closed to him in her chair.

"Don't worry, Osiys. You'll be back soon." Her brow furrowed. "Which is good, because I will need your help."

They were interrupted by Herran and Enoch requesting clarification about certain points regarding the Night Walkers and Canryn's other forces, the details of which Osiys was content to lose himself to. This was his area of comfort, strangely enough. The thing he'd been desperate to be rid of for ten long years now seemed to be the only thing that felt like home, a fact to which he was growing numb. Before long, the details were decided, the plan was set into motion, and the stable boys were being informed of which horses would need to be readied to ride the next morning.

Osiys, Enoch, and Baird would ride and hike to Pallydh over the next several days, taking mostly unused side and mountain roads when they were available. They would come to the sea to the west of the High City, where a comrade of Enoch's would be waiting with a small boat. The four of them then would enter the city through a long-discontinued water channel which ran beneath the city- this would be a blind area to the Canestryn forces as it was no longer on most city maps, such as the kind they'd be using. Enoch suggested bringing some tools for breaking through the light barrier that had been constructed within this water channel, insisting it should not be difficult to disassemble with four strong men and a few pick axes. Enoch would then make contact with another of his comrades who had a direct connection to both Dallan and Lydhea. From there, they would attempt to gain audience with one or both of these members of the High Circle, and convince them to leave the city and return to Brigon with the Starstone.

It seemed like a solid plan- solid enough at least for Osiys to rest his anxieties on for the moment. Herran dusted his hands together and called the meeting to a close, somberly reminding them all not to be late, for they rode at dawn the next morning. After getting another mugfull of tea, Elryh exited the large, warm room, the rest of the party in tow. Even Herran brushed past them, clapping a heavy hand on Osiys' shoulder, and leaving he and Indra sitting there alone at the great wooden table.

Osiys allowed the muscles in his body to slacken. Realizing how tense he'd been, he took a hand to the back of his neck, wincing at himself. Indra quirked a smile at him in amusement.

"Concerned?" She said, mock seriousness playing in the corners of her eyes and in the twitch of her cheek.

"Don't be mouthy." He grinned back at her, humor rippling through his chest. "Don't you know you ought to respect your elders?"

She snorted, which was so out of the ordinary for her generally prim and subtle comedy, that it entirely caught him by surprise, tempting a laugh up from his throat. Her mouth cracked into a grin before falling back into a deeply serious line.

"I was telling the truth you know. I... I'm not sure what to do. I haven't done any of this before. I don't understand what is expected of me. I don't know how to be a..." She bit her lip with a huff.

There was a small silence between them.

"A Starchild," he finished her sentence, eventually, and her eyes filled.

"It's true. I know it must be." Her voice was a squeak in this massive room. "But that doesn't mean I know what to do with the truth."

Osiys sighed, ran a thumb absentmindedly back and forth over his lower lip. "Well, if it's of any help, you still manage to sound full of wisdom, even when you don't know anything."

She looked like she wanted to laugh, but she didn't. It came across more like a wince. A minute or two later, with just the crackling of the fire in the hearth to fill the room with sound, she shrugged.

"I suppose I'm just going to miss you. You might have had a whole life here- love, family, joy- but me? Osiys, I don't remember life without you. I was seven when you came to Canestry. Seven years old. Just a little child. I had no one until you. You are my family, not like that vile thing they call my father, and I don't... I have never had to say goodbye to my family before." Her hands were twisting in the billowing trousers she wore, the fabric creasing and wrinkling the more her agitated hands mussed it. Then her eyes spilled over, and she threw her hands from her lap to her face.

Osiys could do nothing but blink for a moment, til her words sunk into his lungs and he found he couldn't breathe... this was the grief he'd felt before. Family. She was his family. She didn't know how wrong she was about him having left family behind all those years ago— the people who raised the child he'd been meant nothing to him, not compared to her. Not compared to the ten years they'd spent surviving together, learning one another in the soft, insistent sort of way you memorize a poem that makes you weep.

He'd been to the darkest places he assumed one could go, but she was always there— first as a beaming child, then as a wise young woman. In the span of a decade, he'd never been forced to part with her, and the same terror and sorrow as he'd felt in the days leading up to his departure from Canestry washed over him, dizzyingly. The thoughts intruded once more— how long would this war ravage the world, and how long before he'd be counting bodies, only to find hers among them, if he wasn't there?

His body finally responded to the call of the grief in his lungs, and he dropped to his knees from his chair, nearly eye to eye in front of her small, hunched over frame. He reached out, wrapping her in his arms, feeling her sobs in his chest, feeling hot tears streaking down his own cheeks, petting handfuls of her silvery blonde hair in his thick, scarred hands.

"You're right," he whispered, the words gulped down with an escaping sob. "You're my family. You're my family."

She threw her arms around him then, her fingers pressing into his spine and tears soaking the shoulder of his shirt. They wept there until her sobs turned to little shivers, and her hands stroked the length of his back instead of plastering to it.

It was a long time before they summoned the strength to untangle themselves and dry their panicked tears. But even then, the sorrow stayed, stinging Osiys' lungs like a trapped hornet.

YOU

18

WHAT SHE REALLY WAS

JAUYNE, VICHA RYPCHË IN SOUTHERN MEIRYDH
1 month since the sack of Meirydh

She had the unnerving, ridiculous feeling of being caught doing something she shouldn't, and she was flustered, and she hated both of those feelings more than nearly any other.

It was stupid, to feel as though she might be in trouble. This was *her* fucking Province! *She* was the Premier! But still, the black-eyed one's mocking snappishness and the silver-eyed one's forced patience made the tip of her tongue jittery with explanations. It was the insults and the rage that lashed the explanations and the panic back and took over the speaking though, as they usually did.

There was a tingling chill in her fingers, one that made them ache, and she clasped and unclasped them together as she paced beneath the broken window.

Starsdamnit. Another thing she'd broken.

An inkling of the nauseating guilt and anger she'd felt upon finding that little figurine painted the back of her throat in bile. Astra had picked it out for their father one year during the Volcanic Festival of *Vicha Rypchë*. *Vicha Rypchë* was the second-largest of the Meirydhi volcanoes, and the one whose overflow supplied the volcanic springs and heated the nearby Nareilën hot springs and geyser fields.

Jauyne herself had been named after Meirydh's largest volcano, the *Jauynë Rypchë*. When she was little, she'd thought this was evidence of how her parents must love her, to give her a name so full of magic and power. But her sister... her sister had been named star. Astra. And that was when Jauyne had known— she may be a powerful thing, a force of nature so disastrous that frequent reassurance sated total destruction. But her sister was more than than that. Her sister was loved.

They'd been so different: gentle, and harsh. Soft, and jagged. Silk, and steel. Astra had feared fire, woken up repeatedly from dreams where her room burned red until Jauyne spent half her nights curled around the little thing, rubbing her back till she fell to sleep again, her sleep-warm fingers clutching at Jauyne's clothes. She was the only thing that received Jauyne's softness, the only one who looked at it with comfortable awe.

And now she was fucking dead. Killed in a burning city. Her nightmare come to life. And Jauyne hadn't been there to hold her.

Purple lightning razed the sky, reflecting off glass broken into jagged teeth around the stretching scenery. The cold tingle had spread from her fingers, a burning, fizzing freeze not unlike the feeling of the Starstone when it had injured her. It had buzzed in her veins since these two Jopaari strangers had made their untimely appearance, and had only intensified with her own irritability and the throb of pressure in the clouds outside. This was about to be a storm like she hadn't seen in years, and the thought sent goosebumps skittering across her skin.

Something else, an equal intensity building with heat and harrowing depth, climbed through the soles of her feet. All her senses were too alive, too attentive, too sizzling with the lightning and the thunder and the magma seeping under the ground. She could feel the Starstones, the heightened power zipping around her from the people she shared the room with. *Jauyne Rypchë* was readying for an eruption, and Jauyne was readying for one, too.

A touch on her arm, and she jumped, realized she'd stopped before the window. The touch became a soft stroke of warm fingers against the back of her upper arm, and her breath adjusted, deepening, as she allowed this. Zech's hand moved forward, fingers coming round the front of her arm and holding gently.

"Firestarter..." His voice was soft with undercurrents of urgent concern, like she so faintly remembered from the day they'd arrived and she'd gone into shock. "The storm is kicking up. Is this normal?"

His thumb was still soft on the back of her arm, his breath in her hair.

She felt her body move, so far away and somewhere deep inside of her. "This is special," her mouth said, without her. "This is different."

A curl of her stomach affirmed it. Excitement and fear twisted up her guts.

"Why?" He turned her slightly, brought her eyes to his. They were softly lit, more than they usually were.

For a moment, she remembered what she'd said to him in the shack: *You're holding back. That's why this is difficult.*

What had he said?

"What?"

His brows pinched. "Why is it different? Special?"

Her skin prickled again. Silver, slick and cold and full of fire, ran the length of her senses, somewhere other than her eyes. "I think it's coming to me."

"What is?"

She vaguely understood his concern when his finger swiped the apex of her chin and came away wet with tears.

"We never received a Starstone. Meirydh. It didn't arrive in time for... It's coming to me. *Now.*"

The realization slammed into her like the foreboding groan of cracking open earth. Even as she said it, she knew it was true. Meirydh... Her Starstone was falling.

Explosive light washed the world outside in screaming orange, and something inside of her cracked open in a way that made her feel eerily alive.

Zech's eyes went wide. Behind him, Lumen gasped, "holy shit..."

She felt herself grin, even as her vision slanted with lightning. "*Vicha Rypchë* and *Jauynë Rypchë* are erupting."

"*Erupting?* Is that safe?" He was doing that soothing voice still, and she really wanted him to stop now.

She wasn't a person anymore. She was not *safe*. She was lightning. She was the storm clouds choking out the sky. She was volcanic, and she did not need to be soothed.

"Of course it isn't fucking safe." An incredulous snort snuck out as she shot him a sideways look and her body trembled with barely-contained energy. "It's Meirydh. We're all made of peril here."

That slick, cold silver fire ran across the rough-edged surface of her senses again, and need tugged from somewhere deep in her chest. A magnetic pull that nearly turned her stomach with its strength.

I have to meet it halfway...

Her feet moved, pushing past Zech towards the door, and a more corporeal her would have reveled in the flicker of fear that rippled Adras' irises. Lumen's stance shifted, moving in front of his sibling ever so slightly, his hands twitching for the swords strapped on his back. They'd explained the situation, but she'd barely been listening. And this was bigger. This was Meirydh. This was the Stars themselves.

Lumen and Adras let her go, and Zech followed on her tail. "We're coming with you, Jauyne."

"I already told you it's not safe."

"Neither are you. Hasn't kept me away yet."

Lightning lit the sky again— purpled and orange filling the world with eerie doom. But it was hers, and she would not be afraid. Her feet fled faster than she'd ever gone, a speed propelled by Starlit purpose. The steps of the High House and the city unfolded under her as though the marble could worship the kiss of her steps. She moved so fast, it was a wonder she didn't fall on her face, but something was *pulling* her, singing to her with the same voice of cymbals crashing under wooden sticks, wreaking havoc on whatever thread bound her to her body. Black spots danced in her vision, danced to the music of the *Rypchë*. They swelled and collapsed into nothingness.

Come to me, little Meirydhi...

She didn't stop to question her sanity. She didn't hesitate when the words hummed in her fingertips and behind her eyes, when they stoked that cold fire instead of quenching it.

Come to me, little Premier, little lightning bolt, little frigid thing... Come and be warm...

I'm on my way, Rypchë.

Rypchë... The magma beneath her pounding feet laughed, and the Rypchë painted the air orange in the distance. Lightning struck its heart. *So much more...*

Her feet churned bodies and burned grass beneath them, her heart nearly seizing out of her chest with desperate anticipation. As though some other thing held in its palm the red-painted, silver tangle of her veins, and was pulling her nearer with them.

Zech's feet tore at the ground behind her, some brilliant illumination coming from his veins. His head was thrown back, a grin tugging at his mouth as he spun to catch up with her.

Not *holding back anymore...* Not afraid of her. Not afraid of her home.

The sky was a veritable painting of purples and oranges among the black of the clouds and incoming nightfall. Lightning kissed the ground everywhere. Thunder shook the earth. Her veins hissed in pleasure at every strike and rumble. This storm was a thing that echoed under her skin, an unpredictable, writhing, alive thing hemming her in toward the towering volcanoes and surrounding lava pools. It sang for her. It directed her. It moved her in every conceivable way.

Black spots swelled large enough to dizzy her, but something about their depth dragged her closer. She ran for the center of them, leaving them to slump and give way all about her, as she bolted for the largest ones hovering at a distance. Something hot and liquid ran down the side of her face.

Come on, little Meirydhi. I have something for you, only for you. It came from inside her, from the ground beneath her, and her head spun with that burning, fizzing cold, even as the air grew hot around her.

For me... She blinked as the black hit her full-force, swallowing her up for a moment that felt like an age. It was so *fucking cold*. It burned behind her eyes, making them swell and ballooning her skin until she turned numb.

In another blink, all was as it had been. Her eyes and skin were untouched but for the soot falling around her, the presence of which caused her to stop with a suddenness that left her reeling. Holding out an arm with which to halt Zech, she looked around.

It was impossible.

Tilting her face upward, she gazed up the side of the *Jauynë Rypchë*. Its craggy, blackened slopes loomed directly in front of her, and its peak oozed liquid flame. Superheated bliss razed through her gut. The travel from the High City to the *Rypchë* was at *least* a day... She'd been running supernaturally fast, but even then, this was impossible.

Beside her, Zech's body shook with awe and mirrored confusion. She rested her extended, adrenaline-jittered hand on his chest.

"Don't go any closer." Her voice was raspy as she wiped blood from her jaw. "You'll be burned."

He rested his hand on hers, and their veins made a network of sacred magic where they glowed over his heart. "What about you?"

The mountain rumbled again, and the lava pools ahead gurgled with the disturbance. Something in her roared in response.

"It's only calling me." She looked back at his face, shining silvery-grey eyes alert with excitement and reverence. "I'll be alright, watchman."

He gave her hand a yank and grabbed her by the chin, giving her rough and messy kiss. Warmth seeped into her, filled her with a steadiness that gave her adrenaline resilience. She bit his lip, finding his auburn hair with a sooty hand and holding him close to her for a moment.

"I'll be back." She whispered it against his mouth.

"Better be." He nipped her lower lip, scraping his teeth over the dip above her chin. "Go *burn*, firestarter."

Go burn.

She stepped away from him with a little shove and a crazed grin. "I'll burn."

Come on, little Meirydhi...

Her chest tugged her forward, and Zech stood at her back, a force of unmoveable faith.

This pull was different. Or, no, it was the same, but it was... closer. Stronger. Heavier in her body. The lava pools grew larger as she walked forward, their burbling heat creeping up over the edges and oozing toward her as though they knew she was their little *Rypchë* god. There was a rumbling sludge of lava from the peak that slowly wept down the side of the mountain, and there was a response in Jauyne... a heaving giddiness that surged wildly through her gut and out the palms of her hands. Pure delight soared through the small container of her body. She was endless and infinite and invincible here, and her body was just an odd observer.

She gazed into the lava pools as she passed them, the liquid fire reflecting her Sarlight back to her in waves of heat-shimmered air. She wanted to *bathe* in them. For a moment, she thought she saw face looking back at her from one of the simmering pools, a clean and tired version of herself with a grey sweater and ceramic mug clutched in her hands beneath hopeful eyes. A mirage if she'd ever seen one.

A zinging slice of cold shot through the heat, and cranked her head upward.

A brilliant streak of silver cut through the hot, roiling black of the sky. It *screamed* in Jauyne's veins, in her ears, in her skin, and it *demanded* her with a vengeful ownership.

She moved. Fast. Like before. Bolting toward the silver line slicing through the clouds. It was falling, shooting toward the earth— toward the volcano. Jauyne climbed. Gripping hot stone and sharp edges as she took boulders in leaps. Vents leaked lava to either side of her, heating the air to unbearable degrees. Blood crept from her ears and nose. Her cut hands dripped red onto the rock. She was so close...

Wait for me... I'm coming, I swear.

Hurry, little Meirydhi...

A cry of desperation and exertion ripped from her throat as she hoisted herself over a final crest and stood, dripping sooty, bloody sweat, at the summit.

The crater was the most beautiful thing she had ever seen. A simmering, bawling container of glistening orange and gold, weeping riotously over its own boundaries and causing the air to shiver in awe around it. *The Stars beneath the ground... The closest we have to our creators on Allesar...* she'd heard it all before, seen it from a distance, but here, inches from where it birthed itself from the center of the earth, she felt her eyes overflow with veneration and wonder.

There was a part of her that was birthing itself, too. Erupting. Weeping. Spilling over. This was her land. Her soul. And here was where the Stars were calling her name. She reached up toward the swirling clouds with a hand, extended like she could run her fingers through all their rippling shades of black. The ground shivered, and she felt the crackle before it happened...

Her hair bristled. Her skin ran prickling with burning cold. Her heart stuttered with excitement. Starlight hovered behind her eyes.

Lightning struck.

The purple arc kissed her fingers with a searing blaze.

Her heart stopped.

And her body gasped, her Starlight pausing, before she filled with a lurching brightness. She gripped the very edge of the purple scream of energy as it extended a branch to the crater in front of her.

Her very soul tasted flame.

The connection was unbearable joy. A silence so utter and complete, devoid even of the beat of her heart, that only her delight had room to exist. The space between the strike and the release lasted eons... Lightning submerging in the sunken fire of the *Jauynë Rypchë*, in the subdermal fire of Jauyne's Starlight... Purple whip and orange ocean melding into ferocious, incandescent amalgamation...

Jauyne was the polestar of it all.

When the lightning retracted, and the thunder groaned, she stood. The Premier of Meirydh, with smoke still wisping from black-tipped fingers.

And the silver streak plummeted into the heart of the *Rypchë*, just steps from her stance on the summit. The ground shook and split under the power of Starlight, and without a thought, Jauyne leaned forward towards blazing rock, her smoking yet whole hand extended toward the thing that had been calling her name.

It screamed with her closeness. A large clear crystal, double-terminated, settled into a nest of oozing magma at the crater's edge.

Her hand dipped down, curling into the lava and grasping the crystal. Her skin sang, veins hissing with memory and Starlight, the lava coating her hand and sloughing off in great drips of molten fire. It slunk down the sides of the clear crystal, stars and flashes of lightning reflected in its facets.

Home home home home home, it warbled at her.

Tangles and tendrils of metal protruded from the lower end of the crystal, pricking her forearm as she cradled it. Her blood ran hot as streams of it poured from her nose and eyes. Whispers, familiar and too far-off to place, danced in her ears. She bent her head forward to the Starstone, the last licking drops of lava falling from her arms.

"You're home," she whispered to it, and lightning seized, striking the crater once more. "You're home with me."

DON'T

19
RUN AND
DON'T LOOK BACK

OSIYS, BRIGONAN/NAREHEN BORDER ROAD
1 month, 4 days since the sack of Meirydh

The most undetectable road to Pallydh was, as expected, not an easy one, but it was one which the enemy had not yet discovered— well-concealed and perilous. It cut first through the mountains, treacherously slim walkways carved into rock, punctuated by large trees crashed over ravines.

When he looked down, it was several hundred feet to the bottom of the waterfall they were attempting to cross, and his feet were easily upset by the wet moss and algae that had long been growing on the fallen long. It was no wonder Enoch had refused the horses Herran had offered. As his feet once again found solid rock— however slim and crumbling— Osiys gripped the side of the mountain with white knuckles hinging nimble fingers. It took them three days to move through that portion of the journey. They slept sitting on the shallow ridges, strapped tightly to the mountain rock that remained flat at their backs, while their feet dangled thousands of feet above the forest floor.

When Osiys woke, it was to the imagined feeling of falling, and he had to immediately calm his skittering heartbeat. He swallowed, untying himself just as Enoch had showed him. Baird was with them as well, never missing a chance for a sarcastic comment or cheery insult. It was good for him, to have Baird there. A reminder that he wasn't going back to that house of death in Canestry.

A reminder that that part of his life was over. As long as someone from his good, beautiful Brigonan life, he could hang on to the tether of hope that had tied itself to his heart like the thinnest of threads.

He blinked in the morning sun, dazzling even in as it crept over the far horizon. Pink and orange bled through the sky, painting clouds and atmosphere alike in a glorious portrait of hope and promise. His eyes watered from the brightness. He clipped the gnawing blame that held on to his heart with brutal talons, and rose to his feet to follow Enoch. They were clambering down the mountain now, in steep sections that had him skidding flat-footed, pebbles flying over the edge.

The memory of bloodied knees and knuckles flashed in his mind, that aching urge to topple over the rickety wooden posts and freefall til he was with the Stars. He flexed his hands, loosened his jaw, forced out a breath. He wasn't going to be that person any longer. He wasn't going to be weak anymore... no matter how much he deserved a distinctly horrible death. All the things he'd done... He clipped the feeling again, swallowing it into a solid lump. Behind him, Baird was looking all around, giddily taking in the Mountain views.

"Damn, I'm going to miss these mountains." He made a wincing face at Osiys. "I won't miss this trail."

Osiys smiled a bit. Yes, he was glad Baird was with them.

Enoch said nothing, but a small smile tugged at his cheeks.

They continued— down, down— until they reached a broader place, a cave with a large ledge overlooking the forest. They were just above tree line now. So close to that forest floor, the damp smell of growing things drifted up through the coniferous branches, and Osiys inhaled contentedly.

Enoch suggested they spread out on the ledge to eat their midday meal, and Osiys and Baird agreed enthusiastically. Baird scampered to the edge, dangling his feet as he ate a chunk of dried venison and a hunk of bread. Osiys was content to sit a few feet further from the ledge, stretching his legs out in front of him as he tilted back onto his elbows and let the sun beat down on his face. A cool mountain breeze swept through, shushing through the trees, and chilling the sweat beaded on his face.

If only all the world could just be a mountain ledge with sunshine and abundant food and drink... The pleasantness was almost enough to make him forget why he was here with these two, why they chose the brutal mountain pass instead of the ease of the forested road.

Enoch took a gulp from the water jug and wiped his mouth on his sleeve. "What I wouldn't give for some coffee." His voice nearly startled Osiys and Baird; he had scarcely spoken the whole past two days. "My town, just outside the High City, was famous for our coffee. So rich and deep, notes of honey and nuts... They burned the trees down as they came through— the Canestryn soldiers."

Osiys winced. He had been a simple foot soldier in those early days undercover in Canestry, and he recalled marching on the province of Pallydh. He wasn't sure if he was prepared for Enoch to know that yet— for anyone to know. No one would ever be able to hold all of the horrors he'd seen, and, worse, been the harbinger of. Not Indra, with her firm innocence and unnatural wisdom. Not Baird, with his unending humor and compassionate eyes. Not Elryh, with her soft expressions and too-gentle mannerisms. No, he was the only one who would bear it. That shame and hatred clawed its way back up the column of his throat.

"I'm sure it was delicious," was all he could offer.

Enoch smiled. "It was. At least the coffee trees on the other side of the city remain intact, though they're not quite the same."

Even Baird's shoulders seemed to sag.

At last Enoch hopped to his feet, dusting off his pants with his hands, and began to pack up what was left of their lunch. Osiys joined him, tucking the waxy paper around the remaining dried meat and tying it with the cord. He stuffed it into the leather pack.

The sun was at its apex, and Baird squinted against it as he swung his legs back onto solid rock and took a final swig of the water before placing the water jug alongside the wrapped meat in the pack. He clapped a hand on Enoch's shoulder in a quiet show of endearment.

"Well," he set his hands on his hip bones, elbows jutting out. "Better get a move on, I suppose. It would be good to be back under the cover of the trees before nightfall."

Enoch nodded. "If we move quickly, we can be back in the woods even before that. It's not far to the road from here."

They quickly tossed the packs over their shoulders and continued the pressing pace down the mountain, moving quicker as the path widened and became more suitable for brisk movement. Before too long, they were in the lush forest, pushing forward towards the southeast, where the road between Provinces ran. Osiys treasured the scent of the place, the little skittering noises that small creatures made, the rough reddish bark of the towering trees as he brushed his fingers against it. It was peace, here in the Brigonan forest.

He wondered how long it would be before Canestryn torches burned it to the ground.

They had been waiting in the edges of the forest for nearly an hour, and Enoch was getting fidgety. Baird was twirling one of his knives between his thumb and forefinger, occasionally using a nearby tree as target practice. His golden brown curls fell over his forehead, and he brushed them away to concentrate as he let another knife fly free into the great trunk across from him.

Baird had a sword slung across his back and more knives strapped to his legs. Osiys absentmindedly felt his own body for the familiar leather and metal of his own weapons lining his torso and thighs— three throwing knives, a long dagger, and his sword. He fingered the hilt of his knives, comfortingly. He was a good spotter— he'd frequently been placed on the wall for his good eyesight— and his eyes swept the road, back and forth. It was mostly bare earth on either side of it, with the exception of some large scraggly bushes to the opposite side. As it was wide-open, it would be easy to see, should anyone be coming down the road.

Finally, in the distance: two horses.

One was small and grey-dappled, the other a huge white creature. The horses began to slow as they neared the place where Osiys, Baird, and Enoch waited in the woods. On the white steed, sat a man with bronzed skin and traditional Pallydhan clothing. His neck was a column of muscle, his jaw square and wide. His hands moved deftly to grasp the reigns of the dappled horse.

"Finnan," Enoch nodded to him.

The grey horse carried two children— a girl who might have been twelve and a little boy perhaps half her age. Their skin was ebony and their thick black hair rumbled over their shoulders, pulled away from their faces with orange cloth.

Baird sent out a bird call from behind the tree. He was no longer throwing his knives, but held one in each hand, steady and aware. Finnan answered it in turn, lifting a hand to cup his lips as he replied. He began to lead the horses toward the tree line.

Osiys, Baird, and Enoch ambled out of their hiding places and waded through the brush to the edge of the bright dirt road. The children stared at them with huge brown eyes, the girl fisting her hands in her horse's mane as she saw the weapons strapped to the bodies of the three men moving towards her. Osiys's heart strained a bit— that protective fear in her eyes, the determination and desperation. He wished he could soothe her, but instead the frantic beat of his heart echoed what he saw in her eyes.

"These two are children of a friend of mine." Finnan tugged the children down from the back of the horse. They stood slightly behind him, eyeing the three of them. Baird pulled a face, and the girl smiled softly, before twisting it into a humorless smirk. "Hanna and Boris. Their... Their father was killed and their mother taken. They need a safe place to live."

Osiys didn't leave them a moment to feel concern. "Enoch made sure we were expecting them. They will be safe in the High Circle of Brigon."

He and Baird stepped up onto the road to gather the children. Osiys was readying himself to ask about what Finnan was planning to do with the horses when a soft zipping sound raced past his ear. His whole body tensed, and he swept the road with his eyes. A glint— a glint in the bushes. These bastards were hiding in the bushes to ambush fucking *children*.

A figure leapt from the bushes and sprinted forward. Daggers flashed in his hands as he swung back-handed at the dappled horse, leaving a fatal gash in its neck as the creature sprayed blood. It sloshed, warm and thick on Osiys's face, and he gritted his teeth, daggers already in his hands. His heart raced, whether from fear or adrenaline he wasn't sure, as his concentration fell pointedly to the soldier. Their blades met in the air with a sharp clang as Osiys side-stepped to stand in front of Hanna. She screamed, and the sound clung to his ears.

Two more figures dashed out of the bushes; another remained behind, armed with a bow and arrows. The others were pincering them towards the woods. The white horse fell with a gurgling neigh, the brightness of its coat now stained red.

One of them attempted to wedge between Osiys and Baird, but Baird met the man's blade with one of this own, complemented by the vicious snarl on his lips. "Canestryn fucker. You really stooping to hunting kids now? Sick." The man spat, swinging at him again.

Osiys didn't have time to keep him in check or warn him to cut the wrathful conversation. The person in front of him was a skilled warrior, and they were a bit too evenly matched for Osiys's liking. He ducked a swiping blow, just to deliver one of his own— straight under the arm and through the ribs. A harsh stutter came from the man's throat, and Osiys removed his knife, letting the man's blood pour out freely onto the grass.

Pain splintered through his left arm. Shit. He'd forgotten about the archer in the bushes, and now he had a barbed— *barbed! Fuck!*— arrow embedded in his skin. It had definitely broken bone.

He didn't have time for this. He needed to get Baird and these children safe. Needed to get back behind the doors of a refuge where there were warm fires and hot tea and Indra and Elryh and Berg.

His bones groaned. *What in Star's name was that arrow laced with?* A searing, leadening pain was spreading through his limbs, and he struggled to focus, to lift his dagger.

He whirled to Baird who was now taking on two of the attackers. They were ignoring him entirely now, after watching the arrow find its mark, as though they knew... as though they knew he was collapsing, imploding, burning, fading... *Stars be damned!*

Baird screamed.

It was an unnatural, guttural, desperate sound that reverberated through Osiys's skull. Osiys stumbled forward, helplessly, desperately, as the attacker flashed an evil grin at him. Stars, his body was so heavy... He couldn't get to him in time... He— The attacker took the two daggers embedded beside Baird's shoulder blades and dragged them through his flesh, racketing against his ribs, til they hit his hip bones. Baird's scream cut short, his eyes glazed, and his body slumped on the red dirt. Deep red blood gushed from his body, soaking the dirt into a mud that groped for Osiys's boots.

Osiys' body felt as though it was sinking in black, cold water as he watched Finnan and Enoch cut down one of the two remaining attackers. The ground was reverberating now, making his knees warble, and he at last realized that three more men on horses were approaching. The attacker who was still alive shuffled to Osiys' side, shoving him to sit on the ground. Osiys could do nothing as his mind turned to mud and the world whirled around him. "Run," he felt his lips saying. "Run, and don't look back."

The trees seemed to crash into the ground behind Osiys as his head lurched back and an agonizing spasm wracked his body.

Baird is dead Baird is dead Baird is dead.

Baird's eyes were open and glazed, his face still contorted with shock and pain. The flesh of his back was splayed open like gruesome wings.

Good, kind Baird, who had been alongside him since they were just boys, who had urged him on to his lover and supported him, despite his terror and reservations, when Osiys chose to go to Canestry.

To Osiys, it was as if the symbol of all that was joy and lightness and hope in the world had been gutted bloody on the dirt.

NEED

20
I'VE SEEN YOUR STAR CHARTS

The wooden planks of the floor were cold underfoot, sending a chill up Indra's bones till it reached her arm and she shivered with full force. It was then, mid-shiver, that she remembered that she was alone here in Brigon, and that grand and impossible things were expected of her, and that she was entirely unsure whether or not she could fulfill these expectations.

She sighed, louder than she'd expected, and vigorously rubbed her arms with freezing hands.

Why is it so cold?

She stuffed her feet numbly into furred slippers that came up around her ankles and found a velvety soft robe to wrap around the thin silky fabric she had worn to sleep. Glancing at the door, she groaned. She didn't want to go wander the halls, getting lost for what surely must be the fiftieth time in the last several weeks, trying to figure out how to solve some mystery that hung over the whole world.

What she wanted was to go back to bed. With a sudden air of impulsivity that rarely showed itself in her except for dire circumstances, she dove back into the huge, soft bed, pulling the furs and soft fabrics round her shivering limbs, even as she kicked off the slippers.
Indra squeezed her eyes shut, snuggling deeper into her pillow, but the feeling was still there- that sad, uncertain feeling to which she hadn't yet grown accustomed. She nestled her face fully into the pillow and let out a sound of exasperation.

Osiys was the reason she'd left Canestry. If she'd known she would wind up on her own with people she didn't know, in a Province that was foreign to her, with a mystery that involved the whole world, and some grand identity or destiny she hoped wasn't real... well, then she never would have left Canestry.

That was not exactly true. But it would be easier if it was.

"This was not part of the plan," she muttered into the pillowcase.

She flopped around onto her back, pulling the covers up around her chin as she stared at the ceiling with annoyance. It was wood-planked but painted white and then detailed in picturesque images of mountains, flowers, and wild horses. Most mornings, she began her day by gazing up at it, allowing the peaceful scene to calm her before she ventured out into the unknown which was Brigon. But this morning it was as thought the peacefulness of it mocked her. She mentally chided herself for being so petty- so her friend had left for a bit. Why was it causing her to behave like a toddler? He would be back. Osiys always came back for her.

But she had been right, after all, in the great hall when she'd cried into his shoulder and he had cried into hers- they were family. And in her case, he was the only family she had left. There was no circumstance in which her father made the cut for family any longer. She wondered if he ever had. But Osiys... from the moment she'd met him, she'd known he was her family.

Safety, calm, joy... that was what family was supposed to feel like, right? And had anyone ever made a rule that you couldn't go finding what family was meant to give you, if the people who shared your blood denied you those things? Perhaps some would frown on it, she supposed, but if that was the only way to have a family, then she also supposed she didn't really care. So, she wasn't behaving like a toddler- she granted herself this realization. She just... missed her family. A sensation entirely new to her and not in the least enjoyable.

A groan rumbled up from her chest, and she pressed the heels of her hands to her eyes before working her fingers through her long hair. She needed to get up if she wanted any breakfast. There, her stomach growled with insistence. Heaving herself upright, she dashed quickly to the bath room where her clothes had been laid out the night before- a long-sleeved shirt made out of a heavy green satin, with golden embroidery on the collar and sleeves, and velvet wide-leg pants in a dashing evergreen. There was also a warm, black, fur-lined jacket that overlapped in the front to keep out the chill. Black, fur-lined boots had been set beside it all, with knit socks tucked inside. She pulled them all on quickly, goosebumps prickling her skin as she rushed.

Once she was done, she smoothed her unruly hair briefly in the mirror, before giving up and tying it back at the nape of her neck with a strip of matching green velvet fabric. She sighed, surrendering to the purplish half-moons blooming under her eyes, and walked briskly out the door, her boots clicking on the wooden floor.

She made her way to the Great Hall- the one place she seemed to always know how to find in this maze of rooms and hallways stuck precariously to the side of the mountain. One of the guards opened it for her with a nod and a small smile- they were always so kind here, even if they were strangers. Waiting for her at the table was Elryh, the rest having either gone with Osiys or cleared out after their breakfast long ago. Elryh sat in front of the fire, her empty plate nearly scraped clean, a cup of tea in her hands. She turned as she heard the heavy door groan open, and her face broke into a smile. Patting the fur on the floor beside her, she beckoned Indra over to sit beside her.

"Come sit, Indra dear. Get warm. Oh! But first get some breakfast." She motioned to the table.

There was a wooden dome placed on the tabletop, and Indra lifted it to see a steaming plate of eggs, sausages, bacon, root vegetables, and biscuits. Beside the silver dome was a small wooden bowl of fruit, which she picked up along with the large plate, and walked over to the large fur rug balancing the two dishes. Elryh reached up and took the larger plate from her so that she could sit more easily, then placed it on Indra's lap once her legs were folded over the dark brown fur.

"How are you feeling? I cannot imagine this is easy for you." Elryh asked it solemnly, looking into the fire as she readjusted the way her fingers interlaced around her mug.

Indra poked at the plate of fruit, trying to find a familiar piece. She shrugged helplessly, thankful that Elryh had mercifully chosen not to look at her while waiting for an answer. "He's my family. How can't I feel?"

Stubbornly refusing to cry, she popped a chunk of pineapple into her mouth and focused on the way the tart sweetness flooded her tongue, so juicy it made her jaw ache.

Elryh let out a sad little sigh, tilting her head to one side and finally turning her gaze to Indra. "It's alright to miss him. It's alright to miss family. It just..." Her thin mouth twisted as though it was trying to find the words somewhere behind her teeth. "It just means your heart has been tender enough to make some space in there for them, doesn't it? That's what I like to hope, anyhow, when I feel the same."

Indra swallowed the pineapple and met Elryh's eyes with her own glowing, Starlit ones. "Is all your family not here in Brigon?"

A long sip of tea preceded her answer. "Some of my family is in Brigon, yes. My younger brother lives here, in the High City itself. I have a half-sister and a niece who live out in the mountain villages past the High City. I came here to live permanently a few years ago, when I received the invitation from Herran to be on the High Council of Brigon. Before that, when I was very small, I lived with my family out in the villages. When I was thirteen, my parents and young sister were killed in an earthslide." She tilted her head again when she said it with a quizzical expression, as though it was something she had never considered before, as though it was something that required pondering.

Indra felt her breath hitch beneath her shoulder blades.

"I miss them every day." Elryh's voice was soft, wistful. "I lived with strangers, friends, until I could be on my own. Osiys' family took me in for a while, even. But I know what it can be like to miss your family."

A sudden heat rose in Indra's cheeks that wasn't from the warmth of the fire. "Oh, I can't pretend to understand..."

"Shh," Elryh interrupted her with a wave of her hand. "We both miss them. Let's not deliberate who misses more. It's alright to just leave it at that." Her smile was back.

It was a strange way to be comforted, but the comfort settled into her with a warm fullness, just as surely as the biscuits and meat and eggs did. Elryh refilled her tea twice while Indra finished eating.

At last Elryh poked Indra with the toe of her boot. "Best hurry. I'm meant to show you to all the places you'll have access to in order to study the mysterious appearances of the Starstone and answer any of your questions. Here." She reached up to take another mug from the young man who had walked over to them. This one was full of coffee, sweetened with honey and with milk stirred in. Handing it to Indra, Elryh cleared the plates from her lap and handed them to the young man who was standing patiently beside them still. "Come along then!"

Indra hurried to her feet as quickly as she could without spilling the mug of fresh coffee. Elryh walked as though she were waltzing- relaxed, sweeping steps skimming the floor as she made her way to the large doors, Indra in tow. The mug was heavy and warm in her small hands, and gave her something to cling to as her nerves fluttered in the pit of her stomach. She tried to drown them with a gulp of the coffee, unsuccessfully.

"Firstly," Elryh began, glancing sideways to be sure that Indra was keeping up with her, "The Starstones themselves are being kept in the lower chambers of the Greathouse. You can keep your distance from there, as we don't want you to be injured again."

The hearing in Indra's left ear was still dull and plugged feeling. She brushed the tips of her fingers against her left earlobe, subconsciously, wincing at the memory of that awful pain splintering through her head. But the voice... that had been so different, so clear, so soft and bright, unlike the raging scream of the Starstone. Indra blinked out of the memory, Elryh still speaking.

"We have in our care two Starstones- one found here in Brigon, as well as the one which Enoch brought from Nareilë. We know that Osiys and Enoch are going to retrieve the Starstone from Pallydh, and that there are two more- Adras the Oracle of Jopaar is on her way with a mission to bring their Starstone to us, among other details which I have not been made privy to. And there was a Starstone that fell in Chedhiy, which is now missing. They had sent a messenger with it to Meirydh before the attack, but he has not been heard from since. Apparently, a member of their mountain guard went in search of him, but he has not, as of yet, made contact."

Indra was tallying the Starstones in her head. "So that leaves... Meirydh and Canestry. If they are, in fact, falling in each of the Seven Provinces, that is..."

Elryh grinned at her. "That is my Intuition, precisely. Don't you worry about a thing. You will have me to help you as you unravel all of this. As well as Valeryn."

At Indra's quizzical glance, Elryh produced a key from the pocket of her billowing pants, pausing as they reached a door. Elryh turned the key in its lock and opened it, stepping inside and gesturing to Indra to follow her.

Despite herself, a wide-eyed grin bloomed on her face. It was a vast library, like one she'd only dreamt of, as a word-hungry child growing up in a land that wanted nothing more than to suppress widespread knowledge. Her fingers splayed, itching to feel the worn edges of the leather bound volumes contained here.

The library was a wide place, with three small spiraled stairs in the view that her vantage point in the doorway gave her. To her right, they weren't far from the wall, which, along with the high bookshelves, was lined with five large wooden desks. These were each equipped with a lamp, papers, ink, and some other little things which Indra didn't stop her gazing to comprehend. The library extended far to her left, and the shelves, heavy-laden with tomes from countless authors, reached to the height of the ceiling. It was an odd room, with stairs and platforms placed at seemingly random points throughout, with the exception of one platform in the center of the room, which contained a strange circular fireplace with a metal beam reaching to the ceiling. Indra could feel the hunger in her as the sweet, earthy scent of leather and pungent binding glue reached her senses. She was so enthralled, so speechless, that she had entirely forgotten the name Elryh had spoken mere moments before. So, when a tousle-haired young man scrambled up from behind one of the wooden desks to her right, sending papers fluttering and books skidding, Indra quite actually startled enough to jump.

"Oh! Hello! So sorry, I'm afraid I lost track of time." He was shoving his wire-rimmed glasses further up his nose, collecting the papers he'd sent flying. "I was cataloguing the new information we've gotten about the Starstones. I haven't been down yet to study them for myself- it's mostly just been the mages so far- but I was headed there now."

Elryh regarded him with a quiet amusement in her eyes. "This is Valeryn. This," she nodded towards Indra, "is Indra. Valeryn is my younger brother. He is being trained to care for our Province's histories, myths, legacy in written word. He'll help you find whatever you need in this place that might provide valuable insight. He has also been instructed to guide you wherever you need to go in the Greathouse and to study the Starstones firsthand in your place, to avoid injury."

Valeryn waded through the desks and stacks of books, freshly inked paper crinkling in his right hand as he extended his left one to Indra. Black smudges of ink decorated the sides of his hands and forearms, where his shirtsleeves had been rolled up. Indra clasped his hand, unused to being recognized in such a capacity, and it was warm and firm as it enveloped her own.

"Indra is the princess of Canestry and the rightful Premier when her father is unseated. She arrive just shy of two weeks ago, and is here to study the Starstones, as you know, little brother."

Indra's head whirled... and the rightful Premier... She had not even considered this possibility. It was certainly not a part of any plan which her mind had devised. Struggling to hear the rest of Elryh's introduction, Indra strained to force the astonishment out of her thoughts and instead focused on the curve of Valeryn's mouth as he grinned.

"I've seen your Star charts!" He tugged on her hand before releasing it, urging her to follow him as he scrambled back to the desk he'd been working at. "They're magnificent, truly. Such attention to detail, and beautiful flourishes. A work of art, really."

He was brushing other papers off the desk now, revealing her Star chart beneath where they'd lain on the wooden surface, and they floated to the floor. Indra followed, curious, skimming leather and parchment with the tips of her fingers as she brushed past the bookshelves. Elryh laughed lightly from her place by the door.

"I'll leave you two to your hermitage," she teased. "Don't forget to give her a key and show her about, Valeryn."

"Of course not!" He called, not bothering to divert his eyes from the desk. Then, in reply to her pause in the doorway. "Move along, sister!"

She laughed and closed the door behind her, but Indra was already leaning over the desk, amazed and a bit honored to see her very own Star chart being held in such high regard in a library this prestigious. She trailed the lines of ink across the paper, memory pricking the edges of her mouth into a smile. She recalled the day she'd dragged Osiys into the little closet to show him this very same rolled up piece of parchment, recalled the way he'd believed her, recalled the way he'd try to leave without her, recalled the way he'd just left Brigon without her, too. She chewed the inside of her lip.

"I'm sure this has all been a bit overwhelming." Valeryn had stuffed his hands in his pockets, looking at her instead of the chart. "It's alright with me, though. I'm well accustomed to having one's life uprooted. And," he threw his arms wide, stepping backwards with a grin that was more knowing than gleeful, "books always understand. That's why I wanted to apprentice here, you know. I like books better than I like most people."

That claim made Indra's chest bubble with laughter, and his eyes crinkled back at her, sparking with delight. "Yes," Indra nodded at him, looking around at the stairs, ladders, and desks, all sprawling with books. "I've always wanted a library. They were all destroyed in Canestry- all accept the High Mage's library, and I was never allowed in there. It's just as warm and lovely as I used to imagine it might be."

"That makes me so glad! I'll admit I tend to judge others based on their fondness of libraries."

Indra laughed again. It felt good, a lightness she'd needed.

Valeryn rubbed his palms together and leaned over the desk once again. "Alright then. It's high time we get to work."

TO

21

YOUR BEAU THERE

1 month, 1 week since the sack of Meirydh

Adras got the sense that Jauyne was used to people being intimidated by her. Unfortunately for the spindly, harsh little person that she was, Adras was not easily intimidated. Granted, they had had to catch their breath for a few moments upon witnessing just how deep her power ran. And once she returned with the Starstone, skin still smudged with black from her apparent encounter with lightning and lava, Adras had had to reorient themself a bit. But after their many pilgrimages into the Jopaari wilderness, there wasn't much that Adras feared. The anti-alloy factions, yes. The strange beast in the snow cave all those years ago, that had once made a lunge toward their legs with teeth big and sharp enough to sever them from their body, yes.

But the Meirydhi heir— or, Premier now, they supposed— despite her power and snappish attitude, was not something that Adras feared.

Lumen shifted on his feet, his pack hoisting a bit higher on his back. He looked as though he were itching to kill, his edge honed by all the death that surrounded them. Adras couldn't help but echo the sentiment in their chest.

It had been over a month since the slaughter had taken place, and the stiff, purplish bodies were covered in flies and reeked of death. Jauyne was now tiredly walking down the steps of the city, ducking through the open gates as she adjusted her obsidian dagger on her hip and tied her loose wrap shirt into into a hasty, sloppy knot above her brown suede riding pants. Adras could see the outline of the bangle she wore beneath the shirt— a tribute to her home. They absentmindedly drew the tip of a finger down the silver cuff they wore along the shell of their ear, a twin to the golden one Jauyne had reattached to her own ear.

Zech followed not far behind, trying, not too discreetly, to tie the draw-string of his dark leather riding pants. Lumen muttered under his breath

breath something about the Stars giving him patience to deal with these useless children fucking like rabbits. Adras thought it best not to remind him that Jauyne was one year his elder.

"Ready?" Adras didn't wait for the two to get within twenty yards of them before they adjusted the pack that was slung over their shoulders and turned to the worn path that stretched into the Chedhiyn portion of the vast mountain range.

Jauyne cursed under her breath, and Lumen had to visibly restrain himself from mirroring every one of those curses back at her. Adras swallowed a laugh and clapped a hand on the back of Lumen's shoulder, letting him see the humor and irritation in their eyes. Lumen only snorted, but a smile crossed his face.

This was such a strange way to travel— to have to think about the others with them, to consider the number of them when their eyes darted to possible sleeping or hiding arrangements in the wild. They were unused to traveling in a party. Even simply traveling with Lumen had been strange, though comforting, if they were honest. But with Zech and Jauyne, it was a constant practice in patience.

Jauyne was every bit as prickly as she'd been that first night, letting glimpses of the woman beneath the firecat show for mere seconds at a time, but she seemed more dappled with a heavy exhaustion. Adras couldn't decide if they respected the commitment to such a mask, or if it annoyed them to voids. Probably both.

Usually both. Zech was far more accommodating, but the haunted storm that rippled under his skin was something that made Adras wary, and it was clear where his loyalties and feelings laid. Adras struggled to understand the two of them, how they'd managed to find any sort of companionship when they were both so intensely guarded.

They all travelled in utter silence, the only sounds being that of far-off birds cawing and the scratching together of the dry white grasses in the mild breeze.

It was Lumen who suggested the cover of the trees for their night's rest. Adras was impressed— though he hadn't had their training in survival skills, he had listened well and long to what he had been handed, and had grown that skill through patience, frustration, trial and error. The lightning storm had ended hours ago, and though the ground was damp, there were no clouds to shower them in freezing rain. His training was as a warrior and strategist, and he applied both to the way he scouted out their campsite.

They made their way to the small clump of sytril trees and shucked off their packs, all four rolling their shoulders and massaging the backs of their necks.

Jauyne gave a small frown around the clearing but said nothing. Lumen glared sidelong at her. Zech, noting the silent interaction, lifted his eyes to the darkening sky as though he were praying for strength to withstand it. It nearly made Adras bark a laugh, but they swallowed it down, the quirking up of one side of their lips the only indication they'd seen it at all.

Lumen squatted beside his pack, unlatching it and beginning to dig out the food he had stored in one of the inner compartments. "There's a small stream that way." He gestured with his elbow to a space behind the trees opposite the path. "We can wash up and refill our waterskins there."

"I know where the water flows in my own Starsdamned province." Jauyne was muttering to herself, her hands jammed into her own pack.

Lumen splayed a hand to his chest in mock humility. "Oh, pardon me, Premier. Please, tell us the location of all the rivers and streams in your mighty Province."

Adras tensed as Jauyne did, and she let out a low growl to Lumen. A feral creature ought not be prodded; he was just being stupid. "Don't provoke her, dumbass."

The warning was only met with his irritated glare, but Jauyne was already spinning around to face him, her eyes frigid pools of rage, intersected by that nasty scar.

"Fuck off, Jopaari, or I'll show you how I respond to outsiders who mouth off to me."

The grin that crept across Lumen's face dragged a groan from Zech, who no doubt knew Jauyne's next move before she made it. Fast as lightning, and presumably as deadly, the scrawny Meirydhi Premier had unsheathed the long dagger at her thigh and twirled it nimbly. It was made of obsidian that shimmered gold where it caught the light, cut and polished jagged like a bolt of lightning. The power in the woman crackled beneath her skin, flickers of silver light dancing between her fingers and across the lethal edges of the dagger.

It was enough to stir a squirming unease in Adras' stomach, enough to cause them to place a warning hand on Lumen's shoulder; but he just stood slowly, that grin still slinking over his lips. He lifted a hand to finger the hilt of one of his twin swords strapped to his back, the hard-earned muscles in his arm rolling from the motion. "I don't think that would end well for you."

Jauyne's laugh was more incredulity than humor. "I'll have you flat on your back and bound hand and foot before you can even draw those pretty little blades."

He quirked his head to the side, the grin sliding into a smirk. "I appreciate the offer, but your beau there is more my type, darling."

He gave a wink, followed by his tongue running along his teeth as he languidly slung a ravishing look over the full height of Zech, who choked from surprise and went ruddy around the neck.

Jauyne gaped as Zech began to laugh, full-bellied and genuine, until he wiped tears from his eyes with the heel of his hand. Adras couldn't help but huff a silent laugh of their own at the baffled shock on Jauyne's face, and the mischievous arrogance on Lumen's.

Adras planted an elbow in Lumen's ribs, and he dramatically doubled over as she stepped to his side and let her voice hum out dry and humored. "Now that my brother has made the object of his sexual fantasies clear, perhaps we can wash up and collect some wood for a fire?"

Zech gave Adras a nod that could have been construed as friendly before turning to a frowning Jauyne with a chuckle, using a finger to tilt her dagger down. Something he said must have been filthy enough to steal her attention from where she'd been glowering at Lumen's turned back, because she faced Zech with a smirk and shoved him away from her. She sheathed her dagger, and Adras let loose a breath.

Jauyne stalked off to the hidden stream, leaving Adras to wander in the opposite direction for dry brush and wood with which to build their fire. They kept an eye on Lumen and Zech, who both began to fish out bedrolls and food and necessities in uncomfortable silence. Adras swallowed a bitter laugh. How they had all found themselves in this absurd little traveling party was the Stars' guess. And how they'd all make it to the border in one piece was an even riskier guess.

Stretching their tense jaw and rolling their neck, Adras added another fistful of brush to their meager pile. Once they reached Brigon, the work would truly begin, alongside this Canestryn princess who had somehow managed to reach out to Adras's mind, the Starstones their only connection. It was powerful Starlight that awaited them in Indra's person, and it at once both terrified and excited Adras.

A sudden, sharp hum rocketed through Adras' blood, charging the very air with a crackling energy. They snapped their gaze to the camp, their heart lurching. Their feet were pounding the dry grass before their mind could form coherent thought, but they managed to cry out.

"Stop that— put them back!"

The two bundles were still wrapped in their cloth and leather wrappings, but the Starstones had been laid out on the dirt as the packs were emptied. Lumen's face was trained on theirs, confused, but Jauyne burst from the trees on the opposite side of the camp, face twisted into a wince.

"What is that? What are you doing?" It was spat at Lumen, and, to a lesser degree, Zech.

The closer they came to the camp, the more the hum reverberated through their blood, the more their body felt as though it might simply tremble into pieces.

"Me? I—"

Adras cut him off. "Put it back!"

Lumen blinked with confusion, and it was one second too long. Adras grasped the cloth-swaddled bundle that contained the Jopaari Starstone, just as Jauyne reached for the Chedhiyn Starstone in its leather pouch. The air crackled, flickering with light, and Zech's hands flew to the sides of his head with a cry. Pain screamed its way up Adras's arms. A wail echoed in their mind— not their own. Jauyne's?

It's you again... The voice lit the corners of Adras's mind from within, and realization barreled into them.

Indra? Is it you?

Jauyne's snarl of pain echoed next. *Who is this? What are you doing to us?*

Indra audibly recoiled. *I am not doing this! I've not been near my Starstone since it nearly killed me!*

The Starstones have previously connected me with her, Adras admitted, gritting their teeth against the splintering pain in their arm. *We should not have touched our own Starstones at once.*

Then drop yours. The pain was evident in Jauyne's voice.

I'm not sure I trust you not to bully dear Indra.

A prickle of energy shot from the Canestryn Princess. *I am perfectly capable of defending myself. I want to know who you both are.*

I am Premier Jauyne of Meirydh. Jauyne was hoarse with pain. *Who are you?*

My name is Indra. I am the turncoat Princess of Canestry.

Stunned silence emanated from Jauyne, even as Adras thought they could hear notes of sarcasm in the princess's voice. *I was sent to retrieve Jauyne and Zech and bring them to meet you, princess. I am the Allyborn Oracle of Jopaar.*

Are you in pain? Indra's reply was quick.

Jauyne gritted out, *Yes.*

Put the stones down immediately, and get to Brigon as quickly as you can. I will be waiting.

Adras blinked, unseeing, as Lumen painfully pried away another of their fingers from the Starstone, repeatedly growling their name. "Ads, for fuck's sake, where are you right now? I am going to be deeply annoyed if you die and leave me out here with these two."

A thud and huff of air accompanied the sudden emptiness in their hands as Lumen seemingly hit the ground. He was still grumbling as he grunted, catching their falling body with his own. "If you wanted to knock me on my ass, you could have found a less creative way to do it."

"Jauyne... Is she still holding the stone?" Grass roughly scratched at their cheek as Lumen shifted out from under them. Their eyes still saw nothing.

He groaned. "Do I have to save her, too?"

"Lumen!"

There was a sigh and footsteps as he made his way to the opposite side of the clearing. Adras listened to the ensuing scuffle— the grumbling and hissing and snapped demands for thanks— as they desperately tried to recover their sight. Rubbing at their eyes, unsurprisingly, did nothing. Their muscles flickered with remnants of lightning pain.

They attempted to swallow their panic. Indra had sounded well and whole, despite her claims that the last communication through the Starstone had nearly killed her. Perhaps this would simply wear off.

Gulping air, Adras attempted to sit, their body rioting. Jauyne was openly crying out in pain, and the sound was unnerving, coming from her.

"What in seventh dark was that?" Zech was scrambling to his feet behind them. "Stars, what is it doing to her? Jauyne, I'm right here."

"Just hold onto her; she'll drop like a stone when I finally get this out of her hands." Lumen was grappling with the Starstone, huffing with exertion.

Adras' hands and arms still felt full of gaping splinters. A spasm ripped through them with a sudden and unrelenting force, and a spark of pain bloomed in their lip as they bit clean through it. Coppery tang dripped down the back of their throat. The bright taste of panic followed.

The soft thud of bodies hitting dirt registered, followed by the rush of footsteps back to Adras's side.

"Shit. Can you hear me, Adras?"

The stuttering affirmation that left their lips felt slurred. Foreign.

"You need to stay with me, alright, Ads?" Lumen's voice was too high, too tight. "What just happened? How the voids did you bloody your lip?"

Another spasm sliced through them, and they thought they might have screamed. Everything was darkness and shuddering pain and blazing heat. Their body was a series of locked joints and pulsating ribbons of agony. Somewhere that felt very, very far off, Adras had the sense of coolness and light and water... if only they could reach it... if only— another spasm raged across muscle and bone and tendon.

"Zech!" Lumen's voice sounded as though it must be coming from underwater. Adras grasped at empty air.

"Zech." It was an order. It was a command.

It was the last thing Adras heard before the pain shattered their lungs and screeched through their blood like flames.

22

IL ENË LIYD

The begrudging respect that Jauyne felt growing in her towards Adras only did the opposite of warming her to the strange Jopaari Oracle. After all, if she, a newborn Premier without the basic wherewithal to make decent decisions, trusted someone, that person was likely not worthy of it.

Still, Adras had survived what appeared to be a horrific attack of some sort from the Starstones. Even though she herself had been in terrible pain, Adras seemed to have borne the brunt of it, not waking for nearly an entire day. Lumen had been insufferable with fury and panic, but it was understandable, so she had attempted to be kind.

Attempted. Not that it had been well-received.

Jauyne had never thought she'd be so thrilled to see the ever-so-slightly-condescending Jopaari Oracle awake and conscious and talking.

It had been nearly two weeks since that encounter, and the snappish silence had turned into slightly-less-snappish silence, with intermittent bouts of respectfully tactical, if not awkward, conversation. Awkward conversation was the bane of Jauyne's existence— even as a child, she'd preferred long, winding chats that revolved around the book she was currently reading, or astronomy, or perhaps when the next storm was predicted to hit the city.

As an adult, she marveled at how her meager patience for the awkwardness had only seemed to wither. She groaned audibly before she could catch it in her throat.

Adras gave her a sidelong glance, and Jauyne cursed inwardly as she pointed her gaze towards the tree line with intention. The greys and greens of the mountain mist blurring into the blunt beginning of deep green foliage and white tree trunks seemed to settle into her bones with a familiarity that took her by surprise. She swiftly nudged her mind away from the realization that solidity of this land, these colors... they all felt like Zech.

Lumen cleared his throat, and Jauyne felt a bit reproachful of herself when her eyes didn't roll on instinct. Stars be damned, was she going soft?

"It won't be quite nightfall, but we ought to stop early today. I'd rather not confront any border guards in the near dark." Adras shifted the pack on their shoulders with a small smile, then added, "Other than this one."

Because there was nothing inherently wrong with this idea— she almost kicked herself at her own compliance— Jauyne nodded with a quietness that was so cooperative she caught Zech looking at her with concern from the corner of her eye. She shot him a vile look. So help her if he chose to unleash his maddening softness among barely-amicable company. With a subtle motion, he turned over his hands to her in surrender. She turned her eyes back to the mountains that were creeping up to swallow the sky in front of them.

There was something terrifying about their solidness, some terrible sort of steady endlessness that threatened to press down into Jauyne's chest and make her feel safe. And safety was the most dangerous feeling of all. Danger always struck when one gave safety a home in one's heart.

The trees, too, overwhelmed her with solidity. Their trunks were unfeasibly huge. She imagined all four of them could stretch their arms around the papery white bark and still not reach one another's hands.

She hadn't gotten this far before; in fact, to her revengeful amusement, the tree where Zech had blindsided her had been the one they'd camped at the previous night. As they had moved closer under their blankets for warmth, she'd traced a line across the tender skin of his wrists and reminded him that she had rope in her pack if he chose to misbehave again. He'd grinned and whispered back to her, wondering if that threat was supposed to be as enticing as she'd made it sound. That was precisely the moment her regretful acceptance of their foreign company had returned to its usual vibrant loathing.

The mountains were impossibly vast, and she hadn't quite expected the pressure with which their existence greeted her chest. She reasoned with the choked feeling— she was finally going to get help, and it hadn't even been her choice, hadn't been her idea, hadn't been under her authority. At least the chaos of self-loathing was more familiar than the danger of safety.

Rough fingers slid between her own, then gripped tighter when she tried to slip out of their grasp. She didn't look at Zech, but she knew he felt her fright, and she couldn't fault him for being what he was: stupidly good. She squeezed his hand a bit, hoping the surrender would be enough reassurance for him to let her go, and clenched her jaw when he didn't.

Dampness clung to her cloak and crept in towards her clothes as she stepped under the cover of the trees and found herself submerged in mist. Lumen shivered to her left, and her body involuntarily responded in like.

It was as though the forest awakened some deep sense in Zech, and he pushed to the front of their party, the others obediently trailing him in silence. Jauyne could feel the bright, warmth inside of him, sparking and flaring with excitement and adrenaline. His hand buzzed in hers, and she nearly wanted to smile.

She didn't, of course.

Zech wound them through what, to Jauyne, seemed to be a completely aimless path. He stopped every so often to inspect the bark of what to her was a completely inconspicuous tree *here*, or to bend and touch the forest floor *there*, for some unknown reason. They did, however, seem to be navigating towards the mountains.

Little creatures scampered across the forest floor, which was padded with moss and littered with leaves that had made the brave journey downward from untold heights. Now and again, deer stepped pointedly through brush, their sharp hooves and crowns of antlers stealing her breath wondrously. There were so many creatures here that she'd never before seen, so many plants and noises and smells that filled her senses and overwhelmed her; and, for once, her innocence felt like awe instead of shame.

At last, they rounded the trunk of a tree so broad and so tall that Jauyne had to avert her eyes in order to keep her heart from leaping up into her throat. The border watchman of Chedhiy stepped close to the tree, the base of it clear of any brush and litterfall. His fingers danced over the bark in a caress before he looked back over his shoulder at her, at them all.

"Wait here; I'll send a lift down."

"You'll what?" The way she gripped his hand when he tried to pull away thoroughly embarrassed her, and she whipped her hand out of his.

He hid his smirk only a little. Could she get away with smacking him?

"Unless you'd like to try your hand at free climbing without any gloves on—" Lumen wiggled his partially gloved fingers in the air as Zech shook his head. "I don't know what kind of gloves you've got, but they're not Chedhiyn climbing gloves, pal."

As Zech tugged on his own pair of half-gloves, Jauyne peered forward, noticing the nearly-invisible gleam of innumerable short pins poking out from the palms. He kicked off his boots and socks, wiggled his toes in the mossy dirt. With a wink in her direction, he turned, and, to her utter shock and terrified fascination, began scaling the tree.

Pressing his hands against the trunk in steady, upward rhythm, and gripping the papery bark with his feet and toes, he climbed with a quickness that seemed inhuman. She snapped her mouth shut, plastering her arms to her sides to still their frightened shaking, as he disappeared into the gritty barrier of mist.

Her eyes flicked to Lumen and Adras, but they, too, were gaping and dumbfounded at his easy departure. Thoughts rose unbidden to her mind, cynical and catastrophic.

What if he falls? How can I watch him die in front of me? How could he possibly not fall? What the fuck is a lift?

Panic raced the length of her veins, tracking through her body with practiced speed. Horror brought images to her eyes that weren't real, only clouded by other realities. It was as though she could already see his blood against the white of the tree trunks, already feel the thud where he would hit the earth, already—

Her worrying of her lip with her teeth became too rough, and she drew blood. Beside her, Adras was pacing a busy path through the moss.

A hoarse, abrasive sound cut steadily through the damp silence.

The obsidian blade was in her hand without a thought.

The three of them looked round, their backs slowly inching closer together, but the sound seemed to be coming from above them. Swallowing back her fear, Jauyne looked up.

A flat bed of wooden slats lowered slowly down beside the massive tree, ropes creaking, sending all three of them scurrying out from under it in a startled hurry. It settled on the moss almost noiselessly.

Now that it was on the ground alongside them, Jauyne observed it with unbridled skepticism. The little wood-slat floor was double-enforced crosswise and smeared in shades of green and white, presumably to blend in with the trees. From each corner rose a thick tree limb; these were then connected with additional slats of wood that created a sort of barrier. All in all, it looked a bit like a cage, and no way in all the Stars and voids was she putting her life at the mercy of this little rickety thing.

Lumen had crept closer, pressing against the slats and limbs, peering upwards, curiously resting his weight on its edge. Adras followed him gingerly, their brow crinkled with what was either focus or concern, or perhaps both. After a few moments of this tentative inspection, they both clambered onto the strange contraption.

"Well," Adras nodded to her. "Aren't you coming?"

She couldn't seem to move her feet.

"Don't tell me you're afraid of trees." There was laughter in Lumen's voice.

She jutted her chin out, defiant. "Just because I don't have a wish to fall to my death from some obscene height, does not make me afraid of trees." She sounded ridiculous. She felt ridiculous.

Lumen was making a valiant effort at not smiling, which told her that she must look utterly petrified, which was positively humiliating. She had survived a sword to the face and plucked a Starstone right from lava, yet couldn't be maneuvered up the side of a tree without a panic? She wanted to jam one of those stupid tree limbs through her eye. Awkward shuffling came from what she could only assume was the *lift*.

"It's alright, Jauyne." It was Adras' voice. Jauyne's face burned with humiliation. She was so *weak*. She really was fucking afraid of *trees*. "Zech would never put you in danger."

She didn't know how she made it to the lift. Didn't know how she survived the trip to the forest's canopy, nothingness pressing in on her from all sides until she shrunk far inside herself to a place where she was small and invisible. Didn't know how she stepped off the lift and into warm, solid arms. She felt unreal, and the world felt unreal, and she didn't try to fight her way back into corporeality, the way she usually did.

She scarcely registered the jittery grit of Zech's jaw, or the way she was guided across wooden bridges, or the softness of the bed she was tucked into.

Rhythmic, clambering thumps woke her.

The bed was soft. Some thick, feather-stuffed blanket lay on top of her, weighty but not too warm, and her body felt far too weighted and sludgy and achy from the previous day's anxiety. She opened her eyes with a rather reluctant slowness, and a brief prayer to the Stars that this obnoxious noise wasn't just Lumen finding a new way of being... Lumen.

Fuck me, this place is like bad liquor.

Instead, what greeted her eyes was a tiny, curved room, the walls and floor all light-colored wood panels, all dusty as though they hadn't been used in years. The wall behind the head of the bed was still covered in bark, and she realized, with a horrified start, that it was the trunk of a tree.

The sight of Zech pacing in a frenzy was almost a blessing, as she was sure she would otherwise have shattered back into that fractured, small version of herself. And that was something she could not bear more than once— most definitely not in front of Lumen and Adras.

She blearily pushed back the covers and swung her feet off the side of the bed, pressing them against the sanded wood flooring.

"Zech."

He was breathing hard, his eyes pinched in panicked focus, the shimmering silver of his irises sputtering and flaring. She recognized this moment instantly; it had happened before. In the shack. But they couldn't afford for her to go blasting this room to pieces, not when it was all that stood between them and the forest floor so, so, so far below.

She stood, stepped in front of the line he was pacing, caught his hands in hers. He continued muttering to himself, breathing lurching rapidly, tears falling. She ignored the jutting slam of her own heart at the way he always un-became himself in these moments, and slid her hands softly up the length of his arms, across his shoulders, up his neck, til she cradled his jaw. It had started as instinct, but somewhere along the way, between his elbows and his shoulders, the gentleness of her instincts had startled her, and her hands felt awkward on his face.

There was recognition in his eyes that waited for something *more*, something solid to tether to. A wind colder than death brushed through the room, sending the light curtains fluttering. Reassurance stuttered on her tongue. Commands came easily, criticism, too. Caretaking? Not so much. A nervous twinge of nausea turned low in her belly. She took a breath deep enough to drain the room of oxygen, and opened her mouth.

"Zech," she said again. "You need to be here. You need to tell me what is happening..."

"I..." His face contorted with emotion, tried to wrench from her grip.

"Look at me. See me. Come back here now." Her voice was anything but soft: grating, rough, demanding.

A mysterious grief rose up behind her eyes, misting them over. Out of anyone she'd ever known, Zech did not deserve whatever happened to him when the horrors inside him took over. Zech did not deserve the horror of *her*. But she'd try, better this time, less violent.

"I'm here." Her voice still rasped horribly, still didn't sound remotely comforting or gentle, but he didn't seem to mind. "I don't know what's happening in there, but you need to listen to me instead."

He flinched. Looked away.

"No. Look at me. You hear me, watchman? You do as I say, and not a thing more or less."

He gulped a sob, eyes unfocused. "It's worse every time... She's here," he gasped, brokenly.

Chills chased the knobs of her spine. She tried to keep her voice even. "Who is here, Zech?"

"My mother..."

"*Tell her to leave.*" The unhinged shadow of rage in her voice snuck out, despite herself.

His mouth opened. Closed. Again. Again, til Jauyne's body shook with fury. Her teeth chattered with it. Her bones ground against one another with it. She spun, whirling on the room around her at random, flinging her arms out wide.

"You hear me, bitch? I said leave your son *alone.*"

The wind coming through the windows whipped up into a hysterical agitation of dust and leaves and whipping hair. It screamed in a nearly human way, tugged on her hair, shoved her side to side.

"You think you can turn weather against me? Think you can whip me with your windstorm? I'm *Meirydhi*, you clingy little shit. I *am* the storm. *Leave him alone!*" She slammed her foot against the floor, and a splintering crack raked into her ears, dragging terror and self-cursing behind it.

Zech cried out, sinking to his knees. Between the dry thrash of her tangled hair, Jauyne watched him press a hand to his forehead and his chest, Starlight flickering in his veins, as though trying to heal the insanity away. The silver glow pressed towards his fingertips before sinking back down to the center of his hands. He screamed in agitation.

"She wants me to remember!" He was sobbing, clutching his hair in fistfuls.

Raw helplessness took over; she couldn't smash this hurt to the ground. She couldn't demand its submission. And everything she did seemed to make it *worse*. Trying to help just put him in more pain. She wrung her hands, shouted over the wind.

"Remember what?"

His next breath was a hiccuped wail. "Her."

Compassion wreaked havoc with her heart. She sunk down on her knees in front of him, hauled him towards her, grabbed his face and pressed her forehead to his.

She didn't know how to alleviate sorrow if the cause of it couldn't be cut by all of her sharp edges. She'd never been given the chance to offer comfort. No one had ever wanted it from *frigid bitch*. Maybe, for once in her life, she could soothe something instead of disquieting it.

"Zech." She said it softly against his mouth, so softly she wasn't sure he'd heard her. "*Il enë liyd.*"

It was the term of endearment she often heard her mother speak to Astra. Her parents had never used it for her. No one had ever used it for her. It had never passed her lips before, either, and they trembled as she said it now.

Warmth of my heart, it meant.

"You do remember her," she whispered, ignoring the way her voice shook, how horribly vulnerable she felt witnessing vulnerability without the armor of rage. "You already remember her. There is nothing else you need to do, except remember you, who *you* are, *where* you are."

His shaking had lessened, but he was still so far away. He trembled against her, his fingers digging into the back of her arms as she stroked his cheeks with her scarred and calloused thumbs. "Remember *you, il enë liyd*. Remember what's real."

Starlight melted between them. She felt the way it pooled in his palms and tingled down the veins of her arms. She felt it where his breath ran warm and damp on her chin. She felt it in her chest, where pride and empathy flowed so heavily she wondered how she wasn't dripping in it. She felt it, as she always did, like a coolness in the anatomy of her eyes, but it overflowed, ran down her face in cascades.

She had remedied fear with mending instead of cracking open. She wondered if she might have mended something in herself.

She pressed a kiss to his forehead.

THIS

23

THE DISTORTIONS

Silvery-blonde curls were pasted to her cheek with the haphazard drool of sleep. Indra started, smearing back her damp hair as her head jolted upward. A rattling breath snagged her attention and she glanced across the library table, littered with books, notes, and smudges of ink, to where Valeryn sat. His head was lolled over the back of his plush chair, a snore raking though his slack mouth. His right hand still stretched out over the table to brush the tips of his fingers against her own. They stirred, ever so slightly, with each noisy inhale, and Indra bit her lip in a small smile.

Withdrawing her hand, she pulled her mug close, examining with some disappointment her now-cold coffee. With a sigh, she set it back on its messy stack of papers and rubbed the sleep from her eyes. They'd been there all night, as was evidenced by the new light slatting in through the tall, thin panes of glass inlaid between the high shelves. S

he reached her hands high over her head, clasping them as she arched her back, easing her center of gravity back and forth til her spine relieved a small crack. A little muffled groan rolled up from her chest at that. Shaking herself a bit, she pushed her chair back away from the desk with a dull rasp of wood on wood, and stood.

The little cart by the door had been replenished since last night, likely rather recently if the light through the windows could be believed, and there was only one thing on that cart that Indra's exhausted mind cared about: coffee.

Nearly tripping over three separate stacks of books which impeded the walkway as she went, Indra walked herself to the cart and inhaled deeply. A snore from Valeryn punctuated the inhalation. She uncapped the large carafe and tipped its mouth, hot coffee streaming into the new mug she'd obtained from beside it. A happy little sigh left her lips, and she added a little cream, a little honey, then filled a second mug and carried them both back to the makeshift work station which she and Valeryn had set up two weeks ago.

He was still fast asleep, snoring roughly with his head craned back. Indra winced a bit at how terribly uncomfortable it looked. He was sure to be sore when he awoke. Shuffling papers that had proved to be decidedly not useful, she set the stack to the side and cradled the steaming mug between her hands, letting her eyes scan what work she had interrupted with sleep.

The shard of guilt over needing sleep— of all things!— that scored her chest was unearned, she knew, but still it hurt. The longer she took to unravel what was wound closely into these Starstones, the longer she would be living in fear of them. She had lived in fear for too long— of her father, of the strange warped feeling in the walls of her home, of what she feared she might be— to resign herself to that any longer.

Indra quirked her neck to the side, felt the soft crack. Her spine ached. Her eyes ached. Her heart ached.

If only she weren't so sheltered and shaky and stupid...

She glared at the sheets of paper lying on the desk until they blurred with the bitter tears in her eyes. But tears were unhelpful. Tears would get in the way of work. Tears could not be allowed, else they might never stop. So she roughly rubbed them away and scalded the back of her throat with the steaming coffee in her mug.

Valeryn still wasn't awake. He was the only one working as hard as she, stretching his work into the long darkness of night and the cool, pale dawn. He'd still been awake when she'd rested her head on her arms in defeat last night, muttering soothingly to himself about what they knew for sure regarding the Starstones, which was precious little. That consistent, hopeful muttering was what had calmed her enough to stop fighting against sleep, and relent to the pressure which had been building all day behind her eyes.

Unsure of how to wake him, Indra reached out her hand, placing it where he'd extended his own, and softly took hold of his fingers. She smoothed a fingertip over the calloused bump on his middle finger, evidence of years of pen-gripping and note-taking. Still, though, he didn't stir, so she took as much as would fit of his hand in hers and gave it a squeeze.

"Valeryn." Her voice was syrupy from sleep, and his name felt heavy in her mouth. "Valeryn, it's morning. We've got to keep going."

His head jerked forward as he winced and rubbed at the back of it with a groan that sounded decidedly like an obstinate child's. Scrunching up his face with a sigh, his eyes squinted open.

"Yeah. Yeah, alright. I'm awake now." He blinked, and a shaft of morning sunlight haloed him in gold, flecks of dust catching and glinting, creating a sparkling haze. Hazel eyes shifted to the steaming mug she'd set in front of him. "How long have you been awake?"

"Just for a few moments." Her voice was getting a bit sturdier.

He seemed to now realize the way her hand was still gripping his. His eyes travelled from their hands to her face as he gave her fingers a light press and then released them. A yawn eased open his mouth and stretched his arms wide before he curled back in and around his mug. There was a soft slurp of too-hot coffee being gingerly tested on his tongue. A heavy sigh.

"Where are we at, princess?"

She pressed her lips together at the way he insisted on calling her by a title she no longer wore— a title she'd never wear again, after her marked choice to betray the Province of her origin and flee. Those two syllables— princess— were ones that cut her into slices of bitterness. But all she did was level a hard look at the dark-haired, half-awake man slurping his coffee and say, "I have asked you not to call me that."

Mirth cackled in his irises, though he responded simply with, "I'm sorry. It slips out now and again."

A nod. Hers. "It's alright. I'm nowhere closer to answers than I was last night. The only thing looking rather promising is this, here."

She slid papers around on the wood surface til she found what she was looking for, grateful to brush off the feel of his fingertips on hers. It was a diagram he'd drawn in his inspections of the five Starstones they held in the thick-walled stone rooms beneath the High House. It was a place far enough away that she couldn't feel the madness of their pull, their power, their pain.

Each of the three Starstones were different in their own way— shape, form, size— but the same in others. They all were made of some odd conglomerate of the same materials: crystal inlaid in some sort of metal casing at one end, with jutting strands of metal in various colors, sizes, and lengths sticking out of it in all directions. It looked as though someone had done a rather hasty and inefficient job at yanking the

Stones from something larger, something more complete. It always gave Indra an inexplicable wave of yearning and grief when she thought of it.

Licking the rough surface of her dry lips, she pointed to a note which had been hastily scribbled in the corner of the page which carried all of these diagrams.

Each stone responds to various frequencies— Output? All?

"What did you mean by these questions, Valeryn? What would have them respond to all of the frequencies you tried? What's output mean?"

He yawned again, a grumble in the back of his throat. "It's too Starsdamned early. Can I finish my coffee?"

"You asked me," she chided.

He blinked, cracked open his mouth as though he was going to retort, then relaxed. "So I did." A hasty hand scrubbed over his face. "With all the stones together I'm wondering if they might not simply show signs of response to frequencies, but that perhaps they might create one of their own. There was a certain hum, a glow reminiscent of Starlight, that appeared when they were exposed to certain conditions. Recall how it hurt you when Enoch first uncovered the Starstone in the hall. There was some sort of output it was transmitting which only you could perceive. But perhaps it wasn't intended to be used on its own. Perhaps it only injured you because we were using it incorrectly. Perhaps it won't cause harm with all of them together, as they're meant to be."

"That is quite a lot of perhaps-ing."

The corner of his mouth quirked up. "Perhaps."

"It's also quite a starting point. That is helpful speculation. But why was I the only one who could hear it? Why did it only transmit— output?— towards me?"

"If these truly are Starstones, and they are from the Stars, it stands to reason for me that they should have the greatest probability of functioning when in the proximity of those who possess larger quantities of and connections to Starlight. Or that those with the larger quantities and connections might be more sensitive to their frequencies. You have the most Starlight in you of anyone I have ever met, Indra." Something quite a lot like wonder passed over his face, and it made a small, secret part of Indra's chest squirm.

"I feel useless," she said, at last, and Valeryn frowned over the rim of his mug. "I just mean that if your theory is correct, I can't do much of anything at all until we have all of the Starstones accounted for. And we aren't even sure if one has fallen over Canestry, and..."

Indra chewed at her lip, anger and frustration burning at the inside of her stomach. "And we do not have any reason to believe that the Canestryn Starstone would be even remotely accessible when it does fall."

Valeryn set his coffee mug down atop a thick stack of papers and sighed. Reaching out his hands, he caught hers in his own, and tugged lightly, a wordless nudge for her to meet his eyes. Indra thought about ripping her hands free, and at once freeing her chest of that strange squirming feeling, but instead she obeyed, dragging her gaze from her lap to his face.

"You are never useless. Just your presence is enough— you know that, don't you?"

"I—" She swallowed, her throat dry, her heart clattering behind its bone cage.

The library door slammed open, the hard crack of wood against wood causing her to jump, yanking her hands from Valeryn's. Elryh stood framed in the doorway, dark streaks of red smearing her clothes, her face, her neck... Blood. Blood had flattened wisps of hair to her left cheek and her hands were covered with it, shaking and shiny.

"It's the retrieval party." Her voice was loud enough for them to hear, but stilted and choked.

Indra was already stumbling over stacks of books and skidding over loose papers, her sight blurred with the wetness of tears. Her feet moved faster than her thoughts as she scrambled her way to the door, a desperate scream pinned down to her chest. Elryh's eyes were huge and distant as they darted from Indra to Valeryn. Her fingers left blood where they ghosted over her chin.

"What has happened?" Tears slid off her chin, but all Indra could think was Osiys... Osiys... Osiys...

"They got overwhelmed." Elryh clacked her teeth together to stop their chattering, took a deep breath, began again. "All of them did. We don't know why. Baird is—" A huge sob shuddered up from somewhere deep in her chest as she rounded over the vowel of his name. She wept out the rest. "He's dead... They killed him on the road. One wounded. Osiys... Osiys hit by an arrow. Captured."

Indra opened her mouth to say... to say what, exactly? She didn't know, but all the air in her lungs gushed out, and she heard a low, keening cry.

Captured. Captured? How could this have happened? For him to have survived ten Starsdamned years undercover, just to be captured on a simple extraction mission...

The library shelves tilted, but the books did not slide from their messy arrangements. Instead, the side of her head cracked squarely into the doorframe as a pair of arms scooped under her own. The room became a study in refraction, in hearing underwater. Valeryn's voice swam to her through murky warbles; his hand cupping her jaw felt distant somehow. Cool, silver light beams jutted into her vision from no one point, painting his distant concern in shimmers of Starlight.

Voices followed the Starlight, wading through the watery grief to her ears, familiar, and yet not. The pointy, commanding shrill; the languid, firm tenor; the laughing, dark twinkle; the wry, sarcastic snip. Closer, almost, than even Valeryn's touch or the blood shining on Elryh's cheek. The cut of one reality sliced through the other, and she knew.

"They're close." She felt her lips move without really hearing herself. "The other Starstones."

THE HEADY DRUG OF unconsciousness was replaced roughly with the brutal scent of a spice that made Indra's eyes water and throat sting. The world burned behind her eyelids, but the hand held steady behind her head reminded her that all was well. The last time she'd had such a reaction, Osiys had waited by her bedside, disheveled and exhausted until she awoke; this time, he hadn't even left her immediate side. Indra's head screamed with pain, but she forced her eyelids open to assure him she was alright.

Warm brown eyes looked down at her. Brown eyes. Set behind round, wire-rimmed glasses. Set in a face that was decidedly not Osiys's. She drew in a breath that was as bitter as it was sharp as she remembered.

Driving her nails into her palms, she flinched upright, away from Valeryn's touch. He didn't embarrass her by looking hurt. He didn't hold on to her or try to make her lie back down. He just kept his hands flexed behind her, as though preparing for her to fall.

She'd been carried— Valeryn had carried her- out into the hall, rather a ways from the library, and had, evidently, been stopped by a medic. Elryh, crouched in front of her, had been hastily cleaned up, with blood still stuck to her hair but wiped in a rush from her skin, leaving cloudy, coppery stains. There was a bitter sort of apology in her wet eyes, and they flicked hastily to Indra's right.

Indra followed her gaze, choked on the helplessness of her grief and a growing, foreign emotion: fury. It oversaturated everything in scarlet and hung around the four people who stood there.

"Hello," said the one with the soothing, stoic voice. "I believe we've spoken previously. My name is Adras."

"Yes, here she is," said the pale-dark, pointy one. "The reason I had to hand over Meirydh's Starstone." Her sharp chin lifted toward Indra. "Just one thing left to discover, princess: whether or not you were worth it."

PLEASE

24

TYPICAL BRIGONANS

The Brigonans had dragged them into high-altitude chaos, which was typical.

There was so much blood on the floor of the Great House when they arrived; it was all soaked into the long carpet that ran the length of the long hall. Splotches of it led to a door about halfway down, which was punctuated with screams and groaning. Whose blood it was, Zech had no idea. They hadn't been told a thing, just informed that the Premier had been waiting for them and that they were to wait in the hall until someone came to retrieve them. Servants— or whatever they were— bustled about and generally did not look at the group of newcomers who had been thrust quickly into the hall and out of the way.

They'd waited there for several minutes, waiting to be retrieved, as though they were luggage or something. Jauyne paced at an unthinkable speed behind him, gnawing on her lower lip with her teeth and muttering every now and then. Her black hair was all fallen around her face and shoulders, sweaty from the climb they'd made.

He kind of wanted to grab her by the shoulders and find a way to glue her feet in place so he could give her a good shake and then probably also a good Starsdamn fucking because hell, as hideous as it sounded, he rather missed the days they'd spent cooped up in a charred tower surrounded by corpses. There, at least, they'd had no one to bother them or ruin a perfectly good chance for kissing.

He had to admit he actually liked these two, though. Lumen stood with folded arms and a soft scowl, his white hair pulled back in a low knot. He blew away a stray tangle of it, shifting his weight from foot to foot, which Zech supposed was his anxious tell. Fingers twitching towards one of the swords strapped to his back, Lumen stopped trying to blow away the strands of hair, and instead smoothed them back over his head. Black eyes flitted across the hall. Zech wasn't sure he'd ever get used to those eerie, inky irises. Adras nudged their brother with an elbow, seriousness pinching their brows as they whispered something in his ear. Jauyne huffed at them and came close to Zech's side with a rare pause in her rabid pacing.

Her breath was at his shoulder, quick and impatient and sharp like the rest of her. He urged a smile away from his lips at the thought of the rest of her. Reaching inconspicuously for her hand, Zech entangled their fingers, dragging the pad of his thumb across the back of her hand. The exhale she gave in return was a little deeper, fuller, more complete. She dared to rest her cheek against his shoulder and gave him a quick side glance.

"They're probably deciding which is the most effective way of crossing us over."

"Ah yes," he let the sarcasm seep into his voice, heavy and thick. "These two are certainly going to kill us and take all the nonexistent power and wealth we possess."

She tried to tug her hand away, but he held it firm.

"Zech!" She hissed in his ear, "You never know what Jopaari are up to—their laws run different from ours."

He turned to look her in the eye. If he was honest, he was growing a bit weary of the anti-Jopaari rhetoric. "Stop with that. They've given us every reason under the sun to trust them. And they easily could have gutted us both in our sleep on any one of these nights."

Her lip curled back in preparation for a response which he was sure was venomous, when they were interrupted by a servant. Drying her hands on a small towel she gripped in front of her, the woman beckoned them down the hall.

"The Princess Indra had a terrible spell the moment just before you arrived in the building. She said you would be here." The woman waved them on faster as her speed increased. "You will need to leave the Starstones you have with you in this room here." Here she creaked open an old door which led to a small stone room, decorated only with a small table and chair, and what looked to be a trap door on the slate floor.

Jauyne bristled against him, and Zech saw that Adras's response was not much more subtle.

"We will not leave these things in your hands," Jauyne stepped forward, indignant, and Zech could smell the sweat in her hair as it brushed past him. "How can you ask this of us and expect us to trust your people?"

Zech was surprised to see that neither Lumen nor Adras made any attempt to stop Jauyne or apologize for her. Instead, they looked almost... supportive? Which definitely didn't seem right, considering Jauyne and Lumen's super fun little habit of attempting to stab one another.

"I know it is quite a thing to ask," the servant splayed out her hands in front of her with concern. "But the Princess Indra cannot be in their proximity. She will have an attack. This is the second which she has withstood in only two weeks time. The healing mages do not know what might happen If this continues."

Jauyne snorted. "It sounds like the princess needs to gain a bit of mental fortitude."

The two Jopaari finally stepped in, however reluctant Adras' eyes appeared. "You may have Jopaar's Starstone." Their voice wavered only the slightest amount. "We will expect to leave with it freely, under no obligation or condition that would be otherwise attached to it."

"It will be so," the servant nodded. "There are no conditions. It is yours. We mean only to keep both it and the Princess safe."

Adras hesitated for a long moment, their gaze steady on the servant. Not shying away from that gaze, Adras pulled their pack from their back and knelt, unclasping the buckles that kept the smaller pocket closed. The hum of the Starstone was palpable. Zech could nearly taste it, his tongue buzzing with its song. The breath that Adras sucked in seemed to drain the room of air, and Zech's breath stilled in his chest as they lifted the tightly wrapped bundle from the pack and slowly, painstakingly, transferred it to the servant's hands. The way Adras's hands flexed with the absence of it sent a dull ache to Zech's chest.

This is the most precious item that has ever existed. These Starstones are a Starsdamned miracle, and we're just handing them over... Brigon, you best not fuck this up.

Jauyne's Starlight reeled, and Zech could feel the anticipation, taut as a pulled cord, as Jauyne raised her hands. If he was honest, he truly wasn't sure if she was about to strike the servant down or reach for her own Starstone. Her eyes were peerless. The hum he could always feel rippling under her skin was heightened to a shriek. She curled her thin fingers, one pointing forward as she leaned close to the Servant.

"If anything happens to these, if there is even a Starsdamned scratch on them, I will personally come for the house of Brigon."

Zech held back a smirk, even as the servant swallowed hard, desperate to maintain her sense of composure in the face of this wearily ferocious person threatening her Province. Fortunately for the servant, if Zech was any indication, Jauyne was just as likely to end up romancing the house of Brigon as murdering them. Then again, one never really knew with Jauyne, which was precisely why his adoration of her was so genuine.

Slowly— oh so slowly— Jauyne reached into her pack and withdrew that oh so precious Starstone, the one that had made them what they were, that had linked them somehow, so beautifully. A pang of panic jolted through Zech at the thought of losing that, at the idea that perhaps all this connection was, was a forgery and a fake, crafted by a strange, mysterious crystal. He stuffed his hands in his pockets to keep himself from reaching out and stopping her. Jauyne glanced at him over her shoulder, the very same fear reflected in the pupils of her eyes. But she reached for the Starstone anyway, tugging it out of the deep center of the pack, all bound in cloth even around the pouch. The hum rattled his teeth, and he saw Jauyne's jaw clench as she handed the precious bundle to foreign hands. She then drew out the second, the Meirydhi Starstone, the one that had gifted itself just to her, cradled in lava and Star-song.

The woman nodded her assurances, and another servant appeared behind them in the door, ushering them back out into the hall. The four obediently followed him, and Jauyne gripped Zech's hand as, behind them, the trap door closed, enfolding the woman and the Starstones in secret darkness.

"Fuck, what have I done?" The words were a soft groan in his ear, an aching desperation as Jauyne grappled with her actions. "This was a terrible idea. These things are too wild to belong in some fancy-ass High House."

"It's beginning to feel that way," he whispered back, tugging her closer until they were linked at their elbows as well as their hands. "But I suppose we have yet to see how it all plays out. And if they try to pull one over on us, you and I will go down that tunnel and take back what is yours."

"You two look terribly suspicious with all your hushed tones and huddling." Lumen wrinkled his nose back at them.

Before either Zech or Jauyne could reply, they were stopped short, nearly tumbling into Adras and Lumen. Zech had to take a step back to steady himself.

"What's this!" Adras was craning their neck to see beyond the servant whom they had been trailing down the hall.

He stammered for a moment. "I am so sorry, I ought to have brought them another way," he was saying, to some other man with the same wool pants and tucked shirt as seemingly *every other man* in Brigon. His were etched in a deep blue, however, with the embroidery of a small swirl around a small medicine bottle on the collar.

The man ran a blood-speckled hand over a warm, tan face that ached of tiredness. "She ought to be alright. This one was not nearly so terrible as the first she had. They must have been far enough away that it did not harm her. But grief, too, can have this rather... impactful effect. She has lost someone dear to her. We must be patient."

Past the healing mage and the servant guiding their way, there lay on the carpet a young man, with wildly mussed dusty brown hair and round glasses which had slid to the tip of his nose. In his arms, he cradled a girl— hair radiant silvery-gold ringlets, angelic mouth parted in unconsciousness, hands tumbled open and freshly calloused (which was weird compared to the rest of her), brows knit even though she was decidedly passed out. There was something about her— a shimmer or a radiance that Zech didn't have words for. It was similar to the way Jauyne had looked standing at the peak of an active volcano— *her* volcano!— and there had simply been an indescribable awe at what she was, and how she could possibly be contained in such a thing as a body.

"Who..." Jauyne was craning to see the girl, while Zech was frozen in his state of unbelievability.

"She's like you," was all he could manage.

And then they moved— the healing mage, the servant, everyone. And the princess was stirring, those messy tumbles of curls shifting and swirling. Her eyes shuddered open, she reached for open air, she uttered a word, and the man holding her tensed suddenly, then relaxed his hold and eased her up.

Indra's eyes shifted from the man whose lap she found herself in, to the four of them standing there. She looked slack-jawed, exhausted, and confused. And hungry, honestly. She looked like it took a great deal of energy to make her eyes focus, to register that they were there, in this space, with her.

Eventually, Adras took a step forward, their hands flexing in front of them. "Hello." They talked like they would to a wounded puppy, and that seemed kind of condescending. "I believe we've spoken previously. My name is Adras."

There was no concern over babying where Jauyne was concerned. She snapped her head toward Adras with a hiss. "Yes, here she is— the reason I had to hand over Meirydh's Starstone." Zech winced a bit as she continued. "Just one thing left to discover, princess: whether or not you were worth it."

He snagged her by the hand with a small shake, yanking her ear to his mouth to whisper harshly. "Don't be so Starsdamned rude. Can't you see what she is?"

Jauyne tore her wrist away from him with unsubtle violence. Her words were choked and quiet when she replied. "If her sensitivities were excuse for Brigon to steal my last chance to bargain for the rebuilding of my home, I don't give a starry-eyed fuck who or what she is."

A voice less small, and far more firm than he would have expected, rose from the aforementioned starry-eyed girl on the floor. "It's alright," she said.

25
STUBORN SCRAPPY FUCKER

She was no longer sleeping in those Starsdamned death-trap treehouses, at least.

That was the solitary item on Jauyne's mental list of things to be relieved about. That, and the way a real bed and hearty Brigonan food had managed to remarkably fill out her skeletal form. It was shocking what rest and good food in a safe place could do.

Meirydh. Jopaar. Brigon. Chedhiy. Nareilë. Five of seven Starstones which they had been relentlessly poring over for the past six days. The Brigonans had wasted no time in bringing Jauyne and her three companions into the research, which she begrudgingly supposed might as well be item number two on her mental list.

But working with the little turncoat princess— who, for some unfathomable reason, all the others seemed to fawn over and worship and hail as some sort of savior— who seemed pitifully fragile of mind and incapable of lifting a finger, let alone a fucking dagger, was proving to be the bane of Jauyne's unpleasant existence. That this silver-eyed seventeen-year-old could spend a whole lifetime with the enemy and then decide to ride her mare across a handful of Province borders, only to spend her days fainting and shakily fumbling around in the library and making eyes at the spectacle-wearing library-keeper, was not nearly enough for Jauyne to see her as anything more than a frightened child who ran away from home.

Not when Jauyne had seen real devastation— devastation from which she had scarcely escaped with her life, and which still haunted her every sleeping and waking moment— and still managed to make it through the day without needing to fan herself or sniff from a bottle of strong spices. Jauyne knew horse shit when she stepped in it, and the Canestryn Princess was one fainting spell away from being thoroughly underfoot.

Also, Jauyne was capable of being in the presence of the Starstones, with the exception of the day during their travels in which she and Adras had both grabbed for the stones at once, which was more than the princess could bear. She had been informed that the Brigonan Premier had called for a glass partition to be built in the room in which the Starstones were being kept. It was going to be several panes thick, and hopefully would allow all of them— even *Princess*— to view the Starstones all together through it.

For the time being, the Brigonan guards brought her down the trap door and into an adjoining stone room. The dampness of the earth down there clung to her hair and her clothes, and looked as though it had warped the wood of the chair and table— the only furniture in the space. Lamps hung all along the walls, lighting them in a yellowish hue, which felt like an odd contradiction in the chill damp. It was difficult not to feel like a prisoner in the cell-like room, and the metallic clinking of the guards kept causing her muscles to jump and twitch.

Jauyne pressed her hands flat to the tabletop, calming her body with the subtle steadiness of the bowed wood as she waited for the guard to bring her the Brigonan Starstone.

She'd memorized the Meirydhi Starstone first, but took the time on her first evening in Brigon to catalogue everything she'd discovered about it, putting ink and graphite to paper in haste. She'd moved on to the Chedhiyn Starstone after that, then the Jopaari's and then the Pallydhan one. Each one was unique and just... felt different to hold. The large crystals that made up the majority of their bulk were each a different color and consistency of opaque.

The Pallydhan Starstone had the longest metal tendrils of all of them, which didn't seem to particularly matter, but was still something which she noted. The Chedhiyn one was the smallest, fitting wholly in the palm of her hand, and the Jopaari Starstone was the largest, filling both her hands with more to spare.

Jauyne felt the Brigonan Starstone before she saw the guard enter with it, a veritable wall of rock that seemed to violently strike her senses instead of prickling against them, as the others had done to varying degrees. She sucked a breath into the well of her chest.

This stone was freckled white and grey on deep royal blue. It looked solid and heavy, and was cut to a polished point on one end, raw and rugged on the other. The guard set the Starstone down heavily on the table in front of her, and Jauyne tapped her sheets of parchment into an orderly pile as her eyes devoured it. Four thick, curved metal prongs jutted out from the jagged end, gripping empty air, with a nest of tiny green and blue metal tendrils between them.

A quick sketch of the Starstone was put to the parchment, hasty arrows and scribbled notes spreading out from it in a wet, black cloud of ink. There was something bizarre about this stone, about the way it felt so abrasive, as though it were a refusal of her power as opposed to a beacon to it. Jauyne never had responded well to being refused anything, where Starlight was concerned. Reaching out with a suspicious hand, Jauyne brought the tip of her finger to the point of the stone.

Freezing cold raced up her arm in a lightning arc, and she gritted her jaw to cage a scream. She couldn't move. She couldn't breathe. Her body locked itself into a contortion not unlike a claw and seized. Sparks shot in front of her eyes, filling the room with a blazing fire that cut all else from view.

Far away— so far away— a woman laughed... a light, innocent sound that Jauyne desperately wanted to clamp down on.

The bones-deep ache took its time, intensifying and gripping tighter with every second that passed. Against the terrified instinct in every drop of her blood, she wanted to beg, plead to someone, anyone to make it stop.

The sparks rained down around her or in her or on her, and out of them stepped a woman, her face pointed, her nose sharp, her eyes like stained glass reflecting the fire. Those reflective eyes looked down at the toddler who was snuggled in her arms, a toddler who was all wide eyes and black hair. They were dressed strangely— the woman in breeches that billowed around the thighs before tightening close to the knees and calves, and a jacket with countless buckles and flaps and useless silver zippers. Nuzzling their noses together, the woman babbled nonsense to the child, and that light, innocent laugh leapt from her throat. Jauyne felt something hot and liquid slide from between her lips as the woman twirled the toddler, spinning round so that Jauyne saw words scrawled jagged in white paint on the back of her black jacket: *stubborn scrappy fucker.*

She saw, from someplace not attached to herself, her hand reach forward, pleading to the woman.

"Help... help me..." It croaked from her blood-slick lips.

But the woman flinched, eyes darting around as though looking for something in a panic, and bolted, taking the flames, and Jauyne's consciousness, with her.

Her tongue was bit clean through and was heavy in her mouth, which was truly nothing compared to the way her pride felt skewered and heavy-hung somewhere in her gut.

They'd (whomever they were) removed her from the cramped Starstone examination room and stuffed her back into her bed, huge, fluffy pillows stuffed all around her as though they were frightened she'd break. This was, for obvious reasons, utterly insane, seeing as how she had managed to survive a deep wound across the face without this sort of over-worried treatment. Jauyne momentarily wished for a bottle of chlorynyne to dump over herself in order to be done with the fussing she knew she was about to endure.

The Canestryn princess was sitting at her bedside, which naturally meant that Jauyne was about to be locked in a *real* cell for *real* murder, and Zech was pacing annoyingly at the foot.

"Zech, stop that pacing," was what she attempted to say first, but her mouth was full of cloth, and the words came out all soft and stuffy and entirely unintelligible.

She tried to spit it out, working her sore tongue around her mouth as her hands tried to recall their muscular abilities. The princess spluttered a stream of words that were probably relief, just as Jauyne spluttered the cloth out of her mouth, her hands finally obeying the instructions of her brain and gathering the soggy, bloody strip clumsily.

Zech bolted from the trough he'd likely paced into the floor, and was at the opposite side of her bed, looking sternly at her and reaching for her face. Jauyne was about to open her mouth to furiously reprimand him, but he grabbed her by the chin and yanked open her mouth for her, peering in at her bloody tongue as though it held all the secrets he was looking for. Jauyne smacked him with a limp hand and growled lamely beneath his strict pawing.

"Be quiet and let me check you over." He easily pushed her offending hands away and began turning her head side to side.

Jauyne felt around in her mouth with her tongue, testing its flexibility. Her body was tingly. Her brain was cluttered and greyish. She could see sparks and swirls of Starlight everywhere she looked. "Check me all over, huh? Perhaps Princess should leave." An actual giggle left her mouth, and she paused for a moment in an attempt to consider why she was not mortified.

Zech swallowed a laugh, and it sounded a bit like a hiccup behind his tightly stretched refusal of a smile. "I need to make sure there's no permanent damage, but after that little spectacle I have to admit the prognosis doesn't look great."

His words were half nonsense and half the wisest thing she'd ever heard. Starlight had settled on him like a second skin, lagging back mere seconds from his body's motion so that it created a strange, illusory effect. Jauyne followed the Starlight as it lagged behind, letting her head loll. He was frowning now, and the Starlight didn't want to frown. It wanted to grin. It wanted to share secrets.

"Jauyne, can you hear me?" He was closer to her now. "Stars, it's like you're fucking drunk," he muttered as an aside.

"Of course I can hear you, dumbass. You're close enough that I can smell your breath." He'd eaten rabbit, she decided.

His hands continued roving, lit up with his own Starlight just a few inches away from her body, adjusting the flow of Starlight in her body, noting this or that. The low buzz in her blood seemed to follow his hands, and her head began to slowly drain of it, leaving behind her stark senses. Everywhere she looked, Starlight still moved, still huddled around Zech and herself and... the princess of course... but it didn't talk so loudly as before. She couldn't tell what it wanted or why it was there, though the answers felt like a tangible fleck of matter in the back of her throat.

The princess was still there, awkwardly fidgeting with a loose thread in her cropped and embroidered shirt. Her long blonde curls were unkempt and frizzy, lighting up like a chaotic crown where the sun from the window crept through the strands. "I hope you're alright," she said, finally, dragging her silvery eyes to Jauyne's. "It took me days to recover the first time. I must admit, I was a bit frightened I would not get my hearing back in my left ear. All's well now, but..." A small, exasperated sigh huffed out of her. "I know you like to work hard. Just... be gentle."

She was an awfully little thing, and Jauyne felt a new stab of pity for the girl as Zech swept his hands over her jutting rib cage to examine her navel. What it must be like to be so unprepared and frightened of the whole world, while also having some bizarre nudge to blindly trust one's enemy… And so, in that moment of choking pity, Jauyne rasped out, "Thank you, Princess. That is very thoughtful."

"Just… Indra, is alright," she replied, as Zech moved his examination to her pelvis, and after a swift pause and a very proper nod, Indra slipped out of the room, slippers whispering on the polished wooden floor.

Jauyne couldn't resist a snort. "She left awfully quickly when she saw your hands move just now."

Zech did not reply. He simply stared straight ahead at the space where Indra been just a moment prior, his pupils dilated and lips slightly parted. Jauyne remained unconcerned and became vaguely irritated. Whatever was wrong with her could surely be healed, especially in a fully functional Province High House, in which they were honored guests.

"You know that trying to frighten me isn't going to work, Zech. Whatever it is, I've seen worse, remember?" She gestured sarcastically to the scar spanning her face. The only movement he made in return was a slight furrowing of his brow and a deep inhale.

After a moment, he released the Starlight that had been coating his hands and rested them solidly, warmly, over her hip bones. He broke eye contact with the opposite wall and brought his eyes to his hands.

"Zech… what are you doing?" Her tongue was feeling uncomfortably heavy again, and her head ached, but her stubborn need to get to the bottom of things was prevailing with ease. This was the benefit to being an asshole. She extended a shaky, skinny arm and grasped his sturdy wrist with her long fingers. "Tell me."

It sounded more like she was commanding an army than coaxing a lover, but between the injuries and exhaustion and irritation at his hesitation, gentleness was a bit of a stranger to her at the moment.

Zech dragged his eyes up the length of her, pupils still wide, whites of his eyes shining with a tentativeness she hadn't seen in him since the night in the shed when she had thought he might reach out to touch her. "Fuck, Jauyne," he said, and his voice was both the music of a harp and the rasp of a whetstone as he backed away from her. "You're pregnant."

She threw the bloody cloth at him, and it unfurled, landing like a pitiful decoration across his shoulders.

"This is impossible," he stammered. "I would have known. I sleep next to you all the time. I'm a *healer*. I would have *felt* this."

Terror and fury were blooming in her gut. "Get out."

"Jauyne—"

"Get the *fuck* out of my *fucking* room you selfish, crazy *fucker*."

He flinched, and she knew she should feel badly about calling him crazy. Knew she should take five fucking seconds and *think*. But she kept her eyes trained on him as he made for the door, as it shut behind him. And then she let all her frustration and hopelessness and anger overflow.

She did what she had not done since she awoke in a city of the dead. She sobbed so hard she felt her chest might crack.

She sobbed for the wanting that the odd vision had awoken in her— to be held again by her mother as a child, before she was second-favorite. She sobbed for the knowing that no one liked her, that she was just an angry woman incapable of softness. She sobbed for how she'd wounded Zech, and for how he'd wounded her. And she sobbed for the unbelievability that the Stars had thrown yet another stone in her path, another blockage in her quest to piece herself and her home back together. She sobbed, arms tucked around her navel, until she realized something that stilled the tears and throbbingly nudged at her heart:

No longer was she a Premier with no people. Inside of her was not just any child— it was Meirydhi. It was one of her people, a Province-less child who would need a home.

Jauyne wasn't a mother; what sorts of things a mother did, she was sure she didn't know. Her own mother hadn't been much of one at all.

But Jauyne was a Premier. And the Stars had just given her not a child, not really, but a subject. An evidential reason to demand assistance and justice from the remaining Provinces. The gift of someone to lead, to protect, to fight for, to care for, and for which to restore culture. What else had she spent her whole, miserable life learning?

What plucked against her panic-wracked heart with the most secret tenderness, though, was this: she was the last Meirydhi no longer.

THE SECOND CRYSTALLINE SACRAMENT

All true Knowing comes forth in an unhinged force that tests the defnitions of sanity. We remember.

77TH & CRYPTCALL

YOUR FACE GAZES OUT *at you from behind a fresh swipe of the cleaning rag, coppery-brown on the surface of the espresso machine. Heavy, dark smudges hang under your eyes, and the locks of your green hair, tidily braided and hanging around your face, are frizzed and chaotic from the day.*

The shifts after an attack are always the hardest.

It had been this morning, a bomb that split the courthouse of nearby Carmichael into rubble. At this point, no one remembers what the war is about or why it began, or even for how long it has been raging. (Everyone agrees that last bit is odd, but what energy would be put toward a mystery like that, while bombs still fall?)

All that matters is making sure loved ones are safe, which is why after an attack, Cryptcall Coffee pulses with people, the rotating door never ceasing its dizzying spin, as people from every country pour inside, hoping to find their families and friends to say, "it's alright; I'm safe." Hoping to grasp their clothes and clutch their faces and weep with relief.

The ones who weep with horror at the lack of their presence are the worst. They fall to the floor in the blue patches of sunlight and howl until someone removes them. It makes your insides turn to oily, hot ick. It makes you puke dark vomit in the back alley.

Once again, there is no word from the enemy, neighboring Terreskil— no threat and no apology. There is only the raging of the world, the swearing that perpetrators will be brought to justice. But as no one can remember a time where bombs weren't falling on all sides of every continent, this seems unlikely at best.

Your stomach growls.

You're hungry. Not that you've ever not been hungry; even when your insides are slippery with horror and you're puking in the alley, the hunger lingers. But it feels as though it's scooping out your insides with its muchness, now.

A line, so thin and fine it nearly isn't there at all, has appeared above your navel, and you stroke it through the fabric of your dirty apron.

That line is light and the slightest bit shiny.

A scar. Where there was no injury.

It was accompanied by the littlest twang of pain, just when the last bomb fell, as though this war was now being fought on your body, too.

You have not shown anyone. You have not even shown Kip, and you show him everything. You are unsure why you haven't shown him, but it eats at you, and for some reason it feels good to have the gnawing hunger be gnawed at by something else, something ugly and stubborn.

You wonder how much more of this hell the world can take before it gives up, before it yawns open and falls apart and sets its contents to sprawling out through space. How could it be more than this? You feel every bruise the world endures as though your heart were the victim of some errant fist. You feel every flushed, teary face as though the tears are running down your own...

Oh. They are.

Ailbhe crooks her palm, raw from scrubbing baking dishes, around your elbow, tugging softly. "Go rest, Quell. We can take it from here."

Her eyes are red-rimmed and her face worn when you look at her. You always take turns on days like today. She's just been crying into the dishwater, you know. It's your turn.

"Alright," you find yourself saying.

AND

26

OSIYS LOATHED CHEATERS

Osiys loathed cheaters. And what was poison but a way to cheat a man out of his life? Although, he supposed, he hadn't quite been cheated of his life, if he was returning to a state of consciousness. It had cheated him of dignity though, he thought, just then realizing the way his trousers were soiled.

All was darkness, and his entire face throbbed. Cold, cold, cold bit into his forearms and neck. His hands were suspended on either side of his head, close enough to stick against his cheeks with something tacky—blood? He was half-standing, crumpled against the metal wall behind him. Another wall met his nose hard enough to make him curse when he tilted his head forward.

What?

A jolt of hot panic shot to his gut, forcing his screaming muscles to stand fully. He cried out when pain seared his leg, the wound evidently left untreated. Scraggly breath echoing in the crushing space, Osiys palmed the walls.

The space was scarcely big enough for his body, perhaps just six inches between him and the wall in front of him, with his back pressed flat against the back wall. The whole thing felt made of metal, similar to the stuff biting into his arms and neck.

Stars... Did they fucking bury me alive?

A hoarse wail of terror escaped his mouth before he could stop it. His chest was heaving so hard he thought it might brush the wall in front of him, and the heat of panic was rolling into a churning sick. The pitiful cases his mind was raising in an attempt to create calm were simply drowning in the horror.

Quiet... quiet. I need to listen, need to try to hear... something.

This was not how the quick trip was intended to go.

It seemed to take an age for his breath to slow and for his heartbeat to stop echoing in his ears. He pressed the side of his face to the wall in front of him and held his breath.

There was nothing. Endless, mocking silence.

His injured leg was screeching with pain. Shifting his body weight, the injury bumped the wall beside him, and he lost consciousness once more.

A SHUSHING, GRUNTING NOISE filled the pocket-sized space, and Osiys instantly grasped at empty air, blinking bleary, blind eyes. Perhaps it was a fictitious creation of the final remaining hope in his brain.

The dulled clang of metal on metal reverberated through Osiys' bones. It sounded so very close. Tears pricked his eyes as muffled voices exchanged some casual conversation, from what sounded like somewhere above him. The sudden urge to bang his fists against the metal wall rushed at him. He dodged the thought.

"Think he's still alive?"

"If so, he's a quiet one."

"If not, I've just lost fifty to Haschal."

"It appears that all that's left to do is pop it open and see for ourselves."

Osiys' head slammed back against the wall as the world shifted under him, and he felt himself being raised and turned. There was nothing for him to grasp onto, nothing with which to defend himself. The voices had been familiar— the brothers he'd betrayed when he left the ShadowWalkers. They'd been taking bids on whether or not he was living or dead. He'd known they were ruthless and vile, but for fuck's sake...

He wondered what Indra would be feeling, could still feel her little body cling to his as they'd said their goodbyes. She'd be beside herself, fall to pieces. He hoped that Elryh and the library would be enough to soothe her heart, even as the coffin he was being dragged about within, was finally set down with no care for comfort, upon some rocky, uneven patch of land. The movement jostled his injured leg, and he bit down a moan.

He was suddenly conscious of how filthy and disgusting he was. Piss and shit stiffened his britches, and he was sure the smell of him was unbearable. The injury reeked as well, which likely meant infection, and the sweat on him had dried, still plastered there.

Sharp grunts and a series of clicks and locks that hissed and clanged served only to make Osiys' heart race once more. When the final lock was undone, and the rasping squeal of metal joints, in desperate need of an oiling, announced the lifting of his confining door, the glaring sun shot fire into his corneas.

A howling cackle filled his ears.

"Fucking *Stars*, chap! Do you *smell* him?" The laughter grew.

"Look at that shit all over him. Stupid, stupid fucker."

Osiys' vision was all blistering white, spotted red. But a shadow loomed in one half of his sight, and someone grabbed at the neck of his sweater.

"What, thought you could fuck us all over after playing spy?" It was the first voice again, accompanied by a crack of pain to his jaw. "Thought you could come in here and play nice and then take a *giant* shit on all of us? Stupid. Stars, you're so *fucking stupid.*"

"Osiys even your real name?"

His sight was coming back in jagged claws of color, raked through by horrible light and shrieking pain. Someone was hauling him upward, grabbing at his pants.

"Brigonan bastard. Thinking you're better than all of us. Eat shit."

"I'm—" He didn't know what he was planning on saying, but the second man shoved his fingers in Osiys' mouth. An acrid taste pasted itself to his tongue, stinging his eyes with tears.

"Oh, chap that's disgusting. You actually *touched* his shit?" A pause, as Osiys gagged, as he uselessly clambered to wipe his tongue free of his own excrement. "Feed him more. And hurry before we have to take him to Canryn's hall!"

Osiys reached to flail, to buck away, but arms not impeded with wounds and exhaustion forced him down, held his hands in a useless position. Blind terror flecked his senses with pin-pricks of pain. Adrenaline slammed into his gut. He gritted his jaw, pressed his lips thin-closed.

"No you fuckin' don't." A hand squeezed hard at his cheeks, forcing open a space in his mouth. Shit-covered fingers crammed in.

Fighting the urge to gag, Osiys spat hard into the man's face. His sight cleared for a blessed minute, and he watched the ShadowWalker recoil with a curse.

Osiys' voice was a harsh rasp, but still he grated out: "Go to the void, you worthless fucker."

A fist met the space between his eyes.

ME

27
OUR WHOLE SELVES, THE WHOLE WAY

ADRAS, BRIGONAN HIGH HOUSE.
2 months, 2 weeks since the sack of Meirydh

There was real danger in handling the Starstones.

Jauyne, while insisting she was perfectly alright— and punctuating her claims with her middle finger flung up in the air— was far from her usual self. Since her interaction with the Brigonan Starstone nearly a week ago, something unexplained rocked her from time to time. The strange episodes came on entirely without warning and were wildly explosive.

Adras sat on the well-worn wood plank floor of the library, which was lazily half-covered with an askew rug, and stared at a page they weren't reading. Jauyne had been there less than an hour ago, poring over her notes on the Starstones with visible and contagious agitation, gnawing on the end of her pencil and muttering to herself as she balled up one useless paper after another.

Adras tugged one of the crumpled pieces of paper out from under their thigh, where they'd sat on it, and smoothed out the wrinkles onto their lap. Irritated, scratchy handwriting viciously tore into the paper— the aggravation with which Jauyne had scribbled had accelerated drastically in the last few minutes before she'd lost all handle on herself, and this paper must have been one of the last pieces to be mutilated.

Two women, it said. Stars? Where from? First separate?

Adras rubbed a hand over their chin before cupping it there, sinking their head down into it. It was absolute nonsense. Everything Jauyne said was absolute nonsense. Adras begrudgingly forced themselves to face the fact that Jauyne was very possibly insane.

And, at this point, with this limited sort of knowledge and this high rate of injury, no one could possibly examine the Starstones safely; they simply couldn't possibly risk another person.

A sort of furious exhaustion swept through their limbs. Hauling Jayne out, while taking care not to harm her, had been no easy task, even for someone as brutally trained in combat as Adras.

The Meirydhi Premier had been thrashing, screaming, her Starlight flaring precariously and unbidden. It was as though the very air in the room had changed when Jauyne did. A chill had swept round their feet and curled its way up their body— not just cool air but a life-draining cold, filled with the vibrational crackle preceding a storm. Jauyne's eyes had beamed silver, a blinding shimmer that caused her to cry out (whether in pain or frustration, Adras was unsure) and grasp around at her head and her stomach. Finally, she'd uttered some huge keening sob and driven her fist into the surface of the desk where she'd been working. Pale Starlight had screamed from her pale knuckles, and those in the library had taken cover, shielding their eyes from being surely blinded.

The fallout was chaos— Adras fighting through brutal silver light to get to Jauyne, who was openly weeping with rage, her chin jutting forward as her silver eyes raked the ceiling for some unspecified sign. Adras had plowed into the side of Jauyne with force enough to send her slim body flying, but instead it only served to shove her dully and cause her to stumble. Despite the shock, Adras had lashed her arms around Jauyne's, pinning them to her sides and dragging her towards the door.

Jauyne had howled something that sounded more pythfox than human, sobbing and screeching in aggravation. The utter helplessness and incredible frustration coursing through the young Premier had hit them like a physical force when their skin met hers.

Jauyne never stopped fighting them for a moment, thrashing and bucking in Adras' arms. *I need to find them*, she'd screamed, and it was the scream of the wind bending itself around mountain peaks. *They need us! They're dying without us! Don't you understand, you Jopaari asshole? If the seven can't remember the thirteen, the thirteen will die a second death, and the millions of the seven will die the first death!*

Her body had gone all rigid and twitching then, and Seven Stars— may they be honored— she burned to touch. Adras had as much as tossed her out the door, and then looked down at their hands, which trailed soft wisps of smoke. The tips of their fingers, to the crooks of their elbows, glowed a brilliant, blinding silver; it faded as it extended past their elbows, until their shoulders were a dull shimmer over tanned skin.

Their sight had flickered as they'd flexed their glowing fingers, Jauyne convulsing on the floor just a few feet away. Images twitched behind

Adras' retinas in time with her body— patterned silver walls, silver eyes, brightly lacquered silver nails on dark skin, the clink of crystal glasses, the flash of a million stars close enough to touch...

Adras flinched at the intensity of it, realized they'd dug their short fingernails into the sharp line of their jaw. Frowning, they sucked off the small smudge of blood curled into the half moon of their nail. It reminded them of that final ceremony, that final commissioning of the High Priestess, the similar half moons that were tattooed along their cheek. How they missed home... the familiar sharpness of the cold and the comfort of running their hands over the worn wooden doors of the hall.

They were well aware that the High Priestess believed that this was the purpose for which Adras had been born. It wasn't much of a secret, and an excitement lit the woman's eyes so bright with hunger at times, that Adras wondered if perhaps they were less a beloved child of the Priestess, than a curious item which she regarded as singularly precious. The High Priestess collected lost and broken and fascinating things, after all, and what was Adras but a lost and broken and fascinating thing with skin on?

A sigh rasped from their lips, and they wiped their bloody chin across the back of their hand. That particular itch of thought was not one which they wanted to spend the day unable to scratch. There were more important things to concern themselves over, at the moment, such as cleaning the mess that Jauyne had left behind in the library, and deciding what to do about the apparently dangerous Starstones.

The whisper of cloth on polished wood hushed down beside them, and they angled their head to meet Indra's eyes. Smudges of ink stood out starkly against her soft skin, and were echoed by the dark smears of purple that hollowed out the underside of her eyes. The frizzled crown of her hair had been sloppily braided in the aftermath of Jauyne's unleashing. The girl reached out a hand, a bit gingerly, and curled it atop Adras' knee. A very slight smile tilted one side of her mouth up.

"Do you remember when you first spoke to me through the Starstone, Adras?"

Adras nodded, silent. This girl was calm incarnate, and they fully intended to absorb as much of it as they could. They hadn't gotten much time, outside of rigorous searching and study, to speak with one another. She was everything Adras had imagined, and more... so much more that snaked its way through her delicate blue veins.

"You told me that you had answers, but perhaps not the answers you were looking for." Her voice was careful, soft. "What did you mean? What answers do you have for me, Adras?"

Her eyes were like liquid crystal and intent as a fox, and something about her sang like the Stars to Adras.

"Alright," sighed Adras. "I believe you are a Starchild, as am I, as are Jauyne, and Zech." Adras studied Indra's face for signs of incredulity and suspicion as they went on, but there was nothing but openness. "I believe I was born to understand the mystery of the Starstones, and I believe you were born for something I still don't quite understand... but something that is rife with blood and victory."

Here, Indra's brows scrunched and she twisted her mouth to the side. Her hand pulled away. "My father is rife with blood. That is his destiny. I want nothing to do with it."

yet. Who do you want to win? Because in the end, it might require you to spill blood in order to assure he does not rule over the Seven Provinces." She sucked in a tight little breath, and held it, so Adras went on. "I believe we are meant to unravel this together. That we can make a bridge and return a bit of sacredness to the place that's been desecrated. I believe we are here to remember who we are made to be— that we can be more than the role that lesser men have given us to play, that we can choose the improbable path and take it. Bringing our whole selves the whole way."

Indra's eyes were steady and fluid, even as she chewed on the inside of her lip. Her gaze held for a very long time, and Adras felt a silent pleading in their chest, a need to have this girl see the truth of it, a truth they hadn't voiced til now, and which had felt that much more true for having voiced it. Indra's chest rose slowly, intentionally with a long breath.

"Our whole selves?" Her voice was clear as ice and intimately soft.

"The whole way," Adras affirmed.

"Alright," Indra breathed out in a steady wisp. "I believe in doing what is right, no matter what. I believe in trusting in goodness. And I believe Jauyne is telling the truth when she is in a state like she was a few moments ago. I believe those words mean something." She gestured to the wrinkled paper Adras had smoothed over their lap, lips pressed together fervently and chin lifted. When she spoke again, her voice was a gentle hum. "I know what it was like to be in that... space... wherever it is that the Starstones take your mind. There is truth there, even if it's jumbled. You know it, too, don't you? You've been there."

She was right, and Adras knew that. They were also a bit bitter that their own irritation with the Meirydhi Premier had veiled their ability to pick up on what was true.

"Let's pick up the scrap paper," they said.

Indra nodded, face a little flushed, and folded over onto her knees to begin gathering the discarded bits of paper. Some were full sheets with small notes or large scrawls; others were little corners of pages that had been torn off and scribbled on. Indra called to Valeryn to help, and he began sorting through the papers that had fluttered to his feet, under the table over which he was hunched.

It was only a few moments before the three of them had collected all the scraps and had cleared one of the library tables so that they could spread them out more easily. They laid each piece out individually, in no particular order, creating a patchwork quilt of a madwoman's scratchy divulgence.

There were 13 pieces in all, which they labelled for safe keeping.

1– silver silver SILVER SILVER circle spaces seven even measured stones ??STARS

2– Two women? Stars? Where from? First separate?

3– I can see her through door andsheis so far away

4– REMEMBER

5– you forgot. Seven forgot. Seven 7 7 7 7 7 7

6– 7/13 you stupid fucking fugitives

7– the sky isn't real the monuments aren't real everything is SHINY

8– stubborn scrappy fucker.!.!

9– Starstone makes eyes bright makes bodies shiver makes space fucking stupid

10– thirteen die twice seven die once everybody dies dies DIES

11– self: find lullaby that earth spirits/elementals (?) used to sing to sing to baby

12– doors are deaths are portals are worlds are doors

The final scrap of paper made Indra gasp, and Adras scarcely felt the girl grip her wrist.

Because it wasn't possible. It wasn't possible. It was *not Starsdamned possible.*

13– ourwholeselvesthewholewayAdras

AND

28
A DIFFERENT PATTERN, A DIFFERENT TIME

The glass Starstone enclosure had been completed far ahead of schedule.

Herran had quickly prioritized it after Jauyne began experiencing attacks, in addition to Indra. The others of their party who were suspected to be Starchildren were forbidden from viewing the stones directly and had been relegated to second-hand note-taking and research.

There was a part of Indra that felt this as a physical loss, as though some vital part of her had been scooped out of an open wound. The truth be told, the way in which the Starstones seemed to beckon her, urge her, magnetize her was more than frightening, like all the myths and legends the Canestryn sailors used to tell about beautiful sirens luring them with familiar voices and sharp teeth into frothing black waters of their own doom.

Of course, she had not heard these stories firsthand, either. A strange, garbled emotion rushed her head and nearly made her dizzy. Unadulterated rage was part of this emotion— rage at the thought of keeping a child like herself locked away in the High House grounds, cut off from the world and lonely... so, so terribly lonely.

The rage was befriended by a horrific and hollow grief, a terrible emptiness for the uncountable time that day, at the realization that Osiys had been her eyes and her ears to the outside world.

Only now that she was out, breathing air on the other side of the continent and seeing unbelievable things, and meeting such unbelievable people... now he was the one locked away somewhere dark and horrible. He'd been carried in to Canestry just after she'd been carried out, but she knew the truth: if her father was concerned, the only rest that Osiys would receive in Canestry would be the rest granted to him in the sprawling cemetery.

At least it had a far-off view of the mountains.

The thought made her wish to regurgitate her breakfast. Her insides were coated with the oily grime of repulsion.

Something tickled her shin, and Indra jumped, swallowing a squeal. Blinking with huge lavender eyes was the library cat, nuzzling her leg with its soft ears. Because Indra desperately needed comfort, and because this cat was insistently affectionate, she bent and scooped up the creature, its stiff hind legs jutting out in a mild panic as she hoisted it from the ground and brought it to her chest. His tail curled empathetically around her wrist as he stretched his neck to bump his nose to hers. Indra took her fingers and scratched softly between the little creature's ears, and the tiny rumbling noise that it made settled deeply inside her chest. Indra took a truly full breath for the first time that day and realized she was trembling with exhaustion.

There was a dry shuffling noise somewhere behind her, and Indra started so hard she nearly came out of her chair. The cat, too, started, and dug his little claws into the delicate meat of her shoulder. Yelping, Indra tossed him to the floor, where he meowed piteously until she rose from her chair and patted him with reassurance.

She made her way toward the noise, which seemed to be in the far corner of the library, past the fireplace which was now blazing against the oncoming autumn chill. Stepping carefully over haphazard piles of books and discarded notes on scrap parchment, Indra at last came to the far corner, where she peered into a small alcove.

It was warmly lit by a small hanging metal basket that looked as if it was meant to hold all manner of burnable substance— from meticulously rolled incense sticks to candles to dried herbs. Currently, it held three fat, dripping candles, the wax caught by a connected metal plate. Below this strange little chandelier, in an overstuffed and very old blue chair, Valeryn was holding his eyeglasses in one hand and rubbing at his closed lids with the other. He looked so like a little child, especially with his hair all sticking up, that Indra loosed a small giggle.

Tossing her a teasingly flat-lipped glance from beneath his lashes, he proceeded to exhale onto his glasses lens and rub it vigorously on his untucked shirt. "What are you laughing at?"

Indra ignored his embarrassment, bending to the low table in front of him and plucking a volume from the stack there. "Did you sleep in that chair last night?"

"Perhaps." He wiped the other lens clear of smudges.

Indra snorted lightly. Perhaps was his favorite word. She thumbed through the book she'd selected, not really seeing it. If he was exhausted, he wasn't going to be worth much to the research they were supposed to be doing. He needed to be responsible. Why was it always her job to be responsible? "You should stop doing that."

His eyebrows folded in. "I should stop sleeping in this chair?"

Grief and anger were igniting a bit, and Indra hated the sound of her own voice. "You should stop staying up all night and winding up exhausted. We haven't been able to compare notes since Jauyne's major incident in here. It's our responsibility to figure this out and make sure we don't just all... I don't know." She dragged a hand down her face.

"Descend into chaos?" he offered, unhelpfully and with a bit of a smirk.

"War is chaos," she agreed. "It's all the end of all things, if my father is the one waging it. I'm terribly uninterested in being a guilty party to more death."

Indra liked being irritated with him. She liked the rush of autonomy, that she was even capable of disliking the man without being concerned for his wellbeing due to her father's uncanny habit of slaughtering those servants who did not merit high praise from his daughter. Indra wasn't entirely sure if she had even known how to recognize anger or feel it in her veins until now, and, the best thing of all, she knew Valeryn could take that frustration and do with it something which she hadn't yet mastered.

She set down the book, none too gently, even as he stood, reaching his arms high in a gasping yawn. Indra punched her finger into his chest. "I'm so angry."

Valeryn responded to her jab of violence by wrapping her up in arms that were thin but wiry, arms that were firm enough to create a barrier. She startled, yelped, went rigid with shock at the sensation of embrace, something which she had not experienced— not really, not by someone who knew the steeper sides of her experience— since Osiys had been taken. She was safe with Valeryn, she knew, and she allowed herself the luxury of recognizing it. He sighed deeply, and where his chest met hers, she absorbed its calm. Valeryn had let out a soft huff of a laugh at her yelp, and was now rubbing her upper back in slow, timed circles alongside her breath. The ease of it radiated into her physical body.

She'd wriggle away. She really would. She knew nothing of friendship, after all. She certainly didn't deserve friendship when she carried sorrow over her shoulder as naturally as a lunch sack. But this was nice. If only every ounce of affection didn't remind her of Osiys. If only Osiys weren't the only person who had ever showed her any sort of affection prior to coming to Brigon... Her mind was scrambling with the emotional stimulation of being embraced, but something subtler than her consciousness wrapped her arms around the lanky librarian in turn, and let out the breath caught deep in her torso. She allowed herself to melt into him, thawing the stiffness lying dormant in her shoulders and limbs.

The beating of his heart against her breast was rapid. His hand on her back stilled, the other hovering awkward and loose at her waist. Indra paid no mind. She was unused to friendship, still more unused to the physical warmth of caring. But Valeryn seemed equally unsure, so she tilted her face up to him, some attempt at thanks on her tongue.

The soft hook of his finger under her chin as it lifted, followed by the press of his mouth on hers was the last thing she was prepared for. Indra froze, the sense of warmth which had begun to bloom in her chest, withering with terrified frost. Only her lips worked in a motion of betrayal as it welcomed his mouth into the warmth of her own, a foreign movement made for the first time in the frigid panic of instinct. A word of protest stuck to the walls of the closing canal of her throat. She pressed the palms of her hands against his chest, quaking and weak, but he clutched her closer, the fingers that had drawn gentle circles now digging into the tender ropes of muscle between her shoulder blades.

Her body resisted the simple command to step out of the loose circle of his arms. It resisted the command to release his mouth. It resisted over and over and over and so her command screamed in a terrified insistence, and she slammed her shuddering palms into his chest, flinging herself backwards, out of his grip, and tripping over the low table as Valeryn teetered for balance.

"Stars, Indra, what did I do?" His lips were damp and swollen from their contact with hers, and he wiped a bit of saliva from the corner of his mouth as he stepped forward, extending a hand to where she found herself on the floor. "Are you alright? Did you get hurt?"

But Indra scarcely heard him. She could hardly even see through the shimmering air that now swamped the room. She fumbled backwards, dragging her legs off the table where they were still sprawled. Dimly, she heard the hollow thud of books being knocked off by her boots.

"I'm—" she stuttered, the betrayal of her mouth being joined by her eyes. Valeryn's form contorted, shifted, started and stopped in involuntary jumps and skitters.

One moment he was running his hand through his hair— *twitch*— then taking a step forward, hands busily filled with books. One moment he was peering at her with concern in his eyes— *twitch*— and then he was at an entirely different angle, throwing his pencil at the wall. One moment he was perched on the arm of the stuffed chair— *twitch*— the next he was leering over her, mere inches away, a yell separating the lips that had just been pressed to hers.

The breath in Indra's lungs came short and fast, and she flung out her hands. "Stay away from me! Don't touch me! Do *not* touch me! Stars help me..."

He continued to twitch and shiver in her vision, held fast in this bizarre, inhuman dance. A sudden jolt of light filled her, removed whatever weight in her body had kept her feeling plastered to the polished wooden floor, lifted her gently. Her feet took over then, speeding her towards the huge doors, pummeling her through them, despite the crack of her wrist bone as she flung herself to the other side of it.

"Indra?" Valeryn's voice was still audible, heavy with a concern she couldn't decipher, and just the timbre of it raised every fine hair on the back of her neck.

Her head was all fuzzy and hot, and her stomach was leaden, but she drove herself forward in a desperate panic, her little slippers slapping on the wooden floor. Forcing her eyes to blink hard, she prayed to the Stars that her vision was clear. She prayed she wasn't dying. She prayed the same little recited words over and over as she fled.

I love you— don't go, he whispered in her head, and she had no idea how this was possible. Much like he had twitched and stuttered in her vision, his voice warbled into a different pattern, a different time... *I could have fooled you over and over again*. Again it warbled. Panic striped it through. *Come back, Princess, let me help!*

A scream of terror and frustration ripped her throat raw, and she smacked her hands over her ears, her eyes clenching closed. Softly curling forward as she ran, blind and deaf, she was halted by hands gripping her elbows. She thrashed. He wouldn't lay another hand on her. He wouldn't wreak havoc with her sanity. He wouldn't—

"Indra!" The voice was like tinny sandpaper, abrasive enough to scrape through the noise of Valeryn's ghost.

Eyes snapped open to a stern, pointed little face as her hands were pulled from her ears. Jauyne's hands were shockingly strong for how brittle her fingers looked. They were locked round Indra's wrists, dragging them forward away from her head. Those dark brows were creased with what could have been irritation or fury or curiosity— who ever knew, really?— and her thin lips were pressed thinner still.

"Did you touch a Starstone?" The demand was as sharp as her cutting stare.

"Wh— no, those are all being kept below." Something liquid and warm rolled down the side of her head and over her jaw, even as she caught a flicker of gentleness in all the hard lines of Jauyne's face.

"Tell me what happened, then." It was still a command, but it was an empathetic one. "Tell me, Indra."

The horror in her chest held itself at bay for a full five seconds as she gaped a bit at the over-young Meirydhi Premier. The woman had never been kind to her— never anything but harsh and brusque and deliriously on the verge of fury. For the first time, Indra considered that Jauyne might be an actual human being. It was in this moment of consideration that all the horror spilled over in a gush of tears and stumbling words. None of it made sense, and she knew it, but Jauyne hadn't yet interrupted her, which was shocking, so she continued to allow the nonsense words to tumble out in disarray.

Jauyne yanked out a piece of dainty cloth from her pocket— another surprise— and none too gently began mopping at the sides of Indra's head. Her paled face grew flushed with what Indra could only assume was rage as she continued spilling out what had happened (what might have happened?). When Jauyne pulled the cloth back, folding it, Indra saw that it was soaked through and crimson with her blood.

The woman said nothing, but crushed the handkerchief into one of Indra's shaking hands in silent encouragement to wipe her blubbering face. Her expression was dark and full of wicked promise in the space after Indra's outpouring, which was not quite silence due to the sniffling and gasping with which she was filling the hall. Jauyne only brushed her hand over Indra's arm, with no small amount of awkwardness, and took a deep breath.

"I believe you, Indra," was all she said, voice cold and clipped as the bite of a winter wind.

Indra was just then about to say some word of thanks when everything about Jauyne's posture hardened, and her grey eyes struck the end of the hall like flint. Her lip curled back, a vicious violence seeping from the gesture. A wet trickle started out of Indra's right ear again, dripping from the apex of the dangling teardrop pearl she wore on the lobe. Her throat choked up.

"Walk away, bookkeep." Jauyne's voice was smooth and deadly as the edge of the dagger she wore strapped to her thigh. "You won't be opening your vile little mouth in her presence."

"Indra?"

Valeryn's tentative voice was so flooded with worry it made Indra's heart stutter, but still she did not turn around. She stuffed the handkerchief into her ear and bit her lip. Braving a glance at Jauyne's steeled face, she asked, "Is he... twitching?"

Jauyne did not take her eyes from the librarian, which felt deeply reassuring to Indra. "No." She kept her voice quiet. "But I will watch him. He will not touch you."

Valeryn's footsteps carried him closer, and still Indra kept her back to him, trembling in a way that she thought ought to have made her feel humiliated but instead only caused her to brace herself.

"Indra, you're covered in blood! Let me take you to the infirmary!" His voice rapidly excelled in volume.

It was then that Jauyne brushed around her, sweeping out her dagger with an effortless rasp as she did so. "She said she doesn't wish to see you. Go away." Her manner was as casual as steel.

"She can tell me that herself, thank you!" The indignant tone in his voice wavered only a bit as he was faced with one of the most fearsome wielders of Starlight on Allesar, to his credit.

"I believe she did that already. I'm afraid if you take another step, I'll have to consider it an act of violence and respond with a little violence of my own."

Indra thought Jauyne probably could have gone without the laughter sprinkled into the threat, but she was infinitely grateful all the same.

Valeryn, evidently, was feeling braver than he ought to on this particular occasion. The sick, wet crunch of Jauyne's dagger pommel meeting his jaw, followed by the piteous howl from his throat, was a sound Indra would not find reprieve of for a long while. At least it hadn't been the pointy end.

At this point, Indra turned.

Jauyne stood over Valeryn, who was crumpled into a ball and whimpering on the polished floor, her dagger brandished inverted, the blade jutting down and back from her fist round the hilt. Disgust and bitterness swam in the silver of her irises, now softly beginning to glow.

Panic lurched in Indra's stomach, unaware of what choices this unpredictable woman was capable of. As much as she had needed Valeryn to be incapable of following her, she didn't want his intestines on the floor. She reached out, latched onto the wiry band of Jauyne's forearm. "Let's go, Jauyne. You did it." What it was remained yet to be seen, Indra supposed, with a sort of numb sickness.

Jauyne's eyes flicked between the young man on the ground, carefully cradling his jaw in his hand, and Indra, who was resisting the urge to haul away her by the arm. At long last, her gaze snagged on Valeryn, and she said, with a tic of blunt horror in her high rasp, "What are you?" before turning to walk with Indra further down the hall.

Indra knew Jauyne was expecting nothing of her after that rather humiliating scene, because Jauyne never seemed to expect anything of her, which Indra found particularly insulting. It was because of this, and the newfound fury, and the endless questions her heart carried, that she turned down a small side-hall, one that was terribly familiar, and led Jauyne to the door, which then led to a room with a trap door.

Their steps descending into the yellow-lit darkness were strange and purposeful, and Jauyne asked no questions, which, in Indra's experience, Jauyne had never been known to do. Instead, her presence was steely and quiet, and, wonder of wonders, her eyes never lost their dim glow. Was this how others felt when looking into her own eyes?

As they arrived in the room with the glass enclosure, Adras stood from where they had evidently been making themselves quite comfortable in the corner of the room. A small stack of neatly folded knit blankets padded one of the brutally hard wooden chairs. On the little table in the room was a carafe of coffee, as well as what appeared to be two meals' worth of dirty dishes.

Jauyne crossed her arms at the Jopaari Oracle. "Camping out down here, are we? Still prefer the damp, dark, cold?"

"Charming, as always, Jauyne." Adras raised their coffee mug in a sarcastic salute, until they saw Indra. Their face instantly contorted. "What do we have going on here? Never in a hundred turns of the sun did I think I would see you two walking about as a pair, although anyone being bloodied after a stint in Jauyne's presence seems fitting."

"Afternoon, Jopaari," Jauyne tipped an imaginary hat. "Our Princess was suffering mental abuse from our beloved Valeryn."

Adras'gaze turned slowly to Indra. "What happened?"

"It was strange and fuzzy," fumbled Indra, stumbling for language. "He kissed me. I couldn't— I couldn't pull away. I didn't want it."

"Yes yes," Jauyne pushed her way in. "And then he started popping in and out of sight, and flitting about in an eye's blink."

Indra nodded, thankful for the assistance where her pitiful words could not make do. "And the noises... I could hear him talking to me. Like a memory, but it wasn't."

Adras sucked in a hissed breath. "I realize this has been quite a startling day already," they said, regarding her with a bit of what looked like suspicion. "Elryh was on her way to tell you that we have located a possible location for Osiys, and that we are planning to send in a team in order to bring him home."

Indra's blood stopped flowing through her body... *home... Osiys, home...*

Interrupting her shock and the hopeful tears budding in the corners of her eyes, three enormous men shuffled through the doorway. "We are here," said the first, "for Jauyne of Meirydh, for striking an unarmed man and for being in dangerous and unrefined possession of power."

WE

29

THIS IS WHAT YOU REAP

Jauyne snorted. This was what she got for being nice to an annoying person one time. Figured. "That unarmed man was mentally abusing the precious little princess who you all seem so taken with. Should I rather have just let her bleed out from her ears? Or perhaps succumb to pulmonary failure?"

She knew she was sneering. She knew her voice was dripping with contempt. She knew both of these things were putting her in deeper trouble with each moment. She also did not care, and could not have stopped it even if she had. What did she have if not for her contempt, anyhow?

"No offence, miss, but you're not quite the type likely to be seen protecting her."

Jauyne wanted to spit. "It's Premier to you, you stupid hulk of Brigonan muscle. And you have no earthly idea what type of anything I am."

What she didn't say was that why she'd done it had baffled her at first, as well. She still felt the continuous urge to roll her eyes hard enough to stick whenever the Princess was near. Yet still... she had seen the hysterical gleam in the girl's eyes. She had felt the fury and the fragility and the fear rippling from her in waves.

She knew the chaotic frustration of being overtaken by the visions, of not not knowing whether your own eyes and ears were trustworthy. No being ought to suffer that unprotected. No person trapped in that whirlwind would, in her presence, go unbelieved or defenseless.

Indra surprised her then, stepping between Jauyne and the guards with a strength of spirit that left her feeling thoroughly embarrassed.

"No, she's telling the truth." The girl was squeezing the bloodied cloth hands over and over. "Valeryn... something was not right. He wouldn't stay away when I asked him to. There was something quite strange about... He was not himself. Jauyne found me running blind and bleeding through the halls and defended me when Valeryn caught up with us."

The guards exchanged glances that told Jauyne that Indra's sweet little speech had been altogether unhelpful. She took Indra by the shoulders and pulled her back, out of the way. "They've got to blame someone, and it isn't going to be Valeryn, so it is going to be me. I'm the feral Meirydhi, remember?" She fanned her hands around her face with an altogether excessive wriggle. "We get blamed for everything— I'm well used to it, by now."

An actual dark look of rage crossed Indra's face, and Jauyne recognized it well. "Disgusting," she declared. "I'm past tired of the inter-Province violence. This is the kind of disease my father encourages to fester so he can pick us all apart. I won't be party to this. I'm not going to let them cart you off."

Stubbornness was a good look on anyone, but it was particularly satisfying on Indra's face. Blood had begun drying on the sides of her head, matting her golden curls into a tangled, sticky mass. Some was smeared over her cheeks and chin, and all the crusting red, a mask enhanced by that bright spot of furious courage, gave Jauyne a strange sense of pride. This girl would not be easily knocked over or overrun again. Good. Maybe she'd even become interesting, by some Star-sworn miracle.

One guard stepped forward. "We still need to escort her to Premier Herran, miss. This is a rather grave situation. Valeryn is in the sickroom, and he has not yet come to consciousness. The healers are unsure of how deep the injury goes."

Indra stomped a defiant foot and grabbed for Jauyne's hand before she could pull it away. "I won't have this!"

Adras moved beside Indra, and for just a moment Jauyne thought they'd attempt to drag the girl off of her. She hadn't been exactly welcoming to the Jopaari Oracle those weeks ago when she'd been startled away from what would have been fantastic sex. (Jayne had quickly decided that no one ought to be judged for how they reacted to being startled away from fantastic sex.) But Adras simply pressed a hand to Indra's upper back and nodded. "It seems that one of your guests was threatened by a Brigonan man, which is a rather serious situation according to Brigonan law, am I not correct?"

"That will be for Herran to determine, miss."

The air in the room went cold and dry as death. A pinpoint of confusion sprang into a blade of indignant protection that sliced through Jauyne's gut. "Apologize."

"Pardon?" The guard who had stepped forward was already regretting it.

"Adras is not to be called miss. They are Jopaar's Alloyed Oracle. I hear the High Priestess of Jopaar punishes their anti-alloy factions severely. Is that not right, Adras?"

Adras nodded casually, but the slow gulp that bulged from their throat told Jauyne all she really needed to know. She breathed deeply, and the hum of the Starstones was potent, even through the thickness of the glass.

Beside her, Indra buzzed with fury— not just fury, though. There was also Starlight, pumping through the girl's veins and singing along her skin, zipping across it in solar swirls of silver until it connected with Jauyne's skin. The connection was a shock. She could feel Indra, not just where their fingers were jammed together, but the entirety of her. The shape of her was lit up somewhere inside Jauyne's mind, and she was a beacon, an omen, a whole fucking Star.

It nearly knocked Jauyne off her feet. Zech had been right. (Well, he was nearly always right, but she'd never admit it aloud.) She had never imagined this frail little Princess could withstand the presence of so much power, let alone hold it in her body like a furnace.

Without hesitation, Jauyne clamped down on it, on her, on Indra, and let their Starlight mingle. There was a distinct flow, a river— no, a starved undercurrent— rushing through the three of them. Power sizzled. Ferocity did lightning-steps from Adras to Indra to Jauyne. The walls shimmered like waterfalls rinsed in galactic silver as the guards' eyes swam with fear. Jauyne wanted to consume it, to swallow up their fear in great, cavernous gulps and let it sustain her. *This is what you reap*, she thought. *This is what you reap when you disbelieve a weeping, wounded girl and punish the people who protect her. How do you like your harvest?*

And the baby, the thing that Zech was so insistent was growing inside of her, this tiny person, leapt at that moment. Jauyne knew the baby was too small to feel yet. She knew it was impossible. And she knew what she felt, what the jolt of Starlight in her had done. She knew she was carrying a Starchild, and, quite suddenly and quietly, like the murderous whisper of one of Zech's arrows before it found its target, she realized beyond thought that it was all real— this child, this power, these miraculous people she was just beginning to tolerate. If Jauyne was good at anything at all, if she could still be useful or worth even one drop of the woman she had been mere weeks ago, it would all be driven at using this power to protect her people— her one little Meirydhi person.

Jauyne snatched her hand out of Indra's, cutting the connection and dragging her sense inward, away from the violently humming and glowing Starstones. She pulled it towards her, to her abdomen, and rested it, in a frightful and tentative sort of rest, over the place where she knew that baby was growing. A deep sort of cringe rose up, something that made a part of her want to curl over and shriek until she deposited the contents of her breakfast onto the dirt floor, and made another part of her want to weep with joy.

Her only experience of children had been her baby sister, her relationship with whom her parents had rather ruined with their doting on Astra, and contrasting instruction of Jauyne. But this little baby was more than just a child. It was a citizen with no homeland, and Jauyne would be damned if there were any Meirydhi citizen born into a world with no Meirydh.

Her first and foremost goal still shone true and ferocious in her mind. Nothing would dull that. Nothing would part her from it.

So peering through eyes like struck flint, she outstretched her arms to the guards, wrists bared. "Take me to Herran," she said. "I have a deal to discuss."

ALL

30

SQUEALING TROUBLE

ZECH, BRIGONAN HIGH HOUSE
2 months, 3 weeks since the sack of Meirydh

Zech wasn't stupid, and that meant he didn't want to spend his time putting together a puzzle that everyone around him had already solved. Most currently, and specifically: what the fuck happened to Indra, and why the fuck was Jauyne selling herself out in a very un-Jauyne-like act.

He had instinctively pulled on his old Meirydhi clothing, which he had, for the few weeks they'd been in the High House of Brigon, shucked off in favor of the Brigonan styles. But something in his gut was squealing trouble, and if he had learned anything from growing up among a people whose children flung themselves from limb to limb of the tallest trees, it was that knowing how to fall was just as important as knowing how to climb, and that he always ought to trust his gut.

So now he was creeping through the High House in a sweater, and pants that tied on the side, and quiver-belt, and the looks he was receiving would have been much funnier if it wasn't the Princess of Canestry with whom he was intending to have a chat. Yes, she was still and small and soft spoken, but he could still feel that magnetism, that intense, lurching power under the surface, that tugging forward sort of feeling he'd gotten the very first time he'd been in her presence.

His room was nearly opposite the House from her own, and the House was such a great, expansive thing that took ages to traverse. He stepped to the edge of a small outlet hanging over the wide and empty staircase. Resting his elbows on the cool metal, he tilted his face upward, closed his eyes and pretended that it was real tree cover, that it was the same safety and delight and home he'd grown up with, all those years. Stars, he missed trees. How people lived on bald rock without losing their damn minds, he'd never know. The little charade seemed to work... until he opened his eyes. He turned his gaze down to the stairwell itself. A touch lighted on the back of his upper arm. Zech turned, ready to assure the servant he knew where he was going, but it was Valeryn who stood there. A strange metal reached around the side of his jaw, where bruises mottled the skin, and from the corner of his mouth. Zech just looked him up and down, piteously... He knew himself well enough to know that he was not an adept swordsman, and even he could come out of a practice duel with Jauyne with fewer scrapes and bumps. Unless this poor fellow hadn't really believed her when she'd warned him. Zech almost let out a laugh, recalling his own first altercation with Meirydh's dark-haired Premier.

The young man shifted awkwardly from foot to foot, as if unsure how to give a greeting without the common courtesy of using one's mouth to speak. Speaking, evidently, was not an option for him. He flicked his eyes bitterly away from Zech's scrutiny and lifted up a primly creased piece of paper, scrawled with some note above the personal seal of the Brigonan Record-keeper. Valeryn nodded deeply, and Zech felt genuinely disconcerted by the gesture.

Taking the paper, Zech awkwardly nodded to him in thanks (for some reason it felt rude to speak to someone whose vocal capacity was deemed out of operation?) and paused to read the note written there.

For Indra: I don't fully understand, but I'm terribly sorry to have hurt or frightened you. May this be a peace offering. This is an ancient poem which draws reference to the numbers seven and thirteen, which were repeatedly mentioned in Jauyne's notes. I think it may well be very important. *—Valeryn*

Zech smoothed a hand over the crisp, dried ink, feeling the fibres of the paper and the slight raise of the black letters. He met Valeryn's eyes again, and saw humiliation and anger and the last hints of fading surprise in them. He nodded slowly.

"I'll take it to her," he said. "But Jauyne will see this too. You used her notes. She deserves this."

A flash of grimaced vengeance crossed his distorted face. A quick breath. Then, Valeryn turned with an abruptness which seemed to communicate everything, and padded away.

Worry needled at the edges of Zech's thoughts. Valeryn wasn't cruel or wicked, but he was a young man who had been humiliated, and injured, in front of a girl he cared for, and that was the sort of person who often tended towards violence.

Unfolding the papers in a hurry, he scanned them with suspicious eyes. There was no way in the Starsforsaken void that he was going to hand this to Indra without first inspecting it. What if the librarian had just stuffed it full of exaggerated, pathetic pleas for returned love or some other equally horse-shit concept? But it wasn't that at all. In fact, as he read it, Zech felt a chill of disbelief sweep over the skin on his arms, then up the back of his neck and down his spine.

Indra needed to read this. She needed to read it badly. And so did Jauyne.

Zech left the outlet and continued around the staircase, steps quickening with concern. It took a few more moments, but he soon reached Indra's door, a tall, engraved, and pearl-inlaid thing, and knocked rapidly. The whisper-shush of slipper feet on wood reached the door, and she opened it— just cracked at first, then pulled wide as her smile when she saw him.

"Zech! Hello, I wasn't expecting you!" She stepped to the side to allow him entry, and he couldn't help but smile back. Her kindness was as magnetizing as her power. "It's good to see you. I— I really wish you weren't leaving."

Jauyne had insisted that the two of them needed to leave, to stay away from the High City until their child was born. Though she'd promised to explain, they hadn't yet had the chance to sit in privacy for more than a few moments. She was constantly under watch from the armed guard now, out of concern her power might be let loose over something petty. This was ridiculous, Zech knew, because Jauyne cared only about things which were deadly serious. With the exception of himself, of course.

"So do I," was all he replied with, though he opened his arms to her, and she filled them with a brisk hug. Their interactions had all in all been few but familiar, right from the beginning, as though he knew her already, somehow.

"I have something for you," he continued, carefully. "It is... from Valeryn."

He watched her face close, eyes shuttering, mouth pinching, jaw clamping, chin jutting.

"I don't want it."

"Just... trust me on this, Indra. This is something... more universal than the way he wronged you."

She eyed him flatly.

"I swear to you," he bent his head, little envelope held flat against his chest. "I have looked it over. There's nothing in here that will hurt."

Her silver eyes narrowed a bit, then relaxed. "It hurts by association," she sighed. "But I'll have it. Why don't you read it aloud to me?"

Folding her arms over herself in a gesture that looked a little like shielding her body and spirit from whatever remained of Valeryn in the pages, she perched on the edge of her bed. She looked terribly uncomfortable. Zech decided he should get it all over with as quickly as was possible for his tongue to form the words. He unwrapped the papers in such a hurry that one of them tore slightly along the side. He muttered a fuck or two of annoyance at his own clumsiness.

The Seven Stars were the first inhabitants, after the elements themselves, and the great old seers and monsters, and they spread out over all the land, tending to the planet and teaching it the whirling songs of the cosmos. They kissed the ground where they stood and drew up from it dancing Mortals. And as they did, a great song began to chant through the very dirt below their feet:

Memory is a liar

It tells Stars seven lies

The forgotten invents you

With scarlet-streaked hide

Brightest of Starlight

You must tell thirteen truths

Remember your skin

To be conjured anew

One is the dove

Wings of spilled blood

Two is the dragon

The Harbinger comes

Three is the avenger

Wields the legacy trove

Four is the deathless

Unshackled, unscorned

Five is the shifter

Slaughtered in test

Six is the reaper

Defying void's breath

Seven is the guide

The Labyrinth-singing

Eight is the bespeaker

Archives enduring

Nine is the key

The void and the voice

Ten is the serpent

Who tethers to choice

Eleven is the infinite

The walker of Star paths

Twelve is the whole

Greater than two halves

Thirteen is the god

Lightless ruler of the Fall

Curiosity of worlds

The returning holds all

Indra's face looked numb, and Zech could see the fine raised bumps of a chill spread across her collar bones and chest. He stayed quiet as she brought her forefingers and thumbs to her temples and swirled them there, absentmindedly. Her silver eyes were growing terrifyingly bright as she at last turned her face to his. His feet were still frozen to the floor near the doorway, unsure of what he should do. But she stood, flowed over to him as though her muscles were made of silk, and gripped his wrists.

"Jauyne must see this. Her words are in here. This is proof— it's what we have so badly been needing. This proves her fits are visions of the Stars."

Zech wanted to believe her. He wanted to say, *fuck yes! My lover hasn't entirely gone out of her head! We can stay!*, but something sat heavy and cold in his gut, and he knew it was the truth. Jauyne could not stay in this place, with its dense stone walls, and perfectly ordered city streets, where they kept magic behind layers of protective glass. She was too wild for it. Her contact with the Starstone may not have set off full blown psychosis, but an extended period of time in this High City just might.

He shook his head, a bit sadly, and handed the slightly crumpled pieces of paper to Indra. "It's more than proof, but you don't really think she's meant to be here, do you?" He said it simply, and she started a bit. "She's practically feral!" — a laugh— "And especially with... the situation at hand."

Indra paused with her hands on the papers, her smallest finger tucked into the tear he'd accidentally made. "What situation?"

He felt like crying, though he was unsure why. "Jauyne is pregnant, Indra."

"Pregnant?" Her little mouth gaped. "You're absolutely sure?"

"I don't know how I missed it." A sniff escaped. "I... I should have known sooner. I don't know how I didn't know sooner."

"Oh..."

His emotions were being keenly observed, and discomfort wriggled into the spaces his just-falling tears left. Setting down the pages with a rustle, Indra came to stand in front of him, gripped his arms gently.

"I should have known." He continued as though her contact was the breaking of a dam. "She's so angry. And she should be. I should have known."

"Friend, if you should have known, you would have. So perhaps stop looking for ways to find fault with yourself. She can be angry, and you can be innocent, and it doesn't make her anger any less wrong." Her little arms wrapped around him briefly, before she turned and crisply stacked the pages on her writing desk.

"I'll copy all these down and then bring the original to Jauyne to have something to do in the guardhouse."

He nodded. "If it's not too much trouble." She was not quite what he'd expected she would be, if all the High House guards and servants were to be trusted. She was so much kinder, so much more ancient, so much less fragile.

Indra paused, he little ink pot and sheets of paper she was pulling from the desk drawer halted halfway out. She turned to him with a small smile that looked a little sad, seeming to read his mind. "I'm capable of much more than that which I'm given credit for."

She slid the crisp parchment fully out of the drawer and laid it on the desk, resting the ink pot beside it. A long, starkly striped feather— pheasant, Zech noted absentmindedly— was withdrawn from the little drawer as well, and then she slid it closed and drew back the little writing chair.

"I know that I look very fragile— Stars know how many times that word has been used to relegate me to some small, unimportant task— but I singlehandedly stole highly secretive Star Charts from my father's house and smuggled them out to an enemy Province, relying on the aid of a spy. More than that, though," she continued softly, turning away from him and sitting down, "I survived seventeen years in my fathers house, within the same walls, stifled and meek, and still found the courage with which to stand up and walk out. That is what I am capable of."

She seemed to be talking more to herself than him, as though she needed the reminder. The swallow that filled his throat was heavy as he watched her gently uncap the ink pot and dip the pheasant feather into it. She began to copy the poem, deliberately and gracefully.

"You're right," he said. "You're right. I could sense you before I saw you here, you know? I looked at Jauyne and I told her as much— that there was another Starchild, and that it was you. I don't really think you are fragile."

She leant her head over her shoulder, catching what he hoped was the sincerity in his gaze with the corner of her eye. A little smile quirked up the side of her mouth. "I know, Zech. You are a good person."

He tilted his head at her, smiled. It was a weird thing to say, he thought. It wasn't his goodness he was concerned about— more like his sanity. But he watched as she copied down the ancient words and blew softly on the ink to dry it, and when she handed him the time-worn stack of original parchment, he took it. He thanked her warmly, tucked her halfway into a hug, and wished her well, and then he was back in the long halls of the Brigon High House, winding his way towards Jauyne.

He found her in the meeting hall.

Or, rather, he heard her. Starsdamnit, Jauyne...

Her restraint was fracturing, that much was clear, and he could feel the Starlight crackling in her as her raised voice carried through the thick wooden doors, outside of which stood two armed guards.

That's new...

"You know nothing about him that isn't from frightened fucking gossips," she was saying, her voice level but dangerously unhinged. "Don't you say his name to me. You don't deserve for it to cross your lips."

Herran's reply sounded exasperated. "He's a border watchman who's widely known as insane, Jauyne. Honestly, as a Premier, you ought to use some discretion. But don't mind me. Go to the guardhouse, stay there until we have this mess with the Starstones under control, and you'll have the things you've requested."

There were scrambling noises from inside as Zech felt his face grow hot, and Jauyne burst from the doors, visibly seething, Starlight sprouting and shrinking from her body in crackles like lightning. She met his eyes, and hers grew determined as her feet pounded the carpeted hall, leaving black marks in her wake. When she reached him, her hands gripped his face, her eyes lit brightly, and kissed him hard and rough. Teeth dragging out his lower lip, she nuzzled her nose to his in a gesture so soft it startled him.

"You've never been insane, *il enë liyd,*" she murmured fiercely against his mouth. "Let's go."

NEED

31

I CAN FIX THIS TOO

Adras had never thought they would have cause to see the cursed Province of Canestry. This had never bothered them, seeing as they had never desired to see a place this filled with the degradation of all that they spent their life learning to honor. The air seemed to condensate with a heavy sickness as the rescue party drew closer, and they licked their lips compulsively for what was most likely the hundredth time. The horses' hooves made slurping sounds on the muddy ground.

The party had passed Meirydh nearly two weeks ago— a stinking mass of rotting flesh and gaping, blackened wounds. It was an abomination, Adras thought, that so many dead should be left dishonored and vulture-picked. There were nine of them in the party, and not one of them had said a word as they passed the stink that hung in the air next to that once-glorious High City. Adras had brought their cowl up around their nose to block out the smell, but even the thickly-knitted Jopaari wool had not been able to keep it from their nostrils.

Adras was quite used to travel, but was less used to traveling in a group. It was slower going and they found they were rather impatient and irritable when the group was forced to pause or wait due to someone's needs. They weren't even frequent needs, which Adras reminded themself of often, but still it was not a thing to which they were accustomed. Lumen seemed to share their annoyance, chewing his lower lip and sighing a bit as though he alone had somewhere very important to be. He seemed to have something strange up his sleeve, a weird secret kept even from Adras, which hovered in Adras' peripheral like a spy perpetually evading clear sight.

Lumen's strangeness only irritated them further, so that by the time the party reached the brink of Canestryn territory, they were twitchy and finicky with aggravation.

This was terribly unlike them, and this—

somehow— annoyed Adras even more. There was nothing they liked less than feeling unlike themselves, after all the long years of working to understand and externalize what 'themselves' even was, outside the gripping definitions that had been placed on them by the people of Jopaar.

So Adras perched on their inky steed, fingering his mane with restless energy, and called absentmindedly on their Starlight.

The bonds were strong. Angry, even. And Adras had never, in their two decades of near-constant contact with the celestial bodies, known the Stars to feel angry. Their cool light was like ice here, a frigid fury, where elsewhere the coolness was a balm. The freeze-burnt taste of shock, and its lingering curiosity, needled at the edge of their mind, and they teased it, pressing their awareness further towards the city.

Spears of icy light seared their knowing, and Adras gasped. The city was full of Starlight, but it was wrong. There was no love in it, no knowing, no sacredness. They could feel it, slimy and pocketed with cold, running through the high outer walls of the city, through the inner walls of the Premier's High House and the streets of the High City. It ran thick and slow as though weighed down by something profane, and as their awareness intersected it, it became a clinging, caking thing, reaching for them with heavy arms of a cold deeper than any frozen tundra.

Rage scraped into them, a Starlight that was deep and hot and smooth as fine whiskey at the back of their throat, a Starlight that refracted on their conscience like campfire sparks on lake water. The Stars are angry, Canestry. What have you done...

"Adras? What's—" Lumen had reached for their arm, and was now recoiling. A hiss shucking from his lips as he wrung his hand out in the cool evening air. "What the fuck, Ads, you're burning hot! What are you doing to the horse?"

Adras blinked. The slightest silver hummed under their skin, veins alight with the hum. The light diffused under their fingernails and cobwebbed through the tiny capillaries in their hands. Where their fingers had been toying with their horse's mane, the thick strands of hair were softly shimmering in response. The previously coarse black hairs were turning a silky silver. They could feel the rest of their party shifting with an unsettled air. Someone muttered something about the horse's eyes glowing.

That whiskey and campfire Starlight curled in their lungs like the aromatic smoke of a Pallydhan cigar, and a violent joy slicked over their

Star bonds to settle deep in their stomach. The sparks and the whiskey and the smoke and the light hummed with pleasure, a pleasure that became a low cello song. Will you be our champion? The song was the Stars, but with something more glittering and golden, something with more heat. Will you allow us to choose you? Will you choose yourself?

No priestess tea or sacred chant, no hypnotic incense or Starlit ritual, had ever stirred something so hot and true in Adras. None of their years of dedication and training had produced connection like this. What chance was there, truly, that they would be able to turn down the first choice that had ever been wholly theirs to make?

"Yes," Adras whispered. "Yes, I will be your champion."

Then we will be yours, sang the liquid cello Stars. Go.

Adras looked back only once, to Lumen. "Go to the opposite gate. Do not stop. Beware. The walls of this city are sick."

His softly slanted black eyes blinked once, assessing, before he grinned. "Tear them apart." At his words, their horse broke into a gallop.

It was as though their steed was swimming in a current. Its hooves did not beat against the ground— or if they did, they were both still and silent. The wind slammed into Adras' face, and they had the strangest inclination to tilt back their head and roar. Every pin-prick Star in the sky blared bright as day for them, a shining path carved out for them and them alone as the midnight horse with Starlight mane bolted, muscles loosely churning beneath velvet skin, towards the front gate of Canestry's High City.

There was a lightness in their blood, a fuzzy, heated hum like furs in front of the fireplace, that strung them infallibly to every blazing celestial body. Adras hugged the horse's body with her knees, though they scarcely needed to, and spread their arms wide like the dragon wings tattooed on the front of their neck, a laugh loosing from their open mouth. A soft crackling skittered from the Starlight bonds into their chest and down the length of their arms as they raced boldly between two border towers, and a liquid fire sprang to life in the mortar between the stones. The towers melted into wet flame and chunks of stone, pierced through by the screams of watchmen.

Every drop of blood, every chip of bone, every strand of hair burned yes in their ears.

A high warning squealed through the starlit night as Adras drew impossibly closer to the city walls, thin voices pealing out, "Danger at the gates!"

For the first time, Adras had no need to swallow back a lingering inkling of fear and run to where the danger was. For the first time, they were no fascinating object or wounded student or lonely child or brave warrior or wise oracle. Adras was the danger at the gates, and the danger feared nothing at all.

They drew the horse up short at the gate, placed a hand over the wood. Whatever infected Starlight hid within it crawled under the surface and bubbled up, pressing revoltingly against the palm of their hand. That same rage scraped at their insides with a raw burn, and Adras pressed it out, a sacred rite of their own creation. The rage shrieked from their palm— hungry, holy— seeking out the pollution that slunk through Canestry's gates, and Adras screamed with their whole chest, a battle cry.

Foul smoke poured from the grain of the wood, the tainted light becoming a fireless flame that burned nothing at all, instead belching refuse into the clear night air. The dark cloud of it came for Adras, wrapping itself sticky and thick around their outstretched arm. Indignation streamed from the Stars, a wordless blaze of feeling that stretched from the sky to Adras' heart and then screeched down their arm. The sticky vapor liquefied, the last drops of it slipping unpleasantly from their fingers to a steaming puddle on the dirt below.

Tell the gates to open, sang the cello Star-song.

"Open," commanded Adras, and they swung on their hinges.

They rode through freely.

The smooth-hewn stone streets were in an early state of chaos. Soldiers stumbled out of the bunkhouses built up against the outer wall, and late-night party-goers fled as the watchmen yelled. Blaring calls of "city breach!" were going up all around Adras, but they bolted through the bewildered inhabitants of the crowded street. The sickly Starlight ran like a near-invisible river of poison through the very stone of the streets, leading them directly to the High House itself. They watched it wind out in front of them, unfurling a path of blasphemy and destruction which curdled their stomach.

I can fix this, too.

Adras' steed responded with a whinny, and Adras locked one foot into the stirrup, hooked the opposite knee over the breadth of the saddle, and gripped the pommel tightly as they swung sideways. They dangled nearly upside down, reaching a hand for the rock. When their fingers met the road, there was no tearing of flesh, similarly to whatever way the steed's hooves made neither noise nor jostling motion. Instead there was the repulsing squirm of infection beneath the city's skin, and the shriek of rage thrusting from their fingertips.

Clouds of black smoke curled behind them, obscuring the buildings and street from view, and it followed Adras as their horse continued to drive his way forward, deeper into the heart of the city. The soldiers who had been gathering behind them were suspended in the darkness, and Adras heard their anguished and petrified screams echoing off the stone as the gaseous poison passed around and through them.

Their horse tossed his mane, and Adras righted themself with a grunt. He had come to a stop outside of a second gate, this one smaller. It appeared to be the gate directly enclosing the Premier's High House and grounds. Adras nearly spat with disgust. This was where Indra had been trapped for seventeen years. This was the place she'd been harmed, controlled. This was the place where Osiys had invested and sacrificed so much of his life, only to have it stolen back and boxed up within the very same walls. They didn't need to have a connection deeper than the one that already ran between them and these two people to be innately disgusted at their treatment.

In moments, this gate too, was flung open, and Adras dismounted their steed, and left him at the gate, shimmering and silver.

They stepped through on their own two feet. The gate slammed closed, sudden and vicious, behind them. Adras didn't need to turn in order to know there were guards waiting— they could feel the ugly way their armor and weapons glittered with that same poisonous inversion— so they did so slowly.

No fewer than a dozen guards stood against the gate and surrounding wall with lazy confidence. A few whispers skittered through the ranks, and muffled chuckling followed them. One of the soldiers, looking well-decorated and full of hate, stepped forward, a predatory sneer crawling up his face. His metal armor clanged and scratched against itself when he crossed his arms, and the anger of the Stars boiled as he tilted his head in inspection of them.

"It appears they've alerted the whole city over this little lady." He tossed a glance over his shoulder at the waiting soldiers. "Who's shaking in their boots?"

A swell of laughter rolled over the men.

Adras curled their lip. "I am not a lady."

The soldier snorted. "Well I can see that." His eyes shone as they roved the length of Adras' body. "Pray tell, what are you then, little hybrid lady-thing?"

Bile burned at the back of their throat. "I am an Alloy." Adras lifted their chin. "A bit of the astral, a bit of skin, forged in Starfire."

He stared wide-eyed at Adras with brows raised, then sputtered out a laugh, spittle wetting the stone. "Looks like there's nothing to worry about, fellas," he called back, and they joined in his laughter. "She's not quite right in the head. This little lady thinks she's a Star!"

All went silent in Adras' mind, except the steady song of smoke and whiskey and Starlight that came to them from the cosmos. Every connecting thread of Starlight pulled taut, and the thin seam of their mouth stretched in a slow smirk.

"Wrong again. I am not a Star." Adras flexed their fingers by their side, in time with the fresh chorus of laughter. "I'm their champion, fucker."

Cloying darkness exploded from the armor of the men behind him, and it flung itself over their heads, enveloping them in a saturating smoke that seeped through their skin. It dried them out from the inside, consuming them until they were papery husks, too fragile to hold their own armor, and the clang of metal sounded as their breastplates caved in the ashy bones of their ribs and sternum and clavicle. The wet splat of their eyeballs dropping to the stone was punctuated only by the hysterical screaming of the man in front, their determined leader, who had wet himself in petrification.

The stain spread long down his leg as the shadows writhed, crawling over his feet, across the stone, to Adras. He shuddered, collapsing to his hands and knees in the last trickle of his own piss, as the last of the shadows passed him by. Adras tried not to flinch as the shadows collected themselves around the angles and edges of their body. They did not flinch. They trusted the song. As if it felt their trust, the song sang louder, wilder, speared through with a sharpness and melancholy it hadn't been before. All those raging notes turned the sticky smoke to a liquid that burned like cold fire as it dripped from their body. It splashed on the stone and vibrated into void-like nothing— in itself, a dying star.

Adras stepped forward, till the toes of their boots were even with the man's trembling hands. A slurred spike of disgust dropped into their stomach, and they pulled a dagger from their hip. The man yelped pitifully, flinching.

"Don't turn them on me!" The man blathered, fingernails scrabbling in pebbles and urine on the ground. "Don't send the shadows for me! I always knew it was a terrible plan! We were just having a bit of fun with you, I swear! We didn't know any better!"

Adras' lip curled involuntarily. It was always the same with his kind— always just joking. Somehow their jokes always seemed to dry Adras to a frightened husk. Not this time. They pressed the point of the dagger under the tip of his chin, lifted it so that he was forced to look in their eyes. Saliva hung in strands, delicate and obscene, from his silently muttering lips.

"What is your name?"

"Vadris!" In his hurry to comply with their question, another dollop of saliva drooped over the corner of his mouth, onto Adras' dagger. Lumen would have run him through for that offense alone. His tears and mucus from his nose both ran down and over his lips and chin, commingled.

"What am I, Vadris?"

He shuddered, visibly, into the edge of the dagger, and the bodily fluids running over his chin slid under the upper hem of his shirt, red with blood. "You are the champion of the Stars." The whisper was wet and groggy.

"What have I done, Vadris?"

"You've killed all these men." More of his fluids dripped from the sharp edge of their blade. His glassy eyes were too dilated.

"How did I kill them, Vadris?"

"You took all the light out of their armor..." Something like confusion twitched over his visage. "Only the Premier can do that. He said it would protect against people like you."

Adras resisted the urge to laugh at that, even as concern embedded itself deep in their gut. They bent at the waist, leaning close to his ear, and the repugnant scent of sweat and piss and rising bile slammed into their nostrils. Vadris's long hair was splattered in slimy, wet stripes over his temple and forehead, dripping with sweat. Nevertheless, they spoke gently, in the tone one might used to coax a child, into his ear.

"You are going to tell me precisely where Osiys is being kept. And then you are going to go to your Premier, and you are going to tell him that this perversion of Starlight cannot protect any of you from me. Nothing can protect any of you from me. And if you refuse, I will let the shadows feast on you."

He was weeping, openly. Great spluttering sniffs wracked his body. But he only said. "The prisoner is inside the dais. He's inside the dais!"

Adras recalled their dagger, wiping it on Vadris's un-dampened sleeve as he flinched again and again. They stepped back, revulsion finally boiling over. "Get the fuck away from me."

He fumbled backward on his hands and knees, flailing at a fevered pace into a gait that propelled him vertical, till he was pushing himself through the gates and bolting away from them, down the road. Something deep within them had shuddered free, something more violent and primal, something of which the High Priestess would be ashamed. For the first time, Adras shrugged out from underneath that measly feeling of guilt, and turned their sights toward the High Meeting Hall of Canestry.

YOU

32
SARCASTIC DISPLAYS OF HALFHEARTED SQUABBLE

JAUYNE, BRIGON/CHEDHIY GUARDHOUSE
3 months, 3 weeks, 3 days since the sack of Meirydh

Jauyne was regretting everything.

The little Brigon-Chedhiy borderline guardhouse, which the Brigonans had offered to them, looked, and smelled, as if it hadn't been actively used in the last decade. It likely hadn't been, she figured, with the exception of the time they'd stayed there during their trip to Brigon, considering there had never been any contact between the two provinces that wasn't friendly. To be sure, both provinces were somehow simultaneously stubborn and equable, and as such they frequently worked the other into sarcastic displays of half-hearted squabble.

But the friendly quality was long-established, and many of the borderline guardhouses were left either abandoned or scarcely-used.

They had attempted to clean it in the first few hours following their arrival, but even though Zech made a show of stripping off his shirt before working a thin sheen of sweat across his muscled shoulders, a slow, worming dread made its home in her.

It wasn't just the dust that clouded in strangely near-sentient swirls, or the family of mice that they'd shooed from the three cupboards, or the oily gunk slicking Zech's fingers after he'd unclogged the back-filling wash basin.

It was the unsettling feeling that she was trapped here alone with him. Not that she feared he'd try to harm her— quite the opposite. Already, a cloying smothered-ness clung to her lungs. She was not the settling kind. She was the let-her-best-friend-finger-her-and-then-go-back-to-discussing-interprovince-policy kind.

The thought of which made her chest ache with the missing of Lissa— snitching the dinner rolls with pepper jelly to eat them on her balcony, flirting mercilessly before easing into the comfort of their friendship. She wanted to throttle Zech, but this hadn't even been his horrible-idea concoction. She had actually chosen this, and that was the most unbelievable part of all.

Her brain had cleared enough for her to gain some grasp on the possibility that this pregnancy was not his fault. They had spoken about it. There was a tense forgiveness and gentle leaning in from both of them, and she truly was beginning to find solace and comfort inside of this thing they'd become. It wasn't *that* bothering her.

It was the four walls. The stale air. The height of this stupid treehouse, perched between tree and rock. The lack of choice, even within her choice, on all fronts.

Sure, she could have tried to make a run for somewhere less stifled, and Zech would have come with her. She'd chosen not to. She'd chosen this. Sure, she could have drunk the bleeding tea and rid her body of this child taking up residence. She'd chosen not to. She'd chosen this.

A short spike of fear jutted into her chest as the room swam in front of her, and for a moment she nearly smacked herself out of frustration. Now was not the time for tears— when was ever the time for tears?— but it was not tears which where drowning the dusty room and Zech's bare chest in her vision.

A slow warbling started in the skull behind her eyes— a watery hum that soaked her vision and hearing in bogged-down time and untrustworthy distance. The walls seemed to tilt this way, then that— slowly, hypnotically.

Drippy, slurred consonants shrouded her ears: *Did you come to find me?*

"Huh?" She felt the syllable leave her mouth, but it seemed to stick to her teeth. Her tongue was clumsy.

"Jauyne?" Zech spun, and she watched it happen in slow motion, watched all those diamond drops of sweat being flung from his skin, across the room. All she did was blink, and his fingers were digging into her elbow and ribs.

"Off!" She managed, and again, the word was chewy.

"Yeah, I don't think so," he said from very far away, directly beside her. "You can flay me later if you'd like. You need to sit. Something's not right."

"Dizzy," she said, garbled, as though bubbles were popping under her tongue.

"No shit. Do you feel okay otherwise? Does anything hurt?"

My pride, my sense of self, my independence... "No." She felt her body make contact with something both soft and sturdy— the fresh mattress which had been carted in with them.

That water-logged, slurring voice crept back toward her. *Hmm... Interesting. You need to leave. There's more out there. They never would listen, but I remember everything. That induced memory theft doesn't work on me.*

"What?" She smacked her tongue against her teeth in an attempt to release it.

Zech's brows folded into a frown. "I didn't say anything."

"Not..." she smacked her tongue again. "Not you."

The frown creasing his face deepened. "Then, who, Jauyne?"

Walls spun. She squeezed her eyes together. "Don't know."

The damp voice whispered directly into her ear this time. *Strange that he can't see me— oh, that neither of you can, huh? Must be you, little fire-starter. You feel... funny.*

Something wet trickled down the angular lilt of her jaw. It felt like magma. *Firestarter... how can you know his name for me...?*

"Fuck. Your ear is bleeding." He wiped the side of her face a bit roughly, and a groan came from somewhere impossibly deep in his body. "I knew coming here was a shit idea. I should have fought it harder."

His voice was helpfully distracting, and she let her consciousness swivel toward it. He needed to keep talking. "Why?" She murmured, her tongue a bit less tacky.

There was a long pause, and she could feel the tension building in him. Fumbling on the comforter, she at last grabbed hold of his hand. It was clammy with sweat, like the rest of him. "Why?" she repeated.

"Because..." He fidgeted. "This part of the mountains is full of ghosts. I even feel a bit like a ghost when I'm here. Like I'm haunting whoever I used to be."

She swallowed. Of course. Of course. "This is close to where you used to live... Where your family—"

"Yes."

Childhood memories assaulted her without warning— the last time all the Provinces had been together. A celebration; it ought to have been, at least. She'd been only twelve, then, and still she recalled the screams of a boy about her age, high up on a rocky outcropping, pleading with a woman... she'd jumped. She had seen that woman again inside his mind on that night in the shack in the outskirts of Meirydh... How could she have forgotten all that time?

But this... this wasn't near enough to the center of Chedhiy to be where his mother had died. This was where the earthslide had claimed his father and sister. She wondered with more dread what other ghosts littered this corner of the mountain range.

She chanced to open her eyes. The room was still groggy with that absurd watery quality, but it no longer tilted sideways or tried to drag her down to meet its floor. She blinked. Flicked her eyes hesitantly toward Zech. His jaw was tight, but his eyes were gentle where they met hers. Within a moment of that met gaze, the gentleness melted into self-conscious regard.

"I just... I don't like to talk about it. The High Circle made me repeat it so much when it happened. And they told me so many times that I wasn't making sense..."

A little splinter of protective anger angled into Jauyne's ribs. She reached for him before she could stop herself. "That's absurd. What doesn't make sense about an earthslide?"

He eased her up until she sat opposite him, legs tucked. Ugh, her ear was throbbing something nasty. She thought he might not answer when he took her chin between his finger and thumb to tilt her head, inspecting the bloody ear. "I don't know. They sure seemed skeptical." There was a pause where he peered more intently at her ear. "Looks like your eardrum might have popped. Why are you always turning up injured and angry, firestarter?" He huffed a little laugh, even as the heat fled her body.

"The ghost knows you call me that." Hot sick curdled her gut.

The warm hands on her jaw stilled, then turned her face back to his, sharp and sudden. "What?"

"Our little ghost friend, who made the room swim and my ear bleed, called me that, not five minutes ago." She wrenched her chin from his fingers.

He opened his mouth to reply, but a noiseless gust of wind slapped against the little guardhouse, whipping the dust into massive swirls of unreal, life-like forms that dissolved and reformed over and over all about the room. The pressure of the strange, silent wind was utterly unbearable. Jauyne gasped for a breath, but it was as though the wind were sucking air from her lungs to create itself. She dug her fingers into Zech's hand, rage and terror splitting her in two as the wind doubled in intensity and forced them into a huddled mass, clinging to the mattress for fear of being carried off.

Something hard and sharp punctured her upper arm and was ripped out again by the wind before she could cry out. A sharp hiss from Zech told her he, too, was being assaulted by this conscious hurricane. They hid in one another's arms, nothing to be done, until the wind gradually lessened. It still tossed the inky strands of her hair all about, but she wrangled them to the side in time to see the dust, risen up in a female form that stood still above them, disintegrate into tiny particles in the suddenly dead air.

Sputtering with something between disgust and horror, she batted at the fine layer of grime that now coated her clothes and skin. Beside her, Zech coughed violently, an apparent attempt at forcibly dispelling the dust-woman from his lungs.

He finally gasped a clear breath, but Jauyne scarcely noticed. Her eyes were fastened to the floor by her feet, where a piece of distinctive, moth-eaten paper was pinned to the wooden boards by a bloody shard of bone. A wet, red drip splashed onto its surface, the very same color as the words scrawled there, and she put an absentminded hand to the cut on her arm. In her own blood was written a single sentence.

Remember me and do what you're here for, or I'll make them tell you, and that will be messy. Love you.

DON'T

33
TOE TO TOE WITH A FUCKING BEAST

Their hands were covered in a grey film of grime, and they dimly wondered what sort of permanent damage contact with those vile dark contortions of Starlight might do. A bit of his vomit-flecked spittle had splattered on the supple leather of their vest, and they wiped it away with a sickened grimace. They reached out a hand to take hold of the door latch, but it whispered away from their touch.

Adras had their axe and dagger in their hands and flexed toward the widening crack of the door, just as a curved short blade jutted out from the dark. They grunted, lifting their dagger and scraping the cold steel of the sword across the wide hilt, side-stepping its curvature. The thick, dark wood of the door was flung open, and a furious, black-eyed face jutted out of the opening.

"Adras?" Lumen's mouth fell a little slack before cleaving into a sweat-streaked grin.

"About damn time you showed up. Where've you been? showing off? I heard a hell of a lot of screaming out there. Thought I was about to go toe to toe with a fucking beast."

A twinge of relief pinged in their gut, and they returned his smile, albeit smirkier. "I am a beast, Lu. Don't forget it." The sight of the dais far behind him in the massive hall dragged them harshly back to their duty. They raised their axe again, pointing at the raised platform of black stone. "He's in there."

Lumen blinked, incredulous. "In where? I've looked all over the place."

They pushed past him, the smell of his sweat clinging to their nostrils in a sort of familial comfort that was borderline absurd. "He's inside the dais. That man you heard screaming told me."

The grind of hinges swiveling and wooden crunch of a bar being jammed into place sounded behind them, before Lumen's near-silent footsteps caught up with them. They moved fast through the hideous room, on guard in a limber way that had relief and a renewed strength churning through their muscles, but worry flicked against the relief.

"Lu, where's everyone else? Why aren't they with you?"

They knew him well enough to track the pupils, invisible in the rest of the black of his eyes, and they knew his was nervously side-eyeing them now. They didn't have time for this nonsense.

"I asked you a question." It came out snappish and hoarse.

"The rest of them were coming in from the opposite side— we figured a surrounding assault on the Hall would be best. They took out the guards on that side. A couple of them got... enveloped... by this weird black light. Sticky, smoky shit. The rest either got the hell out or followed me in here. Berg and Enoch are guarding the opposite entry."

Just Enoch and Berg... a sick motion twisted in their chest. Getting Osiys out would be much harder than they'd anticipated. The use-polished wooden handle of their axe danced ominously in their left hand, beside which Lumen flicked the hilts of his twin curved blades in little circular twirls within his palms. The unlit chandeliers hung high above them, their shadows twisted and hideous in the dirty light thrown from the much-lower sconces.

The two of them reached the dais, and Adras nodded to Lumen. "Look around the perimeter. On it. Wherever. Find where it opens."

They narrowed their eyes at him when his face twisted in suspicion. But that suspicion was well-earned. This seemed far-fetched. Doubt flickered under their scalp. Vadris could have lied... He should have lied. But Adras clutched the memory of his terror-wide eyes, the reek of him, and assured themself: *Fear doesn't lie. That's left to confidence.*

The dais was made from some black stone that seemed immensely dense and somehow shielded. The steps and edges of it were fitted impossibly tight together— the lines so crisp and perfect, that the design of it seemed both impossible as well as distantly familiar. They let the death-sharp edge of their axe run across its surface, and blue sparks popped into life at the contact.

He has to be here...

They circled to the back of the square dais, testing each step as they took it. Crouching, they placed their hands flat on the strange material and reached out with Starlight, and they felt... nothing. It was a void, an emptiness, that wormed under their fingers. It so unsteadied them, that they toppled back, landing on their ass with a sharp gasp. The only other thing that felt as untouchable as that was—

Lumen was beside them in a fraction of a second. "What? What did you find?"

Adras opened their mouth, closed it, opened it again. "I can't feel anything. The dais— it's like a void."

Lumen stared at them for a moment. "You mean like—"

They cut him off with a curt nod. "We need to find a way in. We have to."

Their brother did nothing for a moment. Then he blinked, slowly, as though the act had been much-deliberated. He took two steps down the dais, then knelt forward til his knees made contact with one step higher. He sheathed his blades on his back, and with a glance at Adras that sent a spiraling shot of realization and panic down their spine, he slammed his hands onto the top of the dais.

They had tried to leap for him, in that blazing second between glance and contact, but too late. Adras rammed against the invisible repellant magnet force that he had become.

A scream ripped from their tongue, and they tasted something like human ash. They pummeled their fists against the growing pressure that groaned outward from Lumen, squeezing painfully inside their ears.

Adras watched as Lumen curled over his flattened hands in a pained arc, only thinly aware of the reedy screeching that scratched its way out of their throat, cocooning the same syllable over and over: "Lu! Lu! Lu!" All sense was gone, all care for who they might attract with the noise— there was only Lumen, who mattered more to them than all the world and the Stars, and the dais and their uninhibited terror.

Lumen's hands were still pressed hard against the black dais, his mouth stretched into an excruciating grimace that was creased with dark blood. His hands and arms seemed to be losing their sense of corporeality, shuddering into a grainy mirage as the short section of dais in front of him did the same. It was as though the dais were dissolving, each little mote suspending in the air before drifting towards him. The floor and base of the dais and the back of the throne which sat upon it were eaten away, withering and disintegrating into hollowed-out panels. Lumen lifted his head towards the specks, and black blood oozed from the corners of his eyes, from his ears, from his nose, from the pores of his skin.

With a malevolent rush, the dais flecks hit Lumen full-force, and he gagged, twitching but unable to retch, as they forced their way into his chest and down his throat. He froze, momentarily, looked toward Adras with stained black lips and an expression of utter agony— they wanted to reach for him, to gather him up and hold him like they had the first and only time this had happened before, to tell him *stop, please please please, stop*— before he toppled backwards down the stairs.

The repellent force surrounding Lumen ripped outward, sucking a wet pop from somewhere in Adras' right ear before shattering the blown glass of the candle sconces. Most of the candles went out, and Adras found themself stumbling for Lumen in the dingy-brown near-darkness.

When their hands found his head, it was sticky and matted with blood. His chest rose and fell in shallow, light breaths that shuddered more than they properly inhaled. They gripped his face in their hands, felt for the life-point on his neck where his heartbeat throbbed.

"Why would you do this?" They swallowed a sob, and it seemed to get caught somewhere behind their ribs. "You didn't even give me a chance to try... You don't know what I could have done... You—" A groan echoed against the dais.

"Lu, can you hear me?"

No answer.

"Lumen, answer me, you reckless child."

Another moan. It wasn't coming from Lumen's body. They scraped their axe free, brandishing it with one hand while they gripped his shoulders against them with her other. "Who is there?"

Their voice was wrenching, even to Adras' own ears.

A scuffling noise filled the gaping hollows left by Lumen's work. The smack of brandished skin on stone, the belabored breathing of someone's body working hard. A cracked voice tried and failed to produce language, and settled for a hacking, wet cough and yet another moan. It tried again. "Are you... Adras?"

His voice cracked the world into sharp, mocking contrasts. Osiys was alive.

"I am." Anxiety made them monotone. "We are here for you. Can you walk?"

"Not sure," his voice was barely sustained. "Will try."

The opposite doors were thrust open, and moonlight poured in over the dais, silver and unreal. Berg and Enoch burst through, weapons drawn, ears drooling blood.

"You actually found him," Enoch gasped, too loud, and Berg let out a wail which clipped in half as he sprinted forward.

In the moonlight, Lumen's hair seemed to glow, and whatever blood was matted in it turned abruptly to dust. The wet black rivulets on his face and body, however, were un-cleanable here, and his life seemed unbearably fragile. His lips were stained as though all of this limpness was because he was simply drunk on wine, except that it was, instead of purplish red, an unsettling black. Adras pressed a firm kiss to his hairline, steadying themself, and turned to Enoch.

"You've got the horses?"

The man nodded, his deep brown gaze hooked on Lumen with a fear he abruptly shuttered. "Just outside, hurry."

"Help me with him."

Quicker than they'd thought it possible, Adras and Enoch hoisted Lumen from the ground, slung their arms around him, and took him to the horses. Bells of alarm had begun ringing closer, and Adras' hands fumbled as they slung up into a saddle, then adjusted Lumen in front of them with Enoch's brief help.

A sudden spark of light shone in their vision, a sharp, citrusy Starlight connection that flung towards their chest. There was no time for curiosity now. No time for anything but running. Leaving. Escaping with Lumen. Assuring Lumen's wellbeing.

Already, their mind was calculating how they might escape with all they'd come for. Enoch had run back inside to assist Berg with Osiys, and was now rushing out, half-dragging the emaciated man with him.

Osiys looked so unlike the young man Adras had once met at a Chedhiyn festival all those years ago— and not due to age, but rather the weeks of starvation and torture that twisted and wrung familiarity from his body. Enoch lifted him gently into a saddle and swung up behind him, while Berg leapt into his own.

Alarm bells rung louder. The pounding steps of the Canestryn guard grew.

Enoch spurred his horse towards the Eastern Gate and tossed Adras and Berg a glance over his shoulder. "This way is much less heavily guarded— follow me!"

Adras clutched Lumen to their chest with one hand and fisted the reigns in the other. He was limp, but solid against them, and he felt so young, so soft, so fragile against the toughness of their Jopaari leathers.

Berg was last, swearing and muttering something about all of them getting Starsfucked. Adras wrinkled their nose despite themself. The coarse heresy of the Brigonan's language still ruffled them a bit.

The horses moved, and the gates were already open— because what invaders and prisoner of war would send themselves hurtling further behind enemy lines? How foolish would that be? Adras groaned internally.

The answer, obviously, was very. Very *very* foolish. And the answer to the first question was them. Adras and Enoch and Berg and Lumen and Osiys. Stars and void, they hoped this wasn't the end.

Beyond the eastern gate, less than half a dozen guards lazed, their weapons resting at their sides. Adras felt the song in their blood, one of whiskey and rage, and with it danced the hum of citrus and the sea, and the chords that ran through all the universe ran to them alone, to bear witness and to be their victory.

Be our Champion, Adras...

Adras tossed back their head in a howl of sorrow and fury— even as Enoch brandished his scimitar, even as Berg lifted his axe above his head— and swept their rolling gaze to the scrambling guards.

As their head arced to the left, and as their howl rang eerie through the Canestryn streets, a curvation of indigo-silver light leapt from their mouth and swam in globulous patterns to swallow the guards whole.

The silver drowned them all.

Adras watched them gasp for air, clawing uselessly at pure light, the hideous profanation of their armor shriveling as the worming black light was sucked from it like poison from a wound.

At last, they swung their head forward once more and urged their mare closer to Enoch, whose deep brown skin had gone sallow. *He is afraid... of me.* The realization struck Adras across the face as they neared him.

"We will reach the guards waiting for us in no time at all," they shouted over the wind, which had begun to whip up the long grasses. "I have a plan."

Enoch swallowed, the rough bulge of his Adam's apple dipping noticeably, but he nodded.

"Good." Adras didn't have time for explanations or anyone's doubt. They were the Champion of Stars, and they would be victorious. "Give me Osiys' robe."

"It's... filthy." Osiys spoke slowly, scarcely audible above the thrashing grasses.

"That's alright. Just give it here."

Osiys unbuttoned the front enclosure, and Adras suddenly felt a deep pity. The clothes he wore beneath the robe were soiled beyond recognition of color or fit. He reeked of human excrement and sweat and blood and fear. The clothing was so threadbare they could see his skin through the weave. He looked away, the cavernous hollows of his eye sockets shading the whites of his bloodshot eyes a sickly grey.

Enoch tossed them the robe, and Adras caught it, quickly tucking it round Lumen. Clamping down a gag, they turned back to Enoch. "Go straight to Jopaar. Do not stop. Ride as far as you can before the horse tires. My people will welcome you, and they will provide him with healing. Please... Please urge him to tell them everything he knows. They will communicate with us in Brigon."

"What!" Osiys' hiss was alive and well. "I'm going home. I need to go home."

"If you make for Brigon," Adras cut in, sharp as the axe on their back, "they will catch up to you and kill you. Your horse is already tired, and so are you. They will make chase after me, Lumen, and Berg, believing we are protecting you. I can fend many of them off... The others we will lose in the lava fields or waste of Meirydh. But if you wish to live, if you wish to heal from the horrors you have survived, if you will to keep surviving long enough to make them pay for this, you need to run."

He looked away once more, shame and frustration too exhausted to build in his frail limbs. But Enoch looked into their eyes and nodded, slowly. "We will make for Jopaar. I can cut away from you before we reach the front of the city. When they make chase after you, we will run to the north."

"Doesn't anyone give a shit about my opinion?" Berg's voice was gravelly, and his lips were pressed tightly together.

Adras knew they should be kind, knew the man was grieving his friend, thrice lost to him, but all that left their mouth was: "Not really, Berg."

The surprise and hurt in his eyes stung, but he only crunched his mouth closed and stared straight ahead. "Well then," he said, "lead on."

BE

34

DRINK, INDRA

Beyond the fug of the corporeal, it called to Indra. She heard it beckoning, from somewhere inside the marrow of her bones, from somewhere beneath her skull, from somewhere deep in the bloody canals of her heart.

It was home. She was home. The tart burst of citrus in her sinuses. The soft lap of saltwater along the dips and curves of her ankle bones. They were given voice and name and they called— wept with joy, even.

I'm home I'm home I'm home I'm home: it sang it again and again. And it was a yellowish crystal, small and trouble-terminated. *Take me use me make me take me use me make me.*

Adras blew in on a breeze, the flecks of them collecting to compose their full form. Kindness crinkled in the corners of their lavender-tinted-grey eyes.

In their hands, they held a knife.

"Take it, Indra," they said, and their voice was not their own.

Indra looked at her hands; they clutched a chalice of crystal. Gems of deep red were inlaid along the bell of the chalice, and the stem was a slender stripe of fragile, clinking glass. Her eyes rose once more to Adras. "I don't understand."

But Adras did not hand her the knife. Instead, they suspended a wrist over the chalice and slid the knife through their skin, veins and arteries slicing, spilling blood— their blood— so vibrant and full of life, into the chalice. Almost immediately, their eyes unfocused and their speech slurred, as hot wet blood slithered into the rim of the chalice.

"Please," they whispered, "drink, Indra."

She choked on air as she lurched awake, stomach roiling and lurching, unable to rid her mind of the sight of Adras' wrists emptying their body of blood. Her embroidered bedclothes were fisted tight in her fingers, and she forced her eyes to account for all the empty corners of her room.

The past few weeks had been brutal— nothing but her mind distancing itself from reality. She was no longer a trustworthy witness to her own life; her eyes betrayed her now, just as her body had, that day in the library. Sometimes, she would look around her room, or up from her journal, or back from the window, to see Valeryn standing in the corner, peering at her with innocent eyes over the cracked spine of a book, cracking her own spine with slicing self-doubt. The first time it had happened, she'd gone very still with terror, and had only managed a small cry when he set down his book and began to move towards her. The guards had seen nothing, despite standing mere inches from the bookkeeper that wasn't actually the bookkeeper.

He hadn't harmed her, though, not really... It had just been a kiss. Just a kiss, and then... panic. Stuttered motion. Confusion. He'd been so kind before then; it wasn't fair of her to be so frightened, and yet she was. She was so, so frightened.

She scarcely left her room. It was far too likely she'd have another attack if she happened to see Valeryn in the flesh, or the library, or get too near where the Starstones were being kept. She felt that slowly her world would shrink to nothing but the walls which kept her here now, that she would shrivel into an absence of a memory as the rest of the world carried on.

And it terrified her.

It terrified her almost as much as this dream, a new one, in which her old home taunted her in a bizarre fashion, before Adras slit their wrists into a cup and expected her to drink it. It was this petrifying fear, coupled with a subtle citrusy call lingering still in her awakeness, that set Indra's feet to moving, that had her sliding on her slippers and tugging on a heavily brocaded house coat and peering around the great wooden door for any potential guards.

There weren't any guards, naturally. Things had been calm for a few days— she'd gotten used to the nightmares, to the sharp slices of pain that came with them; she had also gotten used to the inability of the caring staff to do anything at all. Their suggestions were frankly ridiculous and desperately unhelpful, and because of this, for the first time in her life, Indra blatantly lied.

She told them she was getting better. She told them she was feeling much more well. She told them the hallucinations had ceased. None of this was true. In fact, when she opened her bedroom door and stepped into the massive hall with only a small candle and the hint of moonlight through windows to guide her, she whispered to herself, "I've lost my Starsdamned mind."

The rescue party was not due back for one or two more days yet, she knew, but there was a nagging which sat sharp between the valves of her heart, an insistence that drove her towards the nearest east-facing window. The glass was cold, and her breath made little clouds whirl up against it. It was elegant and tactile, done in a little scene of the sun rising above the mountains, strips of grey and green and white and yellow glass fastened within wire framing.

She felt the smallest of smiles nudge the edges of her mouth upward— she hadn't expected to feel fondness for this place, but even now, she traced the outline of the rising sun with a small, pale finger and realized how comforting the sensuality of these people was to her. The particular insistence on beauty, even in a small, east-facing window at the end of a long hall.

Eddies of wind whistled through the thin opening between the two panels of stained glass, spraying her face in a wisp of bitingly cold air. Unlatching the little metal hook that kept it closed, she pulled the doors of the window toward her, and leaned her face out into the wind. It rushed into her lungs, wiping the breath from them and replacing it instead with freezing mountain air. She struggled to gulp a time or two, and the stunning cold braced her. She could feel her body as though it was hers, as though it was alive and pumping blood and growing fresh skin and prickling with chill. There hadn't been a day in the last few weeks that she'd felt so present in her own skin, instead of simply being a spirit taken to haunting this particular human form.

When she'd caught her breath again, she tilted her face down the mountainside— all those thousands of feet of rock and brush that had once made her skin crawl with terror, which now felt strangely like home— and spotted two horses recklessly racing up the teetering carved-out road. She peered closer. There were distinctly three figures on the two horses, and they were coming up the mountain at a dangerous speed. One of the figures appeared to be half-limp in front of... Adras.

The shooting pain split her head in two, ear to ear, and it was so sudden and so very terrible that her mouth gaped open while forgetting how to scream. She slid to the floor, the polished wood wall smooth on her back. The pain burned; it burned like salt in a wound. And then her nose filled with the salivating scent of a freshly-peeled orange. She struggled to identify the sound ragging heavy in her ears and found it to be her own breathing. And she was salivating— a long strand of drool hung from the corner of her mouth like a pendant on a necklace. She wiped it brusquely away, her senses returning to the sharp equilibrium she'd been ushered into by the wind, and turned, racing for the stairs.

It was so far down— four levels of bedrooms and guards and meeting rooms and guards and dance halls and guards— to reach the entry hall. Indra leapt so hard from the final step that she scarcely caught herself mid-stumble, nearly winding up a pile of skirts and robe and curls on the plush carpet.

Adras was just entering through the massive main door, Lumen's arm hooked over their shoulders as they gripped his hand and hoisted him under his opposite arm. Healers and servants swarmed them, but the feral hiss of the Jopaari oracle sent them skittering back in alarm. Herran had even awoken and was moving towards the two of them, his hands outstretched in worry, his hair crinkled in sleep, gently saying something Indra couldn't hear. But Adras shooed him off with the rest, tugging Lumen closer to their body with a protective panic, when their eyes found Indra's. Tired— oh, they looked so very tired. The hot red rings around their crazed eyes told Indra they'd been running on terribly little sleep, as well as crying, and that was as frightening as anything else.

"Indra!" The voice they used to beckon her was scratched through with exhaustion. "Come with me— this way, they mentioned an open room."

Indra could scarcely string two words together, and certainly not coherent thought, but she managed: "Osiys?"

"He's out." It was curt, and, this time, Adras did not meet her eyes.

Indra ignored the hardness with a relief that soaked her through; she slipped her thin shoulder under Lumen's other arm and slung her arm around the strong meat of his middle. A grimace had him sucking air in tightly, and something small and sharp on the back of his hip dug into her waist.

A burst of citrus exploded on her tongue.

He was... wrong. Now that she was near him, she wanted to wriggle away, or perhaps her skin might wriggle away on its own— he was nothing. He was a shell of a thing. He was Lumen... but... wrong.

The place where his lips met was stained black, and his shimmering white hair was matted all over with blood that looked almost fresh. As if noticing her inspection, a slow, thick runnel of blood oozed from his ear and down his neck. It was nearly black. His eyes were black as ever, but looked somehow unfocused, despite the lack of a visible pupil. He coughed wetly, and more blood strung, suspended in saliva, from the corner of his mouth. It, too, was a vile, diseased blackish color, and it smelled of death.

"Adras—"

"Not a word. Not yet." Adras kicked the door to the room open with a filthy, booted foot. "Help me get him on the bed."

It had been made up in furs and a brocade spread, as most of the beds in the Brigon High House were, and Indra shuffled to it, her muscles burning with the weight of Lumen's strength-strung body slung against her. He slid down to the covers with a weak moan, and Indra rolled back her shoulders and flexed her fingers, which were trembling from exertion.

Adras was kneeling beside their brother, smoothing back his blood-mottled hair with an expression like vinegar. "We need sacred water, a chalice, a knife, some black fabric, and Zech."

Indra gagged hard, but kept her lips clamped whitely together, as pain ricocheted from ear to ear once more. Was this where the nightmare came to pass? Adras' wrist splitting open over the chalice filled her vision, and her stomach rebelled. "Zech is gone," she found herself saying, a distraction from the way her stomach was inverting. "He left with Jauyne the same day you left for Canestry."

Leaving me all alone in a High House... again. Traitorous tears threatened to sting her eyes. *It's not the same. You know it's not the same.*

Realization blankly smacked across Adras' features, their head snapping up. "That's right... this is..." They turned away once more. "This is not good."

"I'm sure I can help..." Indra stumbled. She had never seen the Oracle like this. "I can at least make sure we have the rest. What—" she worried her lip, despite herself— she couldn't very well ask if Adras was planning on slitting their wrists, now. That wasn't very polite. "What is the knife and chalice for?"

"I need something to put the sacred water in. He needs to drink it— get the poison out. But it ought to be activated by a trained healer first. I also must soak the bandages in sacred water, and the bandages required are black— I need a knife to cut up the black fabric." They spun a glance at her. "Your anxiety surrounding that question is something we can discuss another time, though."

Indra gnawed the inside of her cheek bloody as Adras spoke, flushing furiously at Adras' intuitive nod to her anxieties, then ran to gather the items they had requested.

Moments later, she found herself stumbling back into the little room, arms full of an absurd assortment of things. Adras flew up from their statuesque position beside Lumen, whose eyes were now open and blinking softly. They took the knife and the black cloth that was slung over Indra's arm, and instantly began cutting large, jagged strips from it. Indra sat the rest of the items on the small readying table to the side of the bed, near the wall, and uncorked the first large bottle of water from one of Brigon's sacred, Star-touched mountain pools.

Pouring the first bit into the chalice sent chills skittering over Indra's arms and behind her eyes. A strange fuzziness folded its way around her vision. She placed the chalice on the table and emptied that first bottle into the bowl she'd brought with her. It only filled about a third of the small basin, so she opened the second bottle and added it as well.

"Drink, Indra. *Please!*" The last word was a shriek, and she spun, swallowing back the terror that gathered like lead in her throat. She heard the wheeze of her breathing and knew there was nothing that could be done about it.

Adras met her eyes with careful suspicion dosed with curiosity. "What did you just hear, Indra?"

Nearly gagging on the fear, she said, "I heard you. Screaming. Telling me to drink your blood from the chalice." There was a silence that carried all the graciousness of a very proper person who could not think of something remotely proper to comment. "I've been hearing a lot of things," she finally admitted. "I'm afraid... I'm afraid I am going insane. I'm sorry."

Adras blinked once, then a creaky, off-center grin crept up their face. Lumen made a noise that sounded like a drowning person trying to chuckle. Indra winced. But Lumen's hand was fumbling about, awkwardly brushing against bedsheet and clothing and twisting to his back.

"Shh," Adras tried to soothe him. "You're safe now. Everything is... We are going to take care of everything."

Lumen shook his head, insistently. "A pouch. Round my waist. Is in the back."

Indra blushed with shocked embarrassment that she was witnessing a very powerful someone reduced to someone so very vulnerable. It licked at her insides with a discomfort that chafed her raw— who could she count on? Was anyone as invincible as her father seemed? These people were no more Starchildren than she— what had she expected?

Indra looked away— at the ceiling, out the window, at her slippers, at the bowl of sacred water, didn't matter, really— as Adras retrieved the aforementioned pouch, tugging it free from his body with a soft, quick snap of leather cord. They pulled it into their lap, perched on the bed, back to Indra. She could see they were fiddling with the enclosure, but all at once, clarity swept through her with the scent of citrus and the sure-footed desire for home, and she knew she had dreamt the truth.

On the bed, Adras went very still. "You didn't," they choked out.

The same, drowned chuckle surfaced. "'Course I did."

"Why." It wasn't so much a question as a demand.

"Wanted um to know."

"You wanted them to know what?"

He wheezed. "That we could."

It was Adras' turn to laugh, and they did— snaps and crinkles of bitterness pricking through it. "You showed them." They shook their head. "You should have stopped there. You shouldn't have gone for the dais. I thought you knew better."

Indra clenched the long sleeves of her robe, gnawing at them with hands of sweaty desperation. It had not occurred to her before now that she ought to have an exit strategy in place, in case of long, personal conversations of which she was not intended to be the recipient.

But all Lumen mumbled was, "I kn-now. Sorry."

Indra held her breath and tried to force her gaze elsewhere as Adras' stooped to kiss Lumen's forehead. Then they glanced up, towards Indra, as though none of those words had been exchanged.

"Do you have the water?" They gripped something in their tightly clasped hands, and Indra wanted— needed— to know what it was.

No... She already knew what it was. But Indra just nodded, gesturing to the table.

Adras lowered the strips of black cloth into the water. They were speaking feather-edged words, too quiet for Indra to hear, and their left hand still clutched the thing they'd found on Lumen, invisible behind the cage of their fingers. Indra resisted the urge to grab for it. A deep hunger thrummed in her, so steady and luminous she was unsure how she hadn't always felt its presence.

Perhaps she had.

She couldn't remember.

Vibrations wrestled her teeth.

Stars, her head ached.

STUPID

35
BUT ADRAS
DID NOT SNIGGER

ADRAS, BRIGONAN HIGH HOUSE
4 months, 3 weeks since the sack of Meirydh

Adras had larger concerns than Indra thinking they wanted her to drink their blood. Well, not exactly— it was all connected, of course— but rather, less weirdly specific concerns.

Lumen, the precious delinquent, had somehow managed to snatch the Canestryn Starstone, of all things. It was a wonder to Adras that it hadn't driven them mad by the time they reached the city walls, instead filling them with an odd and vibrant rush of crazed energy, let alone on the two-week journey back to Brigon. There was something disturbing about it, a sort of wailing, that nagged the corners of their thoughts, and they were waiting for just a few hours of uninterrupted time in order to sort it all out.

As fate would have it, this was not to be easily had. They scrubbed a hand down their face and attempted to re-attune their mind to the conversation at hand. This proved to be a shockingly difficult task.

Enoch could be criminally boring for a man who hailed from one of the most animated and warm Provinces in Allesar. He wasn't always this loathesome, though; they expected he had gotten even less sleep than they had since fleeing the Canestryn border, which was, horribly, very little.

That had been months ago now, and Enoch and Osiys had returned from their diversion to Jopaar just a few days prior, a woman named Maryt, who seemed evidently quite attached to Osiys, in tow.

At least the chair was mostly comfortable, and they'd arrived in the Great Hall early enough to be fortunate in finding a seat close to the fire, which was popping good-naturedly. It reminded them a bit of their own room back in Jopaar, the one they hadn't seen in a few months, now. The one that death threats used to sneak under, and which Lumen used to sneak through to sit by the fire and whisper about nothing at all.

The coffee in their mug was spiced, however, which they were unused to and which somehow continued to surprise them, not pleasantly, with every cautious sip. They assumed this was to disguise the fact that the imported coffee was only what the Jopaari hothouses could grow, and not the proper stuff tended in Pallydh. They'd tried Brigonan tea, but that, too, tasted weird and foreign. Why didn't anyone in Brigon drink decent tea, anyhow? Stars, if only they could get their hands on some properly tended herbs... The steam rising from the offending cup of coffee distorted Enoch's face in their line of sight, and Adras shook themself before their eyelids drooped.

"The important thing to note is that we have all of the Starstones, save that from Nareilë. With Osiys rescued, Lumen and Valeryn healing, and all but one of the Starstones, we can expect that Canestry will be coming for us sooner rather than later. We need to move quickly."

Herran was rubbing his hand back and forth over his mouth and chin; his brows were creased in concern. Adras had never quite gotten used to the hulking presence of him, the way he towered over everyone, even seated. Just now, he was sighing heavily and worrying an eyebrow.

"How we will be able to retrieve the Nareilë Starstone is a concern. Do we have any allies there who are still living? Anyone who can help? And we will need all available hands studying the Starstones. Indra, do not worry; we will split up the work into groups— Valeryn can remain at a distance. Adras, I want to know what really happened to Lumen back in Canestry. If there is a way that our enemy might seek to use this against us, I need to know."

They nodded, ready to explain that Lumen ought to be the one talking about Lumen, but Herran had already hurriedly moved on to Enoch once more, discussing something about one of the Star Charts which Indra had snuck out of her Province a few months prior.

Lavender and citrus hovered in the air as Indra leaned close to them from the adjacent chair. "They'll be at this a while. I can excuse us, and we can escape to the Starstone observation room, and you can just sit undisturbed for a while." A knowing smile curved the edges of her mouth, and Adras was terribly grateful for this unsuspecting little princess, who now turned her attention to the bear-like Brigonan Premier. "Excuse me, Herran, if there's nothing else we'll need to know, we thought we might get a start at the Starstones again?"

"Ah! Yes, a perfect thought, dear. Indeed, you are dismissed!"

Adras' knees creaked when they stood, and they wondered when that had started happening, because, if they were honest, yikes. Abandoning the cup of terrible coffee at the table with no small amount of relief, they followed the winding path that Indra led them down to the entry level of the Brigonan High House. It seemed needlessly convoluted.

"Indra, wouldn't the other staircase have been far faster?"

The girl's hand fluttered awkwardly on the banister for a moment. "Yes," she began, carefully, "but it is difficult to avoid Valeryn when I go the other way."

Rippling blonde curls portrayed no trace of the shame that her voice did. There was a grief welling up in Adras that came from a lifetime of being not quite what was expected, but trying desperately to believe they were. It was a grief well-acquainted with shame. They caught Indra's free hand in theirs, gripped tightly.

"There is nothing wrong with going the long way," they said to the very surprised silver eyes that looked back at them, and also to the thing beating so inconveniently in their chest. "If you get where you want to go, safely and happily, why should you care if it took a little longer."

One blink of the silver eyes. Two, encircled by tears. Indra cast her arms around Adras and gripped them, hard. Adras was neither comfortable with, nor skilled at, physical displays of interpersonal affection, but this felt more like hugging themself than anything else, and because of that, they returned the gesture with an unexpected height of emotion quivering inside their highly-strung, thoroughly exhausted body.

"Our whole selves," Indra's voice said, muffled with hair, from somewhere near Adras' shoulder.

It took them a moment to understand what it meant, but quite suddenly the moment in the library— was it two months or two years ago, they could scarcely tell— returned to their memory, and a smile that felt more like tears stretched the width of their face.

"The whole way," they whispered back.

When Indra pulled back, after a quick squeeze that left Adras feeling both confused and affection-illiterate, it was with a renewed firmness to her slight, straight shoulders, and a solidness to her being which hadn't been there a moment ago. Adras thought they knew what that felt like, too, but that feeling was somewhere far away.

The little room, split in half by that thick, layered glass, had become a sort of safe haven for Adras. Though the entry room, ladder, and hall leading to the Starstone's enclosure was lined with guards, the room itself was isolated and quiet. No one wanted to be in the presence of the strange stones which had caused such terrifying episodes to people of far greater power than they. The rumors spread about them had become near-fanatical, horrifying tales of the Starchildren sprouting extra eyes or discovering a taste for human flesh or being able to disappear people at will.

It was all so utterly ridiculous and absurdly obnoxious that Adras quite enjoyed the irony of hiding away from it in the precise location they were so frightened of. They weren't sure why the Starstones had not yet had such an affect on them as they had on the others. With the exception of that day on the Tanaraq Plains of Meirydh, when they and Jauyne had both grasped the stones at once, there had been no overwhelming fear or injury to them from the Starstones. In fact, if anything, being in the presence of the strange, otherworldly things seemed to settle something in them.

"I'm going to go over my notes again." Indra closed the door crisply behind them, and made her way to one of the little tables, on which her growing pile of papers and books sat precariously.

Adras sat in the same chair they always did, feeling keenly observed. Hurriedly, Indra looked away.

"Is something wrong?"

"No!" Indra bit her lip. "Well. I just... The Canestryn Starstone felt different to me. Did the Jopaari Starstone feel any different to you? Did it... hurt you?"

The Starstones gazed back at Adras through the glass, like an odd, familiar smile. "No, it didn't. Not until we had two of them together. But on its own... it felt like it was made for me, like it could speak to some part of myself I didn't consciously know was there." They flicked their eyes to Indra, whose jaw was stiff and eyes glassy as she, too, looked at the collection of Starstones beyond the glass.

"I just never got to hold it. It was locked up, just like I was, by people who only cared to use it. It's like there is a kinship between us that I never had the chance to honor."

It struck Adras as a physical twinge, and they sighed, deeply. "It's very strange how Premier-led it's become, isn't it? It's as though they've all forgotten what the Stars are."

Whiskey cello songs. Fierce anger. Melting smoke.

A bob of her head. "Magic," Indra said, simply, then nodded to Adras' tattoos. "Like your dragons."

"But dragons aren't real," they replied, and felt stupid.

The soft porcelain of Indra's cheeks crinkled. "Let's not play that game, shall we?"

A discomfited sigh pressed out of Adras' lips. They nodded. "Once we have them all, what do we do with them?" The Starstones glowed softly, and Adras couldn't be sure if it was delightful or ominous.

"Well," Indra huffed a bit, one hand crooked at the small of her back, the other flipping a few pages back in the uppermost book of her stack. "They aren't just meant for looking pretty. And I don't believe they're trying to hurt us. They're just..."

The silence prodded Adras into realizing how curious they were. "They just what?"

"It sounds crazy."

"So does everything worthwhile at first."

A deep breath, wincing. "I believe they're trying to talk to us. Or let us talk to them. Or... something communicative."

Their mind bent itself into knots. "Why communicative?"

"Well, I was thinking about all of the side effects we have had thus far, and what happened to each of us during contact, as well— the first time, it connected you and I, and we were able to hear one another, clear as day, despite you being all the way in Jopaar, and me being here."

Something tingly and raw began to stir in Adras' chest. "Go on."

"Then there was the episode with all three of us at once— you and me and Jauyne. Once again, it connected all three of us and allowed us to communicate. And individually, it's been a strange conglomeration of communication: ancient poetry, garbled speech, an insistence that there was something to be said or heard or remembered."

Every realization was pinging in Adras' mind, and a harsh, metallic pain was starting in their temple. But Adras was accustomed to pain, and it made them sharper, made them excited. It wasn't until Indra spoke again that they realized how long they had been standing still and silent, staring ahead towards the stones and unmoving.

"I could be wrong, of course," Indra muttered softly.

"No," Adras grabbed her wrist, rough but not unkindly. "No, you're right. I don't know why I know this, but I know. You are right."

They could feel the thrill of joy in the girl's veins, the rapid pulse of her lifepoint, like a sparkling burst of citrus.

"Then how do we prove it?"

"Danger, naturally." They hadn't had a moment to rest, but this was renewing them like a dip in an icy lake. "Ask one of the guards to retrieve Lumen for me."

Time was never quite right around the Starstones, and Adras was sure it had taken longer than the few seconds their brain was aware of to gather Lumen and get him snugly packed into a chair.

He still wasn't quite himself. They had never been sure of what had really happened when his body had absorbed so much Starlight as a child, of what he was capable and how much he kept to himself. His eyes were black, yes, but Lumen was only light. It felt wrong of the world to give him the capacity to absorb such darkness.

Through his awkward protests, Indra brought him another pillow and shoved a mug of coffee into his hands. It was difficult for anyone to look truly miserable with her tiny form flitting about them attentively, but he managed an expression of at least half misery and half amusement. Adras swallowed a laugh and took the seat crosswise from him. Indra folded herself into an impossibly small package in a nearby chair.

Looking half-grumpily over the rim of his mug, Lumen sighed. "The two of you are being terribly mysterious, which I realize is all the latest fashion with you Starchildren, but all the same, I'd love to know why I'm not in my very comfortable bed."

If Adras had been anyone else, they would have sniggered, but Adras did not snigger. They had far too much practice in solemn responsibility for that. "I think you should tell us what happened in Canestry, and then we are going to figure out how to use the Starstones."

To their satisfaction, he blinked with surprise. It was not often they surprised one another.

"The guards were wielding some strange sort of Starlight. It wasn't... right." He swallowed. Glanced at Indra. "Most of the party fled. Realized when we got back here that they must've been hunted down somehow. The others died. Was just me and Berg and Enoch. Then Adras nearly hacked my face off with their axe, we found Osiys—" Indra sucked in a small, spiked breath, and he looked at her with an expression somewhere between concern and curiosity. "—and got the hell out of there."

His casualness was often a balm, but was currently something that felt closer to acid in Adra's marrow. "Stop being a smartass." It was venom, and it got his attention. "You know what I'm asking, Lumen. What did you do at the dais?"

The tarry black of his eyes expanded. They had never demanded this of him before, and there was a piece in Adras' soul, albeit small, that felt immense guilt for it. They never pushed, never questioned, never made him tell any part of his story that he wasn't ready to tell of his own accord. But this wasn't just about him anymore. He wasn't just about him. None of them were just themselves any longer, and even as the thought flicked across Adras' mind, they realized how true it was, how dangerous it was, how utterly unavoidable it was. All of them were bound to one another now— how, and why, it remained to be seen. But the reciprocal bondage of their strange little company was an inescapable reality now.

"Look," they said, less venom, more resignation. "I know I have never made you talk about it. But it is important. You are important. You are not the wounded child you were back then. We are all being forced into the corners where our fear has been hiding. It all matters, and yours is no different."

The words in his unreadable black eyes were about a thousand versions of swears directed pointedly at them, but they held their gaze steady with his.

"You know you can't un-hear it, right?"

Whatever Adras had thought him about to say, this was not it. This thought, in fact, had not even occurred to them, and because of this, their voice was more stilted than they would have liked, when they replied simply, "I know."

He leveled the blackness of his eyes at Indra, and she didn't flinch. "You prepared for this, too?"

"Yes." Her voice was small, but steadier than Adras', which was mildly irritating.

For just a moment, Lumen closed his eyes. He filled his lungs and emptied them. His eyes reopened.

"The Starlight in me is not mine, and it is always hungry. So is the void alongside it."

DON'T

36

SAFE NOW

A haze.

Being clutched close.

The freezing cold.

Rough jostling horse beneath him.

Light and shadow.

Commotion.

The heat of the fire.

Calloused, brown hands smoothing the sweat on his forehead.

The nightmares. The clutching terror.

The cold air seeping in the window.

Blind with fear.

When will the pain start next?

Had he spoken aloud?

"You're safe now," Enoch whispered, hands bolstering. "They cannot harm you any longer."

THE THIRD
CRYSTALLINE
SACRAMENT

All are capable of seeing through veils, if one only recalls that they already see. We remember.

77TH & CRYPTCALL

You are ripped from sleep by your own screaming.

It's a raw gagging in your throat, this grief.

Everything was burning. You saw it. This odd, foreign knowing that sometimes assaults your dreams, poisoned by the terror and grief of your own world's war.

Eyes glowing silver. Blackness swallowing the world. Crystals half-sunk in pools of liquid fire. A woman staring back at you through them.

Something familial is tearing at something crucial inside of you, something that has been screaming for recognition your whole life. You grab at the sheets beneath you, curling your fingers into the soft fabric and pulling until it rips. That's what it feels like must be happening to your stomach, to that spot above your navel. You peel your sweaty hands from the sheets and lift the hem of your shirt, expecting to find a gaping wound, oozing blood.

It's still just a scar. Fuck. Fuck! It's like a blade is being twisted in your gut, slashed across your face.

You cannot breathe. The silver light of the moon streams in the window and makes your skin ghostly and translucent.

You sit up, hoping to chase a deeper breath, finding none. Looking down at your hands, they no longer look like yours. They're slender and pale and trembling. A silver light illuminates them. You're suddenly standing on stones, hearing the impossible screaming of small children. There is so much pain, here, wherever you are. There is so much hell. Is everywhere the same? Is there no hope?

You grip your head, dry heaving.

It's like a high-pitched scream only the stars can hear. Maybe it's the stars themselves. All of them. A trillion stars everywhere screaming, screaming, screaming...

You punch the wall beside you, desperate for relief, for hope, for help, for release... Pain splinters through your knuckles, and everything disintegrates.

BE

37
A WEIRD-ASS COCKTAIL IN THE PIT OF HIS STOMACH

ZECH, BRIGON/CHEDHIY BORDER HOUSE
6 months, 1 week since the sack of Meirydh

Shrieks and roars of terror ripped through the mountain air.

Jauyne is fine Jauyne is fine Jauyne is fine...

At this point, he wasn't sure if it was the foggy exhaustion or the trilling ghosts causing the thoughts that made diving starts for his mind. It didn't matter. He'd always been crazy. He'd always been a bit ghostly himself. He'd always been strangely susceptible to the eerie things others only saw in dreams, or else not at all. It was as though he was a Starsdamned beacon for them, and here on the mountain, a beacon was more tempting to the discontented spirits than ever.

No one else knew this, of course. There were always stories— but when weren't there?— of things that haunted the lonely mountain corridors where border watchmen stayed alone or in pairs, but that was usually shrugged off as one too many late nights, or an extra cup of ale when it wasn't your turn on duty. It had been the easiest job for someone like him, who couldn't have hid his unfortunate predisposition if he'd tried.

But last night had been the worst yet.

Jauyne had thrashed and screamed, eyes unblinking and rolling wildly, flecks of foam building at the corners of her mouth, as she'd howled about death and destiny and that even Zech was a ghost and that she was all alone on the mountain. He'd gotten no sleep at all, even after tying her to the bed so she wouldn't injure herself.

He smeared the innards of a squashed bug across his arm where it had tried to bite him. The stripe of bug guts slashed adjacent to the swipe that strange ghost-dust-woman had taken at him in the crazed wind that had stirred up all the dirt in their new home and undone all his cleaning.

It was scabbed over and peeling off now, but the eerie feeling in his gut hadn't gone away, not even after he'd burned the note written in Jauyne's blood. She was so damn stubborn, refusing to leave, insisting that this was best for them, that they needed to give Indra and Adras time to solve the mystery so they could all go back to the way they once were.

The sun had been up for hours but had yet to actually flash its brilliant gold over the easternmost peak. Zech curled his lip at it. "Go back down," he grumbled, pitifully, in its direction, then rolled his eyes at himself.

Jauyne's screams were turning rapidly to little giggles and hums that were eerily unlike her. She'd snap out of it anytime now. His headache beat like a second heart between his brows, defiantly even and unbudging...

His head slammed up so fast it cracked painfully against the wooden doorframe. Fuck. He'd dozed off. Turning, he saw Jauyne in the bed, sniggering tiredly at him. She raised her bound wrists with a lazy raunchiness.

"I'd normally find this hot." The flatness of her mouth and raised-brow glare only served to churn a heat between his hips. "Except for that little detail that was my insanity."

Zech hunched himself to standing, his boots crunching pebbles as they swiveled. He pitched his hands at his hips. "Except for that little detail, huh?" Stars, it was always such a fucking relief when she came back from wherever it was she went when the ghosts came out to play. It was frighteningly similar to the episodes she'd had near the Starstones, and it disquieted him. But when he continued, he kept the heat in his voice to tease her. She didn't need to know how he'd feared. "You're not insane anymore."

She leveled him with an incredulous gaze. "You're nearly asleep on your feet. The only thing you're doing in this bed is sleeping."

He slunk to her side, humor and relief making a weird-ass cocktail in the pit of his stomach. Easing down on the mattress, he ran his thumb across the pale blue network of veins along her inner wrist, below the pink marks the bindings were leaving on her skin. "Who says I wanna do anything in this bed?"

She made to bite him, still volatile as an animal— no, volatile as a Meirydhi— and he jerked out of her range, her teeth snapping together. He couldn't help it; he laughed a laugh that took the air out of him, and her glare only made the laugh more breathless, more satisfying. Yeah, relief felt damn good.

"Come on, Jauyne." He swiped a tear from the corner of his eye, grinning at her. "I just love when you come back... When you're not..."

The fury flickered across her face. "Crazy?"

"When you're not in pain."

There was hesitancy in her, a piece of her that would always be haunt-thrashed now, he knew. He knew because he would always have that part in him, too.

Slowly, as she watched the recognition form on his face, the heat in her eyes turned from fury to arousal, and the air went kinetic— she was the damp crackle before the storm. She leaned toward him, golden flickers building on her lips, a feral light reeling him in from her eyes. When he moved toward her, she stopped short, shrugged her wrists upward. "Your turn for this, though."

He grinned through the molten feeling deep inside, began working at the knot around her left wrist. "No wonder everybody's scared of you Meirydhi girls."

A frown, laced with challenge— Starsdamn him, challenge was his favorite drug, second only to her— creased her face with a vicious gleam. "Are you telling me you're not afraid of me, Zech?"

"Of course not." It was a delicious fucking lie, more so for her seeing right through it.

Her hand slipped free, and she slapped him across the face. It stung until the tingling burn in his cheek scorched through him. He wanted her to do it again, but instead she took him by the chin, slid her body forward, so close to his.

"You should be."

He remembered the click of her teeth when she'd moved to nip his nose, and he went for her lip. Thin and soft, he captured it in his teeth and tugged, heard her breath sucked through her teeth, felt her fingers pinch harder on his chin. Fumbling to find it, he ripped the bond from her other wrist, and she became a wild creature against him. Grappling, he fought for balance and lost, her full-bellied, wiry body thrashing him fast against the bed.

Those scrawny limbs were ever so slightly less scrawny than they'd been back in Meirydh, and her stomach was swollen into a well-nurtured curve. Her hair still hung long and black, like a curtain of night, over him when she bent forward. She scraped a nail softly over his mouth, across the stubble on his chin, down the line of his throat, and his skin prickled.

"Don't forget the first promise I ever made you."

The plain linen dress she wore was thin and bunched up at her hips and under her stomach from the splay of her knees where she straddled him. The sharp points of her nipples peaked at the front of it, and he dragged a thumb across one, slow, his eyes not leaving hers. "Why? Still feel like gutting me, firestarter?"

"Only—" Her breath halted mid-exhale at the sharp pinch he gave, and he couldn't help but smirk a bit. "Only if you run."

He didn't have more than a moment to make note of the pang of truth in that, the biting confession that lived there, because she dragged her hand, heavy and solid, across his groin, and he went stiff. Her fingers ripped at the laces. She was hungry, and it rippled from her. Nudging her roughly with his knee, he wriggled awkwardly out of his pants and kicked them from the mattress before hauling her back down to his skin.

Oh, fuck it all, she wasn't even wearing anything under that linen dress, and her slick little body on his sent lightning shivers of pleasure up his spine. Every place where their bodies met sparked and sizzled with silver. She bent to kiss him again, dragged herself across him with an agonizing slowness, flicked her tongue behind his teeth. The noises he was making would have been absolutely fucking embarrassing if it wasn't her.

"Mm, changed my mind," she talked against his mouth, and he ate her words. "No time for playing, no time for the ropes. I've missed this; just get the fuck inside me."

He jerked against her, even as he lifted her abruptly by the hips. He held her there for a moment, let the sight of her severe mouth, shiny and swollen with kisses, and messy hair stir a maddening softness in him. Was she a goddess or a hawk— he could never decide. He slammed her downward. Her eyes went wide, and she dropped her mouth open in a noise that was somewhere between a squeak and a moan.

Oh fuck. A goddess. Definitely a goddess.

Those sharp nails of hers dug in as she planted them on his chest, bracing herself.

"Too much?" He asked, and his voice was more breathless than he thought it should be.

Grey eyes glinted like a silver clash of flint. Firestarter. "It's been a while, just give me a second."

That wild fizz of black hair hung wild, and he gently tugged a strand, his other hand tracing over the plane of her sternum. And— ohmyfuckingStars— she began to move. He wasn't gonna last long at this rate. It *had* been a while. When he slid a hand below the soft bulb of her stomach and found that rhythm with his thumb, the one he knew she liked best, she tilted her head back and closed her eyes, her chest shuddering in a deliciously uneven breath.

If she hadn't twisted her hips just so, he would've grinned. Stars, he felt normal for the first time in weeks. He'd needed this. They had needed this. Seeing one another be overcome by the chaos of the Starstones, directly followed by the deeply fucked up haunts of the mountain had taken its toll. To see her as this— the ragingly sensual ruler that she was, riding him into a bliss he'd forgotten existed— was good for him.

He fisted a handful of her hair, thrusted as she rolled, worked his thumb harder. A scream, an actual scream, left her mouth and she jerked her head forward, grinning at him wildly. He was giddy. If his body hadn't been so involved, he might have left it.

"Stars, I missed this." He grunted out the words, twisted her nipple, let her breast bounce free as she rode him harder.

"So did I..." She laughed through a moan. "You fuck just as well as I remember, for a ghost."

Ghost... The heat left his body. His hands whipped away from her. *She's not back. She's still half-crazed. Starsdamn me. It's been all night! She isn't back... She should be back!*

She was plunging herself down on him with a desperate force, but she looked at him, annoyed, through her lashes. "Well don't stop now!"

Her skin was tacky with sweat when he grabbed her hips and forced her to still. "What did you just say to me?" Maybe he'd heard wrongly... maybe everything was fine.

"I said don't stop now! What's the matter with you?" She wiggled, tried to pry his hands off her.

"The other thing."

"What other— oh, you mean about how you fuck pretty good for a ghost? I didn't put it together before we got here, but now that I've actually seen ghosts, after they've talked to me, now I know—"

"I am not a ghost." He hauled her off him with a slick sound.

She had daggers for eyes as she tugged her dress down with no small amount of resentment, scooped an arm protectively around her belly. "Right. Fine. Fuck the crazy girl until she gets too crazy. Don't look at me that way. How *dare* you look at me that way?"

His stomach was pitching. He was angry. He was sick. He was really fucking disillusioned. The air was too cold as he stood to reach for his pants. "Look at you like what?"

"Like you pity me! You have never pitied me before. Not once. If you're going to start now, just walk yourself home to Chedhiy because I don't want you touching me; I don't want you in the same room with me."

"I'm not going to Chedhiy!" His vision swam. Everything was getting soft and grey around the edges of his vision. Everything was getting jagged and bitter around the edges of his feelings. This wasn't happening. *Stop... Not now...*

"Because you fucking pity me!"

He bumped into the cupboard. Bit his tongue. There was blood between his teeth. His vision swam. The roughness of his knuckles wiped red streaks from his lips.

A blink.

More blood on his hands. His knuckles.

Another blink. He was covered in crimson. All his thoughts blurred as seconds, minutes, slipped away from him. She'd been angry. He'd been angry.

He'd... hurt her?

Oh Stars... ohstarsohstarsohstars...

He spun. Blood on the floor. Blood on his clothes. Had he killed her? Had he lost his mind and killed her? Had the haunts told him to?

His breaths screeched through his lungs, aching. The world was smudged. He could hear her calling his name from so far away.

Why would he do this? She'd... She'd called him a ghost. Rage rippled through him, and an echoing headache split ear to ear. There was a wet thing rolling down his face. His neck. He couldn't breathe. Couldn't fucking breathe.

I am not a ghost! Unless I am... Stars, what if she was right? What if I'm a ghost? He felt less corporeal just thinking the words. Another blink. Blood hovered on the less-than-realness of his hands. The roughness of the floorboards peered up at him vaguely through his fingers. *Fuck. Fuck!*

A scream, an actual scream, ripped from his tattered lungs. He felt himself dying in the rockslide all those years ago as a child— the press of the earth getting heavier, heavier, heavier... the way his eyes felt freakishly unsuited to their sockets... the sharpness of pain at his right temple, then... then what? He could never remember what came next. He'd... died?

Then what! Oh fuck, he was dead, wasn't he? That must be how it had happened? Probably? Maybe? Right? If he was a ghost? How else would it have happened? How could he not have known? Had everyone just been humoring him, all these years? They'd all always acted as though he was crazy— why hadn't he believed them? Why had he never questioned the way he could see ghosts?

Of course I'm crazy. Of course I'm fucking crazy. Why would everyone tell me I was crazy if it wasn't true?

His arm contorted in front of his eyes, deep gashes welling up with shriekingly bright blood in the shape of letters, words... *Love you Z.*

A brutal thud slammed into the back of his head, reverberated through his body like an excruciating shiver, and the world of panic and horror turned to nothingness.

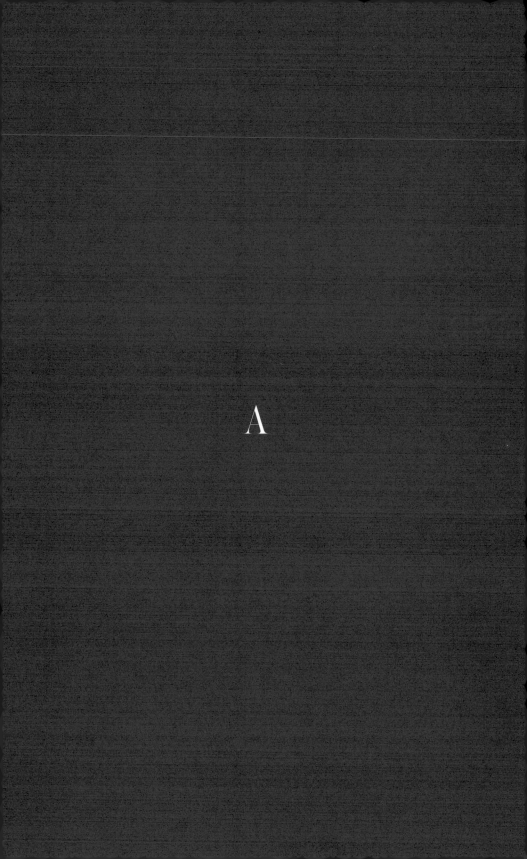

A

38

SHE WAS JUST TRYING TO PROTECT PEOPLE

JAUYNE, BRIGON-CHEDHIY BORDER GUARDHOUSE
6 months, 1 week since the sack of Meirydh

Love you, Z.

Had she hit him too hard? How long was someone supposed to be unconscious for, anyway? That wasn't really something she'd ever needed to know, and now, when she did, of course there was no one to ask.

Rough wooden planks ran wide beneath her body, where she sat with her back pressed up against the bed, and she traced a jagged splinter with an absent finger. Her toes nearly skimmed Zech's forearm, and she resisted the urge to run them down the length of it.

The sky growled, then thudded, like her stomach. The once-fluttering taps of the child inside had rapidly expanded to what she felt were highly unwarranted thrashes of— if this child were anything like her— pure rage. She supposed, though, that this child might be absolutely nothing like her— that it might be far more like this unconscious Chedhiyn border watchman at her feet. Fucking Stars, and she'd been the one to knock him out. (Which didn't feel wholly like her fault, considering she'd been doing him a favor.)

But could ghosts even get you pregnant? Because that sure as fuck didn't make sense. Which led her, for the fifth time that morning, to the inevitable conclusion that she was absolutely bat-shit crazy, entirely off her rocker, and most definitely high on some bizarre Starstone concoction that was somehow still wreaking havoc on her from however far away she was from them, now.

Stars-be-damned, this was not how this was supposed to go. None of this was how it was supposed to go. She gritted her teeth, jamming her jaw closed around the temptation of a sob.

She was just trying to protect people. Again. This little monster of a baby, Zech, Indra…She'd been trying to do the right thing by coming here to the little treehouse on the border, which was albeit also the selfish thing, but who said those two couldn't commingle? Of course it had all gone fuck-sideways. Her whole Province had been murdered, why wouldn't this be doomed to fail, too?

Her head was full of angry, woozy thoughts, and the smoky glitter that coated her vision wasn't helping. It had only gotten worse since the visit of their strange ghost-guest, mucking over everything so that every edge and corner that greeted her eyes was a sick cacophony of shimmering silver and light that swirled like smoke caught in an updraft. It made it next to impossible to walk straight, to tell corporeal from ethereal, to order time or comprehend reality.

Very few things were solid and sturdy in her mind now, but those things were becoming clearer, just as everything else around them softened into non-existence: They desperately needed help. They needed to know if Indra and Adras were feeling it, too. They needed to find a way to be done with the stones, to give them what they wanted and just be done.

Because the fear that crept in at every opportunity was this: *a woman insane could not lead a Province.*

Another thrash pressed outward from within her belly, and she cradled a hand to the offending limb— Stars knew which it was. A flare of pain, like the lighting of a match, flashed at the apex of her legs, and she sucked a gasp between her teeth, curling over herself. A flicker of light dashed across the surface of her belly.

Zech stirred at her feet with a violent twitch, grey-green eyes opening wide as she'd ever seen them. He thrashed toward her, a naked relief glistening over him in that smoke-and-glitter way until she could nearly taste it. One of his hands laced around her calf, warm and loose and heavy.

"I thought I'd..."

"Don't be stupid." Affection ran her voice ragged, and she couldn't fault it, despite herself. "You'd never."

"Even if I'm a ghost?"

She knew it was a test. She didn't particularly care. "Yes." Her voice was flat. "Even if you're a ghost."

Another match lit inside the sensitive nerves at the inner crook of her hips. *It's nothing. Pregnancy's just a bitch.* She exhaled an angry whimper that made her arguably more miserable than the pain.

Grains of glittering dust refracted gleaming sun into her eyes as they gathered aimlessly around one another. Zech shuffled to sitting, moved close to her.

"What just happened?"

"Nothing. Making people is misery. Didn't anyone ever tell you that?"

He shot an eyebrow up, skeptical at best.

She didn't want more questions, couldn't take doting... "Just distract me. I'm sure it will pass. What's that?" She nodded to the sickening skin-carved words in his arm. "Who the fuck calls you Z?"

When his eyes shuttered and his body curled around itself, she knew it was the wrong question... again. She'd done the wrong thing, again. The selfish thing, again. How many more people would cut themselves on her jagged edges?

"My mother did." He winced down at the blood coating his arm and hand. It had congealed, at least. Wasn't running free any longer. She'd made sure of that before she'd sat down. It'd scab over soon.

His mother...

Another sudden leap of flame shot through her veins, and this time it leapt up, up, up... like it was in her brain, like it was in her eyes. She clapped her hands to her face. She could claw it out. She could pull it out! Was that her own shattered scream? A feeling of boiling was sloshing behind her skull, now. Flashes of memory-that-couldn't-be-memory assaulted her.

Not again, not again...

"Jauyne... Jauyne can you hear me?" Zech's voice scrabbled at the edge of her hearing, tinny with a stripe of panic. "I need to know what's wrong. Tell me what's wrong, please!"

But she couldn't. She couldn't form words around the horror gagging her throat. She couldn't speak, couldn't see him anymore. She could only scream as her vision was hacked at with grievous things she'd never experienced.

Her daughter was ripped from her arms as she screamed, screamed, an utterly frigid coldness numbing her fingers, pinching feeling from her nose... and there was her baby and there was Adras and Indra and there was Zech but those bitches were so far away and they had her baby they had her baby *they had her baby* and she was saying goodbye but she didn't want to and why was her baby clinging to Indra and why why *why did she fuck this up too* was she a horrible mother was her own baby repulsed by her *did she deserve this* no no no nonono....

There was no feeling other than heat and cold and pain in her body, and the limits of each seemed to test one another in a horrifying, ripping, expanding way that left her body as nothing but its pitiful servant.

And she screamed. Stars, how she screamed as she hadn't since the carnage of her awakening all those months ago... She screamed their names— *Indra! Adras!*— over and over, a fury of their own, a promise of suffering.

HERO

39

SOFT AGAINST THE BRUTALITY

INDRA, BRIGONAN HIGH HOUSE
6 months, 1 week, 1 day since the sack of Meirydh

Indra had relived Lumen's words and the numb burn of the Starstones nearly every waking moment. It was hard to remember what time was, or how it worked. Frequently, she'd look up from the breakfast she'd been picking at alongside her notes and work, and find that it was already dark. Other times, she would pace for what surely must have been hours, the cat following her path in an oddly conscious sort of support, to discover that a mere five minutes had passed.

It was frustrating and disconcerting to her usually precise mind, and she had requested that someone come to remind her of the time every three hours.

It helped, only marginally.

Lumen had learned of the violent interactions between she and Valeryn and Jauyne and had offered to come to the library with her as a sort of protective barrier... which one again helped, only marginally. Though, once she was fully immersed in her work, it took a significant amount of disruption to garner her attention, for which she was thankful. Valeryn was a notoriously quiet student of the library, holing himself up in a corner behind teetering stacks of books for hours at a time, and only more so since the incident.

She was loathe to admit it, but the poem he'd found had proved immensely fascinating, and she knew it was helpful, even though she struggled to find a basis for that knowledge. What somehow felt of greater consequence to her heart, as sentimental as it was, was this: she knew deeply within her that the Starstones were meant for communication, and Adras believed her.

There were a few extremely important things on which they'd agreed

+ the Starstones were meant for communication— what precisely this meant, or what form of communication, was not explicit, but it was definitely communication.

+ they did not affect Lumen— either negatively or positively— because the Starlight in him ate up whatever they projected before he was capable of using it for himself, and the void in him seemed to simultaneously repel it somehow?

+ all of the Starstones were necessary for the communication to properly work, and possibly all of the Starchildren were needed in order for them to fulfill their greatest capacity.

+ they seemed to have been sent deliberately. The reasoning for this was that only one had landed in each province, and that their timing had been staggered in what felt like a pattern.

+ when these things were discussed, sometimes Indra or Adras would begin to bleed from the nose or ear. This generally happened when they talked about their own Starstone, when they discussed the implications of bringing all of the stones together, or when bringing attention to the strange effects the Starstones seemed to have on the world

+ these effects included, but were by no means limited to: a strangely distorted sense of time, disturbed sleep which did not seem to influence tiredness, more frequent memories that refused to make any proper historical sense, an increase in their sensitivity to Starlight, a wider variety of ways in which the connection to their Starlight manifested, and an increased frequency to those sudden moments of intense and overwhelming knowing.

Indra ran her tongue along the smooth enamel of her teeth. It was still numb in the bizarre way that burned tongues were for days on end. She had noticed it after the meditation that Adras had led her in. Returning to one's body after astral projection, Adras had assured her, could sometimes cause odd little physical side effects. Although, waking up bloodied from her own nose, ears, and eyes seemed a bit on the extreme side of "odd" and also "little". There was a familiar, ethereal prick at the back of her throat; she wasn't sure if it was from anxiety or something more... foreign.

Neither she nor Adras had remembered anything from their six-hour voyage into the astral. The only thing they had to show for it was their bloodied faces and a key, the bow of it a die-cut Starmap, clutched in Adras' fist. The knowing inside her had screamed with wrongness when they returned, a terrible sense of being unmoored on a lightless sea.

The two of them had shown only two people the key, which they had agreed did not belong in the hands of the Premiers, more fuel for the brimming war. Lumen had shuddered at the sight of it, saying that, despite keeping watch over their bodies, he had not seen it appear. Enoch, however, had gasped, an outstretched hand shaking as he ran a finger over the teeth of it.

"Where did you get this?" His voice had been clipped with rush and emotion.

"We awoke with it," Indra had told him.

He had looked at them both with awe that balanced on the knife's edge of fear, shook his head, and reached a hand into his locs. He tugged and wriggled his hand in an odd motion, before pulling it into view again, a matching key hanging from a ribbon.

Adras' fingers had gone white as they squeezed around Indra's wrist.

"This is the key to the box which held the Pallydhan Starstone. I stole it when I left last. If I am correct, and I usually am, that," he gestured to the one in Indra's hands, something sparking in his dark eyes, "is the key to the box in which the Nareilën Starstone is kept."

Even at the memory, a nauseating, confused ache plummeted deep inside, somewhere far too deep to pluck out, something that part of her knew would not ever abate. But the best thing she knew to do when in distress was to make herself useful, and so she had. She wiped fresh blood from her nose.

It was in this state of distressed task-strictness which Adras disturbed her.

"Don't you find it odd that we haven't yet heard from Jauyne and Zech?" Adras was picking at a stubborn hangnail with a frown.

Indra blinked, irritation at her own failing mental faculties needling her. "How long has it been?"

"Three months since they left. Nine days since last contact."

"Can you feel them?" Indra asked suddenly. They hadn't yet discussed the way the threads that connected her to the Stars also now seemed to extend to the other Starchildren, lighting up her veins the way it had the day Jauyne had stood up to the guards in the little Starstone-adjacent room.

Adras' eyes flicked up at her, narrowing a bit. "You, too?"

"They feel…" She splayed her hands. This wasn't something that was meant to be conveyed in language.

Adras' cocked their head, and Indra could feel a soft swelling of Starlight from them— not pointed like an action, but rather like a cautious wave lapping outwards, with them as its epicenter. A flicker of a moment later (or perhaps several minutes; Indra no longer trusted time.) Adras folded their brows together, concerned.

"Something isn't right."

Indra teased the edge of her awareness, her own Starlight a wave of intake and sensation. *Jauyne… Zech…* She felt them, sharp and spiraling. Then, someone else: a third presence pulsed and howled in its existence. Realization grasped her by the windpipe. She met Adras' eyes with panic.

"It's the baby."

Time eddied and flurried as they bolted from the room, shot to the stables, flung themselves along treacherous mountain passages. Lumen followed, trepidation seeping from him.

They were still several minutes' ride away from the little watchhouse when unfettered screams of agony and hysteria began to rend the air into shards of sharpest dread. Indra felt her life-point beating erratically under the stiff brocade collar of her shirt. She led the way, teetering with slow-earned fearlessness against the rock face, a piece of Brigon embedded in her blood, now.

She gritted her teeth. No shards of dread would cut her. No height would dizzy her. The turncoat princess and the paranoid dreamer that lived within her had birthed a new, cresting courage. She was a Starchild; this was only a mountain.

The final bend was abrupt and sharp, and Indra drew her horse up sharply in the surrounding outcropping of rock beside which the watchhouse was built. The sky here was darker and flickered with scarcely-contained flashes of lightning. When it rolled through the air, the thunder was strong enough to make the pebbles below their feet scamper in a panicked dance.

Adras met her eyes as they leapt down from their horse, feet slamming hard into the rock. Silver shimmered, overwhelming grey irises. They nodded sharply, allowing Indra to lead the way toward the watchhouse.

Indra had never led the way toward anything. She bit the inside of her cheek until it bled and refused to tremble. She was a Starchild; this was only a watchhouse.

The air was swampy and thick with the heaviness that always saturated the world before a storm. Every step forward was like wading through a syrupy current. Wailing struck her ears again and again, and each heaving scream sent a freshly sharpened chill down the length of her spine. The watchhouse felt very far away and far too close, all at once. She gripped nothing but the dregs of her courage in her fists.

"Jauyne? Zech?" The wind consumed her words, clipping them into broken things. The wind jammed itself into her lungs uncomfortably as she took a steadying breath. She tried again. "Zech! Jauyne! We've come to help!"

A scream of wind dragged her curls into stretched-out tatters.

"Indra?" Zech's voice, pained and hoarse, yelled through the wind. "Be careful! This wind could toss you off the mountain! I don't know if you want to—"

A gust shoved her feet out from underneath her, too fast for her to even scream. Her fingernails scrabbled on the pebbly rock face, scratching so hard they broke. The wind barreled her over again, tossing her over herself and towards the edge in a tumble. The meager grasp she'd had on the pebbles gasped away. She was going to fall. She had left Canestry to die in Brigon.

Huge hands hauled her upwards by her arm and the back of her shirt, her forehead snagging on a rough rock and spitting blood in her eyes. Lumen tucked her firmly under his arm, his shoulder sitting easy inches above her head, and smeared the blood across her forehead. The world was still tilted with nausea and terror.

"You're alright," he was shouting next to her ear. "I've got you. You're not going to fall. Promise."

She squeezed her eyes shut, forced a deep breath into her chest, swallowed hard. She looked up at him through the blood matted in her eyelashes, and for the smallest moment had the thought that perhaps affection was not as limited, as scarce, as she might have thought.

"Let's go," she shouted, and she was proud that her voice was firm.

With Lumen steadying her, it was easier, though not by much, to drag herself across the landscape of wind-ravaged rock. Pebbles whipped against her face, stinging. On the other side of Lumen, Adras gritted their jaw as a pebble smacked them in the lip, blood spraying.

As she grabbed the door frame, the clouds unleashed themselves, and torrential rain buffeted them. With a yelp, Indra shoved herself through the doorway and was immediately slammed against the adjacent wall in an unnatural bluster. The air seemed to steal what was remaining in her lungs.

Silver light undulated from Jauyne's hunched, writhing form in the opposite corner. A chorus of wailing, horrified howls reverberated eerily from her throat. Zech's eyes met Indra's from the center of the room, the raging wind somehow leaving him unaffected, and the shining silvery-green of them swam with helpless terror. He flicked his gaze back to Jauyne. With one hand, she clutched her stomach. With the other, she gripped a beam into splinters. Shimmering tears ran rivers down her face.

The air was gone, and there was only wind. Indra gaped her mouth open and closed, hoping piteously for oxygen. Lumen hadn't snatched her from the cliff edge only for her to be murdered by this madwoman. A surge of determination she hadn't felt since she'd stolen a page uniform and snuck herself out of Canestry hit her square in the gut.

"Jauyne, please." His voice was soft against the brutality of that wind, and Indra felt it more than she heard it, as though it didn't require his lips to move, as if it spoke in Starlight. "They're here to help. I promise, little firestarter." One of his hands extended to her, silver rippling from his veins in waves that crashed against her turbulence. The other hand he extended to Indra. "Let her come in. Please."

A sound, like moaning wind and the stuttering scratch of pebble over rock, wrung itself from Jauyne, her lips parting in agony. Her eyes were crazed as they opened and closed, glazed with too-little sleep and paranoia. Her voice, too, was more feeling than sound when she cried out. "They're going to take my baby. They're going to take her. I can see it— her in their arms while we die."

Ink blots of her encroaching unconscious crowded Indra's vision. Her lungs burned, knife-sharp pain fizzing into murky tingles. "Jauyne..." She crafted the words in her mind, unsure if her mouth formed them. "Jauyne, I will not touch her. I swear it. I swear it..."

But even as she said it, she heard angry, anguished cries, calling for a daughter... heard a child crying, felt it clinging... The inky black drowned it all out.

PLEASE

40
ALL OF YOU ARE BLEEDING

JAUYNE, BRIGON CHEDHIY BORDER GUARDHOUSE
6 months, 1 week, 1 day since the sack of Meirydh

Her daughter was screaming.

Those perfect grey-green eyes of hers all silver and liquid with tears. And Jauyne wasn't reaching— Starsdamnit, why wasn't she reaching for her?— because oh, oh she was so very far away. Just a face in a window in the frigid cold now. And there was only her daughter's screams and Indra's voice.

Don't go, she said. Don't go, you don't need to do this. We need you... I need you to stay, Jauyne.

And something inside of her was so rigid and so fluid and so impossibly both and all. I love you, she felt her lips saying. *I love you so much, Lil... My il enë liyd, my precious girl. Mama loves you, strong girl. Remember me, Lilith, alright? That's the thing: you need to remember us...* And, oh, the tears. She couldn't stop them, but she could look away, tear away her gaze and turn it outward to the shrieking stars, could tug hard on every bond they gave her, could throw every inch of her wild, broken-hearted power to—

Pain.

Blinding, shattering pain.

As though she weren't in pieces already. As though she wasn't already a million sharp edges, dangerous to touch.

Pain that silenced the whole world and split her right in two.

And whispers... watery, gurgling whispers. With breeze-soft and Star-light-cool touches, sweeping down her arms, her back. The world was a thousand veils, and she could see all of them, layered and wispy and half-real, floating around her, through her. Countless whisper people, smoky glimmer washing them over, passing through the space where she stood, heaving. Pressing closer, despite her terror, their hands petting her without hesitation. The whispers a terrible assault as they echoed, aimless and trapped, around her head.

What's her name?

Her name is Lilith.

Is it her?

She has their blood, she has Starlight.

But is it her?

Don't be stupid.

And then, cutting through... "It was a fantastic attempt, but you aren't going to kill me, so would you please cut out the wind storm and let us help you. You... you rescued me. From him. And now I'm here. To return the favor."

A cool, firm little hand clamped down on her lower back. The wisps of blonde curls edged into her vision, shimmering and shifting like smoke. Jauyne reached out a blood-smudged hand before she could stop herself, tugged a bit on the curl before rolling the fibrous hairs between her fingers, every bit of friction a welcome reminder: *corporeal.*

Indra was really here. For her. She wrapped her fist around the ringlet and was too exhausted to feel shame, even when hot tears muddied the blood on her fingers, turning blonde hair to rust. Indra only grasped her by the wrist and eased her down, down to the floor.

Voices.   Someone disagreeing.   Someone... trying to tell Indra.... No. Indra maintained   her course, hand around   her shoulders. All fours.

Like a cat like a pet like the animal she was.   No.   Indra   said *no.   Like the   Wild.   Fierce   Meirydhi.   you are.*

Screamnowokay?   Ok a y.

Rip p in g.   Saw   the wh o le   Universe.   Al l   kindsofsilver. Pl anets   o ut

th ere,   andherheartsaid   H ome.   an d   Thenitsa id   *Lili th.*

Was it   eve n   wor th it ?   Nofuckingquestion.

The world focused, shrunk back to what was real. Indra on the wood plank floor in front of her, fists intwined with Jauyne's, brows pressed flat with an intensity Jauyne had never seen mirrored before. Her lip was curled, her teeth set as she watched somewhere beyond Jauyne's eyes for a sign...

"Fucking Stars." A heavy-handed pain seized Jauyne low in the abdomen before fisting the rest of her ribs and back in a twisting grip of tension that burned through her muscles and nerves like fire.

"Now! Scream with me." Indra dropped her jaw, eyes locked with Jauyne's, and howled a low bellow that came from some impossibly deep place.

Jauyne knew that place.

She hadn't been sure anyone else had one, not like hers, and certainly not the princess. But the rawness of the pain, and the desperation for the feral, in Indra's eyes woke something primal inside of her. She roared— a sound both heavy and whisper-light, a sound that made every veil in her sight shiver and tremble, a sound that left her body as one thing and became another, more powerful thing in her attentive listening.

How long she spent, on hands and knees, with soaked thighs and raw throat and gripped fists in her own, she could never be sure. Time was already altered. It almost no longer mattered. But then— Adras letting out a cry from behind her, Zech's steady hands on her thigh and the back of her hip, a smaller, cooler hand on her lower back, and then a final call to scream from Indra.

She gave it everything that was left in her body— more than she'd given anything. More than she'd given her will to live for Meirydh. More than she'd given the blast that shattered the shack. And her body flooded with a shimmering flash of silver. She felt it, fast as lightning, brighter than Starlight, every millisecond of it reflected in Indra's glowing eyes.

And then she heard the cry.

Indra caught her as her elbows and knees crumpled, rolling her sideways onto a pile of furs and blankets that Adras had fluffed together on the floor. Nothing was real. Everything was real. None of this was how it was supposed to be, and all of it was exactly as it should be.

Zech's eyes were red and wet looking at her like a god, blood and birthing fluid streaking his arms to his elbows and soaking his clothes. And his hair was fire-streaked and messy, just as it had been in her room those several months ago. He handed an impossibly tiny smudge of blankets and mewling noises to Adras.

Adras was tentative and raw and smiling as they neared, the bundle in their arms. They looked into it— at her baby— and stroked a long finger down that little round bump of nose, silver light trailing from it. Soft whispers uttered from their mouth, and they began to echo.

Echo...

Until the room was full of them, soft and cacophonous. What was it if not a chant, a Jopaari Oracle's muttered spell. What was the blessing of a child-stealer worth... Stars, her skull was only a surface for the whispers to be vaulted against, heightening the hissing, hushing sounds to deafening.

"Give me my child." Her voice was a crack of thunder; her body was a shimmering bolt of lightning. She felt it move through her, ready to do her bidding. "Give me Lilith."

Zech nosed forward, wary. "Jauyne, they—"

He didn't understand. He hadn't seen what she saw. He hadn't seen them take her. "Leave it, Zech."

Adras stilled, jaw set, eyes level but flickering with something unreadable. They stepped forward, knelt, rested the small bundle of blankets in her arms— so soft, so terrifying.

"She's early." Adras gestured gently to Lilith. "Zech and I were making sure that she is alright. I was helping her body prepare for the world. Little ones this young often need that help."

Lightning-hot rage, up her spine. "I am her mother. I can help her."

Adras drew their brows together, stance hardening. "None of us doubt you, Jauyne. Perhaps you should attempt to return the decency at some point."

They were lashing down their power in a way Jauyne had never been able to do, denying it like they could. She could feel it in them, feel the way they wrapped those Starlight bonds around themselves in cords. But the tiny creature in her arms was louder, softer, fiercer than any Starlight she'd ever felt before. Lilith was warm and cold and firm and fluid and sharp and gentle, an electric Star. When she opened her mouth and cried, the room shook.

She couldn't pull her eyes away, couldn't find the rage readily retreating to make room for the strange, warm blooming in her chest. She would kill Adras later if she needed to; no one would remove this Star-kissed child from her arms anytime soon. How did anyone do anything at all but mewl over their infant's cry? Over these huge silver— *silver*— eyes and the thick, coated mess of dark hair? Over those long, pink fingers that flickered with silver and golden light? That light... It rippled outward from her tiny body in waves, sending shivers of bizarre joy through Jauyne's bones.

"Jauyne?" She allowed her eyes to trail a ripple of light outward, to where it passed through Indra, whose skin was taking on an unearthly sheen of Starlight. Dark blood trickled from her nose, dripped from her top lip. Her eyes met Jauyne's, and her voice was clear but far away. "You're bleeding— your nose."

"So are you." She looked to Zech, Adras... "All of you are bleeding."

The words felt odd on her tongue, like she shouldn't have said them. Her voice was a thing that did not belong to her. She felt delirious with... with joy? With terror? She licked her lips and tasted blood, felt it slink along the wet, pink ridges of her gums. Lilith looked up at her, perfect silver eyes rimmed with light— a blessing, a protection.

But here they were, two Meirydhi firstborn, far from home, and the Meirydhi knew no protection greater than the power in one's own veins. Jauyne grinned at her daughter with blood on her teeth. Her fingers were wet with her own blood, and she streaked red across Lilith's forehead.

JUST

41

OF COURSE I'LL REMEMBER YOU

OSIYS, NARELLË HOT SPRINGS LODGE
1 week, 2 days since the birth of Lilith

Long weeks at the hands of the Jopaari had instilled a sense of solidity in Osiys' bones. His gaunt frame and withered muscles had been padded with weeks of filling foods and constant care. The healers had insisted on him going on walks as soon as he was physically capable, and he had strolled the decadent halls of the High Priestess's temple and the square of the main city daily.

Enoch had stayed with him, propping up his feet on the end of Osiys' bed and reading to him from the books on the tall shelves which lined the room he'd been given. Outside his natural climate, Enoch was constantly bundled and frequently fidgeting, never without a cup of steaming tea and always managing to hunker near the fireplace, should any given room have one.

Once, on a day near the beginning, when everything around Osiys looked like a weapon with which to end his misery, and his words were messy and incoherent within wet sobs, Enoch had eased onto the bed behind him and wrapped his arms around him. He'd rested his chin on Osiys' hair and talked aimlessly about his coffee crops and growing up as a child on the sandy cliffs of Pallydh and the smell of the sea after a storm. Pulling back tear-plastered ginger locks with rough brown hands, he'd stayed. Just... stayed. And not mentioned it since.

They had become dear friends. Osiys still battled the curling cruelty in his gut that insisted he didn't deserve such a friend, that he didn't deserve to be alive, let alone be cared for so tenderly. But as one month, then two, rolled by, the cruelty softened and the wiser, truer voice in him sharpened. A thing with which to cut the truth from the lies, instead of a thing with which to cut himself.

Daily, they took the long halls of flickering white stone outside to the main square, where they spent the first hour of the day together in the tea shop, watching the locals go about their daily habits while they sipped the steaming liquid from small crystal cups.

It was there that he'd met Maryt, the woman with slanted eyes and short, dark braids woven above shaved hair. She poured his tea each morning, soon making time to sit with him for long minutes, wanting to hear everything about Brigon. She'd never traveled, she told him, but she was tired of serving tea.

"I don't think I'd ever get tired of serving tea, especially if I got to talk to the handsome Brigonan stranger," he'd winked in return.

She'd called him a smartass, and then she'd kissed him.

He missed it, now, slow mornings in that tea shop, as he found the edge of bravery and trepidation, out on the very same road where Berg had died and he had been wounded... captured... taken back to be tortured...

A sturdy clap landed on his shoulder, and he threw a half-smile to the dear friend beside him. Without him, Osiys surely would not have returned to the road, to travel, to this mission. It had been hard to leave Jopaar. It had been harder yet to leave Brigon once more. They'd stayed only two nights before Indra had folded a simple key into his hand and gazed up at him with guilt-ridden eyes.

The moonlight had shown in the window at the end of the hall, the one inlaid with colored glass, and had lighted on her face, contorted with self-division. The way she'd clung to him, grasping his arms with frantic apology, still chilled him to the bone. Different. She was different, now. The Starlight in her seemed to be seeping from all her angles, a chilly rush to it.

"You're the only one I can trust," she'd whispered.

When he'd snuck down the hall to find Enoch and Maryt, they had both insisted on joining him. How grateful he was for that, now.

The trees were bare and tangled together above him, a delicate nest that dissected the grey winter sky into angular slices. Maryt ran her fingers along one of the scars that roped down his forearm, her touch a grounding tether, even as they approached the place where the trees thinned and the road opened in front of them. A bald expanse. Enoch showed his gleaming teeth, half appreciative of Maryt's presence for his friend, half a wince at the road ahead.

Osiys could feel Enoch's effort at lashing down his own traumatic memories, twined with his effort to remain calm for Osiys, like a physical tension. It did not help.

"Look." The man pointed one long, dark finger, sadly bare of its usual stacks of rings, towards the opposite side of the road. "At least the winter has stripped the brush of leaf as well. There is nowhere for an ambush to hide."

It was true, and it did send a small hiccup of relief through his chest.

"Alright." It was Maryt now, giving his hand a soft squeeze with her own. "I'm going to step into the edge of the tree line and scan for incoming traffic." She turned back to him, her dark brows briefly creasing. "You have your blending gear, correct? Put it on now, and move when I give the signal."

Something fluttered low in Osiys' stomach, and he held onto her hand, bringing it to his lips to press a soft kiss to her knuckles. He knew the fear bled into his voice when he spoke. "Be careful. Be safe. Please."

She shot him a wink and a grin, that darling gap in her teeth making his heart stutter. "Always am. Be good. No heroics today."

Enoch hooked a hand through Osiys' pack, tugging gently as Maryt slunk off to the edge of the trees. "She'll be fine. Get this off of you and pull on your blending gear."

"Yeah." He knew he was mimicking, starting to drift away from his body, moving out of habit instead of presence. "She'll be fine."

Stripping the pack from his shoulders, he unbuckled the front portion and began pulling out the yellow and brown and grey patchwork jacket, and the tall yellow socks.

Nareilë was an odd and wild Province, full of hissing steam and screaming geysers and swampy earth. Everything was slick and damp with the moisture seeping up from the ground. Yellow mosses clung to every surface.

Spies had reached Jopaar just a day before they'd left the freezing Province, saying a plan had been hatched among some of the remaining Nareilëns to steal the box containing their Province's Starstone and hide it in an old dilapidated hunting lodge in their wilderness. It had once belonged to the Premier, but since the Canestryn overthrow nearly six years ago, it had been unused and fallen into disrepair, claimed by the elements.

As Osiys shrugged into the odd patchwork jacket and pulled the yellow socks up high, he repeated the plan to himself, the loop of words soothing him slightly. *Cross the road. Keep north. Enter the lodge. Find the box. Move northwest. Return via Chedhiy.*

Enoch was repositioning his pack over his own blending jacket, shrugging his shoulders to get comfortable under the weight. He gazed toward the road, his face pained and voice still melodic, despite its haggard scrape. "Are you alright, friend? This place makes my heart ache."

Memories clawed at him, but Osiys swallowed them back. "I'm in control. I'll be fine. You won't lose me today."

A luminous bird call pierced the quiet, and his head turned instinctively to Maryt. She was ready for them. It was time.

Within moments, which were punctuated by his own heartbeat in his ears, the three were breaking the tree line in a swift jog. Packed earth pounded under Osiys' feet, sending shocks up his legs. On the road, the petrifying, exposed feeling threatened to strangle him, but he kept his eyes low, trusting Maryt and Enoch to watch what needed watching. He had only to make it across the road.

It felt like it lasted eternities.

But dead leaves and yellow moss met his boots with a sinking crackle, and they were across. The land dipped low, sinking into gentle valley, and soon the swell of the hill behind them, and the murky fog ahead, obscured the road beyond that from view. At last, he blew out a breath, paused, pressed his palms to his knees as his muscles burned along with the tears in his eyes.

He'd done it. He had crossed the road.

Enoch chuckled low, tilting his warm face, shadowed with his short beard, skyward. His eyes listed closed. The relief in him was thick.

Maryt's hands were on his face, her thumbs curling into his short beard. Her grin lifted everything heavy in him, and when she lifted his mouth to hers, he felt her smile.

"You did it, smartass."

He laughed against her mouth. "I crossed a road— aren't you proud, darling?"

The fist that cuffed his ear made him flinch good-naturedly. "It wasn't just any road. And I *am* proud. Now come on; this isn't too far, and we should use the fog as cover as long as we can."

She turned abruptly, her braids whipping, and he followed.

These were eerie, desolate lands. It unnerved Osiys no small amount to see only dull white-ish blur no matter the direction he turned. They were making their way by the changes in the ground below them and the sounds of the landscape around them.

Nareilë had suffered perhaps the worst fate, other than that of Meirydh. Over half the population had been exterminated, died choking and bleeding from their pores when the Canestryn army had filled the geysers closest to the city with poison. When they erupted, the poison hung heavy in the air. Now, his skin seemed to prickle and burn with his paranoia.

They pushed hard, driving forward through the mist without any sign of being tracked or followed. Hours later, when the sound of bubbling and the spraying hiss of the geyser fields reached their ears, they turned north, and Osiys knew that meant they were growing close to the old lodge.

Maryt's hand found his, damp and clammy from the rate of their progress and the humidity in the air, and squeezed. They had all stopped talking hours ago. There was nothing else to say. And their breath ran heavy and labored from the punishing pace they were keeping.

Gradually, the clinging mist thinned, and out of it rose an old dilapidated lodge. Built much like Nareilë's main city in miniature, the surrounding courtyard wall bulged outward toward them in even, bulbous curves, like water jugs, culminating in decorative arches of mud and stone at the top. Once beautiful, it now crumbled in places and moss crept up the sides, forced its way into cracks. The three of them passed silently through the gates, which hung permanently open and broken.

The courtyard itself was overgrown and devastated. It looked as though someone had torn it to pieces. Local flora was uprooted and ripped apart, scattered across the open space instead of tucked into their garden beds. Sagging, soggy colored grasses were strewn about, while vibrant purple flowers had been ripped from their climbing trellises and smashed underfoot.

Osiys' hand released Maryt's, clutching instead around the hilt of his sword. She reached for her belt, tucking throwing stars between her nimble fingers, while Enoch tensed hands around daggers. Nodding to the two of them to spread out, Osiys moved directly forward, towards the curved point of the doorway of the main building.

His whole inner self clenched in grim anticipation. It was obvious they'd been beaten to this location already. What remained to be seen were two things: were the Canestryns still here, lying in wait? And had they found and recovered the Starstone?

One thing was certain. He was not going back to that pit of evil. He would win or he would die, and he would have no other outcome.

The dirt, made muddy by the decomposing wetness of the scattered plants, squelched underfoot. He licked his lips and crossed the threshold. It was dark, with dusky beams of dirty yellow light squeezing through broken windows and cracked mud walls. The building was trashed. Pottery smashed on the floor. Colorful, hand-needled cushions cut open and ripped to shreds. Loose bricks pulled free.

His breath was making so much Starsdamned noise. A shadow passed over the floor, and he flinched, twitching for his sword before he recognized Enoch in the window to his left. The man gave him a half-amused smile that looked only a little grim.

Continuing forward, deeper into the lodge, made his stomach droop. This place had been thoroughly searched. Nothing left un-assaulted in their hunt. There was no way the Starstone was still here. His shoulders sagged.

Scuffling above his head jolted his body back into action. Swiveling towards the stairs, which were built into the far wall and carved with delicate, arched designs, he noiselessly moved for the source of the sounds.

Upstairs, the building was mostly vast rooms, once rich in color and comfort, spread with dreamy textiles and bejeweled with hung art. He crept down the wide hall, peeking into each room as he passed it.

A moan, muffled and miserable, came from far down the corridor. Osiys continued to move with slow, intentional precision, having no desire to be caught off guard during his investigation, until he reached the final door. Wet breathing sounds hung heavy in the air, punctuated by low groaning and whimpers. He leaned his head around the doorway.

On the floor, lay a person. Tight, spiral curls fanned from their head like a short brown halo, but their freckled face was mostly obscured behind a dirty, blood-encrusted gag and blindfold. Their hands were tied with painful tightness, the rough rope binding them to a heavy metal bed frame. The long linen shirt and tight linen pants they wore were filthy and bloody, and a dark bloodstain soaked the lower half of their right pant leg. He would bet anything it was broken.

The wet rattle of their breathing had paused as they heard his footsteps at the door, and he blinked himself into action, eyes sweeping the room for sign of a trap.

"It's alright." His voice was a rasp as he crossed the floor. "I'm here to help."

A sound that could only be construed as a sob choked out around the gag. He was instantly on his knees beside them, fingers working at the knot keeping the gag in place.

Fuck... They've been beaten half to death.

Easing a hand beneath their head, he tugged the gag out of their mouth before resting their head back down and moving to tug the blindfold over their hair. Touching them felt wrong. Sent a wriggling squirm through his veins that made him want to *run*. He didn't know why, but this person *should not have been here*.

Depthless brown eyes looked back at him, searching and unfocused. Blood was oozing from the tear duct of one, and that rattling breath spattered his hand with blood. He couldn't tell how old they were, but fine wrinkles wound from the corners of their eyes.

"What is your name?" He didn't know why he was whispering. "How long have you been here?"

Their lip trembled, split and swollen. "Siobhan. Been days."

"I'll get you out of here." He didn't want to touch their body again.

A gurgling laugh rasped from their throat. "No," they said. "I'm going to die here, and you will not remember me."

"Of course I'll remember you, Siobhan," he said, but wrongness clawed at his gut.

"Look inside... the windowsill. There." A broken finger pointed to the window at the end of the room as they ignored his reassurance. "Then run."

"I can't just—"

They spat blood. "Are you dense? Get the Starstone, then fucking run."

He wheeled back, leaning on his hands. "I—"

A snarl from their gagging, bloody throat.

Shaking his head, his heart hammering, he stumbled to the window. The dirt surface of the sill was wet, but so was everything... There was nothing here to— He stopped short as he realized the sill of this window was a few inches higher than the others. Gingerly, he touched it. The surface wasn't entirely solid.

Siobhan was muttering and moaning so weakly behind him. "Rhett... mama tried..."

He dug his fingers in, and the sill slowly gave way. Clawing at the mud now, he breathed hard in disbelief until his fingers touched something hard and smooth. Carving out more space, his hand grasped a crystal and pulled it out. He wasted no time, turning to Siobhan.

"How did you—"

Eyes glazed and dark, smiling mouth slack, Siobhan was dead.

A slow trickle of dark sludge began from the corner of their lips, tinged disturbingly with an oily green sheen. It flowed thicker, faster, till it coated their chin and neck, began melting skin and still-twitching muscle in front of him. The sludge slurped onto the floor with a hiss.

He fucking ran. Bolted for the door, clutching the crystal.

Momentum carried him down the stairs and through the front door, even as his cognitive rush softened into white-ish nothing like the mist around the lodge.

He nearly barreled through Maryt as he shot from the doorway, chest heaving and panic blaring for reasons he couldn't seem to remember.

"Void and Stars..." Her eyes were on the Starstone gripped in his white-knuckling hands. "You fucking found it."

She traced a finger, hesitantly, over its mud-caked surface. "Where did you find it?"

Emptiness greeted his thoughts. "Upstairs. Windowsill."

Her brow creased, but relaxed as Enoch rounded the corner of the building. He strode forward. "You've found it! Look at you— so panicked. What hap—"

A massive crash erupted from the building behind them, and Maryt's eyes widened. "Run. *Run!* What else was up there?"

Osiys yanked her by the hand as his feet sped away from the lodge, something sick and terrifying twisting in his guts. "I can't remember," he gasped.

COME

42

ULTIMATELY DETRIMENTAL

ZECH, BRIGON/CHEDHIY BORDER GUARDHOUSE
2 months, 2 days since the birth of Lilith

There really wasn't anything to do. Or rather, there was.

There was so much to do, and all of it was monotonous in the best way, so that it almost felt like this had always been his life. He could almost convince himself of it, too, if it wasn't for the ten times a night he woke up— if it wasn't Lilith, it was Jauyne, and if it wasn't Jauyne, it was him. Nightmares and blurry visions ruled both day and night, waking and sleeping.

It was days (Stars knew how many— he couldn't keep track anymore.) before Jauyne let him ask Indra to come to their rescue. She looked as fuzzy and airy as the ghosts that drifted in and out of his vision, but, fuck, he was so tired he didn't even care. He and Jauyne had got maybe four whole-ass solid hours of sleep at once, then.

Any of Adras' concerns about the birth of Lilith and how long she'd had in the womb were soon tossed away, as she was nothing if not perfect. Absolutely fucking perfect. Fuck. Just... she was perfect. He knew adoration, and he knew awe, but he had not, before he watched her round, pink face emerge and caught her in his own two hands, known reality.

Everything had always been half-real and unconfirmed with him. His mother. His ghosts. Even Jauyne, in all her furious vibrancy and sharp-edged bones, had an air of awestruck other about her. But this child... this Star-touched heiress of Meirydh, the tiny queen of fire and earth... she was so real. And she was his reality.

If he thought about it for too long, his head would go wooden with the intensity of her. From her place in her bassinet or her mother's— Jauyne! A mother! A fucking incredible one!— arms, waves of saturated Star-light crashed in infant need and haphazard curiosity. It was powerful and startling, a poignant echoing back to him of the truth of what she was: A whole future and past, tied up in dark hair and pink hands and massive silver eyes.

Even her birth itself was so grounded in reality he'd never be able to forget it. He was a trained and skilled healer, and he had assisted in childbirthings before, but there was nothing like the power and raw fear that had enveloped that little guardhouse in the moments of Jauyne's laboring. The vibrating keen that had flowed from the mouths of her and Indra was a song that still sang through his veins, and the trembling magic of holding his daughter's head, of easing her with blood-slick hands from Jauyne's body as the last push wracked her muscles... it was too much. It still drove him to tears of wonder.

They'd had so many visitors from Brigon, he was beginning to grow homicidal, and quite genuinely concerned that his next vision would be of him pulling Heran's brain out of his nose. He congratulated himself on the creativity of his imagined murderous tryst.

It was what Adras informed him was a month before he could tell night from day and sleeping from waking. He had honestly pretty much forgotten that was a possibility, and Stars what a relief. Indra had a permanent place in their little mountainside house— she seemed overly enthusiastic about it, which was odd considering she'd been half-dead in the doorway not that long ago— and Adras visited every couple of days, usually accompanied by Lumen.

They blew in now with a sharp gust of wind. It was almost warm, he realized. It had become nearly summer in the month since Lilith's birth. Sweat coated the inner fold of Adras' more lightweight cowl, the thin material drooping like Adras and Lumen were, evidently miserable in the lack of frigid cold. He almost laughed at the memory of the first time he'd seen their cowl, wrapped tight around their neck as they entered the Meirydhi High House study where he and Jauyne were tangled together, warm in ways unrelated to the fire.

Lumen stretched his arms, dragging his palms across the wood-and-stone ceiling with a grimace. "Might start to feel like this place is trying to kick us out if the weather keeps this up."

"Wouldn't want that." Jauyne's voice was colored with her smirk, but it wasn't entirely unfriendly, he thought.

Sniggering as he dragged a chair from the little table, Lumen raised his brows at her. She pointedly ignored him, but Zech noticed the sole protrusion of her slim middle finger as she shook out the carefully quilted blanket Adras had brought Lilith from Brigon. (They had somehow convinced the quilters to make squares of volcanoes, and lightning, and daggers, and bonfires, and Chedhiyn trees, and a bow and arrow, and stars, and chlordant berries. It had made him cry, which was impressive; it had made Jauyne speechless, which was more impressive.) Lumen only howled with laughter at her middle finger until Indra gestured wildly for him to be quiet, as she rocked the bassinet with a foot.

He knew Jauyne resisted the itch to stir conflict, to strike lightning into the campfire of their anomaly of a group. But the inner child in his heart, who had grown up alone, lived alone, always alone with the ghosts and watching life from a distance, the reality of those he could touch taking up even a temporary residence near to him was almost more comfort than he felt he deserved. Lumen's cackle, Indra's shushing, Adras' silent eye-rolled smile, Jauyne's middle finger... he sucked them dry of all their realness and swallowed it.

The dry scrape of chair legs on the wooden floor scratched out again, and this time it was Adras, straddling the chair backwards at the end of the bed where Jauyne sat with folded legs and bristling hair. They dragged a hand across their face and shot Lumen a look of solemn irritation.

"There are things we need to discuss. Firstly, as of just a few days ago, Osiys and Enoch have returned with the Nareilën Starstone, and it is intact and well, though they all seem a bit rattled and confused. The stones are now all together behind the glass in the Brigonan High House. Secondly, our spies have indicated that the Canestryn army has been seen moving about, and, more concerning, seems to have replaced their Starstone with something equally worrisome. The Premier can still relocate entire armies."

A solid mass of dark emotion gathered at the back of Zech's throat.

Indra frowned deeply. "How have they done this? If this is true, they could be here at any moment. That darkness my father summons... it's terrifying." She paused, shivering with something like fear or fury, before she seemed to be distracted by another thought. " Adras. Have you been keeping up with research? The last I heard from you about it was well over a week ago."

"Yes, well..." Adras chewed their thumbnail. "I wasn't able to write you letters to bring anymore, because I suspected they were being searched, and the information I had to tell you would have been... ultimately detrimental."

Move entire armies...? Searched...? The anticipation was a physical thing, pressing down on his shoulders. Jauyne's face was crimped with expectant resolve.

"Everything we've seen so far has led us to believe that we need all of the Starstones and, also, all of us, in order to use them for what they are intended for, with the least amount of damage to ourselves and the stones as possible." Adras continued, "Based on the excerpts we found from your episode in the library, Jauyne, and then from following episodes and experiments with each of us, we think it's a communication device that might even allow us to speak directly with the Stars themselves, and because of that, it requires all of us to fully function. It seems to me that there would be a reason why so many Starseeds would be born at once, don't you think? Wouldn't we be meant for something as grand as this? And think of how the Stars— the Stars!— could help us!"

The dry casualness in Jauyne's voice was a forced one. "But do you... do you really think that's possible? I've never heard of such a thing. And what I say under such an episode might not be entirely trustworthy. It's a bit ridiculous."

"It isn't." Indra's chin was jutting towards Jauyne. "You know it isn't. You know this is real, the same way you know your own Starlight. If you doubt it, feel it."

Zech sucked in a breath. They were serious... They were *serious*. He bit his lip in concentration of the revelation, glancing at Jauyne. She was blinking at them all, skeptical, as always, yet hopeful. He took another breath. *Feel it*, Indra had said. This seemed easier said than done for someone with an endlessly untrustworthy mind.

He felt, anyway. He felt the saturated lapping of Lilith's Starlight, flowing outward from her bassinet. He felt Adras' firm shimmer, Indra's billowing shine, Lumen's rolling void, Jauyne's sparking brightness.

He felt his own Starlight, erratic and flourishing within him, the thing he longed for, the thing he feared. Inside, somewhere deep and lucid, was an echo, a truth of something pressed into his heart like an errant, blooming seed. There was a feeling of something very old and very tired, as though it had not slept since the world was young, as if it were trying very hard to stay awake, to keep open its drooping eyes for some very important reason. What the reason was, he wasn't sure, but it leapt at Adras' words with a vigilance and energy he was surprised it had. And he knew that Adras was right.

"What can we do about it?" He found his mouth chattering without consulting his thoughts. "They still have the Starstones. And Jauyne and I have to stay here. And we have Lilith..."

There was a long, hard look exchanged between Adras and Lumen, who nodded towards them. Indra stared at her lap, fidgeting with the hem of Lilith's blanket. Jauyne leaned forward beside him, her dark hair bristling with static and excitement.

"You three are..." Jauyne paused, stifling a little gasp.

Zech looked from her to the other three members of their weird little family. Apparently he was the only Starsdamned person out of the loop. As usual. "They're what?"

Jauyne looked up at him conspiratorially through her lashes, that magnificent scar of hers looking particularly vicious as she raised her brow. "They're going to steal them."

Air decided to strangle him. He beat a fist to his chest and coughed. "You're all *what*?"

"Tell me I'm wrong!" Jauyne flung a pale hand towards the three.

Adras grinned. "You're not wrong."

Whooping, so positively feral he wanted to duck in case of lightning strikes, fled Jauyne's lips as he blinked away tears from coughing, his throat still stinging.

"You're joking." His voice was raspy, and he coughed once more for good measure.

Jauyne tossed her hair, looking hilariously vain. "They've come to see that all the best ways to solve things involve breaking someone's stupid rules."

Indra looked pained, Adras on the verge of smug, and Lumen downright giddy. He couldn't help but laugh. They were a wild lot. How was it that just months ago they'd been at one another's throats? And now they were... what? About to rob a province of Allesar's most precious possessions?

He gave his chin a scratch, holding in a laugh. "Where do we start?"

BACK

43

YOU HAVE TERRIBLE FLIRTING SKILLS

It was a solid plan which they'd formulated together, and with Indra with them, the High Circle of Brigon truly wouldn't suspect a thing. Adras couldn't help but think what a shame this was, how unfortunate these people were to not understand the complexity of the girl. Though well-meaning, their blind dismissal of the existence of Indra's emotions and capabilities wound up much the same as Canestry's smothering of those same things. Herran was a kind fellow, but he was too fatherly, to a fault even. He saw Indra as a wounded bird, forgetting this bird was a *il'ishryd*, the legendary, self-resurrecting firebird of Pallydhan myth. It was said this creature spawned glittering galaxies when it resurrected, splaying burning blue wings across the Star-dotted, black expanse of the night sky.

Adras tossed a glance toward the Canestryn ex-princess as they hurtled along the mountain road. Her hair caught the burnished gleam of the setting sun, lighting those white-blonde curls with flame. It wasn't blue, but it didn't matter. The *il'ishryd* was all Adras could see. Her face was still and fixed, a firmness squaring her jaw since Adras had known her.

They recalled the conversation they'd had with her a few months ago—blood was what they'd seen in her future. Blood that would write, in fresh red ink, hope over her father's wrongs. Then, blood was all Indra had been capable of seeing. Dreams of Adras splitting their veins and begging Indra to drink from them had crowded her mind. Adras disliked it; it made them feel slowly drained each time Indra had relayed the dream to them.

A sigh sputtered from their lungs. How they hoped Indra would not have to spill blood today.

The three of them wound round the last bend in the road, the High City of Brigon suddenly packed tight against them and the High House cresting the peak in front of them. Adras sighed again. They were weary of returning here. They were thankful this would be the last time.

Canryn's troops had been spotted readying themselves, and a few guards positioned carefully near Canestry's border had reported seeing great flashes of black and a sky bending to meet the earth. According to the account Indra and Osiys had made of the night of Meirydh's attack, Canryn was capable of transportation over long distances though this horrifying and bizarre method, but without the Starstone, that should have been impossible. Apparently, this was not the case, and as such, they had no idea when an army might be upon them.

This extraction was a nerve wracking situation for many reasons, then. It wasn't just the safety of Indra and Lumen for which they were concerned. It was the timing— would they extract the Starstones before the attack? Would anyone be injured or killed in this mission?

Indra would go in to update Herran on the wellbeing and preparedness of Jauyne and Zech, creating an excuse as to why Lilith had not been brought back o the High City for protection. Lumen and Adras would make their way down into the space where the Starstones were kept. This would not be an odd sight, as Adras frequently came down to visit them before doing anything else. Together, the two of them would break into the glass enclosure, pocket the Starstones, and creep out to the stables where their horses would be left saddled.

The plan was tight enough. There was no reason it should not work. Still, acid burned in Adras' throat. They wished it was smoke instead.

Lumen shot them a sideways look as they all slowed their horses into a brisk walk and the road they took began to near the gate.

"Would it kill you not to look like you just sucked on a raw fish?"

They blinked. "Excuse me?" It came out ever so slightly more imperious than they intended.

"You look guilty, Ads. Simmer down. Everything's fine."

"Says the one who practically killed himself on a mission a few short months ago. Your standard for *fine* is not unblemished."

He only grinned. "Damn, you're really wound up." A pause, a shifting of his grin. "Where's your smokes?"

"Ran out," they grimaced.

"Nah." He snuck a hand into one of the pockets of his white leather vest, and withdrew it, pinching a rolled paper of herbs.

"Where did you..." Fondness bloomed in their chest and dampened their eyes as he shot them a wink.

"Knew you'd run out. Made sure to grab extras."

They rolled the little tapered bundle back and forth between loosely cinched fingers, the comforting crinkle releasing an even more comforting aroma. "Thanks, Lu."

He responded by striking a match, also procured from within his vest pockets, and extending the little flame to them as they brought the papers to their lips. The inhale was utter paradise. They let the burning tingle expand within their lungs, tasting all the complex notes of the wrapped herbs as they billowed into smoke within their body. The exhale was Starsdamn satisfying, slow curls of white-ish grey leaving their lips and ballooning in the air before being sucked back down through their nostrils for another inhale.

"Ooh," Indra breathed. "Show me how?"

Adras crooked an eyebrow.

Lumen tsked. "Corrupting the children. What would the High Priestess say?"

Attempting to decide between an eye roll and genuine offense took a second too long, and Indra interjected, leaning forward in her saddle to cast an indignant look at Lumen. "Children! You're barely older than me!"

"By *four years*," he snorted.

"Funny." She sat up primly, turning away from him to face the road, her royal upbringing evident in every vertebra of her spine. "You act so much younger."

Adras nearly choked on another inhalation, eyes tearing, and Lumen's exression was somewhere between offended and impressed. He tipped an invisible hat towards the ex-princess, a grin sliding into one dimpled cheek.

The comforting sizzle of the herbs as Adras sucked down the smoke settled between their collar bones and pooled in their chest, a loose calm that unspooled the cords of muscles that had knotted tight against one another. They dragged another breath of the burning herbs as they approached the gate. Several guards were stationed here, now, and they were grateful for Lumen's forethought in stashing their herbs. Adras counted nine armored men, instead of the usual three.

"Ah! Adras, Lumen, Princess Indra."

Adras bit back their irritation at the way no one had ever seemed to care that it bothered Indra to be referred to as such, and instead nodded up towards the homely-faced guard addressing them.

"Hello, Aster. I see you've got some new pals to keep you company."

He winced. "Can never be too careful these days. Half-er the town's back here now. We'll open up for you three now."

Their heart hammered, but they steeled it back down, herb smoke and whiskey Starlight calling to them. As Aster disappeared into the stone watchtower, Adras nodded to Indra. "You know what to do."

Indra nodded back. She did not look afraid at all.

Nudging their horses into the stables, Indra stopped the stable workers from coming to un-saddle them.

"We'll be right back," she assured. At the look of confusion she received, she lied with eerie smoothness, bright eyes round and sincere. "We're attempting to discover the connection between Starlight flow and animals. Where better to start than the horses?"

Adras squeezed her hand for a hard moment as they parted ways at the stable door. Lumen clapped Adras on the shoulder before tucking them under his arm, good-naturedly. Gesturing to the heavy grey that clung to the mountain with the promise of drizzle, he grinned.

"What a perfect day for a heist," he hissed into their ear, just this side of a laugh.

Despite themself, Adras' mouth twitched. "Perfect indeed."

No one minded the two Jopaari siblings as they wound through the High House. Despite being foreign, they'd made their home in the towering mountain rock of Brigon for months now, and were an expected sight to those who called this place a more permanent home.

Lumen joked and laughed with the servants they passed, winking conspiratorially at the young man who tended the fires. He grasped Lumen's arm as he passed, leaning towards his ear with a coarse whisper.

"Hey, come find me later. Missed you."

Lumen bit the lower half of his grin as he poked Adras' arm. "Keep going, I'll catch up."

"What?"

"We're not going to be back later," he whined.

"So you're going to go fuck the fire-tender *now*? In the middle of *this*?" An irritation that felt close to panic kissed their ribs.

"You have to spend at least an hour in there anyway, or people will be suspicious." He wiggled his eyebrows. "This won't take an hour."

"Lu, I *swear—*"

"See you soon!" He kissed the top of their head.

They flailed, hissing after him, "Can you not keep it in your pants for *ten minutes*?"

He thrust his middle finger into the air towards Adras as he caught up with the fire-tender and backed him into an alcove, mouths crushing, his hand around the man's tanned throat.

Adras stood alone in the hallway for a moment, seething, before they allowed themself an exasperated stomp, a noise of frustration tearing from their throat.

He better be hiding more smokes for the stress he's putting me through... won't be back later, my ass.

Raking shaky hands through their hair, and feeling entirely irritated and untethered, Adras wound their way down to the weird little room where the trap door to the Starstone rooms lay. The guard outside the door nodded toward them with a familiarity that had guilt twining with the anxiety in their throat. They reminded themself to breathe. It was probably a good thing that Lumen had decided to abandon them— his *sibling*, for Stars' sake— for a quick fuck. This way, they had time to meditate, to slow their rattling heart and kicking breaths.

When they entered the room, it was just as it had always been. Or rather, since it had been since Adras took a liking to it. The old, rickety table that had once been the only furniture in the space now rested against the wall, and three comfy chairs now sat about the room. A side table sat beside one of them. A cozy rug was sprawled across the floor. Adras sighed with the kind of happiness that was self-aware enough to know it was living on borrowed time.

Softly closing the door behind them, Adras padded across the room to sit cross-legged in one of the seats. They closed their eyes.

Deep inhale.

Count for five on the pause.

Full exhale.

Feel your whole ribcage expand.

Let out the dark feelings.

Memories of High Priestess Reinah guided them through breathing, easing it, returning it to normal. She had taught Adras these exercises when they were just a wee thing. Just a little fearful, lonely, anxiety-ridden creature trying their best to survive in a hostile land.

Whiskey and smoke swirled with Starlight behind their eyelids. It filled the cavity of their chest and licked up into the column of their throat. Songs hummed in their bones where the strange Starlight curled. It beckoned, called, wooed in a way they'd never felt Starlight do before. It was intoxicating, breathtaking, mesmerizing. Breathing became rhythmic as it pulsed in their heart space, heat like that from a fireplace buzzed beneath their skin.

A hand on their shoulder caused them to startle. Lumen blinked down at them, tucking his shoulder-skimming white hair back into the leather tie. His eyes were focused on the Starstones on the other side of the glass. Had it been more than just a few moments?

He hooked his hands over his hips. "How are we doing this, Ads?"

They gave themselves a second or two to rally their consciousness. The room was still faintly coated in the smoky-whiskey-Starlight. It nuzzled at the edges of what was real. Spearing their vision towards the door in the far corner of the room, on the same wall which housed the glass through which they viewed the Starstones, they pointed.

"We go in there, we grab the Starstones, we keep them close to you at all times so that your void hides the power coming from them. I cannot touch them at the same time as another Starchild, so you'll need to split them with me."

Rubbing his hands together with aggressive friction, he nodded. "Let's do it."

It HAD BEEN EERILY easy.

Adras supposed this was what happened when you robbed someone who trusted you: their doors were never locked, and their eyes were always innocent.

The lock on the door in the Starstone room had been crude and half-assed, like they'd assumed no one would want to risk the side affects of contact with the stones anyway. Stupid.Adras had popped it open and been slammed full-force with a power and frustration that screamed from the stones.

It was as if they could speak: *how dare you lock us up? How dare you keep us separated from our Starchildren? How dare you how dare you how dare you...*

Adras had gagged a bit on the intensity of the pressure switch in the air before catching their breath and being able to actually, physically enter the room. When they did, the heaviness, the anger of it, was enough to reassure them that these actions were the right ones, that their hunch about the Premiers being the ones to lead this ethereal battle was correct.

Those who didn't understand a power should never be allowed free reign over its control.

They had quickly grabbed each of the Starstones, sliding them into the pockets of their pack, and of Lumen's. He took the majority of them, leaving Adras with Jopaar's and Canestry's. The strange void inside of him old counteract their Starlight, effectively silencing any shimmering output they gave. With their heart pounding in their ears, Adras had gently closed the outer door to the room adjoining the Starstones, using a small tool to break the inner lock, jamming it. Then, together, they and Lumen had climbed the stairs and stepped out of the trap door, nodding inconspicuously to the guard standing there.

Indra was waiting for them by the stairway leading to the rear exit of the High House, where a path ran directly to the stables. She had a second pack tossed over her shoulder, as she'd gone to grab some of each of their personal things, things they'd be heartbroken to lose should they not be able to return to Brigon ever again. Adras didn't want to think about that possibility, though they knew it was the most likely. They wanted to believe the Premiers would see the wisdom in their actions, would have faith in the Stars that this is what was best.

"How'd it go?" Adras asked quickly, ridding their mind of the accumulating worries.

"Like usual. Nothing strange," Indra responded, a breathless tone to her voice. "You?"

Lumen closed the outside door behind him and began running down the stairs, just at Indra's back. "They don't suspect a thing. Grabbed 'em and then jammed the door behind us."

"Let's hurry, though," Adras pressed, shooting along the path to the stables.

Indra licked her lips nervously but kept pace with Adras, slowing as to avoid suspicion when they came in closer distance of the stables. The Starlight in her eyes flickered and flared with anticipation.

One of the men in the stable looked up in confusion as they entered, walking purposefully towards their still-saddled horses. His brows crinkled inward. "Are you leaving again so soon?"

"We have important news that needs to be taken directly to Jauyne and Zech. It is unexpected, but not concerning," Indra soothed.

"Ah." Adras thought he still looked somewhat ruffled, but most likely due to the nerves that everyone was bristling with, when thinking of the war at their doorstep.

Lumen clapped a hand on his shoulder as they passed, a good-natured grin playing at his mouth. "Cheer up, pal. I'll be back before you know it."

The young man flushed bright red and ducked his head as Lumen winked at him, walking quickly away.

"Ah," Adras smirked, "I knew your terrible flirting skills would come in handy someday."

He threw a playful scowl their direction as he swung into his saddle. "*You* have terrible flirting skills," he muttered, sulkily.

Indra covered a snort with a sneeze.

"Let's get out of here." Adras urged her inky steed forward, out of the stables, Indra's Star-flecked grey mare and Lu's tawny steed streaking behind them.

They managed to stay mostly hidden until they turned onto the street which led to the main gate. Usually, it was wide open and free of people, but now it was so closely guarded, and it was the only way out of the city. The men squinted down at them.

"You've just arrived, friends." Aster's face was contorted in concern. "Is something afoot?"

"No," Indra once again took the situation's reigns. "There are just some new developments that Jauyne and Zech need to be made aware of. We've been sent back to do some clarifying work on Starstone application, as well."

"Mm." He was still frowning, but he nodded to the guard evidently in charge of lowering and raising the gate, and it began to creak open. "I wish you all the best. Hopefully you can make it back into the safety of the city before... hm. Yes. Well. Have a safe trip."

They all three nodded to him in thanks, hands gripping reigns to keep from visibly trembling, and bolted from the city.

Adras didn't feel the itch at their back cease until they'd been traveling for a few hours, and by the time they reached the little guardhouse, there was only triumph mirrored in the faces of Lu and Indra. Jauyne and Zech were waiting in the doorway, visibly tense, Lilith in their arms. At Lumen's whoop of victory, Zech broke into a grin, running to clasp Lu's hand, and Jauyne rolled her eyes, barely hiding a smile of relief.

Following the stern Meirydhi Premier and the watchman of Chedhiy into their odd little guardhouse perched between tree and cliff, the three travelers loosed their packs and rested them gingerly on the ground. They stood in a circle, Jauyne absentmindedly rubbing circles into Lilith's back in a motion that was soft but not gentle. Her shimmering grey eyes flicked between them all.

"How are we doing this?" Her voice was a raspy bark, but without its bladed edge.

"I think Lumen needs to set them out," Adras began. "So that we don't accidentally touch them two at a time. And Indra ought to stand behind him, so he can act as a shield."

Indra flushed. "I'll be fi—"

"You'll stand behind me, little Star creature. Don't be a hero; stay safe." Lumen patted her on the head as her eyes widened, indignant.

"Then," Adras continued, chest flaring with affection toward both the little Canestryn heir and their overgrown puppy of a brother. "Zech, Jauyne, Indra, and I will attempt to use all of the Starstones to make a connection, like we have conjectured is possible. My concern is over how we will be present during that time, or if the Starstones will take over a bit, in a similar fashion to before. If this happens, and the Canestryns attack, we may not realize."

"So I'm to be your knight in sexy armor," Lumen supplied.

Jauyne curled her lip. "Sexy is debatable."

"Awfully high praise, but what have I told you, Meirydhi?" Lumen grinned at her wolfishly. "You're not really my type."

Rolling her eyes, Jauyne made a gagging motion and held up her middle finger, which she let flicker with crackling Starlight. Lumen just laughed.

"The real question," Adras interrupted... whatever this was... "is whether or not Jauyne and Zech will allow Lumen to watch over Lilith while this is happening."

Jauyne startled. "What." It wasn't a question. Just seething response.

But Zech nodded. "We can't be trusted to watch her, if we aren't *all here*."

She opened her mouth and closed it again, panic and fury fighting for control under the surface of her brightening skin. Lumen swallowed, audibly, but bared his palms to her.

"I'd never hurt her, Meirydhi." His voice was gentle, the mocking term almost sounding like one of endearment. "My void can counteract any Starlight, in case the four of you start hacking away at the mountain or we get ambushed somehow."

"I—" Her voice was raw, and she cut it off as she clutched Lilith and clamped down her teeth to fight off a sob.

"I know what it's like to be separated from one's parents as a child. I would never—" There was a ripe vengeance lashing through his usually humored voice. "—ever let that happen. I will keep her safe and bring her back to you."

She nodded around a shuddery breath, but didn't say a word. Zech squeezed her arm. Everyone let out a nervous breath.

"Well, I think that's everything." Adras spoke, but it sounded far away with anxiety and anticipation. "Let's talk to the Stars."

DON'T

44
WE DON'T HAVE MUCH TIME

INDRA ???????
2 MONTHS, 1 week, 3 days since the birth of Lilith

They'd been found. An offshoot of Canestryn's army had found them.

The revolting smell of blood and burning flesh licked up into Indra's nostrils with a squirming rush that sent ripples of nausea through her stomach and throat. It was dizzying. She peeled off the swirl of golden hair that was plastered to her cheek with sweat and blood. Jauyne, eyes crazed and focused, was centering her Starlight into the center of the circle which the seven Starstones made. her entire face was lit up with cool light, her eyes too brilliantly blazing to look at directly.

How that woman could focus with all the clashing noise around was a mystery to Indra. Zech and Adras as well were intensely focused on the Starstones in front of them, though neither were as crazed and otherworldly as Jauyne.

Indra's hands were trembling in front of her, the fear and adrenaline spinning into an unhelpful concoction in her veins, and she couldn't manage to summon hardly any light at all, let alone what would be required to activate these Starstones. With just four Starchildren and seven of the Starstones... Indra shuddered, despite herself.

A scream erupted outside the door, then was sickeningly cut short. The dizzying nausea was back. Where was Osiys? Was he alright? Though she knew the scream had not been his, perhaps the next one would be... or the one after that... or... Her heart was hammering, her breath rushing and rapid.

Why am I the only one unable to breathe...

"Indra!" Jauyne was rasping at her through pale lips, not even removing her focus from the Starstones to reprimand her. "Indra we need you to focus. Now!"

Swallowing the sick that kept rising in her throat, Indra nodded weakly, then squeezed her eyes shut, trying desperately to squeeze the sounds and smells out of her ears and nose, as well.

I am a Starchild. This is only a stone.

The sounds and smells remained, but grew ever so slightly dimmer as she fixed her concentration on the hum that the Starstones emitted, the hum that rumbled in her bones. Even with her eyes closed, she could feel the presence of the other three Starchildren around her; she could even see them, in a sense, by the twining patterns of Starlight which they emanated in the darkness of her vision.

A hair tickled the side of her nose before sticking there into the thick smear of blood. She stubbornly refused to give it her attention, returning instead to the baseline of thrumming energy she could feel from the Starstones, reflected in her own body. Gritting her teeth so hard it hurt, she reached out.

I am a Starchild. This is only a war.

The chaotic buzzing and screeching she felt from the battle was terribly distracting, the clashing colors of red and murky blue and black she saw threatening to overwhelm her invisible senses and blind her. She felt a scream boiling in her throat, and she released it, the sound seemingly punching a tunnel through the mayhem of battle and illuminating her mind with a flood of Starlight.

It was as though all the energy of the Stars was suddenly dumped on her through this carved-out opening, and she felt as though her hair must be standing on end. A buzzing thrill shot through her veins, the Starlight in her body more dense and thrashing than ever before. A flood of it wept from her palms and eyes, pouring into the room and encompassing the final Starstone. It slithered into the cracks of the room, into the final connecting channels between each of the other stones. Zech and Adras nearly jumped with the suddenness of Indra's power.

The overwhelming light began to hum louder and louder, screeching and rumbling until it felt as though Indra's bones were grinding together.

Damn, that hurts...

There was a ringing in her ears now that was too familiar for her liking, and a horrified realization slid into her awareness. Even as the recognizable high-pitched tone began to scream from the stones, her vision stuttered out. Quite suddenly, there was nothing at all— no sound, no sight, no sensation— for what felt like several minutes, before she blinked open her aching eyes to a sight that bewildered and panicked her.

She was in a room, but not the guardhouse room in which she'd just been standing, and not a lush and decadently rustic room like those in Brigon, and not one fashioned of flickering stone and ice like the buildings of Jopaar, and not one of glass and polished stone like the ones in Canestry.

This room was a slick and shiny silver, so spotless it was as though no dirt or dust or blood had ever touched it, until Indra's own boots had stood there. Perhaps not even then, seeing as her boots seemed to make no mark on the floor. Confused and brain-muddled, Indra continued to gape around her, the ringing in her ears becoming a dull, high buzz.

The room was long and sleek, punctuated on the wall behind her by tall doorways, which were framed in linear, geometric ornamentation looking rather similar to the four-pointed starburst of Canestry. The doors had long, even cracks down the center of them and triangular patterns that split from each side of the cracks in silver and deep blue and glowing white. Between these doors, flat panels of glowing blue and white circles hugged the wall. Hard-edged, stepped lights fanned out from the wall above these panels, the glowing beams trimmed in silver and black.

Along the edges of the wall, on the floor, ran long strips of a bold, cubic pattern which were that same glowing white like a falsified Starlight. The center of the ceiling was done in the same triangular design as the doors, and it, too, glowed white, brightening the entire length of the room.

Brilliant, terrifying vastness opened up on the opposite wall, a glass panel taking up most of it. A huge window, Indra realized, but to a night sky that stretched endlessly sideways, and as far as the eye could see. Between Indra and the window to glittering nothingness stood a great table, the same silvery color as the rest of the room, lined with angular silver chairs.

At the end of the long room, there was a massive doorway, its edges clipped and its border trimmed with the same pattern that ran along the floor. A panel similar to the ones behind Indra rested beside it, squares and circles gleaming white.

Indra stepped closer to Adras, who had gone very pale and still, their hands flexed and shaking at their sides. Beside her, Zech had grabbed Jauyne's arm and was shuffling closer to Indra and Adras. Jauyne was on the edge of hyperventilating, the bony plane of her sternum heaving, even as her whole body braced.

Everything felt gingerly unreal. There was no place in Indra's mind that could categorize what she saw, even for all its frantic sputtering. As she opened her mouth to ask what they ought to do, the steady, inset white light on the floor turned blue, and began zipping along the pattern in racing lines. A high pitched wail sounded from the very walls. Indra swallowed a scream.

I am a Starchild. This is only... This is only... only...

She looked around them wildly, panic squeezing her chest. Her bloody, petrified reflection met her in the wide pane of glass across the room. Adras gripped her hand, and nausea heated her stomach.

A sharp and echoing clicking sound began out of the distance and grew louder until Indra could see three people racing towards them from the other side of the huge doorway. They were strange, and strangely clothed, and everything in Indra's body gripping around nothing for a sense of power and safety. She felt the others tense around her, the Starlight emanating from them all inconsistent and muddied with their fear and confusion.

The leading figure, an extremely tall and thin woman with a closely-shaved head and the deepest shade of skin Indra had ever seen, held her hands out in front of her, waving them in a disarming display of concern as she came to a stop in front of them, panting and disheveled.

"Please, friends!" Her voice was rich and warm. "I know you're confused and worried, but we're here to help. It's going to be okay- we will explain everything!"

A white silk shirt, clinging to her shoulders by thin straps, had been crisply tucked into the high waist of black leather pants which loosely skimmed her hips and thighs before tightening around the knees down to her ankles. A band of pearls in a cage-like metal casing curved over the top of her head, framing a face with long lashes and blood red lips.

Batting away black hair that fell around her broad, silk-swathed hips, a second, much shorter, woman bounded after her. Her clothes were deep and vibrant shades of color, and though she, too, wore a thin-strapped shirt, it was tucked into wide-billowing, silky pants. A gauzy bit of cloth capped her shoulders, held together by a silver chain that straddled the deep crease of her bust. Silver jewelry was punched through her tall, curved nose and the center of her lower lip. "We can help you stop the war over Allesar, but we don't have much time. I'm Vim. This is Dymmares." She placed a warm brown hand on the arm of the taller woman.

Both women's eyes shone silver.

"And I'm Asher." The third person, a young man with a sharp jawline and slanted eyes, came to stand beside the other two and gestured to the table and chairs. "Please, have a seat."

Indra said nothing. She felt frozen, but also so weak, so wavering.

Jauyne ripped free of Zech's grip and lunged forward, eyes a glistening silvery white, fists balled. "Who are you!" her voice was high and ragged from the exhausting work of channeling Starlight and surviving a war. "Why are we here! Explain yourselves!"

Zech looked as though he were about to step between Jauyne and the little group of three strangers, but thought better of it. Indra watched him eye the group warily as his muscles tightened, flexing with readiness. Her hands trembled. She had not felt so lost and afraid since the day she walked down the foreign Brigonan hallway to meet Herran for the first time.

The woman with the long black hair (Vim, was it?) stepped forward, moving close to Jauyne with her palms up and ring-stacked fingers extended before her. "We aren't Canestryn, love. Some of this might be my fault though. We want to explain, we want to talk, but we all need to sit and breathe for a minute first. I can't explain anything with your fists in my face." She smirked, winked at Jauyne.

This seemed to entirely disarm and bewilder the young Meirydhi Premier, and she stood there, sputtering, for a moment before finding her resolve and fury again. What happened next was so entirely unbelievable that Indra wasn't entirely sure it happened at all. As Jauyne swung her fist, Vim stood entirely still, unbothered even, and where Jauyne's fist should have struck flesh, it simply continued to swing. Indra gasped as Jauyne, pivoting and flailing off-balance, passed her arm *through Vim's body* as though she were made of water. Zech grabbed Jauyne's other wrist and tugged her to her feet before she plummeted to the ground, saving her the smallest sliver of humiliation. The hair on the back of Indra's neck prickled with horror, and she heard Adras positively spit.

"What kind of magic is this? How dare you capture us like animals and demand us to sit and be still while you do such things?" Blood streamed from their nose, dark and thick.

Vim only groaned and rolled her head backwards, massaging the bridge of her nose. "Starsdamnit, Dymmares, I did too good of a job. They're brainwashed, and we're fucked. Why was I born a prodigy?"

"This isn't magic at all." Dymmares rolled her eyes lightly and brushed past Vim, who only raised her eyebrow at the four Starchildren. "The 'mystical Starstones' you found that are 'pieces of the Stars'? Those are pieces of our ship's technology, fused with crystals I programmed with Starlight and sent down to your planet in order to communicate with you. We knew you were each born with the ability to access Starlight in extremely rare quantities and proximity, and as such, you would be able to activate the devices— sorry, stones— if working together."

"What?" Indra was unable to help herself. The word rolled off her tongue with a depth of incredulous disbelief she didn't know she could find within herself, before she could stop it.

"Please..." Dymmares' voice was gentle now. "We want to explain everything, but we don't have very much time. Let us help save as many lives as possible."

Asher nodded from behind her. "Have a seat, friends."

The three strangers led the way for the unmoving Starchildren, walking behind the table so their backs were to the huge window, and pulling out their chairs.

The four Starchildren looked at one another, full of skepticism and more than a little repulsion at being called "friends", until Adras began walking gingerly to the long table. The others followed them, unsure and deeply uncomfortable. Indra walked to the table, her body moving while her brain still deliberated. She clasped the cool metal of the slim, angular chair back and pulled it away from the table before carefully sitting in it. It was so thin and light, she wondered how it held her weight.

Across the reflective silver table, the three strangers sat. Indra was still unnerved, but uncomfortably drawn to Dymmares' voice and presence.

What is it about her that feels so strange?

Her thoughts were interrupted by Jauyne's demands. "Why should we believe you? And what nonsense are you talking about? Programmed crystals? Ship technology? A smattering of made-up words? What language are you speaking? Speak plainly or let us leave."

Vim, Dymmares, and Asher looked at one another exhaustedly.

"Yep. You did too well, Vim," Asher shook his head with a hint of humor.

"We don't have time for riddles and pointless words!" Jauyne was quick to continue. "Our people are dying! Any chance of saving lives, saving my *daughter*, is weakening every moment that we are away from those stones and our families and friends. Return us at once!"

"You're right," Vim nodded, a pained look haunting the silver irises of her eyes. "We've learned, through pain and failure, that some humans will just always choose the path of hatred and elitism. Their hearts are too rigid, too fearful, too... I don't know. But..." She paused, biting her lip, looking at each of the Starchildren slowly. "I've also learned that some will just always rise out of the mud and misery and somehow still choose to love and heal. You are those people. Do you understand?"

Indra struggled with the conflicting feelings welling up in her: skepticism and familiarity, recoiling and embracing. Blood rolled down her jaw from her ears. "You don't know us," she said softly.

"Actually," Dymmares crossed her hands, interlocking her long, thin fingers on the mirror-like table top, looking into Indra's eyes. "We do know you. You are Indra, the princess of Canestry. You fled your home because you knew what was right, and you knew your homeland would never embrace it the way you did. You have experienced love and loss during this terrible war and kept fighting, kept holding onto what is true. Your connection to Starlight is pure and spotless."

"Stop," Indra flinched as though Dymmares' words were splinters digging into her mind. A razing pain clawed behind her eyes; blood ran from them in streams. "How do you... Where are you learning... I don't *understand!*"

Dymmares allowed her to splutter, watched the blood stream, held her gaze so steadily that it overwhelmed her. "I created Allesar, Indra."

Jauyne laughed bitterly, enraged and horrified as Indra's thoughts swam and she desperately tried to grip the edge of the table for support.

Adras had been quite quiet up until this moment, and now they looked at the three strange people with their head tilted softly, eyes squinting. At last their eyes went wide, and they exclaimed, "I understand now. This is The After, and you... You are the Stars."

Zech nearly jumped out of his skin. "We've died?"

Indra's mind reeled. Had the surge of her Starlight been big enough to tear a hole in what was real and blow them all to pieces? Guilt surged up within her.

"Stars, you're right!" Jauyne was shaking now. "It's the only way to explain all... this."

A light laugh came from Vim. "No, love. We're not the Stars. I created the Stars."

Adras snorted disgracefully.

"Well..." Vim cocked her head, giggling at Adras' reaction to her statement. "I didn't create them. I took an ancient myth about these seven sacred stars and wove it into the creation of Allesar. Or, the creation of the biosphere that is Allesar, I guess. You see, Dymmares here was the one in charge of overseeing the science and engineering of the biosphere. She filled it with oxygen, designed the system that could sustain that much artificial gravity and man-made atmosphere, and filled it with plants, land, seas, and wildlife to mimic the home planets you and your families each escaped from. She brought it to life literally. I was the one in charge of filling it with myth, legend, tradition, activity, art, religion, creativity, family recipes, inside jokes, memories, and in general, all the things you would need in order to have a full and rich life there. I brought it to life metaphorically."

Indra felt Adras convulse beside her, more than she saw it. When Indra looked over, they were bent over the table, heels of their hands digging into their eyes, gasping and trembling. Blood flowed in concerning gushes from their ears and nose and from under the press of their hands. Reaching out to place a hand on Adras' back, Indra looked helplessly at Zech and Jauyne, who were frantically looking back and forth from Adras to the three strangers.

Jauyne flung her arms out, gesturing to Adras. "What are you doing to them! I swear I will find out what you are doing, and I will *end* you!"

From the corner of her eye, Indra saw Dymmares tap on the band of pearls and metal that bridged the dome of her head. She spoke into it urgently. "I need Cashyl to the Core Conference Room. Now."

"It is the same reaction many of you have had to the Starstones, or when you have uncovered certain information, Jauyne," Asher tried to soothe her. "We're getting someone who can help... a healer. He's very wise, I promise. He and his team have been monitoring your vital signs the whole time you've been on Allesar."

"Just get them aid!" Jauyne was panting, her eyes bloodshot and too wide.

Adras was still trembling, and just then, they pulled their fists from their closed eyes, and with a scream that rose up from their gut, they slammed their hands on the table, squinting their bloody eyes open.

"Adras..." Their name sounded small coming from Indra's lips as she flinched away. "What's wrong?"

Adras' eyes were unfocused, whether from fury or fear or shock or some combination of the three, Indra wasn't sure. They finally blinked into focus on Dymmares across the table, a strange fierceness glowing in them. Indra thought, for a moment, that a hungry hope flared in Dymmares' silver eyes.

"I remember you," Adras sputtered, blood splattering from their lips, the pain still glittering across the expression on their face.

Dymmares blinked slowly. Her throat bobbed, and a damp mist covered her eyes. "You do?"

"I. Remember. You." Adras was hissing now, a low, forced voice that could barely snake its way out from their vocal chords. They flicked their gaze to the plump, long-haired woman, who had clapped a hand to her mouth. "Vim, what the *fuck* happened?"

"Adras, you...?" Dymmares couldn't stop blinking at Indra, impossibly trying to turn gears in her mind that were never meant to function.

Indra's stomach clutched. Consternation gripped her throat in a vice. The sound of Jauyne's breathing, out of control with panic, filled the echoing room as she began to stare at the room around them with unbelieving awareness. Indra was so damn tired of being confused and frightened; somewhere deep inside of her, a reservoir of courage she didn't know she had surged upwards.

"Adras, what are you talking about? How do you know this woman?" Her eyes flashed loathingly to Vim. "What have you done?"

Dymmares couldn't take her eyes off of Adras. "How do you know me? You know me? Adras, are you serious?"

"Oh my fucking... yes!" Vim waded through the waters of her shock more quickly than Dymmares, and she skidded her chair backwards before dashing around the table towards Adras. "We've missed you so much, Adras! The submuscular implant must have had some sort of release fault."

She leaned forward, moving to scoop her arms around Adras, who stayed rigid, before realizing she would just pass through their body. The woman opted for circling her arms around Adras anyway, which felt humorously childlike, in a way that would have made Indra laugh in any other situation. Adras' blood smeared across their nose. Indra recoiled from the nearness of Vim, whose existence she still could not wrap her mind around.

Adras ignored everyone, staring Dymmares down. "Dymmares," they growled, "what the fuck happened? This is not... This is *not* how this was supposed to go."

Dymmares swallowed hard before she answered, glancing into her lap to avoid Adras' eyes. "It was Canryn. He figured it all out, was blocking or evading our monitors. We don't know how."

"He wasn't supposed to be able to do that!"

The howl that erupted from their lips caused Indra to nearly jump out of her skin. Adras stepped eerily through the circle of Vim's arms to smash a fist into the table, and Indra felt the vibrations in her own hand which was resting on its surface. Dymmares jumped, as if startled at how Adras could have made contact with the corporeal thing. Indra didn't know how to read this sudden and bewildering change in her friend, and it chilled her marrow.

And what wasn't her father supposed to be able to do? What wasn't he supposed to figure out? Evade? Block? Could one stop breathing out of shock? Were her ribs actually constricting? Stars, she could. not. breathe. Her eyes, desperate for focus in the scene that was now swimming before her, drifted to the blossoming purple and blue bruise filling in the rough ivory curves of Adras's fist.

"I know, Adras." Dymmares' voice carried a dash of irritation in it. "That was kind of the whole damn point."

Adras winced, sucking in air and pressing the heel of their unfisted hand to their forehead.

The irritation melted from Dymmares' face, replaced once again by concern. "Goddammit, where's Cashyl? Adras, what's hurting; talk to me."

"It's my fucking head. Ugh, and the back of my arm... What the-- Oh."

Whatever mumbled explanation Adras was offering for her "oh" blended into a jumbled murmur that swam over Indra's ears. She couldn't stop the questions on repeat in her head, which was aching. She pressed a hand to her temples, ears, jaw, trying to stop the pain. The hand came away bloody and shimmering with Starlight, and she blanched.

"Adras..." Her voice sounded faraway to her own ears.

Adras and Vim continued to shoot words back and forth, both of them with eyes that were intense and confused. Indra felt her whole body start trembling. With a blurred glance, she saw Zech and Jauyne's faces, both of them wincing and pained. Why was she the only one falling apart? Why could she not withstand this mental onslaught the same as the others?

Are these people trying to kill us all...?

Adras's eyes drifted down to her, and she got the impression that they stopped mid-sentence to yell something at her. Something that she couldn't understand... Something she felt she ought to hear...

I'm sorry. She wasn't sure if she said it or only thought the words, but they rolled around behind her eyes until her eyes rolled back along with them, and everything was finally quiet.

DIE

45

NOTHING BUT THIS STARS-FORSAKEN WAR

ADRAS, COSMITAT ASTRA
2 MONTHS, 1 week, 3 days since the birth of Lilith

They'd just been questioning Vim about the submuscular implants in the when Adras saw Indra trembling in the corner of their eye. Acting quickly, they'd tried to ask if she could still hear, if she could still see.

Adras got their answer as they watched Indra's eyes roll back, her body slumping forward and collapsing onto the floor, as her bloody hand streaked their arm.

"Shit, shit, shit. Indra, we need you to wake up." They bent down, scooped a hand under Indra's shoulder, sliding onto the ground beside her to heave her into their lap. "Come on, little *il'ishryd*."

Zech and Jauyne found their feet despite their own pain, to panickedly circle around Indra. He seemed to be trying to gather his Starlight, but each time a silver glow began to hum inside of him, it stuttered out.

Horror splayed over Jauyne's face and she leaned close to him, hissing panicked encouragement and lending a bit of her own power. Adras didn't have time to tell them it was useless.

They twisted their neck to face Vim. "What the voids is in these crystals, V? This is not the first time she's had this reaction."

"I know," Vim shook her head as she clambered around the chairs, trying to get to where the little huddle of Starchildren was. "It's a physical manifestation of her cognitive dissonance. She's only seventeen, Adras... She's not from... She wasn't..."

The connection looped its way into Adras' mind, weaving between the other thousand things fighting for their attention. Half a lifetime of memories were slamming back into place, and Stars it ached.

"She's got to get away from the Starstones." It was a screeched whisper from Jauyne, gritting her teeth. "As do I."

"How do you--" Dymmares began, before a hiss from Jauyne cut her off.

"I just know!"

Dymmares and Vim exchanged a long look. Adras had forgotten how irritating their instant knowing of one another was. "Well?" They snapped at the two of them, dragging their attention back down to Indra.

The two didn't disengage from one another's stare, but Vim broke their silence with brown hands pressed white against her sides. "We've got to."

"You don't know that... We could--"

"We can't salvage this, Dymmares! It's over— we failed; we'll deal with those repercussions later. Right now, we've got a girl's life to save."

"I..." Dymmares' lip quivered, but casting her gaze towards Indra, she bit down on it with resolve. "Okay. Hurry."

Cashyl leapt through the archway, eyes widening at the sight, his brows knitting as he saw Indra in Adras's arms. "Dymmares, I can't work with a holo! I need flesh and blood!"

Dymmares shot him a nasty look and waved a hand at Asher, who ran over and informed the flustered doctor of what was happening. She then followed Vim to where a button-dotted panel was tucked seamlessly into the wall. They each raised fingers and hands to it, muttering among themselves as they punched buttons. Adras struggled to process what was happening around them, struggled to tear their eyes from Indra, who was growing more pale by the moment. Clutching desperately at her hands, Adras felt tears budding in the corners of their eyes.

I'm so sorry. It will all be alright. I'll make it alright... You are so strong, but still you must be so frightened.

Even as Adras reached to peel a blood-plastered curl from her cheek, the princess vanished. They choked and clawed at the empty air where their friend had been just a half of a second previous. A snarl rose behind their teeth.

"Starsdamnit, Vim! Where is she!"

"She's coming back; just give me a second!" Vim was tapping in a code on the panel, tugging a clear crystal point from the concealed pocket of her billowing silky pants, raising the crystal to the control panel.

"Vim!" Adras could feel Zech and Jauyne bristling with terror beside them, and they struggled not to absorb it, not to feel it, not to get lost in it...

"I said give me a second!"

"She doesn't have a second!"

Vim took her eyes from the control panel to meet Adras', just as Indra reappeared, lying on the floor beside her. "Stand in the center of the crystals, uh, Starstones. You'll be right back, I swear!"

"I'll what?"

A shiver ran the length of Adras's body, a freezing tingle that stabbed and shrieked through every last one of their nerves. As the silver room melted around them, they felt a scream rip from their lungs, but no sound seemed to emanate.

Their knees felt wet.

A squelch. Slap.

Sounds of war. Adras' eyes flashed open, ready and alert despite the angry throb in their head. They were back in the room, the Starstones still faintly glowing, and they had crumbled into a kneel in the mud that now saturated the wood plank floor; Rain poured through leaking holes in the ceiling. An arc of frozen, well, everything, surrounded them, as though their presence had disrupted the weather itself. That was new. Zech and Jauyne had fallen to their knees as well, to their right, and were struggling to their feet. Adras' breath was like a Meirydhi windstorm in their ears, ragging and heavy.

The center of the crystals...

"Come on. Stand in the center." They hoisted up Jauyne, who looked just shy of unconsciousness, by her elbow and half-dragged her between the Starstones into the center. "Zech, hurry."

He staggered alongside them, leaned his hands forward to his knees, panting. "Adras," he paused for breath, "What the fuck..."

Adras had their eyes squeezed shut, lips pressed together in a stubborn prayer, despite no longer knowing who they were praying to, ignoring the bawling grief inside them that reminded their last seventeen years had all been a fantastical lie.

The Stars were a lie. The goddamned dragons that littered their skin in ink were a *lie lie lie*.

There's no one to pray to. No stars. There's only us, only right now, only this fucking useless war.

Wood splintered to their right, and Adras' breath caught in their chest with a sharpness that left any remaining hope dead. The Canestryn soldier bolted through the door, towards the three of them huddled between seven pointless hunks of crystal. Every slop of his feet came more and more slowly to their ears. They could see the drops of sweat rolling down his shadowed chin, smell the spicy soap Jauyne used in her hair, feel Zech tuck his hand around their arm, feel a tear slide through the war muck on their face...

How is this fair?

A wall of light shot abruptly into the air, making the three Starchildren start viciously. Within the shortest second, the light shrunk down again, leaving them surrounded once more by silver and foreign metal. Adras coughed, the sharp catch in their chest releasing, even as they crumpled to the floor alongside Jauyne and Zech.

The floor was freezing cold and painfully rigid under their head as the two collided with a dull thud. Their ears felt full of water and the light on the ceiling faded and flared in their unfocused vision. Stars, their body ached... They just wanted to lie here forever. Maybe the cold would numb away the residual exhaustion, confusion, and pain from what felt like an endless string of unprecedented and unwanted events. Had it been an entire lifetime of this onslaught? Adras gravely realized that, yes, it had indeed been an entire lifetime of unknown and fear and confusion.

It's too much...

A sharp hiss, and then a pin prick. They would have winced if the rest of their body didn't hurt far worse than whatever little thing had caused the pinch.

Faces, above them. A man that must have been Cashyl. Vim, loose tendrils of black hair faintly tickling Adras's face.

"Shh, don't get up. It's alright." She brought a hand down to cup Adras's cheek with a warm, damp cloth. It was oddly maternal of her.

Something (Someone?) distracted her for a moment, and she looked to the side, nodded, responded something about what section of the Battlestar they would need to move everyone to, and quickly; then how things ought to be sorted between the Cosmitats and the Starrarium. She looked back down at Adras. "You four have been through more than most bodies or minds are prepared to handle. You activated the crystals, holo-formed up here, and then we ended the holo, woke up your physical bodies, and transported you here. And we still need you to do more for us. Someday, hopefully, we can repay you for all of this... For the time being, you'll feel the effects of that stim-shot, any moment now, and then we can get back to work. Not much longer, I promise, and then you can sleep for days." More distractions, more distant replies. "Alright, I've got to go see Indra now, okay? She's alright, I've just gotta go check in with her and make sure she understands what's going on. I'll be back."

There was a light squeeze on Adras' hand. They tried to move, tried to get up, tried to sit up... They could barely turn their head. So they resigned to where they were, stared at the ceiling lights and the blurs and shifts from the various people bustling around them, felt the vibrational hum in the floor as Zech and Jauyne stirred nearby, felt the embracing warmth of a crinkly heated blanket being placed over their body. There was nothing to be done except to lie still, so they did, and, begrudgingly, found relief in it.

After a few moments, Adras could hear slowly approaching footsteps, followed by a curtain of gold curls hanging over them. Their heart skipped a beat with relief.

Indra...

Indra knelt beside her friend and took a shaky hold of their hand. Adras' vision had improved, and they could see that someone had washed off most of the blood and grit from Indra's cheeks, and splashed some water over the grimier parts of her hair. She had two layers of blankets wrapped round her shoulders-- a woolen one, with a reflective silver one over it, and she was clutching them together at her chest with a fist. Brushing off Dymmares, who seemed intent on making sure she didn't injure herself, Indra adjusted herself to sit cross-legged.

"So..." Her voice was already faltering, and she looked into her lap, gaining courage. "I hear you're not from Allesar... Or that none of us are. Or, well, no, I am. I'm the only one of us without somewhere to belong, now that this is all ending, I suppose." A hefty sigh erupted from her lips. "But there's not time even to think about that now. We still have thousands of people to save from my father's cruelty. My father... This isn't the first time he has been so bent on destruction." She shook her head, shuddering as she sniffled back several tears. "Can you please wake up so I am less alone here? I know that's terribly selfish of me, Adras, but Stars, I feel like I don't even know what's true anymore— just you and Osiys." She started suddenly, gasping as though she'd forgotten he existed until this moment. "Osiys!"

The way Indra's thin fingers gripped theirs with that sudden strike of terrified realization gave Adras all the strength they needed to groan into a seated position, with Indra helping haul her up by the hand. They gripped her hand for balance as the room wavered and shivered in their vision. Adras took a long, slow blink, swallowing down the anxiety she could feel emitting from Indra.

"Are you okay?" Their voice was scratchy, but they hoped the sincerity showed through.

"I'm fine." Indra was agitated now, her memory sharp and senses focused. "We have to go back. We have to get them all out."

"Get them out?" Curse their sluggish brain... It couldn't keep up with all the directions this day had taken.

Vim ran up to them, brushing long tendrils of hair from her face and neck. "Come on, this way. We've already got Zech and Jauyne moving. I know you're both tired, but we'll need you to be the voice of reason for these people who don't know what's going on. They're going to be scared, and they're not going to want to come with us. We need to change that." She heaved Adras up, slinging a shoulder beneath their arm and walking briskly down the hall. Indra floated along beside them, her hand still squeezing Adras'.

"Osiys was still down there, right in the thick of the battle." Her silver eyes looked crazed, like Adras had never before seen them.

Vim cast her a sympathetic look. "I know. We're gonna do our best."

It likely was not as long as it felt, to make their way down the hall to a massive room much larger than any indoor space Adras had ever seen... or perhaps not... memories came back... flashes and feelings... but it had been so long, and this sight still awed them.

The ceiling was hundreds of feet high, bowed and curved, with lights inset along it in long stripes of geometric patterns. It was an exponentially wide room, and Adras wondered at how many hundreds of people could fit inside of it. Before they could properly appreciate it, though, they was being guided to what looked like a makeshift healer's apothecary. Someone was shouting about getting the war clinic ready, and they assumed this was what it was about. Vim sat them down on a long bench, which was really just a slim fan of metal jutting out from the wall. Adras tested their weight on it, gingerly, before leaning back in an attempt at comfort.

Dymmares, carrying a slim piece of metal which on one side glowed and shifted, was hurrying over. She had begun pulling on a protective-looking jumpsuit but stopped halfway, so that the torso and sleeves of it hung from her waist, leaving her silky black camisole as the top of this ridiculous ensemble. Her mouth was tense. "We need to extract the population, as well as the non-violent Canestryns and bring them here, into this Battlestar. From there, we can utilize the Cosmitats and the Starrarium. The Canestryn High Circle, Nightwalkers, and any other violent opposition will be taken to a highly secure and heavily guarded vessel that travels disconnected, but in conjunction with, this one. We will need some of you to split up to do this, as we need to cover as much ground as possible. We've received intelligence that the Canestryn war vessels have learned our whereabouts and are planning to attack in full strength within the next twenty-four hours. Indra, I thought you might want to accompany me to the current site of battle on Allesar to look for Osiys."

Indra nodded quickly.

"Good. Follow Murlyn. He will tell you where to get a jumpsuit and fill you in on all the details regarding interstellar travel."

Indra squeezed Adras' hand briefly before bounding away after a young man covered in grease and clutching a half-drunk cup of coffee. "This is almost over. I will see you soon, Adras."

Adras nodded, a sudden well of concern rising in them and misting their eyes.

"I know this is difficult," Dymmares continued, "but it's time for you to make your choice, or allow me to place you in one of the units."

"Uh..." Adras' brain felt like mud. "Jopaar?"

"Of course." Dymmares smiled tightly. She glanced down and tapped several times on the pad. "Atsu is gonna fill you in. Everything will be fine."

To Adras, she sounded more as though she were trying to convince herself, which made Adras' stomach swirl and cramp uncomfortably. The tall, thin man to whom Vim had gestured, was coming to sit beside Adras. He looked young, early twenties at most, and he had long black hair, half of which was pulled into a knot at the back of his head. Nodding solemnly to her, he sat.

"We're all really thankful for everything you've done for us. You're kind of a legend." The barest hint of a smile ghosted his mouth as he met their eyes for the briefest moment. "Anyway, I'm the pilot and mechanic of the shuttlecraft we're gonna be taking down to the surface. Mine is going to Jopaar, as are you. There's a lot to go through, and we've only got a couple minutes until departure. Think you can walk?"

Adras nodded, gritting their teeth and pushing themself away from the bench to stand. They surprised themself by the steadiness with which their feet pressed into the floor. Flattening their hands together and shrugging their shoulders, Adras lifted their chin towards him. "Lead the way."

LIKE

46
FIND OSIYS. GET HIM OUT.

Indra strapped the delicate-looking leather and metal harness around her body, tugging at where it connected to the roof of the open portion of the starskimmer for reassurance. Still, she white-knuckled the bar beside her.

The carved-out Spire of the Dead, and the stairs leading to it, which she'd climbed with Osiys so many months prior, drifted below them on the right, and a piece of her wondered if she could just reach out to it... if she could touch it, could she go backwards in time before torture and distance had dragged her and her dear friend so far from one another. She swallowed back the lump that had risen in her throat, giving a sharp cough as the grief went down hard, and the tower faded behind them, the golden sun gilding the polished portions of tower like the crown of a king.

The pilot maneuvered them around the last massive peak, and the freezing mountain air stung Indra's eyes as they widened in horror. There was something unnatural and disturbing about seeing the bloodshed being unleashed from this altitude.

Swaths of deep crimson painted the stone in a passion project of deranged art. The blood had begun to soak the grass where many had begun to flee, or had been coralled, into the plains. Opposing forces were meeting the remaining resistance there, pinning them in from both sides, and a terrible wailing drifted over the sharp clinks and sick thuds of slaughter. Her eyes raked the bloody scene desperately, looking for Osiys's auburn hair and green shirt with the gold thread work, despite being much too far above the ground still to be able to identify anyone

A hand on her shoulder brought Indra back to her nauseated body, and she noticed for the first time how her limbs trembled. The copilot was once again reminding her that all she needed to do to have her voice projected was press the small glowing button on the intricately designed pad attached to the wall.

"We're nearly ready for you, Indra. Are you ready for this? Are you okay?"

She forced her eyes to close to the butchering happening below her, but her ears still rung with its sounds. Slowly, she made her head nod. Eyes open. Words form. "Yes. I can do this."

The copilot nodded hesitantly at her before making her way back inside the vehicle, leaving Indra with the rescue crew. Compelling her lungs to inflate, Indra gulped down a few breaths of the cold air, hoping they'd clear her mind. Some part of her knew that her eyes could never be cleared of the sights they had just witnessed, and a fear began to trickle through her belly like a poison. A member of the rescue crew raised a finger towards Indra, signaling her to begin the broadcast as an unnerving lifting feeling filled her stomach and the ship's descent began.

Find Osiys. Get him out. She recited it over and over, the reminder of her goal boiling through her, willing her voice to produce any sort of volume as she opened her mouth and pressed the black button with a trembling thumb.

"Resistance Army. Canestryn Army. I am Princess Indra of Canestry. Listen to me now. This world is not what it seems, and the battle you fight is one that cannot be won by either force. If you wish to know the truth, to find safety for you and for your family, you must put down your weapons and allow me and my comrades in these flying vessels to help you. We can take you to a place where your wounded- both Canestryn and opposition- will be cared for. We can feed you and your families and keep you safe until all of this is sorted out. Please. Put down your weapons."

A dizzying silence stilled the battlefield as Indra found hundreds of faces turned up towards her in shock and disbelief. A thrum of breathy mumbling replaced the clashing noises of battle, and Indra took the opportunity to allow her eyes to fumble in distress over the nearing mass of people below her.

Find Osiys. Get him out.

As she searched, clinging to the steel bar and her last shred of hope, a cry was bellowed from somewhere towards the plains, and she turned her eyes in dread. Canryn lashed the rump of his horse, and the beast bolted forward back into the fray, the Canestryns once again heaving their weapons aloft and bearing down on the weaker forces. A crippling rage soaked through her, and her fist punched the glowing button again.

"I said stop where you are, and put your weapons down!" The other members of the rescue crew winced as her voice screeched into their eardrums, but she was trembling mad and incapable of stopping now. She felt the fury and inconsolable grudge of her loss-filled soul drip from her lips as her voice rang out freshly against the mountain rock. "For those of Canestry who refuse to lay down their weapons and insist on the butchering of innocents, there will be no safety for you. There will be no forgiveness, no opportunity for reconciliation. You choose now, what your fate will be."

Her words were punctuated with the blows of her small fists against an unbending metal wall, which she did not realize until moments later, when the ache splintered up through her wrist, had already caused bruises to begin blossoming along her knuckles. This sort of outlet for an unrelenting anguish was new and satisfying, and her anger was not nearly quenched, so she continued to scream into the little glowing button as she scanned the crowd for Osiys. They were so close to the crowd now, descending on the gore and violence until the scent of sweat and blood clung to the inside of her nostrils.

Find Osiys. Get him out.

The command thrummed through her skull, hammered behind her searching eyes. They were close to the ground now, and the rescue crew were crouching by the edge of the metal, close to open air.

As Indra mindlessly squawked encouragement to the desperate men and women being hemmed in by the Canestryn forces, the starskimmer lowered until the rescue crew were able to slide lightweight metal ladders down to them. Others of the rescue crew wielded strange weapons, prepared to defend the starskimmer and those climbing to safety. Indra's curls whipped against her face and neck, and she wrestled them back into a knot at the back of her head.

As the bloodied warriors scrambled up the ladder, they were met with hands that grasped them, embraced them, ushered them into the safety of the covered area of the starskimmer. They met Indra's eyes with frenzied, panicked ones, and she gently lighted her hands on their shoulders with understanding and hopeful encouragement.

The starskimmer was filling up, she knew, and still her eyes had not found Osiys. She had demanded that the pilot tell her if another scouter found him first, but they had not yet sent word to her, and her hands trembled from the lashing out against metal, as well as from the terror that was crawling up her throat. The battlefield was growing more barren as the number of people on the scout ships grew, and their low passes of the landscape were less often punctuated with pauses for rescue. A sturdy hand lighted on her shoulder, and she turned to see the copilot standing behind her.

"Indra, we think we may have gotten a lock on Osiys. We're headed to the far side of the field now, but there's quite a bit of activity over there still, so you're going to need to be careful. I suggest you go inside. They've all heard your message, and we can extract him safely without needing to put you in further danger."

She was a Starchild. This was only a war.

"I'm not going inside. I need to be here. I need to be here for him."

The copilot pressed her lips together, displeased, but simply barked out, "Fine. Hang on tight. It's going to be pretty rough, princess."

Indra firmly gripped the metal bar beside her, bracing herself and widening her stance as the scout ship dipped low to the ground and turned wide. The copilot and two of her other rescue team members were crouching on the deck, hanging nimbly onto the smaller metal bars that lined its edge. She was barking orders to them, waving her hand this way and that in a display that Indra could not understand. The air was feeling more tense and dangerous now, their bristling readiness infecting her with a sense of foreboding she hadn't prepared for.

As the starskimmer circled the width of the field and doubled back towards the opposite end, Indra watched the other starskimmers break off from their formation and head upwards towards the sky, where she knew the unfathomably huge Cosmitat was waiting to welcome the refugees. One more tilting turn of the ship, and their destination opened up into her view- a circle of hooded men, cloaked in black and blood-stained charcoal, enveloping two figures who were locked in brutal combat.

They're still so far... Find Osiys. Get him out.

The starskimmer was racing towards the circle, but it felt as though time crawled, Indra craning her body towards the scene as though it would help them accelerate. As they came closer, the thousands of feet between them shredding to hundreds... tens... An unearthly howl erupted from the center of the circle that made Indra's bones scream with recognition. Her chest heaved.

"Osiys!" She whipped her head towards the the copilot. "We need to be there now!"

"We're working on it, princess," the woman growled back, her brows folded together with concentration.

The ship hummed over the circle, and Indra nearly wretched.

In the center, Canryn, her father, held aloft a hand, severed from a body just below the elbow. The severed end dripped and spewed blood over his face, and the blood that oozed from a deep gash in his own arm intermingled with it, washing him in an unholy baptism of macabre rain. The red matted into his hair and over the collar of his jacket, wet and sticky with gore. And as he grinned, mouthful of teeth glistening with the dribbling blood, he met Indra's eyes with a pointed narrowness.

The cruelty astonished her, even with all she knew of his sadism. It had been so long since she had been face to face with it, and his was a kind of evil that left her breathless. She dragged her gaze away from his, though the permeating villainy still clung to her, and craned to see Osiys, who was curled on the ground in agony, body arced around his bleeding stump.

"You can't track us anymore, you worthless Free Worlders," Canryn spat out the words, drops of blood flying from between his lips. "And we won't be coming with you today. Unfortunately for you, I have another ride on its way."

The rescue team was already moving into action, even as Indra was plastered to the deck with shock and fear that settled squeamishly in the pit of her stomach. The copilot screamed orders over the hum of the engine and the vile spitting from Canryn's mouth.

"We want them alive, ladies. We need to know how this happened. And Canryn," she glanced down at him pointedly, "won't be here when his ride shows up."

One of the Rescue team crouched on the metal floor, propping up one of their weapons to his shoulder, and fired, sending a bolt of purple light towards Canryn's thigh as his eyes momentarily widened. Her father fell to the ground, convulsing, and the hooded men staggered, exclaiming. The copilot swung herself over the edge of the starskimmer's deck, sliding down the metal bar on the side of the ladder to land on the blood-soaked grass. One other followed her lead, heaving Canryn up onto his back as the copilot demanded compliance from the Nightwalkers.

They bristled, one of them readying a weapon, and the rescue team took another shot, this time hitting the man squarely in the chest with the purple bolt. He seized much more violently than Canryn had, his mouth foaming and blood dribbling from his lip where he bit it.

The man carrying Canryn on his back reached the top of the ladder, and two rescue team members hauled him onto the deck and secured his hands and feet in thick silver cuffs that beeped when they closed around his ankles and wrists. The copilot trained the barrel of her smaller weapon on a bristling Nightwalker as she knelt to examine Osiys. They mumbled a few words back and forth before she hoisted him up, supporting him shoulder-to-shoulder. He looked up towards the ship, and his eyes went wide when they met Indra's. Despite herself, she felt her eyes brim and spill over, a hot relief that dripped from her chin.

She outstretched a hand, beckoning him towards her.

Osiys fumbled forward, wincing, blood leaking from where his hand was once attached to his body, and from a gash just above his hairline. The red ran over his face and caked in his reddish hair, and spatters of blood, whether his or someone else's, covered his whole body in a ghastly rainbow. He managed a weak, relieved smile that angled crooked over his face, before wincing deeply. His remaining hand grasped the rung at the bottom of the ladder, and he stepped on, his jaw gritted with pain and determination. The copilot followed, both she and her colleagues on the deck training their weapons on the Nightwalkers as she braced Osiys from below. He climbed slowly, agonizingly, and the starskimmer began to ascend slowly.

His eyes raised to Indra's as he reached for the next rung, nearly cresting the top. "Indra..." his voice rasped, and tears brimmed his pained and bloodshot eyes. "I thought they had taken you. I'm so glad you're safe, that you're here."

Even now, with a hand severed and blood leaking from him, his concern was for her. His careful protectiveness was a warm blanket that comforted her heart. Indra reached down towards him, her pale hand skimming his blood-caked one as it drifted further to cradle his jaw. "I looked for you everywhere. We came just in time! If we'd not found you..."

She trailed off, emotions flailing with relief and horror, meeting his gaze with a relief that stunted into confusion as his brows angled into a question and his eyes glazed over, unfocused and dead.

It wasn't until seconds after the fact, until the blood poured over his ear and cheek and trickled over her hand, that she heard the sound of metal burying itself in bone and saw the axe sink into the top of his skull.

Her lungs emptied.

Her Starlight screamed out of her in torrents of anguished power.

Gravity dragged him away from her as she stared, her fingers grazing the tip of his chin as he slumped downwards toward the cursed ground they had, mere moments before, heaved him away from. Silence suctioned into her ears, masking everything but her shuddering heartbeat. She watched the copilot grasp at his shirt, saw the way her muscles and joints constricted as the fistful of fabric hung, deadweight, from her balled fingers. Saw her mouth open in a howl for help with the body that dangled from her hand.

Indra was shoved to the side, her head bumping roughly against the metal wall, as two more rescue team members suspended themselves from the deck and sprawled their bodies forward, their hands splaying open to breach every spare inch between them and Osiys's limp body. As one of their hands brushed his cloak, it tore from the copilot's fingers, and he sailed downwards.

His auburn curls rippled ever so softly in the wind, like they had on the day the grinning young man had first tossed seven-year-old Indra a chocolate orange in the High House of Canestry.

THIS

EPILOGUE

<u>**Adras–**</u>

The silk sheets were cool under the length of their arms and legs, and they were objectively much better cared for and comfortable here on Cosmitat Astra.

They'd thought the confusion, though not the war, would be over now. Everything explained. Everything tied up nicely and their memories stacked up how they ought to be.

They were back with the friends with whom they had spent a brutal but magical childhood. They were coping with the disorientation of returning to somewhere familiar and missing somewhere that didn't, technically, exist.

They were keeping a close eye on Indra, who had disappeared somewhere deep inside herself, and Jauyne, who had learned ugly truths about where exactly she was from.

But then the scent had rolled through their senses— smoky, whiskey-licked, singing Starlight. They fisted the sheets, looked out the wide window into an expanse so great it made them tremble with... awe? Excitement?

The voice came again, Starlit and curling up their spine: *Do not forget, Adras. You are our Champion. We are yours.*

Not a dream, despite being just a myth. Or was this, perhaps, some long-term affect of the insanity the Starstones had wreaked on them and their companions?

Their head pulsed with the unanswerable, gnawing voice.

How much had been concocted? How much had been real?

Zech—

Hands so incredibly tiny he constantly feared breaking them wrapped around his ring finger. Lilith's eyes were wide and solemn, extra silvery where they reflected the dull shine of the walls and ceiling. He still wasn't used to it— the Cosmitat they now resided on, spinning through space, or being a father. He brushed his nose to the chubby swell of her cheek and inhaled her infant smell. It calmed the din of noise from the line in which they'd been waiting.

Opening her mouth with an expression Zech knew all too well— the one that said, "You're not remembering correctly. You're crazy. I pity you."— the young woman in charge of connecting family members and returning belongings was suddenly brushed aside by Vim. Her grey eyes were tense as she waved Zech and Lilith to follow her away from the main line.

Something in him itched.

"What's going on? I know my mother had a box of things here. I *remember*. I swear." Lilith mewled in protest when he clutched her too tightly to his chest.

Vim looked at him as though she didn't understand. "I know, love. Of course your family left things here. Everyone did before they were transported to the surface. It's just that..." Vim twisted her hands with anxiety. "I've been keeping your family's things in my own apartment because... Well... We smuggled them in, Zech."

His stomach hollowed.

"When your mother came to me, she was distraught. There was no record of your parents anywhere. No one even seemed to have seen them before. It was like... they didn't exist."

Lumen—

He'd always been their funny little brother, but he'd always had their back. Adras was his whole world. He worshipped them, adored them, felt most at home poking fun at them when they were stressed.

Some things had changed irreversibly. Some things hadn't changed at all. He hadn't sought out his blood family upon arrival in the Astrofleet. They hadn't wanted him as a toddler; they certainly wouldn't want him now, when he was more damaged, not less.

It was time for him to grow up. He'd felt it when Adras changed, when something greater in them called to something invisible and wondrous in the atmosphere. They'd always love him, but he was no longer their whole world. So Battlestar Fairlight was his destination, and despite the view of Cosmitat Astra out his bunk window, Adras might as well have been an entire universe away.

None of his distractions worked without them. None of his coping mechanisms were singularly sustainable. He was a toddler again—damaged and alone, lost inside the swirling nothingness that braided its way through his veins. The void inside him bottomed out, dipping into dangerous jealousy, scandalous grief. He scrubbed a thumb over the coin in his pocket, smooth from years of this soothing repetitive motion.

For the first time since childhood, he considered what he was. And he sobbed.

Jauyne—

She had sat very still as the man, in sterile white and with an impeccable mustache, explained that because she had been given to a foster family by an orphanage emptying its walls, she had left behind very little before having her memory stored and updated to biosphere conditions. She did not belong to her body, to the gaunt, scarred face or the bony fingers that gripped the sides of the metal chair in which her body sat. The man explained several things that passed through her like a late autumn wind and then handed her a clear plastic box with JAUYNE, ORPHAN stamped across the front.

Then, he left her alone. Terribly, blandly alone.

Her hands trembled violently as she popped off the cover and peered inside. There were only three items, and, seeing as she had only been six years old at the time, she had only the vaguest memories of them. There was a badly crafted and brutally chipped ceramic mug, a small card with intricate artwork of a chalice, and a large, folded bundle of black leather.

She pulled the items out gingerly, as if they might not belong to her at all, as if they might disintegrate under her touch, and unfolded the bundle of leather lying in the bottom of the box.

As it fell open, her mind stuttered in disbelieving shock. Three words, painted in white, stared back at her: *stubborn scrappy fucker.*

Indra—

For everyone else, there was an explanation. For her, and all her desperate attempts at goodness, there was nothing. Her life was nothing. She was nothing.

Dymmares—

Failure. Fucked up, worthless failure. You were trained for this from birth, and still you failed. You stupid, pathetic false prodigy.

She was shaking, head to toe. Panic wracking her ribs and wringing out the lump in her throat. She needed Vim. She needed Adras. She needed anyone other than Project Commander Vada. She was going to be verbally gutted and she simply *could not.*

All her answers would be the same: I don't know.

Because she didn't. She had no idea how Canryn had somehow evaded or escaped the memory dampeners. She had no idea how the New Canestryn fleet had found out about the Biosphere Allesar Project. She didn't fucking know.

Fingers wrapped around the tiny metal flask in her beaded blazer, and she hastily unscrewed it and gulped down the searing liquid, chasing it with a mint leaf from the opposite pocket to disguise the scent of it on her breath. Sweat rolled down the knobby column of her spine as the burn of the liquor rushed her torso with a fortifying sear. With a brief glance about, she took three— it was more than instructed, but this was more than she could bear— of her anxiety pills from the same pocket as the mint leaf, and tossed them back dry.

Gnawing cracked lips and hiding the shaking of her hands with furious fists, she pushed open the doors to Project Commander Vada's monitor wing, and went obediently to the consequences of her failure.

To be continued....

MESSAGE
SEND FAILURE

I DON'T KNOW IF you're gettingg these messages ornot but please ret-
hink this please come backyo u dont need to do this please Lilith and me
and we all need you don't be stupid dont be a hero please just com back
dont die like this

ACKNOWLEDGMENTS

I'm not sure I know how to begin acknowledgements for a story that has been in my bones for seven years, but the only thing I can do is try.

TO MORIAH, because no one knew what I needed from life more intimately than you, and no one else could have handed the gift of me to me other than you. Thank you for taking this story as far as it could go, until you couldn't anymore. I finished it. For you. Always for you.

TO IOLA, my violet colored dawn, because you are in so many ways my same fire and water spirit. Great rage, great empathy, great and magnificent enthusiasm. I hope someday you look back at this first book of mine and know that nothing can keep you from your gift. I want to hear every single one of your stories, forever.

TO POPPY, because sometimes I still think I wrote you into my life, starting seven years ago. Because you still feel like a brewing thunderstorm when you're anxious. Because you were never soft-spoken, and that's magic. Because alongside your ferocity, mine is less alone, and we do twice the damage.

TO MAX, because you saw me from the beginning, and were proud and unafraid of what I was. I love you for that and for five million other reasons.

TO STEPHANIE, because you were the first person, besides me, to truly fall in love with this story, to feel what it meant in your bones, to wolf-howl my gift back to me in this way. I will never forget this. Not ever.

TO MALIALANI, because you named me, and you named me accurately, and that is a rarity I'll treasure in my obsidian heart always. You know what it is to be volcanic and to refuse to be soothed.

TO SHELBY, because you are something wilder and more brilliant than you know, and because we have walked each other through so many iterations of being. You'll always be my favorite weird, dark little summer Scorpio, and my favorite platonic meet-cute. Thanks for writing a BFF for Jauyne; Shahar is a bad bitch.

TO KAITLIN, KELSEA, CADE, MOLLY, ANASTASIA, SAMANTHA, JENNA, & MARIEL, because you all cheered me on, helped me problem solve, or talked me off ledges, at various stages in this process. To K & K especially, for my heart would not be as full or as sturdy without you— thank you for reinventing what friendship means to me.